A MARTYR'S SONG

WHEN HEAVEN WEEPS

TED DEKKER

THOMAS NELSON
Since 1798

NASHVILLE   DALLAS   MEXICO CITY   RIO DE JANEIRO   BEIJING

WHEN HEAVEN WEEPS
© Copyright 2001

Published in Nashville, Tennessee, by Thomas Nelson. Thomas Nelson is a trademark of Thomas Nelson, Inc.

Thomas Nelson, Inc. titles may be purchased in bulk for educational, business, fund-raising, or sales promotional use. For information, please e-mail SpecialMarkets@ThomasNelson.com.

Scripture quotations noted NIV are from *The Holy Bible,* New International Version. Copyright © 1973, 1978, 1984, International Bible Society. Used by permission of Zondervan Bible Publishers.

Library of Congress Cataloging-in-Publication Data

Dekker, Ted, 1962–
    When heaven weeps / Ted R. Dekker.
        p. cm. (A martyr's song; bk. 2)
    ISBN 978-0-8499-4516-8 (repak)
    1. World War, 1939–1945—Veterans—Fiction. 2. Evangelicalism—
Fiction. 3. Clergy—Fiction. I. Title
    PS3554.E43 W48 2001
    813'6—dc21   2001017609
                                                                          CIP

Printed in the United States of America

07 08 09 10 11 RRD 10 9 8 7 6

LETTER FROM THE PUBLISHER

The story you are about to read begins with some of the events told in Ted's novel, *The Martyr's Song,* and then continues with Jan's incredible tale of betrayal and love that many claim is Ted's most powerful story to date.

There is no order to the Martyr's Song novels, you may read any in any order. Each is a stand alone story that in no way depends on the others. Nevertheless, if there is one book we recommend you start with, it is *The Martyr's Song,* the story that started it all.

For LeeAnn, my wife,
without whose love I
would be only a shadow
of myself. I will never
forget the day you saw heaven.

BOOK ONE

THE PRIEST

"Christians who refuse
To look squarely into the suffering of Christ
Are not Christians at all.
They are a breed of pretenders,
Who would turn their backs on the Cross,
And shame his death.
You cannot hold up the Cross,
Nor drink of the cup
Without embracing the death.
And you cannot understand love,
Unless you first die."

THE DANCE OF THE DEAD
1959

CHAPTER ONE

Atlanta, Georgia, 1964

IVENA STOOD in the small greenhouse attached to her home and frowned at the failing rosebush. The other bushes had not been affected—they flourished around her, glistening with a sprinkling of dewdrops. A bed of Darwin tulip hybrids blossomed bright red and yellow along her greenhouse's glass shell. Behind her, against the solid wall of her house, a flat of purple orchids filled the air with their sweet aroma. A dozen other species of roses grew in neat boxes, none of them infected.

But this bush had lost its leaves and shriveled in the space of five days, and that was a problem because this wasn't just another rosebush. This was Nadia's rosebush.

Ivena delicately pried through the dried thorny stems, searching for signs of disease or insects. She'd already tried a host of remedies, from pesticides to a variety of growth agents, all to no avail. It was a Serbian Red from the saxifrage family, snipped from the bush that she and Sister Flouta had planted by the cross.

When Ivena had left Bosnia for Atlanta, she'd insisted on a greenhouse; it was the one unbreakable link to her past. She made a fine little business selling the flowers to local floral shops in Atlanta, but the real purpose for the greenhouse was this one rosebush, wasn't it? Yes, she knew that as surely as she knew that blood flowed in her veins.

And now Nadia's rose was dying. Or dead.

Ivena put one hand on her hip and ran the other through her gray curls. She'd cared for a hundred species of roses over her sixty years and never, never had she seen such a thing. Each bud from Nadia's bush was priceless. If there was a graftable branch alive she would snip it off and nurse it back to health. But every branch seemed affected.

"Oh, dear Nadia, what am I going to do? What am I going to do?"

She couldn't answer herself for the simple reason that she had no clue what

1

she would do. She had never considered the possibility that this, the crown of her flower garden, might one day die for no apparent reason at all. It was a travesty.

Ivena picked through the branches again, hoping that she was wrong. Dried dirt grayed her fingers. They weren't as young or as smooth as they once had been, but years of working delicately around thorns had kept them nimble. Graceful. She could walk her way through a rosebush blindfolded without so much as touching a thorn. But today she felt clumsy and old.

The stalk between her fingers suddenly snapped. Ivena blinked. It was as dry as tinder. How could it fail so fast? She tsked and shook her head. But then something caught her eye and she stopped.

Immediately beneath the branch that had broken, a very small shoot of green angled from the main stalk. That was odd. She lowered her head for a closer look.

The shoot grew out a mere centimeter, almost like a stalk of grass. She touched it gently, afraid to break it. And as she did she saw the tiny split in the bark along the base of that shoot.

She caught her breath. Strange! It looked like a small graft!

But she hadn't grafted anything into the plant, had she? No, of course not. She remembered every step of care she'd given this plant over the last five years and none of them included a graft.

It looked like someone had slit the base of the rosebush open and grafted in this green shoot. And it didn't look like a rose graft either. The stalk was a lighter green. So then maybe it wasn't a graft. Maybe it was a parasite of some kind.

Ivena let her breath out slowly and touched it again. It was already healed at the insertion point.

"Hmmm."

She straightened and walked to the round table where a white porcelain cup still steamed with tea. She lifted it to her lips. The rich aroma of spice warmed her nostrils and she paused, staring through the wisps of steam.

From this distance of ten feet Nadia's rosebush looked like Moses's burning bush, but consumed by the flame and burned black. Dead branches reached up from the soil like claws from a grave. Dead.

Except for that one tiny shoot of green at its base.

It was very strange indeed.

Ivena lowered herself into the old wood-spindle chair beside the table, still looking over the teacup to the rosebush. She sat here every morning, humming and sipping her tea and whispering her words to the Father. But today the sight before her was turning things on their heads.

She lowered the cup without drinking. "Father, what are you doing here?" she said softly.

Not that he was necessarily doing anything. Rosebushes died, after all. Perhaps with less encouragement than other plants. But an air of consequence had settled on Ivena, and she couldn't ignore it.

Across the beds of flourishing flowers before her sat this one dead bush—an ugly black scar on a landscape of bright color. But then from the blackened stalk that impossible graft.

"What are you saying here, Father?"

She did not hear his answer, but that didn't mean he wasn't talking. He could be yelling for all she knew. Here on Earth it might come through as a distant whisper, easily mistaken for the sound of a gentle breeze. Actually the greenhouse was dead silent. She more felt something, and it could just as easily have been a draft that tickled her hair, or a finger of emotion from the past, as the voice of God.

Still the scene before her began to massage her heart with fingers of meaning. She just didn't know what that meaning was yet.

Ivena hummed and a blanket of peace settled over her. She whispered, "Lover of my soul, I worship you. I kiss your feet. Don't ever let me forget." Her words echoed softly through the quiet greenhouse, and she smiled. *The Creator was a mischievous one,* she often thought. At least playful and easily delighted. And he was up to something, wasn't he?

A splash of red at her elbow caught her eye. It was her copy of the book. *The Dance of the Dead.* Its surreal cover showed a man's face wide open with laughter, tears leaking down his cheek.

Still smiling, Ivena set down her teacup and lifted the book from the table. She ran a hand over the tattered cover. She'd read it a hundred times, of course. But it never lost its edge. Its pages oozed with love and laughter and the heart of the Creator.

She opened the book and brushed through a few dozen dog-eared pages. He had written a masterpiece, and in some ways it was as much God's words as his. She could begin in the middle or at the beginning or the end and it wouldn't hardly matter. The meaning would not be lost. She opened to the middle and read a few sentences.

It was odd how such a story could bring this warmth to her heart. But it did, it really did, and that was because her eyes had been opened a little as well. She'd seen a few things through God's eyes.

Ivena glanced up at the dying rosebush with its impossible graft. Something new was beginning today. But everything had really started with the story in her hands, hadn't it?

A small spark of delight ran through her bones. She smoothed her dress, crossed her legs and lowered her eyes to the page.

Yes, this was how it all started.

Twenty years ago in Bosnia. At the end of the war with the Nazis.

She read.

THE SOLDIERS stood unmoving on the hill's crest, leaning on battered rifles, five dark silhouettes against a white Bosnian sky, like a row of trees razed by the war. They stared down at the small village, oblivious to the sweat caked beneath their tattered army fatigues, unaware of the dirt streaking down their faces like long black claws.

Their condition wasn't unique. Any soldier who managed to survive the brutal fighting that ravaged Yugoslavia during its liberation from the Nazis looked the same. Or worse. A severed arm perhaps. Or bloody stumps below the waist. The country was strewn with dying wounded—testaments to Bosnia's routing of the enemy.

But the scene in the valley below them was unique. The village appeared untouched by the war. If a shell had landed anywhere near it during the years of bitter conflict, there was no sign of it now.

Several dozen homes with steep cedar-shake roofs and white chimney smoke clustered neatly around the village center. Cobblestone paths ran like spokes between the homes and the large structure at the hub. There, with a sprawling courtyard, stood an ancient church with a belfry that reached to the sky like a finger pointing the way to God.

"What's the name of this village?" Karadzic asked no one in particular.

Janjic broke his stare on the village and looked at his commander. The man's lips had bent into a frown. He glanced at the others, who were still captivated by this postcard-perfect scene below.

"I don't know," Molosov said to Janjic's right. "We're less than fifty clicks from Sarajevo. I grew up in Sarajevo."

"And what is your point?"

"My point is that I grew up in Sarajevo and I don't remember this village."

Karadzic was a tall man, six foot two at least, and boxy above the waist. His bulky torso rested on spindly legs, like a bulldog born on stilts. His face was square and leathery, pitted by a collage of small scars, each marking another chapter in a violent past. Glassy gray eyes peered past thick bushy eyebrows.

Janjic shifted on his feet and looked up valley. What was left of the Partisan army waited a hard day's march north. But no one seemed eager to move. A bird's caw drifted through the air, followed by another. Two ravens circled lazily over the village.

"I don't remember seeing a church like this before. It looks wrong to me," Karadzic said.

A small tingle ran up Janjic's spine. Wrong? "We have a long march ahead of us, sir. We could make the regiment by nightfall if we leave now."

Karadzic ignored him entirely. "Puzup, have you seen an Orthodox church like this?"

Puzup blew smoke from his nose and drew deep on his cigarette. "No, I guess I haven't."

"Molosov?"

"It's standing, if that's what you mean." He grinned. "It's been a while since I've seen a church standing. Doesn't look Orthodox."

"If it isn't Orthodox, then what is it?"

"Not Jewish," Puzup said. "Isn't that right, Paul?"

"Not unless Jews have started putting crosses on their temples in my absence."

Puzup cackled in a high pitch, finding humor where apparently no one else did. Molosov reached over and slapped the younger soldier on the back of his head. Puzup's laugh stuck in his throat and he grunted in protest. No one paid them any mind. Puzup clamped his lips around his cigarette. The tobacco crackled quietly in the stillness. The man absently picked at a bleeding scab on his right forearm.

Janjic spit to the side, anxious to rejoin the main army. "If we keep to the ridges we should be able to maintain high ground and still meet the column by dark."

"It appears deserted," Molosov said, as if he had not heard Janjic.

"There's smoke. And there's a group in the courtyard," Paul said.

"Of course there's smoke. I'm not talking about smoke, I'm talking about people. You can't see if there's a group in the courtyard. We're two miles out."

"Look for movement. If you look—"

"Shut up," Karadzic snapped. "It's Franciscan." He shifted his Kalashnikov from one set of thick, gnarled fingers to the other.

A fleck of spittle rested on the commander's lower lip and he made no attempt to remove it. *Karadzic wouldn't know the difference between a Franciscan monastery and an Orthodox church if they stood side by side,* Janjic thought. But that was beside the point. They all knew about Karadzic's hatred for the Franciscans.

"Our orders are to reach the column as soon as possible," Janjic said. "Not to scour the few standing churches for monks cowering in the corner. We have a war to finish, and it's not against them." He turned to view the town, surprised by his own insolence. *It is the war. I've lost my sensibilities.*

Smoke still rose from a dozen random chimneys; the ravens still circled. An eerie quiet hovered over the morning. He could feel the commander's gaze on his face—more than one man had died for less.

Molosov glanced at Janjic and then spoke softly to Karadzic. "Sir, Janjic is right—"

"Shut up! We're going down." Karadzic hefted his rifle and snatched it from the air cleanly. He faced Janjic. "We don't enlist women in this war, but you, Janjic, you are like a woman." He headed downhill.

One by one the soldiers stepped from the crest and strode for the peaceful village below. Janjic brought up the rear, swallowing uneasiness. He had pushed it too far with the commander.

High above the two ravens cawed again. It was the only sound besides the crunching of their boots.

FATHER MICHAEL saw the soldiers when they entered the cemetery at the edge of the village. Their small shapes emerged out of the green meadow like a row of tattered scarecrows. He pulled up at the top of the church's hewn stone steps, and a chill crept down his spine. For a moment the children's laughter about him waned.

Dear God, protect us. He prayed as he had a hundred times before, but he couldn't stop the tremors that took to his fingers.

The smell of hot baked bread wafted through his nostrils. A shrill giggle echoed through the courtyard; water gurgled from the natural spring to his left. Father Michael stood, stooped, and looked past the courtyard in which the children and women celebrated Nadia's birthday, past the tall stone cross that marked the entrance to the graveyard, past the red rosebushes Claudis Flouta had so carefully planted about her home, to the lush hillside on the south.

To the four—no five—to the five soldiers approaching.

He glanced around the courtyard—they laughed and played. None of the others had seen the soldiers yet. High above ravens cawed and Michael looked up to see four of them circling.

Father, protect your children. A flutter of wings to his right caught his attention. He turned and watched a white dove settle for a landing on the vestibule's roof. The bird cocked its head and eyed him in small jerky movements.

"Father Michael?" a child's voice said.

Michael turned to face Nadia, the birthday girl. She wore a pink dress reserved for special occasions. Her lips and nose were wide and she had blotchy freckles on both cheeks. A homely girl even with the pretty pink dress. Some might even say ugly. Her mother, Ivena, was quite pretty; the coarse looks were from her father.

To make matters worse for the poor child, her left leg was two inches shorter than her right thanks to polio—a bad case when she was only three. Perhaps their handicaps united her with Michael in ways the others could not understand. She with her short leg; he with his hunched back.

Yet Nadia carried herself with a courage that defied her lack of physical beauty. At times Michael felt terribly sorry for the child, if for no other reason than that she didn't realize how her ugliness might handicap her in life. At other times his heart swelled with pride for her, for the way her love and joy shone with a brilliance that washed her skin clean of the slightest blemish.

He suppressed the urge to sweep her off her feet and swing her around in his arms. *Come unto me as little children,* the Master had said. If only the whole world were filled with the innocence of children.

"Yes?"

NADIA LOOKED into Father Michael's eyes and saw the flash of pity before he spoke. It was more of a question than a statement, that look of his. More "are you sure you're okay?" than "you look so lovely in your new dress."

None of them knew how well she could read their thoughts, perhaps because she'd long ago accepted the pity as a part of her life. Still, the realization that she limped and looked a bit plainer than most girls, regardless of what Mother told her, gnawed gently at her consciousness most of the time.

"Petrus says that since I'm thirteen now all the boys will want to marry me. I told him that he's being a foolish boy, but he insists on running around making a silly game of it. Could you please tell him to stop?"

Petrus ran up, sneering. If any of the town's forty-three children was a bully, it was this ten-year-old know-nothing brat. Oh, he had his sweet side, Mother assured her. And Father Michael repeatedly said as much to the boy's mother, who was known to run about the village with her apron flying, leaving puffs of flour in her wake, shaking her rolling pin while calling for the runt to get his little rear end home.

"Nadia loves Milus! Nadia love Milus!" Petrus chanted and skipped by, looking back, daring her to take up chase.

"You're a misguided fledgling, Petrus," Nadia said, crossing her arms. "A silly little bird, squawking too much. Why don't you find your worms somewhere else?"

Petrus pulled up, flushing red. "Oh, you with all your fancy words! You're the one eating worms. With Milus. Nadia and Milus sitting in a tree, eating all the worms they can see!" He sang the verse again and ran off with a *whoop*, obviously delighted with his victory.

Nadia placed her hands on her hips and tapped the foot of her shorter leg with a disgusted sigh. "You see. Please stop him, Father."

"Of course, darling. But you know that he's just playing." Father Michael smiled and took a seat on the top step.

He looked over the courtyard and Nadia followed his gaze. Of the village's seventy or so people, all but ten or twelve had come today for her birthday. Only the men were missing, called off to fight the Nazis. The old people sat in groups around the stone tables, grinning and chatting as they watched the children play a party game of balancing boiled eggs on spoons as they raced in a circle.

Nadia's mother, Ivena, directed the children with flapping hands, straining to be heard over their cries of delight. Three of the mothers busied themselves over a long table on which they had arranged pastries and the cake Ivena had fretted over for two days. It was perhaps the grandest cake Nadia had ever seen, a foot high, white with pink roses made from frosting.

All for her. All to cover up whatever pity they had for her and make her feel special.

Father Michael's gaze moved past the courtyard. Nadia looked up and saw a small band of soldiers approaching. The sight made her heart stop for a moment.

"Come here, Nadia."

Father Michael lifted an arm for her to sit by him, and she limped up the steps. She sat beside him and he pulled her close.

He seemed nervous. The soldiers.

She put her arm around him, rubbing his humped back.

Father Michael swallowed and kissed the top of her head. "Don't mind Petrus. But he is right, one day the men will line up to marry such a pretty girl as you."

She ignored the comment and looked back at the soldiers who were now in the graveyard not a hundred yards off. They were Partisans, she saw with some relief. Partisans were probably friendly.

High above birds cawed. Again Nadia followed the father's gaze as he looked up. Five ravens circled against the white sky. Michael looked to his right, to the vestibule roof. Nadia saw the lone dove staring on, clucking with its one eye peeled to the courtyard.

Father Michael looked back at the soldiers. "Nadia, go tell your mother to come."

Nadia hoped the soldiers wouldn't spoil her birthday party.

JANJIC JOVIC, the nineteen-year-old writer-turned-soldier, followed the others into the village, trudging with the same rhythmic cadence his marching had kept in the endless months leading up to this day. Just one foot after another. Ahead and to the right, Karadzic marched deliberately. The other three fanned out to his left.

Karadzic's war had less to do with defeating the Nazis than with restoring Serbia, and that included purging the land of anyone who wasn't a good Serb. Especially Franciscans.

Or so he said. They all knew that Karadzic killed good Serbs as easily as Franciscans. His own mother, for example, with a knife, he'd bragged, never mind that she was Serbian to the marrow. Though sure of few things, Janjic was certain the commander wasn't beyond trying to kill him one day. Janjic was a philosopher, a writer—not a killer—and the denser man despised him for it. He determined to follow Karadzic obediently regardless of the elder's folly; anything less could cost dearly.

Only when they were within a stone's throw of the village did Janjic study the scene with a careful eye. They approached from the south, through a graveyard holding fifty or sixty concrete crosses. So few graves. In most villages throughout Bosnia one could expect to find hundreds if not thousands of fresh graves, pushing into lots never intended for the dead. They were evidence of a war gone mad.

But in this village, hidden here in this lush green valley, he counted fewer than ten plots that looked recent.

He studied the neat rows of houses—fewer than fifty—also unmarked by the war. The tall church spire rose high above the houses, adorned with a white cross, brilliant against the dull sky. The rest of the structure was cut from gray stone and elegantly carved like most churches. Small castles made for God.

None in the squad cared much for God—not even the Jew, Paul. But in Bosnia, religion had little to do with God. It had to do with who was right and who was wrong, not with who loved God. If you weren't Orthodox or at least a good Serb, you weren't right. If you were a Christian but not an Orthodox Christian, you weren't right. If you were Franciscan, you were most certainly not right. Janjic wasn't sure he disagreed with Karadzic on this point—religious affiliation was more a defining line of this war than the Nazi occupation.

The Ustashe, Yugoslavia's version of the German Gestapo, had murdered hundreds of thousands of Serbs using techniques that horrified even the Nazis. Worse, they'd done it with the blessing of both the Catholic Archbishop of Sarajevo and the Franciscans, neither of whom evidently understood the love of God. But then, *no* one in this war knew much about the love of God. It was a war absent of God, if indeed there even was such a being.

A child ran past the walls that surrounded the courtyard, out toward the tall cross, not fifty feet from them now. A boy, dressed in a white shirt and black shorts, with suspenders and a bow tie. The child slid to a halt, eyes popping.

Janjic smiled at the sight. The smell of hot bread filled his nostrils.

"Petrus! You come back here!"

A woman, presumably the boy's mother, ran for the boy, grabbed his arm and yanked him back toward the churchyard. He struggled free and began marching in imitation of a soldier. *One, two! One, two!*

"Stop it, Petrus!" His mother caught his shirt and pulled him toward the courtyard.

Karadzic ignored the boy and kept his glassy gray eyes fixed ahead. Janjic was the last to enter the courtyard, following the others' clomping boots. Karadzic halted and they pulled up behind him.

A priest stood on the ancient church steps, dressed in flowing black robes. Dark hair fell to his shoulders, and a beard extended several inches past his chin. He stood with a hunch in his shoulders.

A hunchback.

To his left, a flock of children sat on the steps with their mothers who held them, some smoothing their children's hair or stroking their cheeks. Smiling. All of them seemed to be smiling.

In all, sixty or seventy pairs of eyes stared at them.

"Welcome to Vares," the priest said, bowing politely.

They had interrupted a party of some kind. The children were mostly dressed in ties and dresses. A long table adorned with pastries and a cake sat untouched. The sight was surreal—a celebration of life in this countryside of death.

"What church is this?" Karadzic asked.

"Anglican," the priest said.

Karadzic glanced at his men, then faced the church. "I've never heard of this church."

A homely looking girl in a pink dress suddenly stood from her mother's arms and walked awkwardly toward the table adorned with pastries. She hobbled.

Karadzic ignored her and twisted his fingers around the barrel of his rifle, tapping its butt on the stone. "Why is this church still standing?"

No one answered. Janjic watched the little girl place a golden brown pastry on a napkin.

"You can't speak?" Karadzic demanded. "Every church for a hundred kilometers is burned to the ground, but yours is untouched. And it makes me think that maybe you've been sleeping with the Ustashe."

"God has granted us favor," the priest said.

The commander paused. His lips twitched to a slight grin. A bead of sweat broke from the large man's forehead and ran down his flat cheek. "God has granted you favor? He's flown out of the sky and built an invisible shield over this valley to keep the bullets out, is that it?" His lips flattened. "God has allowed every Orthodox church in Yugoslavia to burn to the ground. And yet yours is standing."

Janjic watched the child limp toward a spring that gurgled in the corner and dip a mug into its waters. No one seemed to pay her attention except the woman on the steps whom she had left, probably her mother.

Paul spoke quietly. "They're Anglican, not Franciscans or Catholics. I know Anglicans. Good Serbs."

"What does a Jew know about good Serbs?"

"I'm only telling you what I've heard," Paul said with a shrug.

The girl in the pink dress approached, carrying the mug of cold water in one hand and the pastry in the other. She stopped three feet from Karadzic and lifted the food to him. None of the villagers moved.

Karadzic ignored her. "And if your God is my God, why doesn't he protect my church? The Orthodox church?"

The priest smiled gently, still staring without blinking, hunched over on the steps. "I'm asking you a question, Priest," Karadzic said.

"I can't speak for God," the priest said. "Perhaps you should ask him. We're God-loving people with no quarrel. But I cannot speak for God on all matters."

The small girl lifted the pastry and water higher. Karadzic's eyes took on that menacing stare Janjic had seen so many times before.

Janjic moved on impulse. He stepped up to the girl and smiled. "You're very kind," he said. "Only a good Serb would offer bread and water to a tired and hungry Partisan soldier." He reached for the pastry and took it. "Thank you."

A dozen children scrambled from the stairs and ran to the table, arguing about who was to be first. They quickly gathered up food to follow the young girl's example and then rushed for the soldiers, pastries in hand. Janjic was struck by their innocence. This was just another game to them. The sudden turn in events had effectively silenced Karadzic, but Janjic couldn't look at the commander. If Molosov and the others didn't follow his cue there would be a price to pay later—this he knew with certainty.

"My name's Nadia," the young girl said, looking up at Janjic. "It's my birthday today. I'm thirteen years old."

Ordinarily Janjic would have answered the girl—told her what a brave thirteen-year-old she was, but today his mind was on his comrades. Several children now swarmed around Paul and Puzup, and Janjic saw with relief that they were accepting the pastries. With smiles in fact.

"We could use the food, sir," Molosov said.

Karadzic snatched up his hand to silence the second in command. Nadia held the cup in her hand toward him. Once again every eye turned to the commander, begging him to show some mercy. Karadzic suddenly scowled and slapped the cup aside. It clattered to the stone in a shower of water. The children froze.

Karadzic brushed angrily past Nadia. She backpedaled and fell to her bottom. The commander stormed over to the birthday table, and kicked his boot against the leading edge. The entire birthday display rose into the air and crashed onto the ground.

Nadia scrambled to her feet and limped for her mother, who drew her in. The other children scampered for the steps.

Karadzic turned to them, face red. "Now do I have your attention?"

CHAPTER TWO

IVENA PAUSED her reading and swallowed at the memory. *Dear Father, give me strength.*

She could hear the commander's voice as though he were here in the greenhouse today. She suddenly pursed her lips angrily, mimicking him. "Now do I have your attention?" Ivena relaxed her face and closed her eyes. Now do I have your attention? Well we have yours now, don't we, Mr. Big Shot Commander?

For years she'd told herself that they should have told the children to leave them then. To run back to the houses. But they hadn't. And in the end she knew there was a reason for that.

Behind her the clock ticked away on the wall, one click for every jerk of the second hand. Other than her breathing, no other sound broke the stillness. Reliving that day was not always the most pleasant thing, but always it brought her an uncanny strength and a deep-seated peace. And more important, not to remember—indeed not to participate again and again—would make a mockery of it. *Take this in remembrance of me,* Christ had said. *Participate in the suffering of Christ,* Paul had said.

And yet Americans turned forgetting into a kind of spiritual badge, refusing to look at suffering for fear they might catch it like a disease. They turned the death of Christ into soft fuzzy Sunday-school pictures and refused to let those pictures get off the page and walk bloody into their minds. They stripped Christ of his dignity by ignoring the brutality of his death. It was no different from turning away from a puffy-faced leper in horror. The epitome of rejection.

Some would even close the book here in a huff and return to their knitting. Perhaps they would knit nice soft images of a cross.

It occurred to her that every muscle in her body had tensed.

She relaxed and chuckled. "What are you, the messiah for America, Ivena?" she mumbled. "You speak of Christ's love; where is yours?"

Ivena shook her head and opened the pages again.

"Give me grace, Father."

She read again.

"NOW DO I have your attention?"

Father Michael's heart seemed to stick midstroke. He mumbled his prayer now, loud enough for the women nearest him to hear.

"Protect your children, Father."

The leader was possessed of the devil. Michael had known so from the moment the big man had entered the courtyard. *Yea, though I walk through the valley of the shadow of death, I will fear no evil.*

He barely heard the flutter of wings to his right. The dove had taken flight. The commander glared at him. *Now do I have your attention?*

The dove's wings beat through the air. *Yes, you have my attention, commander. You had my attention before you began this insanity.* But he did not say it because the dove had stopped above him and was flapping noisily. The commander's eyes rose to the bird. Michael leaned back to compensate for his humped back and looked up.

In that moment the world fell to a silent slow motion.

Michael could see the commander standing, legs spread. Above him, the white dove swept gracefully at the air, fanning a slight wind to him, like an angel breathing five feet over his head.

The breath moved through his hair, through his beard, cool at first and then suddenly warm. High above the dove, a hole appeared in the clouds, allowing the sun to send its rays of warmth. Michael could see that the ravens still circled, more of them now—seven or eight.

This he saw in that first glance, as the world slowed to a crawl. Then he felt the music on the wind. At least that was how he thought of it, because the music didn't sound in his ears, but in his mind and in his chest.

Though only a few notes, they spread an uncanny warmth. A whisper that seemed to say, "My beloved."

Just that. Just, *My beloved.* The warmth suddenly rushed through him like water, past his loins, right down to the soles of his feet.

Father Michael gasped.

The dove took flight.

A chill of delight rippled up his back. Goodness! Nothing even remotely similar had happened to him in all of his years. *My beloved.* Like the anointing of Jesus at his baptism. *This is my beloved Son, in whom I am well pleased.*

He'd always taught that Christ's power was as real for the believer today as it was two thousand years earlier.

Now Michael had heard these words of love. *My beloved!* God was going to protect them.

It occurred to him that he was still bent back awkwardly and that his mouth had fallen open, like a man who'd been shot. He clamped it shut and jerked forward.

The rest hadn't heard the voice. Their eyes were on him, not on the dove, which had landed on the nearest roof—Sister Flauta's house surrounded by those red rosebushes. The flowers' scent reached up into his sinuses, thick and sweet. Which was odd. He should be fighting a panic just now, terrified of these men with guns. Instead his mind was taking time to smell Sister Flauta's rosebushes. And pausing to hear the watery gurgle of the spring to his left.

A dumb grin lifted the corners of his mouth. He knew it was dumb because he had no business facing this monster before him wearing a snappy little grin. But he could hardly control it, and he quickly lifted a hand to cover his mouth. The gesture must look like a child hiding a giggle. It would infuriate the man.

And so it did.

"Wipe that idiotic grin off your face!"

The commander strode toward him. Except for the ravens cawing overhead and the spring's insistent gurgle, Father Michael could only hear his own heart, pounding like a boot against a hollow drum. His head still buzzed from the dove's words, but another thought slowly took form in his mind. It was the realization that he'd heard the music for a reason. It wasn't every day, or even every year, that heaven reached down so deliberately to man.

Karadzic stopped and glared at the women and children. "So. You claim to be people of faith?"

He asked as if he expected an answer. Ivena looked at Father Michael.

"Are you all mutes?" Karadzic demanded, red-faced.

Still no one spoke.

Karadzic planted his legs wide. "No. I don't think you *are* people of faith. I think that your God has abandoned you, perhaps when you and your murdering priests burned the Orthodox church in Glina after stuffing a thousand women and children into it."

Karadzic's lips twisted around the words. "Perhaps the smell of their charred bodies rose to the heavens and sent your God to hell."

"It was a horrible massacre," Father Michael heard himself say. "But it wasn't us, my friend. We abhor the brutality of the Ustashe. No God-fearing man could possibly take the life of another with such cruelty."

"I shot a man in the knees just a week ago before killing him. It was quite brutal. Are you saying that *I* am not a God-fearing man?"

"I believe that God loves all men, Commander. Me no more than you."

"Shut up! You sit back in your fancy church singing pretty songs of love, while your men roam the countryside, seeking a Serb to cut open."

"If you were to search the battlefields, you would find our men stitching up the wounds of soldiers, not killing them."

Karadzic squinted briefly at the claim. For a moment he just stared. He suddenly smiled, but it wasn't a kind smile.

"Then surely true faith can be proven." He spun to one of the soldiers. "Molosov, bring me one of the crosses from the graveyard."

The soldier looked at his commander with a raised brow.

"Are you deaf? Bring me a gravestone."

"They're in the ground, sir."

"Then pull it *out* of the ground!"

"Yes, sir." Molosov jogged across the courtyard and into the adjacent cemetery.

Father Michael watched the soldier kick at the nearest headstone, a cross like all the others, two feet in height, made of concrete. He knew the name of the deceased well. It was old man Haris Zecavic, planted in the ground more than twenty years ago.

"What's the teaching of your Christ?"

Michael looked back at Karadzic, who still wore a twisted grin.

"Hmm? Carry your cross?" Karadzic said. "Isn't that what your God commanded you to do? 'Pick up your cross and follow me'?"

"Yes."

Molosov hauled the cross he'd freed into the courtyard. The villagers watched, stunned.

Karadzic gestured at them with his rifle. "Exactly. As you see, I'm not as stupid in matters of faith as you think. My own mother was a devout Christian. Then again, she was also a whore, which is why I know that not all Christians are necessarily right in the head."

The soldier dropped the stone at Karadzic's feet. It landed with a loud *thunk* and toppled flat. One of the women made a squeaking sound—Marie Zecavic, the old man's thirty-year-old daughter, mourning the destruction of her father's grave, possibly. The commander glanced at Marie.

"We're in luck today," Karadzic said, keeping his eyes on Marie. "Today we actually have a cross for you to bear. We will give you an opportunity to prove your faith. Come here."

Marie had a knuckle in her mouth, biting off her cry. She looked up with fear-fired eyes.

"Yes, you. Come here, please."

Father Michael took a step toward the commander. "Please—"

"Stay!"

Michael stopped. Fingers of dread tickled his spine. He nodded and tried to smile with warmth.

Marie stepped hesitantly toward the commander.

"Put the cross on her back," Karadzic said.

Father Michael stepped forward, instinctively raising his right hand in protest. Karadzic whirled to him, lips twisted. "Stay!" His voice thundered across the courtyard.

Molosov bent for the cross, which could not weigh less than thirty kilos. Marie's face wrinkled in fear. Tears streaked silently down her cheeks.

Karadzic sneered. "Don't cry, child. You're simply going to carry a cross for your Christ. It's a noble thing, isn't it?"

He nodded and his man hoisted the gravestone to Marie's back. Her body began to tremble and Michael felt his heart expand.

"Don't just stand there, woman, hold it!" Karadzic snapped.

Marie leaned tentatively forward and reached back for the stone. Molosov released his grip. Her back sagged momentarily, and she staggered forward with one foot before steadying herself.

"Good. You see, it's not so bad." Karadzic stood back, pleased with himself. He turned to Father Michael. "Not so bad at all. But I tell you, Priest—if she drops the cross then we will have a problem."

Michael's heart accelerated. Heat surged up his neck and flared around his ears. *Oh, God, give us strength!*

"Yes, of course. If she drops the cross it will mean that you are an impostor, and that your church is unholy. We will be forced to remove some of your skin with a beating." The commander's twisted smile broadened.

Father Michael looked at Marie and tried to still his thumping heart. He nodded, mustering reserves of courage. "Don't be afraid, Marie. God's love will save us."

Karadzic stepped forward and swung his hand. A loud crack echoed from the walls, and Michael's head snapped back. The blow brought stinging tears to his eyes and blood to his mouth. He looked up at Sister Flouta's roof; the dove still perched on the peak, tilting its head to view the scene below. *Peace, my son.* Had he really heard that music? Yes. Yes, he had. God had actually spoken to him. God would protect them.

Father, spare us. I beg you, spare us!

"March, woman!" Karadzic pointed toward the far end of the courtyard. Marie stepped forward. The children looked on with bulging eyes. Stifled cries rippled through the courtyard.

They watched her heave the burden across the concrete, her feet straining with bulging veins at each footfall. Marie wasn't the strongest of them. Oh, God, why couldn't it have been another—Ivena or even one of the older boys. But Marie? She would stumble at any moment!

Michael could not hold his tongue. "Why do you test her? It's me—"

Smack!

The hand landed flat and hard enough to send him reeling back a step this time. A balloon of pain spread from his right cheek.

"Next time it'll be the stock of a rifle," the commander said.

Marie reached the far wall and turned back. She staggered by, searching Father Michael's eyes for help. Everyone watched her quietly, first one way and then the other, bent under the load, eyes darting in fear, slogging back and forth. Most of the soldiers seemed amused. They had undoubtedly seen atrocities that made this seem like a game in comparison. *Go on, prove your faith in Christ. Follow his teaching. Carry this cross. And if you drop it before we tire of watching, we will beat your priest to a bloody pulp.*

Michael prayed. *Father, I beg you. I truly beg you to spare us. I beg you!*

CHAPTER THREE

IT WAS Nadia who refused to stay silent.

The homely birthday girl with her pigtails and her yellow hair clips stood, limped down the steps, and faced the soldiers, arms dangling by her side. Father Michael swallowed. *Father, please!* He could not speak it, but his heart cried it out. *Please, Father!*

"Nadia!" Ivena whispered harshly.

But Nadia didn't even look her mother's way. Her voice carried across the courtyard clear and soft and sweet. "Father Michael has told us that people filled with Christ's love do not hurt other people. Why are you hurting Marie? She's done nothing wrong."

In that moment Father Michael wished he had not taught them so well.

Karadzic looked at her, his gray eyes wide, his mouth slightly agape, obviously stunned.

"Nadia!" Ivena called out in a hushed cry. "Sit down!"

"Shut up!" Karadzic came to life. He stormed toward the girl, livid and red. "Shut up, shut up!" He shook his rifle at her. "Sit down, you ugly little runt!"

Nadia sat.

Karadzic stalked back and forth before the steps, his knuckles white on his gun, his lips flecked with spittle.

"You feel bad for your pitiful Marie, is that it? Because she's carrying this tiny cross on her back?"

He stopped in front of a group of three women huddling on the stairs and leaned toward them. "What is happening to Marie is nothing! Say it! Nothing!"

No one spoke.

Karadzic suddenly flipped his rifle to his shoulder and peered down its barrel at Sister Flouta. "Say it!"

19

A hard knot lodged in Father Michael's throat. His vision blurred with tears. God, this could not be happening! They were a peaceful, loving people who served a risen God. *Father, do not abandon us! Do not! Do not!*

The commander cocked the rifled to the sky with his right hand. His lips pressed white. "To the graveyard then! All of you! All the women."

They only stared at him, unbelieving.

He shoved a thick, dirty finger toward the large cross at the cemetery's entrance and fired into the air. "Go!"

They went. Like a flock of geese, pattering down the steps and across the courtyard, some whimpering, others setting their jaws firm. Marie kept slogging across the stone yard. She was slowing, Michael thought.

The commander turned to his men. "Load a cross on every woman and bring them back."

The thin soldier with bright hazel eyes stepped forward in protest. "Sir—"

"Shut up!"

The soldiers jogged for the graveyard. Father Michael's vision swam. *Father, you are abandoning us! They are playing with your children!*

Several children moved close to him, tugging at his robe, embracing his leg. Blurred forms in uniform kicked at the headstone crosses and hoisted them to the backs of the women. They staggered back to the courtyard, bearing their heavy loads. It was impossible!

Father Michael watched his flock reduced to animals, bending under the weight of concrete crosses. He clenched his teeth. These were women, like Mary and Martha, with tender hearts full of love. Sweet, sweet women, who'd toiled in childbirth and nursed their babies through cold winters. He should rush the commander and smash his head against the rock! He should protect his sheep!

Michael saw the dove in his peripheral vision clucking on the roofline, stepping from one foot to the other. The comforting words seemed distant now, so very abstract. *Peace, my son.* But this was not peace! This was barbarism!

The twisted smile found Karadzic's quivering lips again. "March," he ordered. "March, you pathetic slugs! We'll see how you like Christ's cross. And the first one to drop the cross will be beaten with the Father!"

They walked with Marie, twenty-three of them, bowed under their loads, silent except for heavy breathing and padding feet, staggering.

Every bone in Michael's body screamed in protest now. *Stop this! Stop this immediately! It's insanity! Take me, you spineless cowards! I will carry their crosses. I will carry all of their crosses. You may bury me under their crosses if you wish, but leave these dear women alone! For the love of God!* His whole body trembled as the words rushed through his head.

But they did not reach his lips. They could not because his throat had seized shut in anguish. And either way, the insane commander might very well take the butt of his gun to one of them if he spoke.

A child whimpered at Michael's knee. He bit his lower lip, closed his eyes, and rested a hand on the boy's head. *Father, please.* His bones shook with the inward groan. Tears spilled down his cheeks now, and he felt one land on his hand, wet and warm. His humped shoulders begged to shake—to sob—to cry out for relief, but he refused to disintegrate before all of them. He was their shepherd, for heaven's sake! He was not one of the women or one of the children, he was a man. God's chosen vessel for this little village in a land savaged by war.

He breathed deep and closed his eyes. *Dearest Jesus . . . My dearest Jesus . . .*

The world changed then, for the second time that day. A brilliant flash ignited in his mind, as if someone had taken a picture with one of those bulbs that popped and burned out. Father Michael's body jerked and he snapped his eyes open. He might have gasped—he wasn't sure because this world with all of its soldiers and trudging women was too distant to judge accurately.

In its place stretched a white horizon, flooded with streaming light.

And music.

Faint, but clear. Long, pure notes, the same as he'd heard earlier. *My beloved.* A song of love.

Michael shifted his gaze to the horizon and squinted. The landscape was endless and flat like a sprawling desert, but covered with white flowers. The light streamed several hundred feet above the ground toward him from the distant horizon.

A tiny wedge of alarm struck Michael. He was alone in this white field. Except for the light, of course. The light and the music.

He could suddenly hear more in the music. At first he thought it might be the spring, bubbling near the courtyard. But it wasn't water. It was a sound made by a child. It was a child's laughter, distant, but rushing toward him from that far horizon, carried on the swelling notes of music.

Gooseflesh rippled over Michael's skin. He suddenly felt as though he might be floating, swept off his feet by a deep note that resounded in his bones.

The music grew, and with it the children's laughter. High peals of laughter and giggles, not from one child, but from a hundred children. Maybe a thousand children, or a million, swirling around him now from every direction. Laughter of delight, as though from a small boy being mercilessly tickled by his father. Then reprieves followed by sighs of contentment as others took up the laughing.

Michael could not help the giggle that bubbled in his own chest and slipped out in short bursts. The sound was thoroughly intoxicating. But where were the children?

A single melody reached through the music. A man's voice, pure and clear, with the power to melt whatever it touched. Michael stared out at the field where the sound came from.

A man was walking his way, a shimmering figure, still only an inch tall on the horizon. The voice was his. He hummed a simple melody, but it flowed over Michael with intoxicating power. The melody started low and rose through the scale and then paused. Immediately the children's laughter swelled, responding directly to the man's song. He began again, and the giggles quieted a little and then swelled at the end of this simple refrain. It was like a game.

Michael couldn't hold back his own laughter. *Oh, my God, what is happening to me? I'm losing my mind.* Who was this minstrel walking toward him? And what kind of song was this that made him want to fly with all those children he could not see?

Michael lifted his head and searched the skies. Come out, come out wherever you are, my children. Were they his children? He had no children.

But now he craved them. *These* children, laughing hysterically around him. He wanted these children—to hold them, to kiss them, to run his fingers through their hair and roll on the ground, laughing with them. To sing this song to them. Come out, my dear . . .

The flashbulb ignited again. *Pop!*

The laughter evaporated. The song was gone.

It took only a moment for Father Michael to register the simple, undeniable fact that he was once again standing on the steps of his church, facing a courtyard filled with women who slumped under heavy crosses over cold, flat concrete. His mouth lay open, and he seemed to have forgotten how to use the muscles in his jaw.

The soldiers stood against the far wall, smirking at the women, except for the tall skinny man. He seemed awkward in his role. The commander looked on with a glint in his eyes. And Michael realized that they had not seen his awkward display of laughter then.

Above them the dove perched on Sister Flouta's roof, still eyeing the scene below. To Michael's right, the elderly still sat, as though dead in their seats, unbelieving of this nightmare unfolding before them. And at his fingertips, a head of hair. He quickly closed his mouth and looked down. Children. His children.

But these were not laughing. These were seated, or standing against his legs, some staring quietly to their mothers, others whimpering. Nadia the birthday girl sat stoically on the end, her jaw clenched, her hands on her knees.

When Father Michael looked up his eyes met Ivena's as she trudged under her cross. They were bright and sorrowful at once. She seemed to understand something, but he could not know what. Perhaps she too had heard the song. Either way, he smiled, somehow less afraid than he had been just a minute ago.

Because he knew something now.

He knew there were two worlds in motion here.

He knew that behind the skin of this world, there was another. And in that world a man was singing and the children were laughing.

JANJIC LOOKED at the women shuffling across the courtyard and bit back his growing anger with this demented game of Karadzic's.

He'd dutifully kicked over three gravestones and hefted them to the backs of terrified women. One of them was the birthday girl's mother. Ivena, he heard someone call her.

Janjic could see that she'd taken care to dress for her daughter's special day. Imitation pearls hung around her neck. She wore her hair in a meticulous bun and the dress she'd chosen was neatly pressed; a light pink dress with tiny yellow flowers so that she matched her daughter.

How long had they planned for this party? A week? A month? The thought brought nausea to his gut. These souls were innocent of anything deserving such humiliation. There was something obscene about forcing mothers to lug the ungainly religious symbols while their children looked on.

Ivena could easily be his own mother, holding him after his father's death ten years earlier. Mother, dear Mother—Father's death nearly killed her as well. At ten, Janjic became the man of the house. It was a tall calling. His mother died three days after his eighteenth birthday, leaving him with nothing but the war to join.

The women's dresses were darkened with sweat now, their faces wrinkled with pain, their eyes casting furtive glances at their frightened children on the steps. Still they plodded, back and forth like old mules. Yes, it was obscene.

But then the whole war was obscene.

The priest stood still in his long black robe, hunched over. A dumb look of wonder had captured his face for a moment, then passed. Perhaps he had already fallen into the abyss, watching the women slog their way past him. *Pray to your God, Priest. Tell him to stop this madness before one of your women drops her cross. We have a march to make.*

To his right the sound came, like the sickening crunch of bones, jerking Janjic out of his reverie. He turned his head. One of the women was on her knees, trembling, her hands limp on the ground, her face knotted in distress around clenched eyes.

Marie had dropped her cross.

Movement in the courtyard froze. The women stopped in their tracks as one. Every eye stared at the cement cross lying facedown on the stone beside the woman. Karadzic's face lit up as though the contact of cross with ground completed a circuit that flooded his skull with electricity. A quiver had taken to his lower lip.

Janjic swallowed. The commander snorted once and took three long steps toward Marie. The priest also took a step toward his fallen sheep but stopped when Karadzic spun back to him.

"When your backs are up against the wall, you can no more follow the teachings of Christ than any of us. Perhaps that's why the Jews butchered the man, eh, Paul? Maybe his teachings really were the rantings of a lunatic, impossible for any sane man."

The priest's head snapped up. "It's *God* you speak of!"

Karadzic turned slowly to him. "*God* you say? The Jews killed *God* on a cross, then? You may not be a Franciscan, but you're as stupid."

Father Michael's face flushed red. His eyes shone in shock. "It was for *love* that Christ walked to his death," he said.

Janjic shifted on his feet and felt his pulse quicken. The man of cloth had found his backbone.

"Christ was a fool. Now he's a dead fool," Karadzic said. The words echoed through the courtyard. He paced before Father Michael, his face frozen in a frown.

"Christ lives. He is not dead," the priest said.

"Then let him save you."

The burly commander glared at the priest, who stood tall, soaking in the insults for his God. The sight unnerved Janjic.

24

Father Michael drew a deep breath. "Christ lives in me, sir. His spirit rages through my body. I feel it now. I can hear it. The only reason that you can't is because your eyes and ears are clogged by this world. But there's another world at work here. It's Christ's kingdom and it bristles with his power."

Karadzic took a step back, blinking at the priest's audacity. He suddenly ran for Marie, who was still crumpled on the cement. A dull thump resounded with each boot-fall. In seven long strides he reached her. He swung his rifle like a bat, slamming the wooden butt down on the woman's shoulder. She grunted and fell to her belly.

Sharp gasps filled the air. Karadzic poised his rifle for another blow and twisted to face the priest. "You say you have power? Show me, then!" He landed another blow and the woman moaned.

"Please!" The priest took two steps forward and fell to his knees, his face wrinkled with grief. Tears streamed from his eyes. "Please, it's me you said you would beat!" He clasped his hands together as if in prayer. "Leave her, I beg you. She's innocent."

The rifle butt landed twice on the woman's head, and her body relaxed. Several children began to cry; a chorus of women groaned in shock, still bent under their own heavy loads. The sound grated on Janjic's ears.

"Please . . . please," Father Michael begged.

"Shut up! Janjic, beat him!"

Janjic barely heard the words. His eyes were fixed on the priest.

"Janjic! Beat him." Karadzic pointed with an extended arm. "Ten blows!"

Janjic turned to the commander, still not fully grasping the order. This wasn't his quarrel. It was Karadzic's game. "Beat him? Me? I—"

"You question me?" The commander took a threatening step toward Janjic. "You'll do as I say. Now take your rifle and lay it across this traitor's back or I'll have *you* shot!"

Janjic felt his mouth open.

"Now!"

Two emotions crashed through Janjic's chest. The first was simple revulsion at the prospect of swinging a fifteen-pound rifle at this priest's deformed back. The second was the fear at the realization that he felt any revulsion at all. He was a soldier who'd sworn to follow orders. And he had followed orders always. It was his only way to survive the war. But this . . .

He swallowed and took a step toward the figure, bent now in an attitude of prayer. The children stared at him—thirty sets of round, white-rimmed eyes, swimming in tears, all crying a single question. *Why?*

He glanced at Karadzic's red face. The commander's neck bulged like a bull-frog's and his eyes bored into Janjic. *Because he told me to,* Janjic answered. *Because this man is my superior and he told me to.*

Janjic raised his rifle and stared at the man's hunched back. It was trembling now, he saw. A hard blow might break that back. A knot rose to Janjic's throat. How could he do this? It was lunacy! He lowered the rifle, his mind scrambling for reason.

"Sir, should I make him stand?"

"Should you *what?*"

"Should I make him stand? I could handle the rifle better if he would stand. It would give me a greater attitude to target—"

"Make him stand, then!"

"Yes, sir. I just thought—"

"Move!"

"Yes, sir."

A slight quiver had taken to Janjic's hands. His arms ached under the rifle's weight. He nudged the kneeling priest with his boot.

"Stand, please."

The priest stood slowly and turned to face him. He cast a side glance to the crumpled form near the commander. His tears were for the woman, Janjic realized. There was no fear in his eyes, only remorse over the abuse of one of his own.

He couldn't strike this man! It would be the death of his own soul to do so!

"Beat him!"

Janjic flinched.

"Turn please," he instructed.

The Father turned sideways.

Janjic had no choice. At least that was what he told himself as he drew his rifle back. *It's an order. This is a war. I swore to obey all orders. It's an order. I'm a soldier at war. I have an obligation.*

He swung the rifle by the barrel, aiming for the man's lower back. The sound of sliced air preceded a fleshy *thump* and a grunt from the priest. The man staggered forward and barely caught his fall.

Heat flared up Janjic's back, tingling at the base of his head. Nausea swept through his gut.

The father stood straight again. He looked strong enough, but Janjic knew he might very well have lost a kidney to that blow. A tear stung the corner of his eye. Good God, he was going to *cry!* Janjic panicked.

I'm a soldier, for the love of country! I'm a Partisan! I'm not a coward!

He swung again, with fury this time. The blow went wild and struck the priest on his shoulder. Something gave way with a loud snap—the butt of his rifle. Janjic pulled the gun back, surprised that he could break the wood stock so easily.

But the rifle was not broken.

He jerked his eyes to the priest's shoulder. It hung limp. Janjic felt the blood drain from his head. He saw Father Michael's face then. The priest was expressionless, as if he'd lost consciousness while on his feet.

Janjic lost his sensibilities then. He landed a blow as much to silence the voices screaming foul through his brain as to carry out his orders. He struck again, like a man possessed with the devil, frantic to club the black form before him into silence. He was not aware of the loud moan that broke from his throat until he'd landed six of the blows. His seventh missed, not because he had lost his aim, but because the priest had fallen.

Janjic spun, carried by the swing. The world came back to him then. His comrades standing by the wall, eyes wide with astonishment; the women still bent under stone crosses; the children whimpering and crying and burying their heads in each others' bosoms.

The priest knelt on the concrete, heaving, still expressionless. Blood began to pool on the floor below his face. Some bones had shattered there.

Janjic felt the rifle slip from his hands. It clattered to the concrete.

"Finish it!" Karadzic's voice echoed in the back of Janjic's head, but he did not consider the matter. His legs were shaking and he backed unsteadily from the black form huddled at his feet.

To his right, boots thudded on the concrete and Janjic turned just in time to see his commander rushing at him with a raised rifle. He instinctively threw his arms up to cover his face. But the blows did not come. At least not to him.

They landed with a sickening finality on the priest's back. Three blows in quick succession, accompanied by another snap. The thought that one of the women may have stepped on a twig stuttered through Janjic's mind. But he knew that the snap had come from the father's ribs. He staggered back to the wall and crashed against it.

"You will pay for this, Janjic," Molosov muttered.

Janjic's mind reeled, desperate to correct his spinning world. *Get a hold of yourself, Janjic! You're a soldier! Yes indeed, a soldier who defied his superior's orders. What kind of madness has come over you?*

He straightened. His comrades were turned from him, watching Karadzic, who was yanking the priest to his feet. Janjic looked at the soldiers and saw that a line of sweat ran down the Jew's cheek. Puzup blinked repeatedly.

The priest suddenly gasped. *Uhhh!* The sound echoed in the silence.

Karadzic hardly seemed to notice the odd sound. "March!" he thundered. "The next one to drop a cross will receive twenty blows with the priest. We'll see what kind of faith he has taught you."

The women tottered—gaping, sagging.

The commander gripped his hands into fists. Cords of muscle stood out on his neck. "Maaarch!"

They marched.

IVENA SLOWLY lowered the book with a quiver in her hands. An ache swelled into her throat, threatening to burst out. After so many years the pain seemed no less. She leaned back and drew a deep breath. *Dear Nadia, forgive me.*

Ivena suddenly leaped from her chair. "March!" she mimicked, and she strutted across the cement floor, the book flapping in her right hand. "Maaarch! One, two. One, two." She did it with indignation and fury, and she did it without hardly thinking what she was doing. If any poor soul saw her, marching through her greenhouse like an overstuffed peacock in a dress, they might think her mad.

The thought stopped her midmarch. But she wasn't mad. Merely enlightened. She had the right to march; after all, she was there. She had staggered under her own concrete cross along with the other women, and in the end it had liberated her. And now there was a kind of redemption in remembering; there was a power in participating few could understand.

"Maaarch!" she bellowed, and struck out down the aisle by the tulips. She made the return trip to her chair, smoothed her dress to regain composure, glanced about once just to be sure no one was peeking through the glass, and sat back down.

Now where was I?

You were marching through your greenhouse like an idiot, she thought.

"No, I was putting the power of darkness back in its place. I know the ending."

She cracked the book, flipped a few pages to find where she had left off and began to read.

CHAPTER FOUR

FATHER MICHAEL remembered arguing with the commander; remembered Karadzic's rifle butt smashing down on Sister Marie's skull; remembered the other soldier, the skinny one, making him stand and then raising the rifle to strike him. He even remembered closing his eyes against that first blow to his kidneys. But that blow ignited the strobe in his mind.

Poof!

The courtyard vanished in a flash of light.

The white desert crashed into his world. Fingers of light streaked from the horizon. The ground was covered with the white flowers. And the music!

Oh, the music. The children's laughter rode the skies, playing off the man's song. His volume had grown, intensified, compelling Michael to join in the laughter. The same simple tune, but now others seemed to have joined in to form a chorus. Or maybe it just sounded like a chorus but was really just laughter.

Sing O son of Zion, Shout O child of mine
Rejoice with all your heart and soul and mind

Michael was vaguely aware of a crashing on the edge of his world. It was as if he lived in a Christmas ornament and a child had taken a stick to it. But it wasn't a stick, he knew that. It wasn't a child either. It was the soldier with a rifle, beating his bones.

He heard a loud snap. *I've got to hurry up before the roof caves in about me! I've got to hurry! My bones are breaking.*

Hurry? Hurry where?

Hurry to meet this man. Hurry to find the children, of course. Problem was, he still couldn't see them. He could hear them, all right. Their laughter rippled over the field in long, uncontrolled strings that forced a smile to his mouth.

The figure was still far away, a foot high on the horizon now, walking straight toward Michael, singing his incredible song. He would have expected music to reach him through his ears, but this song didn't bother with the detour. It seemed to reach right through his chest and squeeze his heart. Love and hope and sorrow and laughter all rolled up in one.

He opened his mouth without thinking and sang a couple of the words. *O child of mine* . . . A silly grin spread his cheeks. What did he think he was doing? But he felt a growing desperation to sing with the man, to match the chorus with his own. *La da da, da la!* Mozart! An angel with the purest melody known to man. To God!

And he wanted to laugh! He almost did. He almost threw his head back and cackled. His chest felt as though it might explode with the desire. But he could not see the children. And that stick was making an awful racket about his bones.

Without ceremony, the world with all of its color and light and music was jerked from him. He was back in the village.

He heard himself gasp. *Uhhh!* It was like having a bucket of cold water thrown at him while taking a warm shower. He was standing now, facing Marie's fallen body. The spring gurgled on as if nothing at all had happened. The women were frozen in place. The children were crying.

And pain was spreading through his flesh like leaking acid.

Oh, God. What is happening? What are you doing to your children?

His shoulder did not feel right. Neither did his cheek.

He wanted to be back in the laughing world with the children. Marie stirred on the ground. The commander was screaming and now the women started to move, like ghosts in a dream.

No. The colors of Father Michael's world brightened. *No, I do not belong with the laughing children. I belong here with my own children. These whom God has given me charge over. They need me.*

But he didn't know what he should do. He wasn't even sure he could talk. So he prayed. He cried out to God to save them from this wicked man.

THE COURTYARD *had become a wasteland,* Janjic thought. A wasteland filled with frozen guards and whimpering children and moaning women. The ravens soared in an unbroken circle now, a dozen strong. A lone dove watched the scene from its perch on the house to his right.

30

Janjic swallowed, thinking that he might cry. But he would swallow his tongue before he allowed tears. He had humiliated himself enough.

Molosov and the others stood expressionless, drawing shallow breaths, waiting for Karadzic's next move in this absurd game. An hour ago Janjic was bored with the distraction of the village. Ten minutes ago, he found himself horrified at beating the priest. And now . . . now he was slipping into an odd state of anger and apathy drummed home by the plodding footfalls about him.

The girl with a flat face and freckles—the birthday girl dressed in pink—suddenly stood up.

She stood on the third step and stared at the commander for a few moments, as if gathering her resolve. She was going to do something. What had come over this girl? She was a *child*, for heaven's sake. A war child, not so innocent as most at such a tender age, but a child nonetheless. He'd never seen a young girl as brave as this one looked now, standing with arms at her side, staring at the commander across the courtyard.

"Nadia!" a woman called breathlessly. Her mother, Ivena, who had stopped beneath her heavy cross.

Without removing her eyes from the commander, the girl walked down the steps and limped for Karadzic.

"Nadia! Go back! Get back on the steps this minute!" Ivena cried.

The girl ignored her mother's order and walked right up to the commander. She stopped five feet from him and looked up at his face. Karadzic didn't return her wide stare, but kept his eyes fixed on some unseen point directly ahead. Nadia's eyes were misty, Janjic saw, but she wasn't crying.

It occurred to Janjic that he had stopped breathing. Sound and motion had been sucked from the courtyard as if by a vacuum. The children's whimpers fell silent. The women froze in their tracks. Not an eye blinked.

The girl spoke. "Father Michael has taught us that in the end only love matters. Love is giving, not taking. My friends were giving me gifts today because they love me. Now you've taken everything. Do you hate us?"

The commander spit at her. "Shut up, you ugly little wench! You have no respect?"

"I mean no disrespect, sir. But I can't stand to see you hurt our village."

"Please, Nadia," Ivena said.

The priest stood quivering, his face half off, his shoulders grotesquely slumped, staring at Nadia with his one good eye.

Karadzic blinked. Nadia turned to face her mother and spoke very quietly. "I'm sorry, Mother."

She looked Karadzic in the eyes. "If you're good, sir, why are you hurting us? Father Michael has taught us that religion without God is foolishness. And God is love. But how is this love? Love is—"

"Shut your hole!" Karadzic lifted a hand to strike her. "Shut your tiny hole, you insolent—"

"Stop! Please stop!" Ivena staggered forward three steps from the far side, uttering little panicky guttural sounds.

Karadzic glared at Nadia, but he did not swing his hand.

Nadia never took her round blue eyes off the commander. Her lower lip quivered for a moment. Tears leaked down her cheek in long, silent streams. "But sir, how can I shut up if you make my mother carry that load on her back? She has only so much strength. She will drop the cross and then you'll beat her. I can't stand to watch this."

Karadzic ignored the girl and looked around at the scattered women, bent, unmoving, staring at him. "March! Did I tell you to stop? March!"

But they did not. *Something had changed,* Janjic thought. They looked at Karadzic, their gazes fixed. Except for Ivena. She was bent like a pack mule, shaking, but slowly, ever so slowly, she began to straighten with the cross on her back.

Janjic wanted to scream out. *Stop, woman! Stop, you fool! Stay down!*

Nadia spoke in a wavering tone now. "I beg you, sir. Please let these mothers put down their crosses. Please leave us. This would not please our Lord Jesus. It's not his love."

"Shut up!" Karadzic thundered. He took a step toward Nadia, grabbed one of her pigtails and yanked.

She winced and stumbled after him, nearly falling except for his grip on her hair. Karadzic pulled the girl to the father, who looked on, tears running down his cheek now.

Ivena's cross slipped from her back then.

Janjic alone watched it, and he felt its impact through his boot when it landed.

Nadia's mother ran for Karadzic. She'd already taken three long strides when the dull thump jerked the commander's heads toward her. She took two more, half the distance to the commander, head bent and eyes fixed, before uttering a sound. And then her mouth snapped wide and she shrieked in fury. A full-throated roaring scream that met Janjic's mind like a dentist's drill meeting a raw nerve.

Karadzic whipped the girl behind him like a rag doll. He stepped forward and met the rushing woman's face with his fist. The blow sent her reeling, bleeding profusely from the nose. She slumped to her knees, silenced to a moan.

And then another cross fell.

And another, and another until they were slamming to the concrete in a rain of stone. The women struggled to stand tall, all of them.

A streak of fear crossed Karadzic's gray eyes, Janjic realized. But he wasn't thinking too clearly just now. He was trembling under the weight of the atmosphere. A thick air of insanity laced by the crazy notion that *he* should stop this. That he should scream out in protest, or maybe put a bullet in Karadzic's head— anything to end this madness.

The commander jerked his pistol from his belt and shoved it against the priest's forehead. He spun the girl toward the priest and released her. "You think your dead Christ will save your priest now?"

"Sir . . ." The objection came from Janjic's throat before he could stop it.

Stop, Janjic! Shut up! Sit back!

But he did not. He took a single step forward. "Sir, please. This is enough. Please, we should leave these people alone."

Karadzic shot him a furious stare, and Janjic saw hatred in those deep-set eyes. The commander looked back at the girl, who was staring up at the priest through the pools of tears that rimmed her eyes.

"I think I'll shoot your priest. Yes?"

Father Michael gazed into the little girl's face. There was a connection between their eyes, shafts of invisible energy. *The priest and the girl were speaking,* Janjic thought. Speaking with this look of love. Tears streamed down their cheeks.

Janjic felt a wedge of panic rise to his throat. "Please, sir. Please, show them kindness. They have done nothing."

"Sometimes love is best spoken with a bullet," Karadzic said.

The girl stared into the eyes of her priest, and her look gripped Janjic with terror. He wanted to tear his gaze away from the girl's face, but he couldn't. It was a look of love in its purest form, Janjic knew, a love he had never seen before.

Nadia spoke softly, still staring at the priest. "Don't kill my priest." Her voice whispered across the courtyard. "If you have to kill someone, then kill me instead."

A murmur ran though the crowd. The girl's mother clambered to unsteady legs, gulping for air. Her face twisted in anguish. "Oh, God! Nadia! Nadia!"

Nadia held up a hand, stopping her mother. "No, Mother. It will be okay. You will see. It's what Father Michael has taught us. Shh. It's okay. Don't cry."

Oh, such words! From a child! Janjic felt hot tears on his cheek. He took another step forward. "Please, sir, I beg you!" It came out like a sob, but he no longer cared.

Karadzic's lips twitched once. Then again, to a grin. He lowered his gun from the priest. It hung by his waist.

He lifted it suddenly and pressed the barrel to the girl's head.

The mother's restraint snapped and she launched herself at the commander, arms forward, fingernails extended like claws, shrieking. This time the second in command, Molosov, anticipated her move. He was running from his position behind Janjic as soon as Ivena moved, and he landed a kick to her midsection before she reached Karadzic. She doubled over and retched. Molosov jerked the woman's arms behind her and dragged her back.

Nadia closed her eyes and her shoulders began to shake in a silent sob.

"Since your flock has failed to prove its faith, you will renounce your faith, Priest. Do that and I will let this little one live." Karadzic's voice cut through the panic. He looked around at the women. "Renounce your dead Christ and I will leave you all."

Ivena began to whimper with short squeaky sounds that forced their way past white lips. For a moment the rest seemed not to have heard. Father Michael stiffened. For several long seconds his face registered nothing.

And then it registered everything, knotting up impossibly around his shattered cheekbone. His tall frame began to shake with sobs and his limp arm bounced loosely.

"Speak, Priest! Renounce Christ!"

THE PHONE rang, and Ivena jerked upright. Her heart slammed in her chest. *Oh, Nadia! Oh, dear Nadia.* A teardrop darkened the page by her thumb. She closed her eyes and let the book close on one finger.

The phone rang again, from the kitchen.

Oh, Nadia, I love you so much. You were so brave. So very, very brave!

Ivena began to cry then; she just could not help it. Didn't want to help it. She bowed her head and sobbed.

She had done this a hundred times; a thousand times, and each time she reached this point it was the same. The hardest part of remembering. But it was also the most rewarding part. Because in moments like this she knew that her heart was breaking with her Father's, looking down at miserable man; at the leper; the whore; the common pedestrian in Atlanta; Nadia. The ache in her heart now was no different from the ache in God's heart for his stray creation. It was there only because of love.

And she did love Nadia. She really did.

The phone rang incessantly.

Ivena sniffed, twisted to stand, and then thought better of it. Whoever it was could wait. It was only ten o'clock and she had no deliveries today. They could call back. She was nearly finished here anyway; no use running off prematurely. Nothing mattered as much as remembering. Except for following.

Ivena took a gulp of cool tea and let the phone ring out. When it did, she adjusted herself on the chair, sniffed again, and then began to read.

FATHER MICHAEL'S world kept blinking on and off, alternating like intermittent static between this ghastly scene here and the white-flowered field there. He was jerked back and forth with such intensity that he hardly knew which scene was real and which was a figment of his imagination.

But that was just it. Neither world came from his imagination. He knew that now with certainty. He was simply being allowed to see and hear both worlds. His spiritual eyes and ears were being opened in increments, and he could hardly stand the contrast. One second this terrifying evil in the courtyard, and the next the music.

Oh the music! Impossible to describe. Raw energy stripping him of all but pleasure. The man was only a few hundred meters distant now, arms spread so that his cloak draped wide. An image of Saint Francis, but more. Yes, much more. Michael imagined a wide, mischievous grin on the man, but he couldn't see it for the distance. The man walked toward him steadily, purposefully, still singing. The giggling children sang with him in perfect harmony now. A symphony slowly swelling. The melody begged him to join. To leap into the field and throw his arms up and dance with laughter along with the hidden children.

Across the courtyard, the tall cross leading to the cemetery stood bold against the other world's gray sky. He had pointed to that very cross a thousand times, teaching his children the truth of God. And he had taught them well.

"You may look at that cross and think of it as a gothic decoration, engraved with roses and carved with style, but do not forget that it represents life and death. It represents the scales on which all of our lives will be weighed. It's an instrument of torture and death—the symbol of our faith. They butchered God on a cross. And Christ emphasized none of his teachings so adamantly as our need to take up our own crosses and follow him."

Nadia had looked up to him, squinting in the sun—he saw it clearly in his mind's eye now. "Does this mean that we should die for him?"

"If need be, of course, Nadia. We will all die, yes? So then if we have worn out our bodies in service to him, then we are dying for him, yes? Like a battery that expends its power."

"But what if the battery is still young when it dies?" That had silenced those gathered.

He reached down and stroked her chin. "Then you would be fortunate enough to pass this plain world quickly. What waits beyond is the prize, Nadia. This"—he looked up and drew a hand across the horizon—"this fleeting world may look like the garden of Eden to us, but it's nothing more than a taste. Tell me," and he looked at the adults gathered now, "at a wedding feast you receive gifts, yes? Beautiful, lovely gifts . . . vases and perfumes and scarves . . . all delightful in our eyes. We all gather around the gifts and show our pleasure. *What a glorious scarf, Ivena.*"

A chuckle ran through the crowd.

"But do you think that Ivena's mind is on the scarf?" A run of giggles. "No, I think not. Ivena's mind is on her groom, waiting breathlessly in the next room. The man whom she will wed in sweet union. Yes?"

"I don't recall seeing a cross at the last wedding," Ivena had said.

"No, not at our weddings. But death is like a wedding." The crowd hushed. "And the crucifixion of Christ was a grand wedding announcement. This world we now live in may indeed be a beautiful gift from God, but do not forget that we wait with breathless anticipation for our union with him beyond this life." He let the truth finger its way through their minds for a moment. "And how do you suppose we arrive at the wedding?"

Nadia answered. "We die."

He looked down into her smiling blue eyes. "Yes, child. We die."

"Then why shouldn't we just die now?" Nadia asked.

"Heaven forbid, child! What bride do you know who would take her own life before the wedding? No one who understands how beautiful the bride is could possibly take her life before the wedding! It is perhaps the ugliest thing of all. We will all cross the threshold when the groom calls. Until then, we wait with breathless anticipation."

One of the women had sighed with approval.

Somehow, looking at the large concrete cross now did not engender any such mirth. He looked down at the child and felt as though a shaft had been run through his heart.

Nadia, oh, my dear Nadia, what are you doing? I love you so, young child. I love you as though you were my own. And you are my own. You know that, don't you, Nadia?

She looked at him with deep blue eyes. *I love you, Father.* Her eyes were speaking to him, as clearly as any words. And he wept.

"Don't kill my priest. If you have to kill someone, then kill me instead," a voice said.

He heard the words like a distant echo . . . words! She had actually said that? *Don't be foolish, Nadia!*

A flash of light sputtered to life about him. The white field again!

The music flooded his mind and he suddenly wanted to laugh with it. It felt so . . . consequential here, and the silly little game back in the courtyard so . . . petty. Like a game of marbles with all the neighborhood children gathered, sporting stern faces as if the outcome might very well determine the fate of the world. If they only knew that their little game felt so small here, in this immense white landscape that rippled with laughter. Ha! If they only knew! Kill us! Kill us all! Put an end to this silly game of marbles and let us get on with life, with laughing and music in the white field.

The white world blinked off. But now the commander had the gun pushed against Nadia's forehead. "Renounce your faith, Priest, and I will let this little one live! Renounce your dead Christ and I will leave you all."

It took a moment for him to switch worlds—for the words to present their meaning to him.

And then they did, with the force of a sledge to his head.

Renounce Christ?

Never! He could never renounce Christ!

Then Nadia will die.

This realization cut through his bones like a dagger. She would die because of him! His face throbbed with pain; the muscles there had gone taut like bowstrings. But never! Never could he renounce his love for Christ!

Father Michael had never before felt the torment that descended upon him in that moment. It was as if some molten hand had reached into his chest and grabbed hold, searing frayed nerves so that he could not draw breath. His throat pulled for air to no avail.

Nadia! Nadia! I can't!

"Speak, Priest! Renounce Christ!"

She was crying. Oh, the dear girl was crying! The courtyard waited.

The music filled his mind.

Fresh air flooded his lungs. Relief, such sweet relief! The white field ran to the horizon; the children laughed incessantly.

"I will count to three, Priest!"

The commander's voice jerked him back to the courtyard.

Nadia was looking at him. She had stopped her crying. Sorrow overcame him again.

"One!" Karadzic barked.

"Nadia," Father Michael croaked. "Nadia, I—"

"Don't, Father," she said softly. Her small pinks lips clearly formed the words. *Don't, Father.* Don't what? This from a child! Nadia, dear Nadia!

"Two!"

A wail rose over the crowd. It was Ivena. Poor Ivena. She strained against the large soldier, who held her arms pinned behind her back. She clenched her eyes and dropped her jaw and now screamed her protest from the back of her throat. The solider clamped a hand around her face, stifling her cry.

Oh God, have mercy on her soul! Oh God . . . "Nadia . . ." Father Michael could barely speak, so great was the pressure in his chest. His legs wobbled beneath him and suddenly they collapsed. He landed on his knees and lifted his one good arm to the girl. "Nadia—"

"I heard the song, Father." She spoke quietly. Light sparkled through her eyes. A faint smile softened her features. The girl had lost her fear. Entirely!

Nadia hummed, faint, high-pitched, clear for all to hear. *"Hm hm hm hmhmm . . ."* The melody! Dear God, she had heard it too!

"Three!" Karadzic barked.

"I saw you there," she said. And she winked.

Her eyes were wide open, an otherworldly blue penetrating his, when the gun bucked in the commander's thick, gnarled hand.

Boom!

Her head snapped back. She stood in the echoing silence for an endless moment, her chin pointed to sky, baring that tender pale neck. And then she crumpled to the ground like a sack of potatoes. A small one, wrapped in a pink dress.

Father Michael's mind began to explode. His own voice joined a hundred others in a long epitaph of distress. "Aaaaahhhhhh . . ." It screamed past his throat until the last whisper of breath had left his lungs. Then it began again, and Michael wanted desperately to die. He wanted absolutely nothing but to die.

Ivena's mouth lay wide open, but no sound came out. Only a breath of terror that seemed to strike Michael on his chest.

The priest's world began to spin and he lost his orientation. He fell forward, face first, swallowed by the horror of the moment. His head struck the concrete and his mind began to fade. Maybe he was in hell.

CHAPTER FIVE

IVENA WAS reading through tears now. Wiping at her eyes with the back of her hand and sniffing and trying to keep the page clear enough to read. The sorrow felt like a deep healing balm as it washed through her chest in relentless waves.

It felt that way because she knew what was coming next and she could hardly wait to get there! Her fingers held a slight tremble as she turned these few pages. They were worn ragged on the corners. The book stated elsewhere that you could not find mountains without going through valleys. In all honesty she didn't know whether her Nadia's death was a mountain or a valley. It really depended on perspective.

And truly, the perspective was about to change.

JANJIC STARED, his eyes wide and stinging. All about him voices of torment screamed; pandemonium erupted on the courtyard floor. Father Michael lay face-down, his head not five inches from the girl's shiny white birthday shoes.

Karadzic reached out and snatched another child by the collar. The boy's mother wailed in protest, started forward, and then stopped when Karadzic shoved the gun toward her. "Shut up! Shut up! Everyone!" he thundered.

Janjic was running before his mind processed the order to run. Straight for the priest. Or perhaps straight for Karadzic, he didn't know which until the last possible second. The man had to be stopped.

How the commander managed to get his pistol around so quickly Janjic had no clue, but the black Luger whipped around and met him with a jarring blow to his cheek.

Pain shot over his skull. It felt like he'd run into a swinging bat. His head jerked back and his legs flew forward, throwing him from his feet. Janjic landed heavily on his back and rolled over, moaning. What was he doing? Stopping Karadzic—that's what he was doing.

Janjic dragged himself from the commander, urged by a boot kick to his thigh. His mind swam. The world seemed to slow. Five feet away on the ground lay a girl who'd just given her life for her priest. For her God. For Christ's love. And Janjic had seen in her eyes a look of absolute certainty. He had seen her smile at the priest. He had seen the wink. A *wink*, for goodness sake! Something had changed with that wink. He was not sure what it meant, except that something had changed.

Dear God, she had hummed! She had *winked!*

"Puzup, get him to his feet," Karadzic ordered above the din.

Puzup stormed past Janjic and yanked the priest to his feet. Paul gaped at the scene, his expression impossible to interpret. Janjic pushed himself to his knees, ignoring the pain that throbbed through his skull. Blood dripped to the concrete from a wound behind his ear. He turned back to the commander and stood shakily. Ten feet separated them now.

The priest wavered on his feet, facing Karadzic. If the father had passed out from his fall, they had awakened him. The little boy the commander had hauled from the steps stood shaking and bawling. Karadzic pressed his pistol against the boy's ear.

"What do you say, Priest? What's this love of yours worth? Should I put another one of your children out of their misery?" Karadzic's eyes were rocks behind bushy brows, dull gray tombstones. He was grinning. "Or will you renounce your stupid faith?"

"Kill me," Father Michael's voice quavered.

Janjic stopped trying to understand the madness that had gripped this priest and his flock of sheep. It was beyond the reaches of his mind. Yet it reached out to him with long fingers of desire.

"Take my life, sir. Please leave the boy."

The smile vanished from commander's face. "Then renounce your faith, you blithering idiot! They are words! Just words! Say them. Say them!"

"They are words of Christ. He is my redeemer. He is my Savior. He is my Creator. How can I deny my own Creator? Please, sir—"

"He is your redeemer? He is her redeemer too?" He motioned to the girl on the ground. "She is dead, you fool."

The priest stood trembling for a few moments before responding. "She sees you now. She is laughing."

Karadzic stared at Father Michael.

The women had stopped their cries and the children sat still, faces buried in their mothers' skirts.

"If you must have another death, let it be mine," the priest said.

And then the rules of the game changed once more.

The girl's mother, Ivena, who had grown eerily calm, suddenly wrested herself free from Molosov but did not rush the commander again. Molosov grabbed one arm but let her stand on her own. "No," she said softly, "let it be mine. Kill me in the boy's place." She stood unflinching, like a stone statue.

Karadzic now stood with the pistol to the whimpering boy's ear, between a man and a woman each asking for death in the boy's place. He shifted on his feet, unsure how much power he truly held over this scene.

Another woman stepped forward, her face twisted in pity. "No. No, kill me instead. I will die for the boy. The priest has already suffered too much. And Ivena has lost her only child. I am childless. Take my life. I will join Nadia."

"No, I will," another said, taking two steps forward. "You are young, Kota. I am old. Please, this world holds no appeal to me. It would be good for me to pass on to be with our Lord." The woman looked to be in her fifties.

Karadzic slashed the air with his pistol. "Silence! Perhaps I should kill *all* of you! I am killing here, not playing a game. You want me to kill you all?" Janjic had known the man long enough to recognize his faltering. But there was something else there as well. A glimmer of excitement that flashed through his gray eyes. Like a dog in heat.

"But it really should be me," a voice said. Janjic looked to the steps where another girl stood facing them with her heels together. "Nadia was my best friend," she said. "I should join her. Is there really music there, Father?"

The priest could not answer. He was weeping uncontrollably. Torn to shreds by this display of love.

The gun boomed and Janjic flinched.

Karadzic held the weapon above his head. He'd fired into the air. "Stop! Stop!" He shoved the boy sprawling to his seat. His thick lips glistened with spittle. The gun shook in his thick fingers, and above it all his eyes sparkled with rising excitement.

He stepped back and turned the pistol on Nadia's mother. She simply closed her eyes. Janjic understood her motivation to some degree: The woman's only child lay at her feet. She was stepping up to the bullet with a grief-ravaged mind.

He held his breath in anticipation of a shot.

Karadzic licked his wet lips and jerked the weapon to the younger woman who'd stepped forward. She too closed her eyes. But Karadzic did not shoot. He swiveled it to the older woman. Looking at them all now, Janjic thought that any one of the women might give their lives for the boy. It was a moment that could not be understood in the context of normal human experience. A great spiritual love had settled on them all. Karadzic was more than capable of killing; he was in fact eager for it. And yet the women stood square-shouldered now, daring him to pull the trigger.

Janjic swayed on weak legs, overcome by the display of self-sacrifice. The ravens cawed overhead and he glanced skyward, as much for a reprieve as in response to the bird's call. At first he thought the ravens had flown off; that a black cloud had drifted over the valley in their place. But then he saw the cloud ebb and flow and he knew it was a singular ring of birds—a hundred or more, gliding overhead making their odd call. What was happening here? He lowered his eyes to the courtyard and blinked against the buzz that had overtaken the pounding in his skull.

For a long, silent minute Karadzic weighed his decision, his muscles strung to the snapping point, sweating profusely, breathing heavily.

The villagers did not move; they drilled him with steady stares. The priest seemed to float in and out of consciousness, swaying on his feet, opening and closing his eyes periodically. His face drifted through a range of expressions—one moment his eyes open and his mouth sagged with grief, the next his eyes closed and his mouth opened in wonder. Janjic studied him, and his heart broke for the man. He wanted to take the gentle priest to a bed and dress his wounds. Bathe him in hot water and soothe his battered shoulder. His face would never be the same; the damage looked far too severe. He would probably be blind in his right eye, and eating would prove difficult for some time. Poor priest. *My poor, poor priest. I swear that I will care for you, my priest. I will come and serve . . .*

What was this? What was he thinking? Janjic stopped himself. But it was true. He knew it then as much as he had known anything. He loved this man. He cherished this man. His heart felt sick over this man.

I will come and serve you, my priest. A knot rose to Janjic's throat, suffocating him. *In you I have seen love, Priest. In you and your children and your women I have seen God. I will . . .*

A chuckle interrupted his thoughts. The commander was chuckling. Looking around and chuckling. The sound engendered terror. The man was completely mad! He suddenly lowered his gun and studied the crowd, nodding slightly, tasting a new plan on his thick tongue.

"Haul this priest to the large cross," he said. No one moved. Not even Molosov, who stood behind Ivena.

"Are you deaf, Molosov? Take him. Puzup, Paul, help Molosov." He stared at the large stone cross facing the cemetery. "We will give them what they desire."

FATHER MICHAEL remembered stumbling across the concrete, shoved from behind, tripping to his knees once and then being hauled up under his arms. He remembered the pain shooting through his shoulder and thinking someone had pulled his arm off. But it still swung ungainly by his side.

He remembered the cries of protest from the women. "Leave the Father! I beg you . . . He's a good man . . . Take one of us. We beg you!"

The world twisted topsy-turvy as they approached the cross. They left the girl lying on the concrete in pool of blood. *Nadia . . . Nadia, sweet child.* Ivena knelt by her daughter, weeping bitterly again, but a soldier jabbed her with his rifle, forcing her to follow the crowd to the cemetery.

The tall stone cross leaned against a white sky, gray and pitted. It had been erected one hundred years earlier. They called it stone, but the twelve-foot cross was actually cast of concrete, with etchings of rosebuds at the top and at the beams' intersection. Each end flared like a clover leaf, giving the instrument of death an incongruous sense of delicacy.

The pain on his right side reached to his bones. Some had been broken. *Oh, Father. Dear Father, give me strength.* The dove still sat on the roof peak and eyed them carefully. The spring bubbled without pause, oblivious of this treachery.

They reached the cross, and a sudden brutal pain shot through Michael's spine. His world faded.

When his mind crawled back into consciousness, a wailing greeted him. His head hung low, bowed from his shoulders, facing the dirt. His ribs stuck out like sticks beneath stretched skin. He was naked except for white boxer shorts, now stained in sweat and blood.

Michael blinked and struggled for orientation. He tried to lift his head, but pain sliced through his muscles. The women were singing, long mournful wails without tune. Mourning for whom? *For you. They're mourning you!*

But why? It came back to him then. He had been marched to the cross. They had lashed him to the cross with a hemp rope around the midsection and shoulders, leaving his feet to dangle free.

He lifted his chin slowly and craned for a view, ignoring the shafts of pain down his right side. The commander stood to his left, the barrel of his pistol confronting Michael like a small black tunnel. The man looked at the women, most of whom had fallen to their knees, pleading with him.

A woman's words came to Michael. "He's our priest. He's a servant of God. You cannot kill him! You can not." It was Ivena.

Oh, dear Ivena! Your heart is spun of gold!

The priest felt his body quiver as he slowly straightened his heavy head. He managed to lift it upright and let it flop backward. It struck the concrete cross with a dull thump.

The wailing ceased. They had heard. But now he stared up at the darkened sky. A white, overcast sky filled with black birds. *Goodness, there must be hundreds of birds flying around up there.* He tilted his head to his left and let it loll so that it rested on his good shoulder.

Now he saw them all. The kneeling women, the children staring with bulging eyes, the soldiers. The commander looked up at him and smiled. He was breathing heavily; his gray eyes were bloodshot. A long thin trail of spittle ran down his chin and hung suspended from a wet chin. He was certifiably mad, this one. Mad or possessed.

The lunatic turned back to the women. "One of you. That's all! One, one, one! A single stray sheep. If *one* of you will renounce Christ, I will leave you all!"

Father Michael felt his heart swell in his chest. He looked at the women and silently pleaded for them to remain quiet, yet he doubted his dismay showed—his muscles had lost most of their control.

Do not renounce our Lord! Don't you dare speak out for me! You cannot take this from me!

He tried to speak, but only a faint groan came out. That and a string of saliva, which dripped to his chest. He moved his eyes to Ivena. *Don't let them, Ivena. I beg you!*

"What's wrong with you? You can't hear? I said *one* of you! Surely you have a sinner in your pretty little town, willing to speak out to save your precious priest's miserable neck! Speak!"

Bright light filled Michael's mind, blinding him to the cemetery.

The field! But something had changed. Silence!

Absolute silence.

The man had stopped, thirty meters off, legs planted in the flowers, hands on his hips, dressed in a robe like a monk. Above his head the light still streaked in from the horizon. And silence.

Michael blinked. What . . .

Sing O son of Zion; Shout O child of mine
Rejoice with all your heart and soul and mind

The man's words echoed over the field.

Child of mine! Michael's lips twitched to a slight grin. Rejoice with all . . .

The man suddenly threw his arms out to either side lifted his head to the sky and sang.

Every tear you cried dried in the palm of my hand
Every lonely hour was by my side
Every loved one lost, every river crossed
Every moment, every hour was pointing to this day
Longing for this day . . .
For you are finally home

Michael felt as though he might faint for the sheer power of the melody. He wanted to run to the man. He wanted to throw out his own arms and tilt his head back and wail the same song from the bottom of his chest. A few notes dribbled past Michael's lips, uncontrolled. La da da da la . . .

A faint giggling sound came from his left. He turned.

She was skipping toward him in long bounds. Michael caught his breath. He could not see her face because the girl's chin was tilted back so that she stared at the sky. She leaped through the air, landing barefoot on the white petals every ten yards, her fists pumping with each footfall. Her pink dress fluttered in the wind.

She was echoing the man's melody now, not like Michael had done, but perfectly in tune and then in harmony.

Father Michael knew then that this girl hurtling toward him was Nadia. And in her wake followed a thousand others, bubbling with a laughter that swelled with the music.

The song swallowed him whole now. They were all singing it, led by the man. It was impossible to discern the laughter from the music—they were one and the same.

Nadia lowered her head and shot him a piercing stare as she flew by. Her blue eyes sparkled mischievously, as though daring him to give chase.

But there was a difference about Nadia. Something so startling that Michael's heart skipped a beat.

Nadia was beautiful!

She looked exactly as she had before her death. Same freckles, same pigtails, same plump facial features. But in this reality he found that those freckles and that thick face and all that had made her homely before, now looked . . .

Beautiful. Nearly intoxicating. His own perspective had changed!

He took an involuntary step forward, dumbfounded. And he knew in that moment that his pity for both Nadia's appearance and her death had been badly misplaced.

Nadia was beautiful all along. Physically beautiful. And her death held its own beauty as well.

Oh death, where is thy sting?

For the first time his eyes saw her as she truly was. Before, his sight had been masked by a preoccupation for the reality that now seemed foolish and distant by comparison. Like mud pies next to delicious mounds of ice cream.

A wind rushed by, filled with the laughter of a thousand souls. The white flower petals swirled in their wake. Michael couldn't hold back his chuckles now. They shook his chest.

"Nadia!" he called. "Nadia."

She disappeared over the horizon. He looked out to the man.

Gone!

But the voice still filled the sky. Michael's bones felt like putty. Nothing else mattered now. Nothing.

They suddenly came at him again, streaking in from the left, led by this beautiful child he'd once thought was ugly. This time she had her head down. She drilled him with sparkling, mischievous eyes while she was still far off.

He wanted to join her train this time. To leap out in its wake and fly with her. He was planning to do just that. His whole body was quivering for this intoxicating ride that she was daring him to take. The desire flooded his veins and he staggered forward a step.

He staggered! He did not fly as she flew!

Nadia rushed up to him, then veered skyward with a single leap. His mouth dropped open. She shot for the streaking light above. Her giggles rose to a shrieking laughter and he heard her call, crystal clear.

"Come on, Father Michael! Come on! You think this is neat? This is *nothing!*"

It reverberated across the desert. *This is nothing!*

Nothing!

Desperation filled Michael. He took another step forward, but his foot seemed filled with lead. His heart slammed in his chest, flooding his veins with fear. "Nadia! Nadia!"

The white field turned off as if someone had pulled a plug.

Michael realized that he was crying. He was back in the village, hanging on a cross before his parishioners . . . crying like a baby.

CHAPTER SIX

JANJIC WATCHED the priest's body heaving with sobs up on that cross, and he pushed himself unsteadily to his feet. Nothing mattered to him now except that the priest be set free. If need be, he would die or kill or renounce Christ himself.

But with a single look into the priest's eyes, Janjic knew the priest wanted to die now. He'd found something of greater value than life. He had found this love for Christ.

Karadzic was shaking his gun at the priest, glaring at the villagers, trying to force apostasy and carrying on as if he thought the whole thing was some delicious joke. But the priest had led his flock well. They didn't seem capable of speaking out against their Christ, regardless of what it meant to the priest.

"Speak now or I'll kill him!" Karadzic screamed.

"I will speak."

Janjic lifted his head. Who'd said that? A man. The priest? No, the priest did not possess the strength.

"I will speak for my children." It *was* the priest! It was the priest, lifting his head and looking squarely at Karadzic, as if he'd received a transfusion of energy.

"Your threat of death doesn't frighten us, soldier." He spoke gently, without anger, through tears that still ran down his face. "We've been purchased by blood, we live by the power of that blood, we will die for that blood. And we would never, never, renounce our beloved Christ." His voice croaked. "He is our Creator, sir."

The priest turned his eyes to the women, and slowly a smile formed on his lips. "My children, please. Please . . ." His face wrinkled with despair. His beard was matted with blood and he could hardly speak for all the tears now.

"Please." The priest's voice came soft now. "Let me go. Don't hold me back . . . Love all those who cross your path, they are all beautiful. So . . . so very beautiful."

Not a soul moved.

A cockeyed, distant smile crossed the priest's lips. He lowered his head, exhausted. A flutter of wings beat through the air. It was the white dove, flapping toward them. It hovered above the father, then settled quietly to the cross, eyeing the bloodied man three feet under its stick feet.

The sound came quiet at first, like a distant train struggling up a hill. But it was no locomotive; it was the priest and he was laughing. His head hung and his body shook.

Janjic instinctively took a step backward.

The sound grew louder. Maybe the man had gone mad. But Janjic knew that nothing could be further from the truth. The priest was perhaps the sanest man he had ever known.

He suddenly lifted his head and spoke . . . no, he didn't speak, he sang. With mucus leaking from his nostrils and tears wetting his bloodied cheeks, wearing a face of unearthly delight, he threw his head back and sang in a rough, strained voice.

"Sing, o child of mine . . . "

And then he began to laugh.

The picture of contrasts slammed into Janjic's chest and took his breath away. Heat broke over his skull and swept down his back.

The laughter echoed over the graveyard now. Karadzic trembled, rooted to the earth. Ivena was looking up at the priest, weeping with the rest of the women. But it was not terror or even sorrow that gripped her; it was something else entirely. Something akin to desire. Something . . .

A gunshot boomed around Janjic's ears and he jumped. A coil of smoke rose from Karadzic's waving pistol.

The resounding report left absolute silence in its wake, snuffing out the laughter. Father Michael slumped on the cross. If he wasn't dead, he would be soon enough.

Then Janjic ran. He whirled around, aware only of the heat crashing through his body. He did not think to run, he just ran. On legs no stronger than puffs of cotton, he fled the village.

When his mind caught up to him, it told him that he also had just died.

JANJIC DIDN'T know how long he ran, only that the horizon had already dimmed when he fell to the ground, wasted, nearly dead. When moments of clarity came to him, he reminded himself that his flight from the village would mean his death. The Partisans did not deal kindly with deserters and Karadzic would take pleasure in enforcing the point. He had drawn a line in the sand back there with the commander. There was no avoiding Karadzic's wrath.

But then he remembered that he was already dead—a walking ghost. That was what he had learned in the village watching the priest laughing on the cross.

And what about the fact that his heart was pumping blood through his veins? What about these thoughts, bouncing around his skull like ricocheting pellets? Didn't they avow life? In some mundane, banal reality perhaps. But not in the same way he'd just witnessed. Not like the life that belonged to the villagers. In spite of the child cut down in cold blood; in spite of the priest's martyrdom, the villagers possessed life. Perhaps because of it. And what life! Laughing in the face of death. He had never even heard of such faith! Never!

Which was why he had to go back there.

Janjic spent the night huddled in the cold without a fire. His neck throbbed where Karadzic's pistol had cut a deep gash from a spot just behind his right ear to his shoulder. Images of the village came at him from the dark, whispers from the other side. A young girl in a pink dress falling to the concrete, wearing yellow hair clips and a neat little hole through her temple. A priest suspended from a cement cross, laughing. Did you hear me laughing? the girl had asked the priest. Laughter. It seemed to have possessed them both. The currency of life beyond. It was the laughter that had made the killing a truly horrifying event. *Face it, Jan, you have seen worse before and left with a shrug.* But this. This had reached into his chest and set off a grenade!

He had a dream in his drifting. He was in a dark dungeon, strapped to a beam. Perhaps a cross. He could see nothing, but his own breathing echoed about him, impossibly loud in the black space. It terrified him. And then the world lit with a flash and he stared at a great white field.

He'd awoken then, sweating and panting.

Sometime past midnight, Janjic stood and headed the way he'd come. He had no idea what he would do once there, but he knew that in fleeing he had committed himself to returning.

He reached the village at daybreak, stumbling over the same hill from which they had first gazed into this tranquil valley. He pulled up, breathing steadily through his nostrils. High above, gray clouds ran to the horizon, an unbroken blanket. The air lay still and silent except for the twittering of a sparrow nearby. The church rose like a huge tombstone below, surrounded by carefully placed houses. A thin fog drifted through the northern perimeter. Several homes spawned trails of smoke from their chimneys. On any other day Janjic might have come upon the scene and imagined the warmth of the fires that crackled in the bosom of those houses.

But today Janjic could not imagine fire. Today he thought only of cold death. A knot rose to his throat. The cemetery was shrouded by a dozen large poplars. Behind those drooping leaves stood a tall cross. And on that cross . . .

Janjic descended the hill, his heart beating like a tom. Now the unseen forces that had driven him from the village reached into his bones, raising gooseflesh along his arms. He'd heard an Orthodox priest pray for protection once. "Yea, though I walk through the valley of the shadow of death, I will fear no evil." Janjic whispered the prayer three times as he approached the tall trees.

Then he was beside them, and he stopped.

The gray cross stood tall beyond dozens of smaller crosses. A black dog nuzzled the earth at its base. But the body . . . The body was gone. Of course. What had he expected? Certainly they would not have left his body for the birds. But then where had they laid his body? And the child's?

Janjic stumbled forward, suddenly eager to find the priest. Tears blurred his vision and he ran his wrists across his eyes. *Where are you, Father? Where are you, my priest?*

The earth had been disturbed at the foot of the cross; heaped into a smooth mound roughly the length of a body. A tall body. And next to it a smaller mound. They had buried the priest and Nadia at the foot of the cross.

Janjic ran for the graves, suddenly overcome by it all. By the war and the monsters it had spawned; by images of peaceful women and delighted children; by a picture of the little girl falling and the priest hanging. By the echoes of that laughter and that final resounding boom!

The tears were so thick in his eyes he could not see the last few yards except for vague shapes. The dog fled and Janjic let his body fall when his boots first felt the ground rising with fresh dirt. He fell facedown on the priest's grave, sobbing from his gut now, clutching at the soil.

He wanted to beg forgiveness. He wanted to somehow undo what he had done by visiting this peaceful village. But he could not form the words. He gasped deeply, barely aware of the dirt in his mouth now. Every muscle in his body contracted taut, and he brought his knees up under him. It felt like death and he welcomed it, completely oblivious to the world now. He slammed his fist on the earth and sobbed.

Forgive me, forgive me! Oh, God, forgive me!

Janjic lay there for long minutes, his eyes clenched against an assault of images. And he begged. He begged God to forgive him.

"Janjic."

His name? Someone was speaking his name.

"Janjic."

He lifted his head. They'd gathered in a semicircle at the entrance to the courtyard, ten meters off, the women and the children. All of them.

Nadia's mother stood before him. "Hello, Janjic." She smiled with ashen lips.

He pushed himself to his knees, raising up on shaky legs. The world was still swimming.

"So you have come back," Ivena said. Her smile had left. "Why?"

Janjic glanced about the villagers. Children gripped their mothers' hands, looking at him with round eyes. The women stared without moving.

"I . . ." Janjic cleared his throat. "I . . ." He reached his hands out, palms up. "Please . . ."

Ivena walked forward. "The priest didn't die right away," she said. "He lived for a while after the other soldiers left. And he told us some things that helped us understand."

A ball of sorrow rolled up Janjic's throat.

"We can't condemn you," she said, but she was starting to cry.

Janjic thought his chest might explode. "Forgive me. Forgive me. Please forgive me," he said.

She opened her arms and he stepped into them, weeping like a baby now. Nadia's mother held him and patted his back, comforting him and crying on his shoulder. A dozen others came around them and rested their hands on them, humming quietly in sympathy and praying with sweet voices. "Lord Jesus, heal your children. Comfort us in this hour of darkness. Bathe us in your love."

And their Lord Jesus did bathe them in his love, Janjic thought. He continued to shake and sob, a tall man surrounded by a sea of women, but now his tears were mixed with warmth.

When they had collected themselves enough to stop the crying they talked in short scattered sentences, decrying what had happened, consoling each other with talk of love. Nadia's love; Father Michael's love; Christ's love.

When they had stopped talking, Janjic walked over to the cross. Bloodstains darkened the gray concrete. He gripped it with both hands and kissed it.

"I swear this day to follow your Christ," he said and kissed the cross again. "I swear it on my own life."

"Then he will have to be your Christ," Ivena said. She took a small bottle the size of her fist from Marie. A perfume bottle, perhaps, with a pointed top and a flared base.

"Yes. He will be my Christ," Janjic said

She held the bottle out to him. It was dark red, sealed with wax. Janjic took it gingerly and studied it.

"Take it in remembrance of Christ's blood, which purchased your soul," she said.

"What is it?"

"It's the priest's blood."

Janjic nearly dropped the vial. "The priest's blood?"

"Don't worry," another spoke. "It's sealed off; it won't bite. It holds no value but to remind us. Think of it as a cross—a symbol of death. Please accept it and remember well."

Janjic closed his fingers around the glass. "I will. I will never forget. I swear it." A great comfort swept through his body. He lifted his hands wide and faced the sky. "I swear it! And I too will give my life for you. I will remember your love shown this day through these, your children. And I will return that love as long as I live."

His prayer echoed through the courtyard like a bell rung from the towers. The villagers looked on in silence.

Then somewhere, behind one of the mothers' skirts or under sister Flouta's rose-bushes, perhaps, a small child giggled. It was an absurd sound, foreign in the heavy moment. It was an innocent sound that danced on strings from heaven. It was a beautiful, lovely, divine sound that sent a tremor of pleasure through the bones.

It was a sound that Janjic would never, never forget.

IVENA CLOSED the book and smiled. Glory!

For the third time that hour, the phone rang in the kitchen, and this time she walked to get it. She plucked the receiver from the wall on its fifth ring.

"Yes?"

"Ivena. Are you all right?"

"Of course I am."

"I've been calling for an hour."

"Because I don't answer my phone you think I am dead, Janjic?"

"No. Just concerned. Would you like me to pick you up?"

"Why would you pick me up?"

"The reception," Janjic said. "Don't tell me you forgot."

"That's tonight?" she asked.

"At five-thirty."

"And tell me again why I must attend. You know I'm not crazy about—"

"It's in your honor as much as mine, Ivena. It's your story as well. And I have a surprise I would like you to share in."

"A surprise? You can't tell me?"

"Then it would no longer be a surprise."

She let that go.

"And please, Ivena, make the best of it. Some of those there will be quite important."

"Yes. You've already told me. Don't worry, Janjic; what could an old woman like me possibly say to upset important men?"

"The fact that you even ask the question should be enough."

"Pick me up, then."

"You're sure?"

"Of course."

"Five o'clock?"

"Five is fine. Good-bye, Janjic."

"Good-bye."

She hung up.

Yes indeed, Janjic Jovic had written a brilliant book.

BOOK TWO

THE SINNER

"I tell you that in the same way there
will be more rejoicing in heaven over
one sinner who repents
than over ninety-nine
righteous persons
who do not need
to repent."

LUKE 15:7 NIV

CHAPTER SEVEN

"What a terrible thing it is for children to see death, you say.
We have it all wrong. If you make a child terrified of death, he won't
embrace it so easily. And death must be embraced if you wish to
follow Christ. Listen to his teaching. 'Unless you become like a
child . . . and unless you take up your cross daily, you cannot
enter the kingdom of heaven.'
One is not valuable without the other."

The Dance of the Dead, 1959

JAN PICKED Ivena up in his limousine at five and it quickly became obvious
that she was in one of her moods.

"I'm not sure I'm in the spirit for silly surprises, Janjic."

"Silly? I hope you don't feel that way when you've seen it."

She gave his black suit a look-over, not entirely approving. "So. The famous
author is honored again."

"Not entirely. You'll have to wait." He grinned, thinking of what he'd
planned. In reality the event was more like two rolled into one. Roald's idea. The
leaders wanted to honor them and he had this surprise for them. It would be
perfect.

"I read the part of Nadia's death again this morning," Ivena said, staring
forward.

There was nothing to say to that. He shook his head. "It's still hard to imagine my part in—"

"Nonsense. Your part is now the book."

They rode in silence then.

The war had ended within two months of that most sobering date. The history books read that Tito's Partisans liberated Sarajevo from Nazi occupation in April of 1945, but the war left Yugoslavia more bloodied than any other country engaged in the brutal struggle. One million, seven hundred thousand of her fellow citizens found death; one million of those at the hands of other Yugoslavs. Yugoslavs like Karadzic and Molosov and, yes, Yugoslavs like him.

Janjic spent five torturous years in prison for his defiance of Karadzic. His imprisonment had proved more life-threatening than the war. But he did survive, and he'd emerged a man transformed from the inside out.

It was then that he began to write. He had always been a writer, but now the words came out with gut-wrenching clarity. Within three years he had a three-inch stack of double-spaced pages beside his typewriter, and he'd confidently told Ivena that no one would publish them. They were simply too spiritual for most publishers. And if not too spiritual then certainly too Christian. For those publishers who did publish Christian material the pages were far too bloody. But they did contain the truth, even if the truth was not terribly popular in many religious circles. At least not this part of the truth. The part that suggested you must die if you wanted to live. He doubted anyone would ever publish the work.

But he wrote on. And that was a good thing because he was wrong.

He finished the book in June of 1956.

It was published in 1959.

It topped the *New York Times* bestseller list in April of 1960.

"There are times to forget, Ivena. Times like today. Times when love tells us that it's worth even death."

She turned to him. "So your surprise today has to do with love? Don't tell me you're going to ask her?"

Janjic grinned, suddenly embarrassed. "I'm not saying a thing. It wouldn't be a surprise then, would it?"

She *humphed*, but her lips curved with a small grin. "So love is in the air, is it? My, my. We can't seem to escape it."

"Love has always been in the air, Ivena. From that first day. Today I begin a new journey of love."

She smiled now. "You have much to learn about love, Janjic. We all do."

THE HOTEL'S grand ballroom was crowded with well-wishers, sipping punch and smiling in small groups an hour later. Seven tables with white embroidered tablecloths and tall red candles hosted enough shrimp and artichoke hearts to feed a convention. Three large crystal chandeliers hung from the burgundy domed ceiling, but it was Karen who shone brightly tonight, Jan thought. If not now then in a few minutes.

He watched her work the guests as only the best publicists could—gentle and sweet, yet so very persuasive. She wore an elegant red dress that flattered her trim figure. Her lips parted in a smile at something Barney Givens had said. She was with the leaders in the group—she always gravitated toward the power players, dazzling them with her intelligence. The twinkle in her brown eyes didn't hurt, of course. The subtle curve of her soft neck, stretched in laughter as it was now, did not impede her influence either. Not at all.

Working as the publicist for one of New York's largest publishing houses, Karen had come to one of his appearances at the ABC studios, more out of curiosity than anything, she'd said. The image of the pretty brunette sitting on the front row stayed with Jan for weeks, perhaps because hers were the most intelligent questions asked of him that night. Evidently the experience had impacted her deeply and she'd read his entire book late into that night. Exactly one month later they met again, at a lecture upstate, and this time Roald's scheming had come into play. Three months later she'd left New York for Atlanta, intent on igniting a new fire under *The Dance of the Dead*. They'd hired her as both agent and publicist, on a freelance basis. The brilliant publicist five years his junior had sparked a second wind to a waning message that launched the book into its third printing. Then its fourth, and its fifth and its sixth printing, each one expanding to meet the demand she had almost single-handedly created for his story.

Ivena might be right when she suggested that Karen was *a highbrow woman*, as she put it, but in many respects Jan owed his career to her *highbrow* brilliance.

Karen suddenly turned her head and caught his stare. He blushed and smiled. She winked and addressed Barney without missing a beat. This time Barney and Frank beside him both threw back their heads in laughter.

Jan leaned against the head table, admiring her. At times like this she could make his knees weak, he thought.

Ivena stood across the room talking to the ministry's accountant, Lorna. She wore a simple yellow-flowered dress that accented her grandmotherly look. But Jan was deceived by neither her white hair nor her gentle smile. They weren't talking cross-stitching over there—Ivena never talked of such trifles. *Drink her words deep, Lorna.*

To his right, a camera crew scanned the audience; Roald had invited them when Jan confessed his idea. His surprise.

"It's perfect publicity. They'll love it," he'd said.

"Now *you're* the publicist?"

"No, but we can't very well consult Karen, can we?"

"The whole world will know," Jan protested.

"Exactly. That's the point. You're the voice of love. Now you show some love of your own. It's perfect!"

"Who then?"

"ABC. I can talk to John Mathews about getting it on the news."

Jan couldn't have talked Roald out of it if he'd wanted to. The ABC crew was filming, and adding their commentary at leisure. It was now or never.

He picked up a fork, took a deep breath, and struck the side of his glass. The chime cut through the scattered conversation. He struck it again, and the din died down.

The camera had already swung to face him.

"Thank you. It's a pleasure to see you all here tonight. Thank you for coming." Jan's heart stomped through his chest. Roald was right: The world's eyes were on him.

He turned to face Karen, who smiled unsuspectingly beside Frank and Roald. "Most of you probably think my book, *The Dance of the Dead,* has forever changed my life. And you would be right. You might think that it's a culmination of a life, but there you would be wrong. It's only a beginning. I am, after all, still a young man."

Chuckles rippled through the room. Jan caught Ivena's eye.

"Ivena tells me that I have much to learn of love." He winked at her and she graciously dipped her head. "And she's right. I stand before you—before all of my friends, before the world—with the hopes of beginning a new journey into the heart of love tonight. A journey that will complete me."

Betty, their correspondence manager, gave a motherly smile and cast a look toward Karen. Some of them had guessed already, of course. His affections for Karen were hardly a secret.

"She came to us three years ago. She's brilliant and kind. She is breathtaking and she is stunning. But more than any of those, Karen makes me a man, I think. And I make her a woman."

Jan's coworkers had all but begged for this moment for over a year now. He could see their eyes brighten in the periphery of his vision. He stretched an inviting hand toward Karen. She moved through the crowd without removing her eyes from his. They were misted now, he thought. She reached him and took his hand. He bent and kissed it lightly.

Over her shoulder, he saw that even Ivena smiled wide.

"I can't believe you're doing this," Karen said in a low voice.

"Believe it," he returned quietly.

When he straightened, the small black box was in his hand, withdrawn from his pocket while bent. He snapped it open. A three-carat diamond solitaire sparkled in its black velvet perch. Someone gasped nearby—perhaps Lorna, who stood not five feet from them. Yes, it was rather extravagant. But then so was Karen.

She was smiling unabashedly now.

He held the box out to her and looked in her eyes. "Karen, will you take a journey with me? Will you give me your hand in marriage?"

A heavy silence gripped the room. The sound of ABC's camera hummed steadily.

A twinkle lit her eyes. "You're asking me to marry you?"

"Yes."

"You want to spend your life with me?"

"Yes." He swallowed.

She dropped her eyes to the box and reached for it. Her hand held a slight tremble, Jan saw. *She's going to . . .*

Suddenly he didn't know *what* she was going to do. You never quite knew with Karen. She ignored the ring, uttered a little shriek and threw herself at him. Her arms wrapped around his neck and she pulled him tight.

"Yes! Yes, I will."

He nearly dropped the box, but managed to snap it closed in his palm. Karen kissed him pointedly on the lips—more of a ceremonious display than an expression of passion. She drew back and winked at him. Then she immediately took the ring box from him, turned to face the camera and held it up proudly. The hall erupted with applause, nicely accented with catcalls and hoots of approval.

The next half-hour wandered by in a hazy dream for Jan. They all congratulated him and Karen, one by one. Interviews were held and camera bulbs flashed. Karen was glowing.

Roald approached them, smiling wide as the rounds of congratulations died down. "I couldn't offer more joy, my friends." He put a hand on each of their shoulders. "It's a perfect day for the perfect couple."

"Thank you, Roald," Karen said, dipping her head. She glanced at Jan with a twinkle in her eye. "I couldn't imagine more myself."

Roald chuckled. "Well, if you wouldn't mind entertaining the guests for a few minutes, Karen, the leaders would like to speak with Jan. We won't take him for long, I promise."

"Don't leave me stranded too long."

"You? Stranded? The cameras are still here, Karen. I'm sure you'll find a way to make use of them."

"I'll be right with you, Roald," Jan said.

The man hesitated and then stepped back. "Take your time." He walked from them.

"So we're really doing this, are we?" Karen asked.

Jan faced her, grinning. "Evidently. How does it feel?"

"It feels like it should, I think. Having the cameras here was a perfect touch. Your idea?"

"Roald's."

"I thought so. Good man."

"Yes." He glanced around and saw that the company was mostly engaged. He leaned forward and kissed her lightly on the lips. "Congratulations," he said.

For a moment they stood in silence. She reached up and straightened his tie, a small habit she performed too routinely. "You're such a handsome man. I'm so proud of you."

"I meant what I said, you know? Every word."

She kissed him on the cheek. "Yes, I do know, Mr. Jovic. And I meant what I said."

"What did you say?"

"I said yes."

He smiled and nodded. "Yes you did. Now if you'll excuse me for a few minutes while I take care of Roald and his friends."

"Take your time," she said.

He left her and angled for the meeting room across the hall. Roald intercepted him. They walked past a dozen guests, nodding graciously. "They're waiting already," Roald said. "I didn't mean to interrupt the moment but Barney has a flight in two hours and Bob promised his grandson a trip to the theater tonight."

"Ivena?"

"She's waiting as well," Roald said with grin.

"Good," Jan said. They entered the meeting room and closed the door on the noisy hall.

IVENA SAT adjacent to Janjic, listening to the scene unfold with a hubbub of monotony before her. They sat around the oval table, seven gray-haired evangelical icons from all corners of the country, sober yet delighted at once, staring at Janjic, their prize, who sat awkwardly at the head. They'd spent the first round congratulating him on the engagement and were getting down to the real meat. At least that was how Ivena saw the setting.

Janjic held himself in a distinguished manner—he could slip into the perfect professional sheen when the occasion demanded it. But beneath his new American skin the Serbian she had known could hardly hide. At least not from her. She saw the way he nonchalantly smoothed his right eyebrow when he was impatient, as he did now. And the way his mouth curved in a gentle but set grin when he politely disagreed. As it did now.

He'd filled out over the years and he'd always stood much taller than her, but under the commanding facade he was still a young man, looking for escape. His face was well aged for thirty-eight years—the war and five years in prison were mostly responsible. It didn't matter, he was still strikingly handsome. Crow's-feet already wrinkled the skin around his eyes from his constant smiling. His dark blond hair swept back, graying above his ears and curled at his collar. The white American shirts with their ties always looked a little silly on him, she thought. For all her fussing over him, Karen obviously disagreed.

Ivena watched Janjic shift his hazel eyes around the table, taking in their stares. Roald Barns, the president of the North American Evangelical Association, and the man who had brought them to this country five years earlier, sat opposite him.

"I think what Frank means," Roald said, motioning to the boxy man next to him, "is that we have an obligation to excellence. *The Dance of the Dead* has sold more than any religious book in this century. Excluding the Bible, of course. And that means it's become an extension of Christianity, so to speak. A voice to the lost world. It's important to keep that voice pure. I'm sure Jan would agree to that."

"Yes, of course," Jan said.

These evangelical leaders had come to honor him and to judge him in one fell swoop, Ivena thought—all dressed in starched white shirts and black ties. God forbid Janjic ever become a carbon copy of these men.

Ivena had held her tongue long enough while these men spoke their rounds of wisdom. She decided it was time to speak. "It really depends on what voice you're trying to keep pure, doesn't it, Frank?" she asked.

All heads turned to face her. "The message of the book," Frank said. "The message of the book needs to remain pure. And the lives of we who proclaim that message, of course."

"And what is the message of the book?" Ivena returned.

"Well, I think we already know the message of the book."

"Yes, but indulge me. Janjic tells me that it's my story as well as his. So then what does this story tell you about God's relationship with man?"

The leaders exchanged glances, off balance by her sudden challenge.

"It's the story of innocent bloodshed," Bob Story said to her left. The short, round evangelical leader shifted in his seat. "The death of martyrs, choosing death instead of renouncing Christ. Wouldn't you say?"

"In part, yes, that summarizes some of what happened. But what did the story *teach* you gentlemen? Hmm? I want to know because, unless I'm missing the tone of the past ten minutes, you are more concerned with protecting the image of the church than spreading the message of the martyrs. I believe you think that you have a flawed spokesman in Janjic, and it terrifies you."

The room suddenly felt hollowed of air. Janjic looked at her as if she'd lost her senses. But then she was right, and they all knew it. They loved the success of his book, but they did take exception to him now and then.

"True, yes? Janjic has written a magnificent book called *The Dance of the Dead* and he's been embraced by a world hungering for the unadulterated truth. But Janjic's just an ordinary man. An excellent writer, obviously, but a man with his share of flaws. Perhaps a man with *more* than his share of flaws, considering the scars the war has left on his heart. And now that he's been chosen by the world as a spokesman for your Christianity, you're quite nervous. Am I wrong?"

They stared at her unblinking.

A hotel waiter entered the conference room, perhaps to offer desserts, but with one look around the table, he thought better of it and turned on his heels. The air conditioner hummed behind Ivena, spilling cool air over her neck.

Roald was the first to recover. "I think I can speak for the group when I say that we have complete confidence in Jan. But you're right, Ivena. He has been chosen by the world, as you say. Although not without our help, I might add." They chuckled. "And he is a spokesperson for the church. Frank's correct—by virtue of his own success Jan has a unique set of standards, I would say. Not unlike any other role model—a sports hero, for example. To whom much is given, much is required."

Barney Givens cleared his throat. "I think Roald's right. We're not questioning God's work in either of your lives. It's a wonderful thing, more than any one of us could ask for. Your book, Jan, has done as much for this country's spiritual health as Billy Graham's crusades are doing. Don't take us wrong. But you have to remember that you do represent the church, son. The eyes of the world are on you. You have our honor, but you also have our caution."

"I didn't ask to represent the church," Janjic said. "I had God in mind when I wrote the book. Have I caused a specific offense, or are we just playing with words? I'm feeling schooled here."

"Nonsense," Frank said. "We're simply cautioning you to watch your step, Jan. You have a wonderful personality, young man, but you do tend to fly off the handle at times. I understand how difficult it must be to live with the memories of the war; I survived the battlefields of World War I myself. But that doesn't change our responsibility to hold the highest standard. Now's the time to consider pitfalls—not after you've stumbled into them."

"And how many women or children did you see butchered in your war? How many years did you spend in prison?"

"I'm not referring to stress from the war, and you know it. I'm talking about moral pitfalls, Jan. Any questionable appearance. It would reflect badly on the church."

"We're just cautioning you," Ted Rund said. "You've been known to be rather unorthodox. I, for one, couldn't be more pleased over what's happened, my friend. But you're speaking for the church now. You've been on virtually every television show in the country. We're in times of upheaval. The moral state of our country is under a full-throttled assault and the church is being scrutinized under a new light. You're one of our most effective spokesmen. We're simply holding you accountable."

Jan leaned back and tapped his fingers on the table. They were obviously not telling him everything.

"What did I do? Tell me how I offended you," Jan said.

Roald and Frank looked at each other, but it was Frank who answered.

"What you did was call our character into question last week in front of two million viewers."

"*Your* character? You mean with Walter Cronkite?" Jan asked incredulously. "He asked if the church today understands the love of Christ. I said no. You found that offensive?"

"I believe 'not at all' were the words you chose. And yes, *our* character. We represent the church; the church represents Christ's love, and you have the gall to say on a national show that we don't understand that love. You don't think that undermines the leadership?"

Ivena interrupted them quietly. "You still haven't answered ny question, gentlemen. What is the real message of Janjic's book?"

They looked at her dumbly, as if her mind were not functioning properly.

"Let me tell you then," she said. "The message is that God loves man passionately. That one moment with God is worth death. He gave his own life for nothing less. I'm not sure any of you has learned the nature of God's love yet."

Except for the sound of Bob Story's spoon clinking through his coffee the room fell to silence. They had come from all over the country for a conference in Atlanta and carved out a few hours in Janjic's honor; surely they had not expected this. Jan looked at Roald and offered that set grin of his, as if to say, *"She's right—you know she is."* Roald held Jan's eyes for a full second and then looked at Ivena.

"I think that Ivena's right," he said. "We're all learning about God's love. Ivena has simply expressed this truth in a way that's as unique as Jan's story. And please do not misunderstand us; we are thrilled at the work God has done with *The Dance of the Dead.* I think my own effort speaks for itself. We just ask you to be cautious, Jan. You've risen among the ranks, so to speak. A lot of people look to your example. Just watch your step, that's all. What do they say? 'Don't bite the hand that feeds you'?"

Several of them chuckled. Ivena thought about telling them that Janjic did not need their hands, but she thought better of it.

Jan nodded. "Good enough. Point taken." That seemed to satisfy them.

"I propose a toast," Roald said. He pushed his spectacles up on his nose. "To *The Dance of the Dead.* May she live forever."

They drank to a chorus of "Amens." Surely they must know that in reality, the life of Janjic's bestseller was nearing an end. It had soared high and far, but the story had run its course over the last five years, a fact that brought Ivena pause in light of their conversation. Why were Roald and this conservative bunch so concerned about Jan's image now?

The meeting disbursed ten minutes later with firm handshakes and one last round of affirmations. The leaders were off, leaving Jan alone with Ivena in the empty room. The sounds of laughter swept in through the open door; the party was winding down.

"I should be leaving now, Janjic."

"So soon? And you haven't even congratulated me yet."

Ivena reached a hand to his cheek. "Congratulations, my dear Serb." She smiled. "I'm sure she will make you very happy."

"Thank you. Would you like Steve to take you home?"

"I'll take a cab."

"Then I'll walk you."

JAN SKIRTED the party and walked Ivena to the street. Not until they were outside did Janjic confront her about the exchange in the room. "You really think that was the best time to question their spiritual sensibilities, Ivena?"

"It was perhaps the *only* time. I don't run with them every day."

"Of course, but you were pretty direct. Actually I shouldn't complain—I think it played in my favor."

"And how is that, Janjic?"

"Compared to you they see that I'm a gentle breeze. I may have brief periods of disorientation and grab the nearest telephone pole at the sound of a car's backfire, but at least I don't line the county's top religious leaders up and school them in the love of Christ." He chuckled and then cleared his throat.

"When we return to Bosnia they will be a distant memory," she said.

"I'm happy in America. You're happy in America. Why do you cling to this silly notion of returning to the land that nearly killed us both?"

"It's a notion that won't fade. We will see, Janjic."

She wasn't sure if the hunch they would one day return to see her daughter's grave one last time came from her own latent desires or if there was more at work there, and she'd given up trying to discern three years ago.

"I'm not sure Karadzic would take my return too kindly. I've turned him into an infamous monster."

"A reputation well deserved," she said.

They walked for the curb.

"I had the dream again last night," he said. "It was so vivid."

She glanced up at him. He'd had the same dream every few nights for twenty years now—the nightmare the psychiatrists liked to blame on the war. But she had her own ideas. She stopped and turned to him.

"Tell it to me."

"You know it. There's nothing new."

"Tell it to me again. It will help you."

He swallowed. "Okay. I'm in a pitch-black room, strapped to a wooden beam behind me. It's the same: I can't see anything, but I can feel everything—the ropes digging in, the sweat leaking down my naked body. I think I am being crucified."

He stopped and breathed deep. Then he continued. "I can hear my own breathing, in long ragged pulls, echoing as if I'm in a chamber. That's all I can hear, and it terrifies me. It stays like that for a long time, as if I'm suspended between life and death." He blinked. "And then the lights are thrown on. And I'm not in a dungeon; I'm staring at a white field." He stopped and looked down at her.

"And that's where it always ends." She stated it rather than asked it.

"Yes. And it means nothing to me."

She reached up and rubbed his arm. He nervously ran his fingers through his hair. "The doctors may be right; maybe it's only my mind playing tricks, pretending to be Father Micheal on the cross."

"Those doctors are full of nonsense. Take it from me; the dream has meaning beyond this world. I'm sorry I can't tell you what that is, but one day we will know. I'm certain of it."

"Maybe you're right."

"Perhaps the dream speaks more to what you have *not* experienced than to what you have, hmmm?"

"Meaning what?"

"Meaning that there's still more to learn about love, Janjic. Meaning that *The Dance of the Dead* only tells part of the story. God knows you have more to learn of love."

He looked at her with mild surprise. "As do we all. But now you're suggesting that I haven't learned the lesson of the priest, right alongside of Roald?"

"Not necessarily. But I do worry for you at times, Janjic. Sometimes I wonder if you've become more like those around you than they've become like you. You defend the truth with vigorous words, but your life is changing."

Now his mild surprise was accompanied by a blink. "You really think so?"

70

"Come on, Janjic. Is it really such a secret?"

"I don't know. But changing a few things on the surface doesn't remake the man."

"No. I wasn't referring to your skin. I mean your heart. Where do your affections lie, Janjic?"

"My affections are with God. And my affections are with Karen. You may not approve, but it's me, not you, who'll marry her."

"What I'm saying has nothing to do with Karen! I'm speaking of Christ."

"You're too strong, Ivena. I've written a book on the affections of Christ, for heaven's sake! Give me some credit."

"You witnessed a dramatic expression of affection between God and man, and you've committed your observations to a book. Just because you saw the love of the priest does not mean that you've learned how to love in the same way." She paused. "Perhaps the fact that you have been unable to write since the book tells us something."

She'd never spoken quite so plainly about the matter, and he looked at her with shock. "You say that with such conviction! I also spent five years in prison for opposing Karadzic. Still you question my love for God? That it has given me writer's block?"

"You understand the love in ways most do not. But still, have you loved him that way? Loved Christ? Or have I, for that matter? And I'll tell you something else: Until we do, we'll never find peace. You've seen too much, my dear Serb."

Traffic hummed by on the street. Janjic waved at a yellow cab that veered toward them. "Yes, maybe I have seen too much. And you as well." He faced her. "You're right, one day we'll find our way through this. In the meantime, please don't rob me of the love I have for Karen." He smiled and opened her door. "Give me at least that much."

"Don't be so sure that I don't approve. You mustn't confuse caution with disapproval, my dear Serb." She climbed into the cab. "Call me soon, Janjic. Come for supper when you can."

"I will. Thank you for coming."

"It was my pleasure." She shut the door.

She left him standing there alone, watching her go. All dressed up in the wrong clothes, but so handsome nonetheless. Famous and now engaged to be married. So very wise and so very tender, yet in his own way lost without knowing it.

Her Janjic.

CHAPTER EIGHT

IVENA'S WORDS burned a hole in Janjic's soul that night. He was newly engaged, for goodness' sake—singing the song of true love—and Ivena had the audacity to suggest that his words were louder than his life. The ringing truth of her suggestion tempered him.

The next day started no better, and he decided to take an hour to sort out his mind at the park before Karen returned to the office after her morning meeting. She was evidently neck-deep in discussions with their publisher over the next edition, and as always she preferred to handle the details on her own. This time the publisher had come to Atlanta and Jan didn't even bother to suggest he attend the meeting. He was a writer, not a businessman.

It was then, sitting on a bench in Piedmont Park, that he first saw her. She was still a shimmering figure at the park's perimeter, a faceless ghost in the midday heat. She looked small and frail under the massive weeping willows that swayed with the wind. He didn't know why his eyes were drawn to her—his mind certainly wasn't. It was busy grappling with the growing dilemmas that seemed to have infected his soul since Ivena had graced him with her words. Maybe it was the woman's direct approach that drew him; or perhaps it was the intensity with which she walked, swinging her arms barely, but hustling along at a good clip nonetheless.

Jan shifted his mind back to Ivena's words.

The people had bought *The Dance of the Dead* in a feeding frenzy, desperate for meaning in a changing world. It was as if a generation had decided en masse to reflect on its past sins and had chosen this one book in which to look for absolution. The story of the young Serbian soldier who had found meaning through the brutality of war and his imprisonment following that war. There was a soul to his story that drew them. Like curious onlookers at a Big Foot exhibit.

He'd told them in bold terms at every university campus and every book signing and every radio show that *The Dance of the Dead* was a story first and foremost about the martyr's desperate love for Christ, not Jan Jovic's redemption. They would mostly nod their heads with glazed looks and ask about the girl or his ordeal in war crimes prison after that fateful day. He would tell them and tears would come to their eyes. But they were not falling to their knees and begging forgiveness as he had. They weren't throwing away their lives for Christ as Nadia had done. They weren't climbing on their crosses and laughing in delight as the priest had.

Therein lay part of the problem, he thought. His life had become a spectacle. An exhibit. But in the end they all walked away from the exhibit, shaking their heads in wonder, unwilling to climb in to join Big Foot in his lonely search for identity.

And now Ivena's little tidbit of truth: Perhaps he himself had peered at the exhibit without climbing in. Maybe he himself hadn't learned as well as he expected his audience to learn.

The woman still approached steadily. An American woman hustling her way through a park, dressed in black pants and a white shirt, going nowhere fast, as the cliché had it. He leaned back and watched her absently.

The Dance of the Dead. In the priest's village it had been a dance of rapture, begging to be joined by those who watched. A great awakening to the other side. But here in America it was inevitably different. They were more interested in having their ears tickled than their hearts changed. Perhaps he could write another book after all, one that characterized these new steps taught in the churches here. He could call it *The Death of the Dance.* That would have the publishers scrambling.

Jan leaned over and rested his elbows on his knees. His mind fell back to that day. It had been the love of Christ that had pierced his soul in the village. The sentiment swelled in his chest and rose to his throat. Dear, precious Nadia. And *Ivena!* He still couldn't imagine the grief of her loss. It was a part of his insistence that she come to America with him and he supposed it was a good thing. She alone really understood.

"Hi, there."

He jerked upright, startled by the voice. It was the woman! In his quandary she had walked right up to him and now stood not five feet away, trying to smile.

"Yes?"

She glanced behind her shoulder and he followed her look. Nothing but empty park and an old couple walking a dog. She sniffed and turned back to him.

A small shiver seemed to work its way over her body and she tried to smile again. A flat grin pulled at her pale lips. Her eyes twinkled bright blue, but otherwise her face appeared void of life. Dark circles hung under each eye and her cheeks looked powdered white though he could see that she wore no makeup. Her blond hair lay in short, stringy tangles.

Jan couldn't help his slow gaze over the woman. The plain white T-shirt rode up her arms, too small even for her delicate frame. Her blue jeans hung past flip-flops to the ground where they were frayed.

She lifted a hand to her lips and bit at a worn nail. Now, half hidden by her hand, her smile took up life. "I'm sorry. I hope I'm not too much of a shock for you," she said. "If I am, I could go. Do you want me to go?"

She said it with a tease in her voice. If he wasn't thoroughly confused, she was a junkie, strung out or coming down or doing whatever drug addicts did. He almost told her to leave then. To get lost. To find her pimp or her pusher or whomever she was looking for someplace else. He was a writer, not a pusher. He almost told her that.

Almost.

"Ah . . . No. No it's all right. Are you okay?"

"Why? Don't I look okay?"

"Actually no. You look . . . strung out."

"And you have a cute accent, mister. How old are you?"

He glanced around. The park was still empty. "I'm thirty-eight."

She reached out a hand and he took it. "Glad to meet you, Thirty-eight. I'm Twenty-nine."

He smiled. "Actually, my name is Jan. Jan Jovic."

"And mine's Helen."

"It's a pleasure to meet you."

"The same, Jan Jovic." She shot a quick look behind her again, and Jan saw concern flash through her eyes. But she recovered on the fly and looked at him, wearing that deliberate smile again. She tilted her head back, closed her eyes and ran fingers through her hair. It struck him then, while her chin pointed to the sky, that Helen was a pretty woman. Even in this anemic state she bore a faint angelic quality. She walked a few steps to the left and then returned to the spot directly before him, as if pondering some deep question.

"Are you sure you're okay?"

She eyed him, still wearing her mysterious grin.

Jan shrugged. "You look like you have something on your mind. And you keep looking back."

"Well, to be honest, I am in a bit of pinch. But it's got nothing to do with you. Boyfriend problems." She shrugged apologetically. "You know how love is—one day on, the next day off. So today it's off." She sniffed and glanced behind.

"I wasn't aware that love turned on and off so easily," he said. "So why did you come over to me?"

"Then you haven't had a lover lately, Jan. And I came over because you looked like a decent man. You have a problem with that?"

"No. But women like you usually don't walk over to men like me because we look decent."

"Women like me? And what kind of woman's that?"

She had a quick mind—the drugs hadn't destroyed that yet. "Women who are having boyfriend problems," he said.

"Hmm. You haven't, have you?"

"I haven't what?"

"You haven't had a lover lately."

He felt heat wash over his face and he hoped it didn't show as a blush. "Actually I've never been married. But I am—"

"And no lovers?"

"I'm a minister of sorts. I don't just take lovers. If there's a lover in my life it is Christ."

Her eyebrows arched. "Oh? A minister. A reverend, huh?"

"No. Actually I'm a writer and a lecturer who speaks on the love of God."

"Well, holy cripes. The pope himself!"

Jan smiled. "I'm not Catholic. And what do you do, Helen? I take it you aren't a nun."

"Pretty observant, Reverend."

"I'm not a reverend. I told you, I'm a writer."

"Either way, Reverend, you are a man seeking to save lost souls, am I right?"

"I suppose so. Yes. Or at least to lead them to safety. So what do you do?"

She took a deep breath. "I'm . . . I am a lover." She smiled wide.

"You're a lover. A lover who throws love on with a switch and flees her boyfriends? You are a . . . What do you call it? A woman of the str—"

"No, I'm *not* a hooker! I'd never stoop that low." Her eyes flashed. "Do I look like a hooker to you?"

He didn't answer.

"You probably wouldn't know a hooker if one crawled up on your lap, would you? No, because you're a man who peddles the love of God. Of course, how silly of me."

"I'm sorry. I didn't mean to offend you."

"No offense taken, Reverend." She used the title deliberately, with a slight smile, and Jan thought that if she'd been offended, she had already let it go. "You're as pure as the driven snow, aren't you? Probably never had so much as dirt under your nails."

"If you knew my life story you would not say that," he said.

She blinked, not quite sure what to make of that comment. The air of defense deflated about her. He shifted his gaze past her. Two figures entered the park from the direction she had come, walking fast. Helen saw his look and turned. She spun back and clenched her jaw.

"You know, maybe you could help me." She bit her lip and a shadow of fear flashed through her eyes. Jan looked at the men again. They strode together, dressed in dark suits, clearly intent on crossing the park.

"What's wrong? Who are they?"

"Nothing. No one. I mean, I don't want to involve you." She looked back to them quickly. Her fear was rising, he thought.

Jan shifted to the front of the park bench. They were after her. He could see it in the attitude of their heads and the length of their strides. He'd seen men brimming with ill intent a thousand times in his homeland; had come to recognize them with a casual glance. These two now approaching with long strides meant Helen harm.

She spun back to him and this time her resolve broke. Helen dropped to one knee, in a proposal posture; her eyes wrinkled, pleading. She grabbed his right hand with both of hers. "I'm sorry! You have to help me! Glenn swore he'd kill me the next time I left. They've been following me all day. I swear they'll kill me! Do you have a car?"

Her hands were cool on his and her face begged. Hers was the face of a victim—he'd seen a hundred thousand of them in the war and they haunted him still.

"Glenn?" he muttered, standing. But his mind was not asking about this Glenn of hers. It was weighing the world in the scales of justice, balancing the touch of this lowlife against an obscure sense of correctness that had taken up residence in his mind.

He could hear Karen at the office now. *You did what?*

He blinked. *I rescued a junkie from two hoodlums today.*

"Glenn Lutz," Helen said. "Please! I've got nowhere to go." She twisted to see the approaching men. The snappy, confident woman had dissolved into desperation.

They were no more than thirty yards off now, angling directly for them.

You did what?

I rescued a junkie from two hoodlums today, and it made me feel alive.

Jan bolted from the bench, pulling Helen stumbling behind him. "Come on! Are they armed?"

"You have a car?"

He glanced back. The men had dispensed with their professional facade and tore after them. They both held handguns, jerking in their sprint.

Jan uttered a surprised cry. "Hurry! Around the corner!" The men were closing and suddenly Jan was thinking he'd made a mistake. His heart pounded as much from the rush of adrenaline as from the run.

She raced beside him now, matching his pace with two steps for each of his, but as fast nonetheless.

But the men behind were still gaining. And the car was still out of sight.

The next time he saw Karen might very well be from a hospital bed, speaking past a bandaged face.

You did what?

Well, I tried to rescue this junkie . . .

"Where's the car?" Helen panted in near panic.

They were on the sidewalk now. He flung a hand forward, pointing. Behind him shoes clacked onto the concrete. And then one stopped. Kneeling to fire?

"Where is it?"

A white Cadillac suddenly pulled away from the curb and roared full-throttle toward them, flashing its lights. Helen pulled up beside him and Jan snatched her hand.

"Come on!"

The Cadillac squealed to a stop alongside them.

Jan yanked the door open, spun Helen around and shoved her into the back-seat. He cast one last glance to the side and saw that both men had pulled up and hid their weapons. He clambered in after Helen.

"This is your car?" She was staring through the tinted window at their pursuers, panting and exuberant.

"Yes. Thank God, Steve!"

Steve pulled a squealing U-turn and punched the accelerator to the floor. "Good night, Jan! What on earth was *that?*"

Jan didn't answer directly. "You okay?" he asked Helen.

"Yes."

"What was that, Jan?" the driver asked again, glancing repeatedly in the rearview mirror. "What on *earth* was that?"

Jan gripped his hands to fists to still their tremble and he giggled.

It was a short chuckle-like giggle, but it was the first time he'd giggled in a long time. "Whoooeee!" he hooted. "We made it!"

Steve grinned wide, infected by Jan's relief. Helen let out a cry of victory. "Yeehaaa! Boy, did we!" She slapped Jan's thigh in an elemental gesture of congratulations. "Boy, did we!"

They sped around a corner. "Jan, *what* on earth was that?" Steve demanded again.

Jan looked at Helen with a raised brow. "I don't know, Steve. I really don't know."

CHAPTER NINE

GLENN LUTZ peered past the smoke glass wall on the thirtieth floor of Atlanta's Twin Towers to the crawling city below, ignoring the sweat that snaked down his nose.

It was green and gray down there, a hundred thousand bushy trees deadlocked with the concrete in a slow battle over the territory. The gray was slowly winning. Pedestrians crawled along the streets, like ants scampering to and fro in their senseless rush. If one of them were to look up and see past the reflective glass surrounding Glenn they might see the city's best-known city councilman frowning down, hands on hips, feet planted wide, dressed in white slacks and a Hawaiian shirt, and think he was gloating over his power.

But Glenn Lutz did not feel any of wealth's pleasures just now. In fact he felt buck naked, stripped of his power, robbed of his heart. Like a man just learning that his accountant had made a mistake. That he wasn't the city's wealthiest man after all. That in fact he was quite decidedly broke. That he could no longer afford the hefty lease payment on the top three floors of Atlanta's most prestigious towers and must be out in twenty-four hours.

Glenn pulled his lips back over crooked teeth, bit down and closed his eyes for a moment. He lifted thick fingers to his chin and pulled at his prickly jaw. Sweat darkened his shirt in large fans under each arm—he hadn't showered in two days and this pointless pursuit of Helen had left him frantic. He hadn't brushed his teeth either, and he was reminded of the fact with a blast of his own breath. Two days of alcohol had not entirely weakened the heavy odors of dental decay.

Glenn turned from the window and glared at the wall opposite him. It was solid mirror from black tile to ceiling and now his image stared back at him. It showed a tall man, six foot five and thick like a bull. The flesh was firm. Bone-white, hairy, and layered in cellulite maybe, but solid. His stomach could use some trimming. Helen had told him so just three days ago and he had slapped her face with an open palm. The memory sent a chill through his arms. Never mind that she'd had her arms wrapped *around* his stomach when she'd made the remark.

His mind softened. *Helen, dear Helen. How could you do this to me? How could you leave me so empty? We had a deal, baby. We're knit from the same cloth, you and I. What can you possibly be thinking?*

Glenn ground his molars. Indirect lighting cast a soft atmospheric hue over the mirrored walls. His eyes stared back at him, vacant, like two holes drilled through his head. It was his most remarkable trait, he thought. His driver's license said they were dark brown, but beyond ten feet any reasonable soul would cross themselves and swear those eyes were black. Jet black. He had started dyeing his hair light blond to accent the eyes a week after high school graduation. Now his hair hung nearly white around stubbled jowls.

Glenn lifted his chin and frowned. Truth be told, slip a black robe over his shoulders and he would look more like a warlock than some business tycoon. Now *that* would do wonders with the women. On the other hand, forget the coat; the image in the mirror was enough to terrify most women as it was.

Most. Not Helen. Helen was special. Helen was his goddess.

He glanced around the office. Over here in the business tower there was nothing to show but a single bare oak desk set on the shiny black tile. The decorator's idea had been to create a stark impression, but Glenn had fired her before she'd completed the job. Thankfully the foulmouthed wench had finished the suite on the adjacent tower; the Palace he called it. That had been three months ago, just before he'd met Helen, and to say that the Palace had delivered would be an absurd understatement. It was either pleasure to the bone or raw pain over there. Ecstasy or agony. The chambers of exotic delights. Which was appropriate considering the fact that he ran one of the country's largest drug rings out of the suite.

The phone on his desk rang and he started. He swore and strode for the black object. He snatched up the receiver. "What?"

"Sir, we really do have to talk. You have calls stacking up and—"

"And I told you not to bother me with this junk!"

"Some of them look important."

"And what could be so important? I'm occupied here, if you didn't notice."

"Yes, of course I noticed. Who wouldn't notice? And meanwhile you have legitimate business piling up around you."

Glenn felt heat flush his neck. Only she could say such a thing. He took a deep breath. "Get in here," he said, and slammed the receiver onto its cradle.

Beatrice strutted in with her chin leveled. Her black hair was piled high in a bun and her lips curved downward, matching the arc of her large nose. She was fifty pounds overweight and her cinched belt exaggerated the folds of fat at her belly. It was a symbiotic relationship with her. If she didn't know so much he might have ditched her long ago.

"What's so important?"

She slid into a burgundy guest chair and lifted a yellow steno pad. "For starters, you missed the council meeting last night."

"Immaterial. Give me something that matters."

"Okay. The renovations on the lower floors of the Bancroft Building are running into a snag. The contractor's screaming about—"

"What does this have to do with me?"

"You *own* the building."

"That's right. I *own* it. I don't build them, I buy them."

"They're saying it'll go over budget in excess of a million dollars."

"I don't care if it goes over budget two million. Right now I don't care if it goes over five million!"

She blinked at the outburst. "Fine. Then I guess you won't be interested in the rest of these matters either. What's a few million?" She was trying to bait him.

"That's right, Beatrice. And if anybody does anything stupid, I'll deal with them later. But not now."

She unfolded her legs as if to stand. "Yes, not now. Now you're taking care of more important business."

"Don't step over this line, Beatrice."

"She'll ruin you, Glenn."

"She's my life."

"And she'll be your death. What's come over you with this woman?"

Glenn didn't respond. It was a good question.

Beatrice looked at him and shook her head. "I've seen them come and go, Glenn, but never like this one. She's controlling you."

Shut up, you witch! He remained silent while her words spun through his mind. She was right in a small way. He could hardly understand his obsession with Helen himself. Helen had waltzed into his life only a few short months ago, a ghost from his past, and now she had possessed him. But Helen . . . Helen wasn't so easily possessed. She held that power over him, and his desire for her ran like fire through his blood, in spite of—or maybe because of—her refusal to be possessed.

"You want her only because you can't have her," Beatrice said. "She's nothing but a piece of trash, and you're slobbering over her like a dog. Come on, Glenn. You're neglecting your own interests. Look at you; you look like a pig."

"Out," he snarled, trembling now.

She stood with a *humph* and walked for the door. She was the only being on the planet who would dare make such statements. Glenn watched her bulging profile and fought an urge to leap after her and pound her into the tile. Beatrice turned at the door. "When was the last time you took a bath?"

"Out! Out, out!" he thundered.

She drilled him with a sharp stare and then strutted off with her chin level and proud, as if she'd somehow set him straight.

Glenn slammed a fist onto the desk and stormed for the far wall. He hit the glass with both palms and it shuddered under the blow. One of these days it would break and send him tumbling to his death. He pressed his forehead against it and peered at Atlanta, stretched out like a toy city. Nothing down there seemed to have changed in the last few minutes. It was still gray and green and scampering with ants.

"Where are you, Helen?" he muttered. "Where are you?"

THE CADILLAC rolled through Atlanta's western business district, silent except for the air conditioner's cool blast. They passed a large shiny Woolworth's storefront on their right; pedestrians strode along the sidewalk smartly dressed in dark business suits and dresses. Jan collected his thoughts before turning to Helen.

"So. Who were they?"

She looked out her window. "Do preachers always drive such expensive cars?"

"I'm not a preacher. I'm a writer. I wrote a book that did well."

"I suppose you take it any way you can get it. Not that I don't approve; I do. I just didn't expect your shiny white ride to fly in just when it did, that's all."

"I'm glad I could be of service. Which leads us back to my first question. Who were those two men?"

She shifted her eyes back to the passing road. "Where are we going?"

TED DEKKER

"To a friend's house. If I'm not mistaken, I just risked my neck back there for you. The least you can do is tell me what for."

"They were two of Glenn's men."

"And Glenn? Tell me about Glenn."

"You don't want to know about Glenn, Reverend."

"Please don't call me Reverend anymore. And again, I think I've earned the right to know about Glenn."

She smiled at him, a tad condescending. "Yes, I suppose you have, haven't you? But trust me, you don't *want* to know about Glenn. He's like a prison—just because you've earned a stay doesn't mean you *want* to go. But then you've probably never been to prison, have you?"

The notion to wallop her upside the head with one of his books crossed his mind. And then another thought: that even a year ago the impulse wouldn't have entered his mind at all. He stared at a hardcover copy of his book that peered at them from the seatpocket netting. Its surrealistic image of a man's bloodstained face stretched in laughter against a bright red sky even now seemed to mock him. Ivena was right, he'd seen too much.

Jan spoke without removing his eyes from the book. "Actually, I have spent time in prison. Five years."

Her grin softened slowly. Jan spoke while he had the advantage. "And yes, I do want to know about any man who threatens my life, regardless of the situation."

"What prison?"

"Tell me."

She turned away. "I told you. Glenn Lutz."

Now they were getting somewhere. "Yes, but you didn't tell me *who* Glenn Lutz is."

She looked at him with a raised eyebrow. "I can't believe you've never heard of Glenn Lutz. The developer? He's even on the city council, although God knows he's got no business there."

"And he's the kind of man that would have henchmen?"

"He's got money, doesn't he? When you've got money, you've always got something going on the side. In Glenn's case he's got a whole ton of money. And if people knew what he had going on the side . . ." She let the statement go. "Trust me, Preacher, you don't *ever* want to know him."

She flipped her stringy tangles back and ran her fingers through them in a futile combing attempt. Her pale skin was smooth; her jawline sloping back to a fair neck, like a delicate wishbone. She closed her eyes, suddenly sobered by her account of Glenn Lutz.

If this young woman was a junkie, which she surely was, she wasn't meant to be a junkie, Jan thought.

"And what does this man have to do with you?" he asked.

"I really don't want to talk about him, if you don't mind. He wants to kill me; isn't that enough?" Her voice wavered and suddenly Jan felt regret for having asked the question at all.

"He's your boyfriend?" Jan asked.

"No."

He nodded and looked through the front windshield. They were winding through an industrial part of town now, not so far from Ivena's house. Red-brick buildings passed on either side. Steve's reflection smiled at him in the mirror. He nodded and returned the man's gesture of support.

You did what?

I rescued a junkie from two goons in the park, but she really has no business being a junkie. Really she is quite witty.

And if not a junkie, what should she be?

I don't know.

Jan turned back to Helen. "You said Glenn wanted to—"

"Actually, I thought I said I didn't want to talk about the pig." She looked at him apologetically. "Didn't I say that? I mean, it wasn't two minutes ago and I could swear I asked you not to speak about the man."

Jan glanced to the front. Steve had lost his smile.

"Look, Reverend. I know you don't run into my type every day. I'm sure this is quite a shock to you—riding in your white Cadillac beside some lowlife running for her life. But in my world you can't just go around talking about every deal that goes down or you might find yourself on the wrong end of one of those deals." Her voice had softened. "If you knew what I'd been through in the last twenty-four hours, you might not be so critical."

He turned to her. "And if you knew what I had been through in the last twenty-four years you would not be so defensive."

They looked at each other for a long moment, each caught in the other's direct stare. Her eyes brimmed with tears and she turned. *Easy, Jan. She's a wounded one. You know about wounding, don't you? Perhaps she's not so different from you.* He cleared his throat and sat back.

They rode in an awkward silence for a few minutes.

"So," he finally said. "Now that I've saved your neck, is there any particular place you would like to go?"

The brick buildings had evolved into a heavily treed suburban neighborhood and Helen studied the homes. "He's got eyes everywhere."

"Glenn?"

She nodded.

"Then perhaps my friend can help until you decide what to do."

Helen looked at him. "Is he as kind as you?"

"He is a she. And yes, she is very kind."

"Girlfriend?"

"No." Jan smiled. "Heavens no. We're just very close."

"Then I think that would be okay."

"Good." Ivena would know what to do. Jan would drop Helen off at Ivena's house and ask her to set the girl on a course that removed her from any immediate danger. Perhaps call the authorities if Helen would allow it. He breathed deep. It was a thing to think about, this strange encounter. Something to think about, indeed.

CHAPTER TEN

Q: "You've been criticized by some for your attention to detail in the suffering of the martyrs. They say it's not decent for a Christian writer to dwell on such pain. Do you cross the line between realistic description and voyeurism?"

A: "Of course not. Realism allows us to participate in one's suffering and voyeurism takes pleasure from it. The two are like white and black. But many Christians would shut the suffering of the saints from their minds; it's not what Christ had in mind. He knew his disciples would want to forget, so he asked them to drink his blood and eat his body in remembrance. The writer of Hebrews tells us to imagine we are there, with those in suffering. I ask you, why is the church so eager to run from it?"

Jan Jovic, author of bestseller The Dance of the Dead
Interview with Walter Cronkite, 1961

THE TINY green shoot at the base of Nadia's dying rosebush had grown two inches overnight. Two inches of growth was too much for one night. Unless her memory of the previous morning was a bit fuzzy and it had already been two inches then.

Ivena bent over the blackened plant and blinked at the strange sight. The small shoot curled slightly upward, like a relaxed finger. The texture of its skin was different from any rose stem she knew of. Not as dark either.

She gently stroked the base of the shoot. By all appearances it was a graft, which could only mean one thing: She had grafted this shoot into Nadia's rosebush.

And then promptly forgotten it.

It was possible, wasn't it? She could've been so distressed over the prospect of Nadia's bush dying that her mind had wiped out a whole sequence of events. It could've been a week ago, for that matter, and judging by the growth it had been a week ago. At least.

The doorbell chimed and Ivena jerked up, startled. It was a delivery, perhaps. The bulbs she'd ordered last week. She pulled off her gloves, wiped her hands on her apron and wound her way through the small house to the front door.

She peeked through the viewer and saw two forms on the porch, one of which was . . . *Janjic! What a pleasant surprise!* She opened the door.

"Janjic! Come in, come in!" She leaned forward and allowed him to kiss each cheek. He was dressed in a well-worn beige shirt without a collar, Bosnian style, and his cologne smelled spicy when he bent for her kiss.

"Ivena, I would like you to meet Helen."

The dark lines around Janjic's eyes wrinkled with a nervous smile. He ran a hand through his hair. Ivena looked at the young woman beside Janjic. Any friend of Jan's would be a friend of hers, but this one was odd to be sure. For starters, the blue-eyed girl looked as though someone had drained the blood from her face. She smiled nicely enough, but even her lips were pale. And her hair hadn't been washed in several days at the least. The T-shirt and jeans made her look very young. Gracious, what was Janjic up to?

"Hello, my dear. My name is Ivena. Come in. Please, come in. And what of Steve?" she asked, looking to the Cadillac. "Will he join us?"

"No, I can't stay long," Janjic said, smoothing his brow.

They entered the house and followed her to the small dining room. She had bread in the oven and its warm scent wafted through the house. Why Americans purchased their bread when they could make it easily enough Ivena could not appreciate. Bread was to smell and to feel; it was to make, not just eat.

"Would you like a drink, Janjic?"

"I'm not sure—"

"Of course you would. We must have a drink together while you tell me of your new friend." She turned and winked at Jan.

"Yes. Yes, all right." Jan pulled a chair from the table, and Ivena could see that his cheeks had reddened slightly. Helen did not respond. Her eyes darted nervously about the house. She looked like a wild bird newly caged. A dove, maybe, with her soft white skin, but skittish and uncomfortable just the same.

"Sit, my dear. It's okay. I'll get us some tea."

Five minutes later they sat around a small blue pot and three porcelain cups of steaming tea, sipping the hot liquid. But really, only Jan and Ivena sipped. The girl picked hers up once and brought it to her lips, but she replaced it on the saucer without drinking. Ivena smiled politely and waited, wondering at the presence of this strange woman sitting between them.

Jan looked as though he wasn't quite sure how to begin so Ivena helped him out. "Just tell me, Jan. What would you like me to know about Helen?"

"Yes. Well, we have a problem here. Helen's in some trouble. She needs help."

Ivena looked at Helen and smiled. "But of course you do, my dear. I could see this much the moment I opened the door."

"That bad, huh?"

Ivena nodded. "I'm afraid so. What is the problem, child? You're hurting, I see."

Helen blinked.

"No offense, dear. But you look as though you just crawled from a sewer," Ivena said.

The skin around Jan's hazel eyes wrinkled with an apologetic smile. "You'll have to forgive Ivena, she doesn't really like to mince words."

"And would you *rather* I minced words, Janjic?"

"Of course not. But Helen might prefer some discretion."

Ivena tilted her head. "I may have passed my fiftieth year, but honestly, it hasn't yet affected my sight." She faced Helen. "And my sight tells me that the last thing your dear Helen needs is the mincing of words. She might very well need a bath and some hot food, but she's seen enough of wordsmithing, I'm sure."

Helen watched them with wide eyes, turning from one to the other.

"What do you say, dear?" Ivena asked.

"Wha . . . About what?"

"Would you like me to speak directly or mince my words?"

Helen glanced at Jan, then gathered herself. "Speak directly."

"Yes. I thought as much. So where did my famous author find you?"

"Actually, Jan may have saved my life," Helen said.

Ivena raised her eyebrows. "Saved your life? You did this, Janjic?"

"She was being chased in the park and I had the Cadillac. It was the least I could do."

"So now you have brought her here for safekeeping, is that it?"

"It wasn't my idea, I swear," Helen said quickly. "He could've dropped me off on a corner. Really."

Ivena looked at the girl carefully. For all the dirt and grime hovering about her, she possessed a refreshing look in her face. A certain lack of presumption. "Well, I would certainly agree with him, my dear. I can see that the corner is no place for you. He was right in bringing you here, I think. Did Janjic tell you how I came to be his friend?"

"No. He said that you were as kind as he."

"Indeed? And do you find him a kind man?"

"Sure. Yes, I do," Helen said, looking at Jan, who smiled awkwardly.

"Then I suppose that there's hope for everyone," Ivena said. "That includes you, my dear."

"You're saying I need help? Like I said, the corner would've been fine. I'm not askin' for your help here."

"Maybe not. But you would like it, wouldn't you?"

Helen held Ivena's gaze for a moment and then shifted her eyes and shrugged. "I can manage."

"Manage what?"

"Manage like I always managed."

Ivena lifted an eyebrow, but she held her tongue. Perhaps this little ragged junkie had been led to them. Perhaps Helen played a part.

"What do you think, Janjic?"

"I don't know," he answered.

Helen gazed from one to the other.

Ivena nodded. "And you want me to keep her?"

"Maybe."

"Wait a minute," Helen said, glancing between them. "I don't think—"

"Well, she certainly can't stay at the office," Ivena interrupted. "Karen would have none of it, I can promise you that."

"Karen?" Helen asked.

"Janjic's agent," Ivena said with a small grin. "His fiancée."

Helen looked at him with a raised eyebrow. "Have you considered the possibility that I might not want to stay here?"

"And you would go where?" Ivena asked. "Back to whoever put that bruise on your neck?"

Helen blinked. "No." She obviously hadn't expected that.

"Then where else?"

"I don't know. But I can't stay here! You people have no idea what my life's like."

"You don't think so? Actually, it seems pretty plain. You've never understood love and so in your search for it you've managed to mix with the wrong people. You have abused your body with drugs and unbecoming behavior and now you are fleeing that life. And perhaps most importantly you are now sitting between two souls who understand suffering."

Helen stared at Ivena as if she had just reached a hand across the table and slapped her. Ivena spoke softly. "You are fleeing, aren't you?"

"I don't know," Helen said.

"You despise your past, don't you? In moments of clarity, Helen, you hate what has happened to you and now you would do anything to get away, wouldn't you? You would risk your own life to escape this monster breathing down your back."

A heavy blanket seemed to fall over them. Their breathing thickened. It was her simple way with the truth. Yes, of course she'd managed to offend some in her time. But truth-seekers always welcomed her direct approach as they might welcome a spring of water in the hot desert. And *she* certainly didn't have the stomach to handle the truth with kid gloves; it seemed rather profane when held next to her own schooling in Bosnia. When stood up next to Nadia's death.

"You have been badly wounded, dear child. I see it in your eyes. I feel it in my spirit. It's something we share, you and I. We've both had our hearts torn out."

A mist covered Helen's eyes. She blinked, obviously uncomfortable, perhaps panicked at the emotion sweeping through her.

A knot rose to Ivena's throat and she swallowed. In that moment she knew that a child screamed to be free before her. Deep behind those blue eyes wailed a soul, confused and terrified.

She looked over to Janjic. He was staring at Helen, his mouth slightly agape. He too had seen something within her. His Adam's apple bobbed. Ivena turned back to the girl. A tear snaked down her right cheek.

"You'll be safe with me, Helen."

Helen looked quickly about the room, scrambling for control now. She wasn't used to showing her emotions, that much was obvious. She cleared her throat.

"It's okay. You may cry here," Ivena said.

It proved to be the last straw. Helen lowered her head into her hands, stifling a soft sob. Ivena rested a hand on her shoulder and rubbed it gently. "Shhhh . . . It's okay, dear."

Helen cried and shook her head. Veins stood out on her neck and she struggled to breathe.

"Jesus, lover of our souls, love this child," Ivena whispered. She let her own emotions roll with the moment. This sweet, sweet sorrow that grew out of the pit of her stomach and flowered in her throat.

She looked at Janjic.

His eyes stared wide in shock.

It occurred to Ivena that he was not necessarily seeing or feeling what she was seeing and feeling. Ivena inquired with raised brows. *What is it, Janjic? What is the matter?*

Janjic swallowed and cleared his throat. He pushed his chair back and rose unsteadily, gathering himself. "Maybe I should leave you two," he said. "I have a meeting with Karen that I should get to." He nodded at Ivena. "I will call you later."

Helen did not lift her head. Ivena continued to rub her shoulders, wondering at Janjic's odd behavior. Or perhaps she was reading more into it than was warranted. Men often felt uncomfortable around weeping women. But Janjic was not usually such a man.

"Thank you, Janjic. We will be fine."

He took one more look at Helen and then walked out.

Ivena heard the front door open, then close. She let Janjic's oddity leave her for the moment and addressed the young woman bent over her table. "There's nothing to fear, dear child. Hmmm?" She ran a finger along Helen's cheek. "We will talk. I will tell you some things that will make you feel better, I promise you. Then you may tell me whatever you like."

Helen sniffed.

A fleeting image of her dead rosebush with its strange new graft flew through Ivena's mind but she dismissed it quickly. Perhaps she would show Helen her garden later.

GLENN LUTZ paced the black tile floor, running his fingers along his stubble, feeling as though his stomach had been cinched to a knot. Waiting for any news at all. He should call up Charlie and have him put his police cruisers on the street looking for her, that's what he should do. But he'd never asked the detective and his cronies to go that far before, not for a girl. Charlie would never understand. Nobody would understand—not this.

But men had died for love before. Glenn thought he understood why

Shakespeare had written *Romeo and Juliet* now. He felt the same kind of love. This feeling that nothing in the world mattered if he couldn't take possession of the love he wanted.

And when he did haul Helen in he would have to teach her some gratitude. Yes, she needed to understand how destructive this crazy game of hers really was. If what Beatrice said about his business interests suffering was true—and of course it was—then it was really Helen's doing, not his. It was her doing because she had possessed him. And if she had not possessed him, then Satan himself had possessed him.

A rap sounded. Glenn jerked his head toward the double doors. "Come." He took a deep breath, gripped his hands behind his back, and spread his legs.

Buck and Sparks walked in. They were already back—alone. Which could only mean one thing. Glenn swallowed an urge to scream at them, now, before they spoke—he knew what they would say already. Fresh beads of sweat budded on his forehead.

The men stepped lightly on the tile, though walking lightly was not an ordinary thing for men weighing over two hundred and fifty pounds. They reminded him of two buffaloes dressed in ridiculous black suits, tiptoeing through a bed of tulips, and again he suppressed his rising fury. Of course they were nothing of the kind, and he knew it well. He employed only the best, and these two were that and more. Either one of these two could crush him with a few solid blows, and he was not a small man. Still, he would think of them as he liked. It was how he warded off intimidation, and it worked well.

They came to a stop across the room and faced him, still wearing their sunglasses.

"Get those ridiculous things off your faces. You look like two schoolchildren caught smoking in the can."

They obliged him, but they still didn't offer a reason for their unsolicited appearance. For a few moments Glenn just stared at them, thinking he really should go over there and bang their heads together. He turned his head slowly to the side, keeping his eyes on them. He cleared his throat and spat on the floor. A glob of spit splattered on the tile. Still they said nothing.

"You're afraid to tell me that she's gone, is that it?" Of course that was it and their silence sent heat up his neck. "You're standing there petrified because you've allowed a single girl, weighing no more than one of your legs, to get away from you, is that it?" He squinted at them.

But they still didn't speak.

"Speak!" Glenn yelled. "Say something!"

"Yes," Buck said.

"Yes? Yes?"

A thought rudely interrupted his intended barrage—*She's gone, Glenn.*

He held his tongue, breathing in shallow pulls. They'd let her go and for that they would have to pay. But what did that mean? *That means that Helen's gone. Gone!* A streak of panic ripped up his spine. A deep terror that brought a quiver to his hands.

It was followed immediately by another fear that these two pigs had seen his dread.

"Where?" he snapped.

"In the park, sir. A man took her in his car."

Now the heat mushroomed in his skull. He dropped his hands to his sides. A man? He could not steady the tremor in his voice. "What do you mean, a man? *What* man?"

"We don't know, sir."

"He drove a white Cadillac," Sparks interjected.

"You're telling me that she left in another man's car?"

"Yes."

Glenn fought a wave of nausea. The room drifted out of focus for a brief moment. "And you followed them? Tell me you followed them."

Sparks glanced at Buck. It was all Glenn needed to know. "But you did get a license plate number?" His voice sounded desperate, but for the moment he no longer cared.

"Well, sir, we tried, but it all happened very quickly."

"You tried?" Glenn whined mockingly, frowning deep. "You tried!" he screamed. He was slipping over a black cliff in his mind—he realized that even as he lashed out. "I didn't pay you to *try.* I paid you to bring her back! Instead she's escaped you three times in two days. And you've got the gall to walk into my office and tell me you didn't even have the sense to take down a license number?"

They stared at him, frozen.

He had killed a few men and it was always in this state of mind that he'd pulled the trigger. This kind of blinding fury that made the world swim in a black fog. Glenn closed his eyes and stood there shaking, speechless, unable to think except to know that this was all a mistake. It was an impossible nightmare. He hadn't just happened upon Helen—he'd been led to her. The hand of fate had rewarded him with this one gift, this one morsel of bliss. He had rescued her from the pit of hell and he wasn't about to lose her. Never!

There are people here, Glenn. These two buffaloes are watching you go berserk. Get a hold of yourself!

He breathed once very deep and opened his eyes. Sweat stung his eyeballs. He stepped toward them. Perhaps a little taste of insanity would be good for them. It would put the fear of God in them, at the very least. He walked briskly for the desk, retrieved a black semiautomatic pistol from the top drawer and strode for the men. Their eyes widened.

He lifted the gun and shot them quickly, each in the arm, *blam, blam,* before even he had a chance to think it through. The detonations thundered in the room. Actually, he shot Sparks in the arm; his shot went high on Buck and clipped his shoulder. Sparks moaned and muttered a long string of curses but Buck merely placed a hand over the torn hole in his shirt. His eyes watered, but he refused to show pain. For a brief moment Glenn thought they might come after him and he reacted quickly.

"Shut up! Shut up!"

Sparks stilled, gritting his teeth.

Glenn wagged the gun at them. "If she's not in this office within three days you're both dead. Now get off my floor!"

They stared at him with red faces.

He clenched his eyes and took a deliberate breath. "Go!"

They turned and strode from the room.

Glenn walked to his desk and sat heavily. If this didn't turn out right he might very well use the gun on himself, he thought. Of course there were other ways to track her down. He would employ every resource at his means to find her. A white Cadillac. How many white Cadillacs could there be registered in this city? Twenty? Fifty? The fool who'd picked her up had just made the biggest mistake of his life. *Oh, yeah, you'd better start packin' heat, baby, because Lutz is gunnin' for you.*

He dropped his head to the desk and moaned.

CHAPTER ELEVEN

THE IMAGE of Helen, leaning over the table crying, had softened as Steve drove Jan across the city, but it still left its imprint and he couldn't wrap his mind around the terrifying sorrow that had accompanied that image.

"So, Steve," he asked with a thin smile. "What do you make of our daring rescue?"

The chauffeur chuckled. "She's a feisty one, sir; that's for sure."

"You think she's sincere?"

"I think she's hurting. Hurting people tend to be sincere. It was good of you, sir."

"Don't call me sir, Steve. You're my elder; maybe I should call *you* sir."

"Yes, sir."

Jan smiled and let the statement stand. It was a small game they played and he doubted it would ever change. The chauffeur pulled up to the ministry and parked.

Jan stepped from the Cadillac and walked toward the towering office complex, trying to shake the annoying little buzz that droned on in his skull. The city was hot and muggy. An old black Ford with whitewall tires moaned by. The sound of beating wings drew his attention to the roofline where two gray pigeons flapped noisily for better footing. It occurred to him halfway up the steps that he'd neglected to close the door. He turned and jogged for the car, grinning apologetically to Steve, who'd already opened the driver's door to come around and shut it.

"Sorry, Steve. I'll get it."

"No problem, Mr. Jovic."

"*Jan*, Steve. It's Jan." He shut the door and headed back. At times he was embarrassed to have a driver. True, in the beginning he could not drive in a country where everyone drove at double speeds, but that had been five years ago. Somehow the driver thing had just stuck. It came with the position, he supposed.

A large illuminated sign featuring a white dove hung over the brick entrance. *On Wings of Doves*, it read in golden letters. The name of his ministry. And what was his ministry? To quicken within the world's heart the deep love of God—the same love shown by a little child named Nadia, the same love of Father Micheal. The same love Ivena suggested Jan didn't really possess at all. Ivena, now, she had lost her daughter and the love poured out of her in rivers. He wasn't sure exactly how he was to show the love of the priest anymore.

Father, show me your love again, he prayed. *Do not allow this world to swallow the fire of your love. Never. Teach me to love.*

An image of the woman, Helen, riding beside him in the car flashed through his mind. *"Do preachers always drive such expensive cars?"* she had asked.

He pushed into the office building and made his way to the elevators. Betty, the correspondence coordinator, was on the elevator, on her way to the mailroom to "set John straight," she said.

"And what are we setting John straight about today?" Jan asked.

Betty grinned softly, bunching her round cheeks into balls. She was nearing sixty and John was half her age; it was a ritual, a mothering thing for Betty, Jan often thought. She had adopted the mailroom manager as her son. She, the short, heavyset, gray-haired wise one, and John, the tall bodybuilder with jet-black hair—mother and son.

"He's gotten the crazy notion up his sleeve that we really can't answer three hundred letters a day, and so he's telling his people to send no more than two hundred letters down to our department on any given day." She waved at the air. "Nonsense!" Betty leaned forward as if to tell Jan a secret. "I think he likes flexing his muscles, if you know what I mean."

"Yes, John does enough of that, doesn't he? But be easy with him, Betty. He's young, you know."

She sighed as the bell for the sixth floor rang. "I suppose you're right. But these young ones need some guidance."

"Yes, Betty. Guide him well."

She clucked a short laugh. "And congratulations again, Jan."

"Thank you, Betty."

She stepped off and Jan rode on, grinning wide. The thought that all those letters in dispute were requests rather than checks ran through his mind. The ministry was slowly being sucked dry by them. My, my . . . where had all the money gone?

They rented the five lower floors to tenants and ran the ministry from the top three, an arrangement that gave them office space at virtually no cost. It had been another one of Roald's brilliant touches. Of course, they didn't really need all three floors, but the space allowed Jan and Karen to occupy the whole top floor as well as providing Roald a spacious if temporary office for his frequent visits. The mailroom occupied the sixth floor and the administrative offices occupied the seventh.

Jan walked in and smiled at the office secretary, Nicki, who was filling her cup with fresh coffee. "Afternoon, Nicki. They say too much of that stuff will kill you, you know."

She turned to him, flashing a broad smile. "Sure, and so'll hamburgers and soda and everything else that makes this country great."

"Touché. Any messages?"

"On your desk. Roald and Karen are waiting in the conference room." She shot him a wink and he knew it was because of Karen. Their engagement would be a hit around the office for at least another week. The thought of seeing Karen again suddenly set free a few butterflies in his stomach. He smiled sheepishly and walked into his office.

Jan glanced over the large oak desk, empty except for the small stack of messages Nicki had referred to, and headed back out. The ministry's administration was handled almost entirely by the staff now. And with Karen at the helm of public relations, he was relegated to showing up and dazzling the crowds, giving his lectures, but not much more. That and worrying about how to sustain this monster he'd created.

He opened the door to the conference room. "Hello, my friends. Mind if I join in?"

Karen stood from the conference table and walked toward him, brown eyes sparkling above a soft smile. Her hair rested delicately on a bright blue dress. Goodness, she was beautiful.

"Hello, Jan."

"Hello, Karen. Welcome back." She reached him and he kissed her cheek. The thought of an openly romantic relationship in the office still felt awkward. Although it hardly should; she was going to be his wife. "I missed you."

"And I missed you," she said quietly. She glanced over his choice of clothing and smiled, a tad disingenuous, he thought. "So I take it you've been playing today."

"I guess you could call it that. I was at the park."

She mouthed a silent, *Ahhh*, as if that put the puzzle together for her.

Roald Barnes grinned a pleasant smile with all the maturity and grace expected of a graying elder statesman. He wore a black tie cinched tight around a starched collar. "Hello, Jan," he said.

Jan looked at Karen. "How was the meeting this morning? Still on speaking terms with our publisher?"

"The meetings, plural, were . . . how should I put it? Interesting." She was slipping into her professional skin now. She could do it at a moment's notice—one second the beautiful woman, the next a sharp negotiator leveling a rare authority. At times it was intimidating.

"Bracken and Holmes refused the seventh printing."

"They did, huh? My, my. And what does this mean?" He crossed his legs and sat back.

She took a breath and exhaled deliberately. "It means we have to face some facts. Sales have faded to a trickle."

He looked at Roald. The older man's grin had all but vanished. "She's right, Jan. Things have slowed considerably."

"You think I don't know this? What are you saying?"

"We are saying that *The Dance of the Dead* is nearly dead."

"Dead?"

The word seemed to throw a switch somewhere in Jan's mind. He buried an urge to snap at the man and immediately wondered at the anger he felt. The man's choice of words could have been better, but he was only speaking the same truth that had lurked in these halls for weeks now.

"What happened to *May she live forever?* Things of this nature don't just die, Roald. They have a life of their own."

"Not in this country, they don't. If people aren't buying—"

"It's not simply a matter of people buying. I've said so a thousand times. I say it at every interview."

Jan was suddenly feeling very hot in this small room without really knowing why. Roald knew well Jan's basic resentment with characterizing the success of the book in mere numbers. After all, the book was about God. Between every page there was the voice of God, screaming out to the reader; insisting that he was real and interested and desperate to be known. How could such a message be reduced to numbers?

"I think what Roald's trying to say," Karen interjected with a firm glance over to Roald, "is that on the business end of things our income's drying up. Another printing would have helped."

"You know very well, Jan, that what's hot one year may be cold the next," Roald said. "We've enjoyed five enlightening years. But enlightenment doesn't pay the mortgage. And the last time I checked, your mortgage was rather significant."

"I'm aware of the costs, my friend. Perhaps you forget that this story was bought with blood. With blood and five years in a prison that might leave you dead within a week. You may say what you like, but be careful how you say it!" Heat washed over his collar. *Easy, Jan. You have no right to be so defensive.*

Roald became very still. "I stand corrected. But you also should remember that this world's filled with people who don't share your sentiments toward God. People who *committed* the very atrocities you've written about. And don't forget, it was I who made this book possible in the first place. I'm not your enemy here. In fact, I've bent over backward to help you succeed. It was I who convinced you to publish your book in the United States. It was I who first persuaded the publisher to put some marketing muscle behind the book. It was even I who brought Karen on board."

"Yes indeed, you did. But it wasn't just you, Roald. It was the book. It was the priest's blood. It was my torture. It was God, and you should never forget that!"

"Of course it was God. But you can't just throw your own responsibility on God. We each play our part."

"Yes, and my part was to rot for five years in a prison, begging God to forgive me for beating a priest. What was your part?"

"I don't hear any complaints about the house. Or the car, or the rest of it, for that matter. You seem pretty comfortable now, Jan, and for that you may thank me and Karen."

"And I'd give it up in a word if it mocked the lives that purchased it." *Would you, Jan?* "If you don't understand that, then you don't know me as well as you once thought. This mountain of metal and mortar is an abstraction to me. It's the love of God that I seek, not the sale of my books." *At least for the most part.*

"If you drift off to obscurity, what becomes of your message then? We live in a real world, my friend, with real people who read real books and need real love."

They sat staring at each other, silent in the wake of their outbursts. It wasn't so uncommon, really, although rarely with this intensity. Jan wanted to tell Roald that he wouldn't know real love if it bit his heart out, but he knew they'd gone far enough. Perhaps too far.

"Well, well," Karen said softly. "Last time I checked we were all on the same side here." She wore a thin smile, and Jan thought she might actually be proud of him for standing so firmly. It *was* inspiring, wasn't it? In a very small way it was like Nadia standing tall in Karadzic's face. In a very tiny way.

The heat of the moment dissipated like steam into the night.

"Now, like I was saying before this train derailed itself," Karen said, "the meetings were *interesting*. I didn't say they were disastrous. Maybe I should've been a little clearer; we might have avoided this robust philosophical exchange." She stared Jan in the eye with those beautiful brown eyes and winked. "Bracken and Holmes may have turned us down, but there are other players in this big bad world of ours. And as it turns out, I just may have found a new life for *The Dance of the Dead*, after all. No pun intended, of course."

"Which would be?" Jan asked.

She looked at Roald, who was now smiling. So he knew it as well. Jan stared at her. "What? You've been turned down by the publisher, so what was this other meeting? You've set up another speaking tour?"

"Speaking tour? Oh, I think there will be speaking tours, my dear." She was playing it out, and in the echoes of Jan's exchange with Roald it was playing like a sonnet.

"Then say it. You obviously know as well, Roald, so stop this nonsense and tell me."

"Well, what would you suppose is the most ambitious way to present your book to the masses?"

"Television? You have another television appearance."

"Yes, I'm sure there'll be more of those as well." She leaned back and smiled. "Think big, Jan. Think as big as you can."

He thought. He was about to tell them to get on with it when it came to him. "Film?"

"Not just film, Janjic. Feature film. A Hollywood movie."

"A movie?" The idea spun through his head, still not connecting. What did he know of movies?

"And if we play our cards right," Roald said, "the deal will be ours within the week."

"And what is the deal?"

Karen lifted her pen to her mouth and tapped it on her chin. "I met with Delmont Pictures this morning—the fourth meeting, actually. They've offered to buy the movie rights to the book for five million dollars."

"Delmont Pictures?"

"A subsidiary of Paramount. Very aggressive and loaded with cash."

Jan sat back and looked from one to the other. If he wasn't mistaken here, they were telling him that Delmont Pictures was offering five million dollars to make a movie of the book.

"When?"

Roald chuckled. "Deal first, Jan. Schedules will come after a deal's made. Actually, it's a wonder we still have the movie rights at all. Most publishers take the rights when they first contract. There was a piece of divine intervention."

"When did you negotiate this?"

"Over the last few weeks."

Jan nodded, still unsure. "So you're telling me that they want to make a movie of *The Dance of the Dead.*"

Karen exchanged a quick glance with Roald. "In a matter of speaking. They want to make a movie about *you,*" Karen said, biting her pen and speaking around it. "About your whole life. From your days as a child in Sarajevo through the publishing of your book. A sort of rags-to-riches story. It's perfect! Imagine it! You couldn't fictionalize this stuff if you tried!"

The Dance of the Dead contained his life story to some degree, of course. But it was much more a story of spiritual awakening. "Rags to riches? My story's not a rags-to-riches story."

Roald cleared his throat and now Jan knew why the older man had taken him to task earlier. He had known this would be a sticking point—this *rags-to-riches* take on Jan's life—and now he'd already aggressively argued his position in a preemptive strike. The man was no idiot.

"Now you listen, Jan. Listen carefully. This is a deal you want to take. This is a deal that'll place your story on the hearts of untold millions who would never dream of reading your book. The kind of people who probably could use the story the most—people too busy with their own lives to take the time to read; people so thoroughly involved in mediocrity that they've never even thought about living for a cause, much less dying for one. Now"—he placed both hands on the table before him—"I realize that they want this spin of theirs on the story, but you must accept this proposal. It will save your ministry."

"I wasn't aware that my ministry needed saving, Roald."

"Well it does. It's doomed."

It is the souls of men that are doomed, not buildings and ministries, Jan wanted to say, but he decided against it. He'd challenged Roald enough for one day. Besides, there was a ring of truth to what the elder statesman said.

"He's right, Jan," Karen said. "You know he's right." It was half statement, half question.

He looked at her and saw that she was begging him. *Please, Jan, you know that there are times to play tough and there are times to trust and accept. And you can trust me, Jan, because you're more than a business partner to me. You are a man to me. Say yes.*

101

A thought occurred to him then, looking at her. The thought that she was desperate for this deal. Perhaps as desperate for the deal as for him.

"Yes," he said, gazing deep into her eyes. She was beautiful. She was striking and gentle and brilliant. "Maybe you're right."

She smiled and a moment passed between them.

"You are amazing," he said, shaking his head.

She smiled and her eyes twinkled with another statement. *We're perfect together, Jan Jovic.*

Roald lifted his coffee cup for a toast. "Now then, I'll say it again, and this time you'll understand. *The Dance of the Dead:* May she live forever."

Jan grinned at the man and lifted his own cup. The entire meeting with the leaders now made sense. "May she live forever," he repeated.

They laughed then. They hauled Nicki in and told her about the Delmont Pictures deal and talked through the afternoon about the new possibilities this would open up for the ministry. They even sent Steve out for some sparkling apple cider, and asked Betty, John, and Lorna to gather all the employees in the mailroom where they announced the deal. A hundred toasts and twice as many congratulations were thrown around despite Karen's caution that it wasn't finalized. Not yet. *But will it be?* Well, yes. *There you go then! Congrats! And congrats on the engagement as well. You two were born for each other.*

Betty hugged John, nearly twice her size; Steve tossed his driver's cap into the air with a holler; even Lorna, the skinny conservative finance manager, surprised them all by pretending to dance with her teacup before turning beet red at their laughter.

The execution of the contract was set to move forward at breakneck speed. Assuming they could come to terms with the scope of the project as it related to Jan's life, they would sign documents in the Big Apple on Friday. Their first payment would come at signing—a clean million dollars.

"We'll have to celebrate with dinner," Jan told Karen in a quiet moment alone.

"Yes, we will. And we have a lot to celebrate." She winked. Every look between them seemed to drip with honey, he thought. Karen sighed. "Unfortunately I have a conference call with the New York studio at six-thirty our time. How about a late dinner or dessert?"

"I'll settle for dessert. Eight o'clock?"

"Eight it is." She stroked his cheek with the back of her finger. "I love you, Jan Jovic."

"And I love you, Karen."

CHAPTER TWELVE

IT WASN'T until five that Jan remembered the young blonde he'd left in Ivena's care. He called Ivena on the phone.

"Hello." The sound of her baritone voice brought the morning's events crashing in on Jan.

"Hello, Ivena. It's Janjic."

"Well, Janjic. Nice of you to call."

"I have some news," he said, but suddenly he wasn't thinking of the news. He was thinking of the woman. "How is she?"

"Helen? You wish to know how Helen is? Perhaps you should join us for dinner and see for yourself. She was your catch, after all."

"I wasn't aware I was fishing. But dinner may not work. I'm meeting Karen at eight." He paused. "Is she okay?"

"You will have to see for yourself, Janjic. What is the news?"

"They want to make a movie of the story."

The phone went silent.

"It won't be made without your consent, of course. But it would be a wonderful opportunity to bring our story to many who'd never read it. And it'll pay well."

"The money is nothing. You remember that, Janjic. Never think of the money."

"Of course."

"When you left this afternoon, Janjic. There was a look about you."

Suddenly the phone felt heavy in his hand.

"You saw something?" she asked.

He swallowed. "Not really, no. I . . . I don't know what it was."

"Then perhaps you should come to an early dinner, Janjic." She said it as a command. Funny thing, it was now precisely what he wanted to do. He could eat with Ivena and meet Karen for dessert at eight.

103

"Come, Janjic. We will wait."

"Okay. I'll be there at six."

"We will have the kraut ready."

And that was that.

JAN GAVE Steve the night off and drove the Cadillac himself. Maybe it was time to stop the chauffeuring altogether. Of course, he'd have to find another position for Steve; he couldn't just let the man go. But being driven around was feeling silly today.

He drove to the Sandy Springs district where both he and Ivena now lived, though on opposite ends. It was an upper-middle-class neighborhood, neatly cut into perfect squares, each heavily laden with large trees and manicured flowering bushes. Roald had recommended the area when they had first arrived and it had seemed far too extravagant for Jan. But then most things in America had seemed extravagant to him during those early days. Now the old custom homes and the driveways lined with their expensive cars and boats hardly made an impression at all.

For the second time that day Jan walked up the path to Ivena's small house, surrounded by sweet-smelling rosebushes in full red bloom. He rang the doorbell and stood back. His palms suddenly felt clammy. Something had happened this morning when Helen caved in on herself at Ivena's table—a shock of emotion had lit right through him. He could hardly explain it, but it had struck a chord in his mind. Like a tuning fork smacked too hard and left to quiver off key. The note had filled him with sorrow.

Jan pushed the bell again and the door swung in. Ivena stepped aside and invited him with an open arm. "Come in, Jan. It's good of you to come."

He stepped in. A kettle sang in the kitchen; the smell of sausage and kraut hung in the warm room. Dinner in Bosnia. Jan smiled and kissed Ivena on each cheek. "Of course, I would come." He straightened and looked about the living room. "So where's Helen?"

"In the kitchen."

Then suddenly she was in the doorway that led to the kitchen, and Jan blinked at the sight of her. She stood in bare feet, it was the first thing he saw. The second was her bright blue eyes, piercing right through him; those hadn't changed. But everything else had. For starters she wore a dress, one of Ivena's dresses; Jan recognized it immediately. It was the blue one with yellow flowers, a dress Ivena hadn't worn for some time, complaining that it was too small. It fit Helen's thin frame remarkably well, certainly a bit large, but not ridiculously so.

It wasn't the only change; Helen had showered as well. Her hair lay slightly unkempt, short and very blond. He couldn't tell if she wore makeup; her face shone with its own brightness.

Jan smiled wide, unable to hide his amusement. Helen and Ivena giggled together as one, as if they had just shared this secret with him and expected him to be pleased with it.

Helen lifted both arms and curtsied. "You like?" She turned slowly, unabashed, posing with an arm cocked to her hairline, as if this were a fashion runway on which she stood instead of a checkered vinyl kitchen floor. Ivena rocked back and laughed. The levity was infectious. Jan stared at them, stunned, wondering what they'd gotten into over the afternoon.

"So, you like, Janjic?" Ivena asked.

You like? Since when did Ivena use such words? "Yes, I like," he said.

Helen twirled around and let the dress rise up until it showed well-tanned thighs. "First dress I've had on in ten years. I guess I'll just have to get me some of these."

Jan chuckled.

"You see, I clean up pretty good, don't you think? Of course, I had some help from Ivena."

He was at a loss for words.

She walked toward him now, one hand on her hip, strutting for show and lifting her chin just so . . . Goodness, she was quite beautiful. She moved without a hint of presumption, as if he and Ivena were children and she the baby-sitter showing them how it was really done out in the big world. She walked right up to him and presented her hand to him. "Then let me show you your seat, good sire." A twinkle skipped through her eyes and she grinned.

Jan looked over at Ivena, hoping for rescue, but she only smiled, quite pleased to watch, it seemed. He felt his jaw gape slightly, but felt powerless to pull it shut. *Don't be silly, Jan. It's a harmless game!*

He reached out and took her hand.

Now, up to this point in the day, Jan had taken everything pretty much in stride. It wasn't the most usual day to be sure. Not with rescuing Helen and the odd emotions he'd felt at seeing her cry. Not with seeing Karen again or the announcement from her that his book was about to sell to Delmont Pictures for an ungodly amount of money. It wasn't a usual day at all. But he had taken it all in stride, if for no other reason than his life had been filled with unusual days.

But now his stride faltered; because now, when his fingers made contact with Helen's, his world erupted.

Pain surged through his chest, igniting a flash of light in his mind. It happened so suddenly and with so much force that he couldn't contain a gasp. His vision filled with a white field, flowered as far as the eye could see; a flowered desert. A sound carried across the desert—the sound of crying. The sound of weeping. A chorus of voices crying and weeping in dreadful sorrow.

Jan stood there, holding her hand, and he gasped, unable to move forward. Immediately a part of him began to back-pedal, scolding him to collect himself. But that part of him consisted of nothing more than a distant wailing, smothered by the raw emotion that seemed to reach into his chest and give his heart a good squeeze. It was an *ache* that surged through his chest at the vision. A profound sorrow. Like the emotion he'd felt at seeing her cry, amplified ten times.

And then it was gone, as quickly as it had come.

He bent over and coughed, hitting his chest as he did so. "Oh, boy. I'm sorry. Something caught in my chest."

"You okay?" Helen asked with a furrowed brow.

"Yes." He straightened. "Yes."

She turned for the dining room. "Then follow me."

He followed, pulled by her small hand. Had they seen his face? It must have turned white. He couldn't bring himself to look at Ivena; surely she'd seen.

The table was set with Ivena's china and three crystal glasses. A large red candle cast flickering light over the silverware; a bouquet of roses from Ivena's garden stood as a centerpiece; steam rose lazily from the sausages. Helen ushered him to the seat at the table's head and then slid gracefully into her own on his left.

"Ivena and I decided that the least we could do was to prepare your favorite dish," Helen said. "Seeing as how you rescued me with all that bravery." She grinned.

Jan's heart still hammered in his chest. He'd had a waking dream or a flashback to the war, but not of any setting he could remember. Still, something felt vaguely familiar about it.

Ivena's voice came distant. "Janjic?"

"I'm sorry. Yes, thank you. It reminds me of home," he said. The tension he felt was in his own mind, he thought. Helen at least seemed oblivious to it.

Ivena asked him to bless the meal, which he did and they dished food onto their plates. Much to Jan's relief, Ivena launched into a discussion about flowers. About how well the rosebushes were doing this year, all but one. Apparently the rosebush she'd brought with her to America was suddenly dying.

Jan nodded with the conversation, but his mind was occupied with the electricity that still hung in the air, with the unusually loud clinking of their forks on china, with the flickering of the flame. With that white, weeping desert that had paralyzed him at her touch. At Helen's touch.

And what would Karen think of this little dinner at Ivena's? What would *he* think, for that matter. But he already was thinking, and he was thinking that Helen was an enigma. A beautiful enigma. Which was something he had no business thinking.

He ate the sausage slowly, trying to focus on the discussion and entering it as he saw fit. Helen's hands held the utensils delicately; her short fingernails were no longer rimmed with dirt. She was a junkie, that much he could now see by a tiny pockmark on her arm. Heroin, most likely. It was a wonder she wasn't thinner. She chewed the food with small bites, often smiling and laughing at Ivena's antics over the differences between America and Bosnia. In some odd way they were like two peas in a pod, these two. This most unlikely pair. The mother from Bosnia and the junkie from Atlanta.

Slowly a deep sense that he'd been here before settled over him. He'd seen this somewhere. All of it. This mother and this daughter and this sorrow—he had seen it in Bosnia. It was in part the reason behind that bolt of lightning. It had to be. God was opening his mind.

". . . this movie of yours, Janjic?"

He'd missed the question. "I'm sorry, what?"

"Ivena says that they're making a movie of your life," Helen said. "So when are they making it?"

"Yes, well we don't know yet."

"And how can they show a film of a life that is not yet lived?" Ivena asked. "Your life's not finished, Janjic."

Jan looked at her, tempted to ignore the comment. "Of course my life isn't over, but the story's finished. We have a book of it."

"No, the book explains some events, not your entire life. You've seen the finger of God in your youth, but that hardly means it is gone."

"Ivena seems to think that I'm still Moses," Jan said. "It's not enough for me to see the burning bush; there's still a Red Sea to cross."

Helen chuckled nervously. "Moses?"

Jan glanced at Ivena. "Moses. He was a man in the Bible." He wiped his mouth with his napkin. "It was also a name given to me in prison. Did Ivena tell you about the village?"

She stared at him with round eyes and he knew that she had. "Some."

Jan nodded. "Yes. And when I returned to Sarajevo I was arrested for war crimes. Did she tell you?"

"No."

"Hmm. Karadzic persuaded the council to throw me in prison for five years. The warden was a relative of Karadzic's. He called me Moses. The deliverer." Jan took another bite of sausage, trying now to ignore the weight of the moment. "I'm surprised I survived the experience. But it was there that I first read the words of God in a Testament smuggled in by one of the other prisoners. It was after prison that I began to write my story. And now Ivena seems to think it's not finished." He put another bite of sausage in his mouth.

"Yes, we've all had difficult lives, Janjic," Ivena said. "You don't possess the rights to suffering. Even dear Helen has seen her grief."

Jan looked at Helen. Twenty-nine, she'd said. "Is that so? What's your story?"

Helen looked at him and her eyes squinted very briefly. She looked away and took a bite of sausage. "My story? You mean you're wondering how a person ends up like me, is that it?"

"No, I didn't say that."

"But you meant it."

Ivena spoke quietly. "Don't be defensive, child. Just tell him what you told me. We all have our stories. Believe me, Jan's is no prettier than yours."

She seemed to consider that for a moment. "Well, my dad was an idiot and my mom was a vegetable and I became a junkie. How's that?"

Jan let her stew.

After a few seconds she spoke again. "I was born here, in the city. My dad disappeared before I really knew him. But he was pretty well off and he left us some money; enough to last me and my mom for the rest of our lives. We were okay, you know. I went to a normal school and we were just . . . normal people." She smiled in retrospect. "I even won an eighth-grade beauty pageant down at O'Keefe Middle School—that's where I went."

She sipped her tea and the smile faded. "There was this kid at my school two years ahead of me, white trash we used to call them, poor and from the dirtiest part of town back then, down by the old industry district. At least that's where everyone said he was from, but I don't think anyone really knew for sure. His name was Peter. He used to watch me a lot. Ugly kid too. Mean and fat and ugly. Used to just stare at me across the schoolyard with these big black eyes. I mean, I was pretty, I suppose, but this sicko had an obsession. Everyone hated Peter."

Helen shuddered. "Even thinking about it now makes me sick. He used to follow me home, sneaking around behind me, but I knew he was there. Some of the other kids said he used to kill animals for the fun of it. I don't know, but it scared me to death back then."

Jan just nodded and listened to her, wondering what this childhood fright had to do with the woman sitting before him now.

"That was when my mom got sick. The doctors never could figure out what it was, but one day she was just sick. At first it was just throwing up and being weak, so that I had to take care of her. And then she started acting really strange. I didn't know it then, but she'd started using acid. Acid and heroin. And the stuff wasn't everywhere back then. You know where she got it? Peter! The creep from my school! Peter was supplying my mother with drugs!"

"Peter. The one who was following you home," Jan said. "How did you know it was him?"

"I came in one afternoon—I was out getting some groceries—and he was there, in the house, selling her dope."

"What did he do?"

"Nothing. I think he wanted to get caught. I threw him out, of course. But by then my mom was a zombie. If she didn't have drugs in her system, she was puking from her sickness, and if she did have drugs, she was out to lunch. And the kid wouldn't go away. He was always there, feeding my mom her drugs and staring at me. I started using within a few months, after I pulled out of school. We ran out of money about a year later. It all went for the drugs."

"You lost it all? Just like that?" She had cared for her mother too, Janjic thought. Just as Jan had cared for his own mother before the war in Sarajevo.

"Peter was robbing us blind. I never gave in to him; I want you to know that. The whole thing was about his demented obsession to make me his girl." Helen shifted her eyes to the wall. "My mom died from an overdose. The way I figure it, Peter killed her with his drugs. The day after my mom's burial he and I had a huge blowup. I hit him over the head with a two-by-four and took off. Never went back. We were dead broke anyway. Honestly, I think I might've killed him." She grinned and shrugged her shoulders.

"Killed him?" Jan said. "You never saw him again?"

"Never. I hitched a ride to New York that same day. Never heard a thing. Either way, if I did kill him, I figured he had it coming. One way or another he'd killed my mom and trashed my life."

She looked up at them with her deep blue eyes, searching for a nod of approval. But it wasn't approval that Jan felt sweeping through his bones. It was pity. It was a biting empathy for this poor child. He couldn't understand the emotions in their entirety, but he couldn't deny them either.

"How old were you?"

"Fifteen."

"You see, Janjic," Ivena said, "she's a child of the war as well."

"You're right. I'm so sorry, Helen. I had no idea."

Helen shifted in her seat. "Relax. It's not so bad. It could be a lot worse."

"Poor child," Ivena said. "You have never been loved properly."

Helen straightened. "Sure I have. Love is the only thing I've had my fill of. They love me and they leave me. Or I leave them. Honestly, I do *not* need your sympathy." She held up a hand. "Please, I don't do sympathy well."

Neither Jan nor Ivena responded. They'd both seen enough of the wounded to know that they all needed sympathy. Especially those who had persuaded themselves they did *not* need it. But it wasn't a gift that could be forced.

"So how did you return to Atlanta?" Jan asked.

"I came back six months ago. But that's another story. Drugs and love don't always mix so well, trust me. Let's just say I needed to get out of New York, and Atlanta seemed as good a choice as any."

"And Glenn?" Jan asked.

Helen set her glass down and turned it slowly. "Glenn. Yeah, well, I met Glenn while back at a party. He likes to throw these big bashes. Glenn is . . . bad." She swallowed. "I mean he's really bad. People think of him as the powerful city councilman; that his money comes from real estate . . ." She shook her head. "Not really. It comes from drugs. Problem is, anybody who crosses him ends up hurt. Or dead."

"And have I crossed him already?" Jan asked.

"No. I don't think so. This was my choice. I left him. It had nothing to do with you. Besides, he's got no clue who you are."

"Except that you came in my car. Except that you're now in Ivena's house."

She looked at him but didn't offer an opinion.

"And he's your . . . boyfriend, right?"

Her eyes widened briefly. "No, I wouldn't put it that way. He puts me up in this place of his. But no. I mean no, not anymore. Absolutely not. Nobody's gonna hit me and think they can get away with it."

"No," Jan said. "Of course you're right." Heat flared up his back. Who could strike such a person?

Karadzic could, a small voice snickered. He shook his head at the thought.

"Helen would like to stay with me for a while," Ivena said. "I have told her"— she looked at Jan—"that I would accept nothing less. If there's any danger, then God will help us. And we're no strangers to danger."

"Of course. Yes, you should stay here where it's safe. And perhaps Ivena can buy you some new clothes tomorrow. I'll pay, of course. It's the least I can do. We will put our ministry funds to good use."

"You will trust two women with your bank account?" Ivena asked with a raised brow.

"I would trust you with my life, Ivena."

"Yes, of course. But your money?"

"Money's nothing. You've said so a thousand times, dear."

Ivena turned to Helen with a sly smile. "There is my first insight, young woman. Always downplay the value of money; it will make it much easier for him to hand it over."

They laughed, glad for the reprieve.

Jan left the house an hour later, his head buzzing from the day.

God had touched his heart for Helen's sake, he decided. Maybe because she was an outcast as he himself once was. His odd enchantment with her certainly couldn't be natural.

It had been God, although God had never touched him in such a specific way before. If only his whole ministry were filled with such direct impressions. He could touch a contract, say, and wait for a surge of current to fill his arms. If it didn't, he would not sign. *Ha!* He could pick up a phone and know if the person on the other end was to bode well for the ministry. He could take Karen's hand and . . . Goodness, now there was a thought.

Maybe he'd imagined the whole thing. Perhaps his emotions had gotten the best of him and caused some kind of hallucinogenic reaction, tripping him back to the weeping in Bosnia; another kind of war-trauma flashback.

But no, it had been too clear. Too real.

He drove the Cadillac toward Antoine's where he'd agreed to meet Karen for dessert. And what should he tell her of this day? Of Helen? Nothing. Not yet. He would sleep on this business of Helen. There was plenty to talk about without muddying the waters with a strange, beautiful junkie named Helen. There was the engagement and the wedding date. There was talk of love and children. The movie deal, the book, the television appearances—all of it was enough to fill hours of talk by Antoine's soft lights.

CHAPTER THIRTEEN

"What is love? Love is kind and patient and always enduring.
Love is kisses and smiles. It is warmth and ecstasy.
Love is laughter and joy.
But the greatest part of love is found in death.
No greater love hath any man."

The Dance of the Dead, 1959

IVENA MEANDERED through her kitchen at nine the next morning, humming the tune from "Jesus, Lover of My Soul." Helen still slept in the tiny sewing room down the hall. Poor girl must have been exhausted. What a sweet treasure she was, though. Abused and dragged down life's roughest paths to be sure, but so very sweet. Today she would take Janjic's signed checks—he'd given them five—and shower Helen with a little love.

Ivena turned one of four taps by the greenhouse door and the overhead misters hissed inside. She opened the door. The musty smell of dirt mixed with flower scent always seemed to strengthen with the first wetting.

She'd shown Helen the garden yesterday evening and the flowers seemed to have calmed her. Ivena had known then, seeing the spindly gray stalks of her daughter's rosebush, that it was for all practical purposes dead, despite the strange green shoot at its base. She was still having difficulty remembering if she had—

"Huh?" Ivena caught her breath and stared at the dead bush.

But it wasn't dead! Or was it? Green snaked up through the branches; vines wrapped around the rose stalks and spread over the plant.

Ivena stepped forward, barely breathing. It looked as though a weed had literally sprung up overnight and taken over the rosebush! But that was impossible!

113

The bush had seven main branches, each one as black and lifeless as they'd been yesterday. But now the green vines ran around each one in eerie symmetry. And they all came from the base of the plant; from the one shoot that had been grafted in.

But you did not graft that shoot, Ivena.

Yes, I must have. I just don't remember it.

Ivena reached her hand out to the strange new plant and ran a finger along its stalk. How had it grown so quickly? It had appeared yesterday, no more than four inches in length and now it ran the height of the plant! The skin was very similar to that of a healthy rose stalk, but without thorns. A woody vine.

"My goodness, what on earth do we have here?" Ivena whispered to herself. Maybe it was this vine that had killed her rosebush. A parasite. Perhaps she should cut it off in the hopes of saving the rose.

No, the rose was already dead.

"Ivena."

She whirled around. Helen stood in the doorway, her hair tangled, still dressed in her pajamas.

"Well good morning, my dear." Ivena walked toward her, shielding the bush. "I would ask you how you slept, but I think I have my answer already."

"Very good, thank you."

"Wonderful." They stepped into the kitchen and Ivena closed the door to the greenhouse behind her. "Now you'll need some food. You can't shop properly on an empty stomach."

HELEN WATCHED Ivena with an odd mixture of amusement and admiration. The Bosnian woman wore her gray hair quite shaggy. She held her head confidently but gently, like her words. Both she and Janjic shared one stunning trait, Helen thought. They both had eyes that smiled without letting up, bringing on pre-mature wrinkles around their sockets. If there were other human beings with Ivena's unique blend of quirks and sincerity, Helen had never met them. It was impossible not to like her. In the woman's presence the small voice that called Helen back to the drugs sounded very faint. Although it was still there—yes it was, like a whisper in a hollow chamber.

They ate eggs for breakfast, and then readied themselves for a few hours of American indulgence, as Ivena put it. She seemed amused by the five checks she waved about. When Helen asked her why, she just smiled. "It's Janjic's money," she said. "He has far too much."

Helen insisted Ivena take her far from the central city district—with Glenn's men on the prowl, anything within a five-mile radius of the Twin Towers was out of the question. Even here it took Helen a good hour to satisfy herself that the chances of Glenn finding her were nearly nonexistent.

Ivena drove them to a quaint shopping district on the east side, where most of the merchants spoke with heavy European accents. They parked Ivena's Volkswagen Bug on one end of the district and made their way through the shops on either side of the street.

"Honestly, Ivena, I really love the halter top. It's so . . . fitting, don't you think?" *Glenn will love it.*

"Yes, Helen. Perhaps," Ivena returned with a raised brow. "But the red blouse, it is a lady's choice."

"I don't know, it looks a little old for me, don't you think?" *He'd kill me if I wore that thing!*

"Nonsense, dear. It's fabulous!"

They held the choices up to Helen's neckline, each arguing their case; trying not to be too forceful. A moment of silence ended the debate. It was then that Ivena, the final judge, issued her verdict. "We'll get both."

"Thank you, Ivena. I swear I'll wear them both." *Glenn . . .*

Get a grip, Helen. Glenn's history.

"Yes, I'm sure you will, dear."

And so the day went, from shop to shop. With halters and blouses; with jeans and skirts; with T-shirts and dresses; with tennis shoes and pumps; with everything except for lingerie. In the end they spent a thousand dollars. But it was just money, Ivena said, and Jan had altogether too much of the stuff. They walked and they laughed and then they spent another hundred dollars on accessories.

The beauty salon presented a challenge because two choices simply couldn't be made without resorting to wigs, and Helen would have nothing to do with wigs, despite Ivena's urging. Helen favored the short sporty look. It was sexy, she said. "Sexy? And you think a full-bodied woman's look is not sexy?" Ivena countered. The beautician tried to interject her opinion, but Ivena kept cutting her short. "It's Helen's hair," she finally announced. "Do as she wishes." And she retreated to a waiting chair. Helen walked out wearing a big smile and her hair just below the ears in a cropped style that even Ivena had to admit was "quite attractive."

Three times Helen thought about the life she'd left, and each time she concluded that this time she would stay straight if it killed her. She couldn't ignore the feeling of butterflies that accompanied the brief memories—a yearning for the drug's surge of pleasure—but watching Ivena carry on about a dress, she could not imagine crawling back to her old life.

It was three o'clock by the time they returned to Ivena's flower-laden home. It was four by the time Helen had wrapped up her fashion show, displaying every possible combination their purchases allowed and then some. Ivena looked on, sipping at her iced tea and boldly proclaiming how beautiful Helen was with each new outfit.

It was five when Helen began to come unglued.

Ivena had gone out to deliver a batch of orchids to a floral shop. "Make yourself at home—smell some flowers, warm up some sausage," she'd said. "I'll be back by six." Helen retreated to her tiny room, Ivena's sewing room actually, and sat on the bed, running her hand through the clothes piled beside her. She wore a dress, the one Ivena had proclaimed the winner of the bunch before leaving—a pink dress, much like the one Ivena had loaned her yesterday, but without all the frills.

She sat on the yellow bedspread in a sudden silence, with her legs swinging just off the floor like a little girl, feeling the fabric between her fingers, when her eyes settled on the blue vein that ran through the fold in her right arm. The room was dim but she could not miss the small mark hovering there. She pulled her hand from the clothes, opening and closing it slowly. The muscles along her forearm flexed like a writhing snake. It had been some time since she'd used the vein. Heroin was too strong, Glenn insisted. It ruined her. He couldn't stomach a rag doll sapped of passion. With Glenn it was all the new rich man's drug. Cocaine.

Glenn.

She blinked in the dim light and felt butterflies take flight in her belly again. She let familiar images crash through her mind. Images of the Palace, as he called it, where she'd lived for the last three months, on and off, but mostly on. Images of the parties, teeming with people under colored lights; images of mirrors mounded with cocaine and dishes with needles; images of bodies strewn across the floor, wasted in the wee morning hours. They were images that seemed ridiculous sitting here in the old lady's sewing room. She'd heard of sewing rooms, but she'd never expected to actually see one. And now here she was, *sitting* in one, surrounded by a pile of clothes that were presumably hers.

What do you expect to do, Helen? Use these people the way you've used the rest?

Suddenly the whole thing felt not just silly but completely stupid. And just as suddenly a craving for the mound of white powder ran through her body. An ache rose to her throat and she swallowed against it. She closed her eyes and shook her head. What was she doing?

Helen lifted a hand to her neck and rubbed the bruised muscles near the spine. She had put up with her share of abuse no doubt, and she could give it as well as she took it. A slap here and little punch there; it was all business as usual. But this strangling business—Glenn had nearly killed her! She'd had no choice but to run.

Here where there were no people she let tears fill her eyes. Now what? Now she was a little girl sitting on the bed, swinging her legs, wanting to be rescued.

Wanting a hit . . .

And she had been rescued, hadn't she? By a preacher, of all things. And his crazy old friend.

No, Helen, don't think of them like that. These are good people. Precious.

"Precious? And what would *you* know of precious?" she growled. The tears began to slip down her cheeks and she wiped them angrily with her wrist.

Helen stood to her feet, and the sudden movement left her dizzy. She blinked away the tears and paced the room. Face it, honey, this is not your world. This life with the flowers and the sausage and the strange accents and the old woman's crazy talk of love, like it was something Helen knew nothing of. All the hugs and the tears . . .

. . . and Jan . . .

. . . you'd think the world was turning inside out or something. Helen cleared her throat. Truth be told, she couldn't see why Ivena's daughter's death was such a huge deal anyway. Sure it was bad enough, but when you got right down to it, a bullet to the head wasn't so crazy. Not the big monstrous deal Ivena seemed to make of it. Like it was some new revelation of love or something. These two . . . weirdos . . . these two weirdos were just different, that was all there was to it. She was a fish; they were birds. And she was suddenly feeling short of breath up here with the weird birds. She needed to get back to her pond. After all, a fish could not live on the beach forever.

He's what they call a gentleman, Helen. A real man. The kind you've never seen. And don't pretend you don't know what I'm talking about, girl.

"Shut up!" Goodness, he was a preacher! She felt heat flare on her cheeks. *He's not even American.*

No, but he's god-awful handsome and his accent's pretty cute.

Helen hit her forehead with her palm. "You're being an idiot!"

The truth of her own words struck her and she halted her pacing mid-stride. The images of the Palace mounded with Glenn's drugs slid through her mind, whispering the promise of pleasure. Of heaven here on earth. The sound of her breathing filled the small room. Like that fish gulping up on the shore. She had no business here. This was a mistake, a stupid mistake.

Which meant she had to leave. And she *wanted* to leave, because now that she was allowing good sense to prevail, she knew that she had to have a hit. In fact, she wanted a hit as badly as she could ever remember wanting one.

It came roaring back. The urge rose through her chest with such force that for a moment she lost her orientation. She was in Ivena's sewing room of all places, a crazy place to be. She didn't belong here. She'd lost her mind!

Helen snatched a pair of Nikes, pulled them over her bare feet, and ran out to the living room. It would be best to leave out the back, in case the old woman . . .

. . . Ivena, Helen. Her name is Ivena and she's not old . . .

. . . drove up front. Helen hurried to the attached greenhouse, suddenly eager to be free. Desperate to get back into the water. She ran out to the backyard. But there were no gates in the tall fence surrounding the lawn. She gave up and ran right through the house and out the front door. It occurred to her only then that she had no ride. She should call Glenn. He would send a car. He'd be in a stew— the thought made her shiver. You pay your dues, baby. We all pay our dues. It was one of Glenn's favorite sayings. His idea of *dues* was a bit extreme.

She raced back into the house, snatched up Ivena's phone and called Glenn's private number. His secretary, the old hooknosed witch Beatrice, answered and demanded to know where she was. Helen gave her the nearest cross street and hung up. *Take a flying leap from the top story, Beatrice. And don't forget your broom.*

Now she ran with the butterflies that fluttered through her belly. She took a turn at the sidewalk and did not stop for two blocks, thinking only once that she should've ditched the dress—she must look like some kind of pink butterfly in the stupid thing. But her craving for the Palace washed the thought away.

Helen sucked in the warm southern air and settled into a walk. It was going to be a good night. Not at first, of course. At first it might not be so good at all, but that would pass. It always did. A picture of all those clothes piled on that bed back there flashed through her mind. *Sorry, Ivena. At least I left them. At least I didn't take them.*

Sorry, Jan.

Don't be stupid.

A long white limousine was already waiting at the corner of Grand and Mason, drawing the stares of stiff-lipped pedestrians in all directions. Yes indeed, it was going to be a good night.

BEATRICE WAS waiting for Helen when the elevator doors opened at the top of the West Tower, her nose hooked and her chin lifted like a snotty schoolmaster. She looked Helen's dress over and her lips twisted to a wrinkled frown. "So, the slug has crawled home wearing a dress. You think that's supposed to impress him?"

"Shut up, Witch. I'm not trying to impress anybody."

Beatrice's eyes grew round and then squeezed to slits. "He's gonna tan your hide when he sees you in that ridiculous getup." She turned on her heels and marched for the double doors leading to the Palace.

Helen hesitated, staring at those wide black doors. Her stomach seemed to have lifted into her throat. Glenn was in there, doing only God knew what, but in reality doing only one thing: waiting for her. Yes, and in truth she was waiting for him as well, right? Or at least for what he could offer. Which was bliss. Yes, indeed, Glenn could definitely offer her bliss.

She swallowed and stepped onto the thick black carpet after the witch, chills now running the length of her spine. *You're a fool, Helen. You have a death wish?* She thought about that and the chill was quickly replaced by a tingle. *No, honey, not death. Sweet life. Sweet, sweet mind-numbing life!*

Beatrice walked in without knocking; she was the only one who could survive such boldness. Helen followed, stepping lightly, as if doing so would somehow make her entrance less obvious. The sprawling room reminded Helen of a casino she'd been in once; lots of mirrors, lots of colored light, none of it natural. Glenn was not in sight.

Beatrice retreated with a *humph* and pulled the doors shut behind her. Helen peered about the room, her heart now thumping in the silence. To her right, one of those large mirrored balls rotated above a dance floor, slowly spinning a thousand tiny white dots through the room. Otherwise the Palace lay absolutely still. When she'd left the party three nights earlier, a dozen bodies twisted slowly on the pink marble dance floor. Directly ahead, a large lion head roared down to a red leather couch. A couple had been sprawled on that sofa, wasted to the world that night. Other guests had passed out on a dozen similar couches, each under beasts that glared down at them. There were a hyena and a rhinoceros and a buffalo—all within her sight. The others wound about the suite. To her left a long bar sparkled with a hundred colored bottles, each hosting its own intoxicant.

The last time she'd seen Glenn, he'd been leaning on that bar, talking to some huge black man with his back toward her. He was not there now.

"So . . ."

Her heart seized and she spun to his voice. Glenn stood ten yards to her right with his arms to his sides, in the shadow of a Greek pillar, huge and thick like the stonework beside him. A red-and-yellow Hawaiian shirt hung loosely over his torso; white slacks ran to the floor where they met his bare feet. He took a step forward then stopped, spread his legs, and clasped his hands together like a soldier at ease. From this distance his eyes looked like holes drilled through his skull; as black as midnight. His chin was stubbled and his hair unkempt.

Helen gulped and fought the overwhelming urge to flee. This had been a mistake. A terrible error on her part—coming here, back to this monster. He liked things dirty, he said, because he *could*. Weaker men had to stay clean to impress those in power. But not he. On several occasions she had suspected that he'd gone a week or more without bathing. When she was high the fact somehow held its own appeal, but now with a clear mind the very sight of him brought bile to her throat.

"So. Where have you been?" he asked.

"Hi, Glenn." She said it straight, but her voice wavered slightly. "I've been around."

"Around, huh? Why did you leave me?"

She smiled as best she could. *You can't be weak, Helen. He despises weakness.* "I didn't leave you, Glenn. I'm here, aren't I? Nobody forced me to come here." She wanted to say, *You think you own me, you pig?* but she held her tongue.

Glenn walked toward her. He did not stop until he towered over her, within arm's reach, drilling her with those dark eyes. He lifted a hand and touched her cheek with a knotted finger, rolling it back and forth, intent on the feel of her flesh. "You look so much like your mother, you know."

Her mother? Glenn knew her mother? Helen blinked. "You knew my mother?"

"Just an expression, dear," he said, gazing with a cocked head at his fingers touching her. His body odor hit her nostrils and she turned her head, trying not to show her disgust.

"What is it, darling?" he said in a soft, labored voice. "Do I frighten you?"

His breath smelled of dead flesh. Helen felt the pressure of tears fill her sinuses. "Are you *trying* to frighten me?" she asked. *Be strong, Helen. You know how he likes that.*

A soft moan ran past his lips. "Do you have any idea how much I've missed you? I was worried sick." His finger trembled on her cheek. "I feel lost without you, you know that, don't you? Look at me."

She held her breath and clenched her jaw and looked at his face. His unshaven jaw rested open and he ran his fat tongue over those crooked teeth. "Do you love me?" he asked.

A thousand sirens of protest raged through her mind. "Yes. Of course I love you." She had to get some dope into her system. She had to before she threw up on the man's smelly shirt. "You have some snort for me, honey?"

His lips peeled back over yellowed teeth in a smile of sorts and a string of spittle bridged his open mouth. He was enjoying his power over her. "Where did you get the dress, Helen?"

"The dress?" She looked down at the pink dress, wishing she would have had the sense to leave it at Ivena's. She chuckled. "Oh, this? Goodness, nowhere. I stole it. I—"

Crack! A blow struck her cheek and spun her around to the door. She gasped and instinctively jerked a hand to her mouth. It came away red and wet. Tears stung her eyes. Behind her Glenn was breathing heavy. She had to walk the line carefully now—this line between his anger and his desire to play. She turned back to him.

"What's the matter, Glenn?" she asked, forcing a grin. "Your little treasure disappears for three days and you come unglued, is that it?"

He blinked, unsure how to take the indictment. "You look like a schoolgirl," he said. "Your hair's different."

"Yeah, and you prefer the street girl look. Then give me what I want and I'll give you your street girl."

He brought each foot forward one step. "And what is it that you want, Helen?"

She'd meant the drugs, of course. They both knew that. But now he was daring her to say anything but him. "I want you, of course," she said.

She hoped it would appease him. It did not. His hand flashed from his hip and across her head before she could react. The blow sent her staggering to her right. This time she cried out and sprawled to the floor. It felt as though her ear had been ripped off by the blow, but she knew better. She gritted her teeth and pushed herself to her knees. She could kill the monster! If she had a knife now she would rush him and stuff it into the folds of his belly.

"You want me, do you? And that's why you were off with another man?" he thundered. He was red in the face now.

"That was nothing," she returned, standing unsteadily. "You sent two men after me, what do you expect?"

"I expect you to stay home, is what I expect! I expect you to at least try to stay alive, which means staying away from other men." His hands were balled into fists at his sides.

"Well, if you'd quit hitting me I might want to stay home!"

He grunted like a bull and swung again, but this time she stepped out of the blow's path and skipped back. "You fat pig!" She had entered his game now. "I came back, didn't I?" That was it. That was her ace. The fact that his men had not caught her and still she was here of her own will.

She sidestepped and ran across the room. *Come on, baby. Play the game. Just play the game and it'll be okay.*

Glenn lumbered after her. "I swear, if you ever, and I mean *ever*, leave me again, I swear I'll kill you!" he said. Someday he might actually make good on that promise to kill her, she thought.

She leaped behind a large couch and faced him. "Unless you die of *heartbreak* first!" She said it with a grin and tore out of his way just as he crashed into the sofa. "Give me some dope, Glenn."

Glenn pulled up in the center of the room, threw his fists to either side and roared at the ceiling. She spun around, the first genuine smile now spreading her mouth. *Now* he was playing. Now he was definitely playing. And that was good. That was really good. Adrenaline rushed through her veins.

"Give me some snort, Glenn. I'll be your girl."

He ripped his shirt open, popping the buttons with a single pull. His flabby belly bulged white. She couldn't stand to touch him without the drugs in her system. "Give me the drugs, Glenn!" She called out frantically now. "Where did you stash them?"

He taunted her with an ear-to-ear grin. "Drugs? Drugs are illegal, dear. You want to be illegal in my palace? You want some dope?"

"Yes. Yes I do."

"Then beg. Drop to your knees and beg, you dirty pig."

She did. She dropped to her knees, clasped her hands and begged. "Please! Please, tell me . . ."

He grinned like a kid. "In your bedroom."

Of course! Helen twisted to the door leading to the apartment he referred to as hers. She clambered to her feet and ran for the door. Glenn pounded across the room in pursuit. She slammed through the door and scanned the room for the dope. Her bed lay exactly as she'd left it—a comforter strewn cockeyed across it, three pillows bunched at the head. When he'd first presented the hidden apartment to her, its psychedelic yellow decor had taken her breath away. Now it made her head spin. She only wanted the stuff.

And then she saw it; a small pile of white powder on the mirrored end table across the room. Glenn's hot breath approached from behind and she bolted for the stash. She stumbled forward and fell to her knees just out of the stand's reach.

His big hand landed on her shoulder. "Come here, precious."

She clawed her way to the end table, desperate now. She had to have the stuff in her system. Had to. She swung her elbow back hard and landed it on his bare chest. He grunted.

The blow stalled him enough for Helen to reach the powder, shove her nose into the mound and inhale hard. Her nostrils filled with the suffocating drug, and she fought the urge to cough. A bitter pain burned at the back of her throat and through her lungs.

Then three hundred pounds fell on her back and rolled off to the floor, squealing like a stuck pig. Glenn squirmed on the carpet and giggled. *You are a sick man*, Helen thought. *A very sick man.* But the drug had already started to numb her mind and she thought it with a twist of irony. Like, *I am with a sick man. With a smelly pig and I'm feeling good. And that's because I'm sick too. We're just two sick pigs in a blanket. Glenn and me.*

She dived on top of him, slapping his fat and squealing along with him. Suddenly he wasn't a pig at all. Unless pigs could fly. 'Cause they were flying and Helen thought that maybe she was in heaven and he was her angel. Maybe.

Then Helen just let herself go and held on to her angel tight. Yes, she decided, she was in heaven. She was definitely in heaven.

123

CHAPTER FOURTEEN

JAN'S MANSION, as Ivena called it, lay at the end of a street, its arched entrance bordered by tall spruce trees, its front door bearing a simple greeting etched on a cross. *In living we die; In dying we live.* Behind the house a scattering of maple leaves drifted across a blue swimming pool nestled in a manicured lawn—an absolute necessity in this heat, Roald had told him. Jan had yet to use it. The house was of Southwestern decor, inside and out, from its ceramic shingle roof to the large rust tiles that covered the kitchen floor.

In all honesty, Jan felt awkward in the large house. He used the master bedroom, the kitchen, and the living room, which left four other rooms untouched. The exercise room sat collecting dust down the hall and the dining room had seen use only once—when Karen and Roald had first come to christen the house. The whole thing had been Karen's idea—give Jan an elegant house that completed the rags-to-riches image she was building around him. Roald had jumped on the idea and found the house.

Jan and Ivena sat in the living room under the indirect lighting of two amber floor lamps, staring past a large picture window at the shimmering pool late that night.

"So then," Jan said. "She's gone. What can I say?"

"We have to find her. Don't you see, she's doomed."

"Perhaps, Ivena, but so are a million other women in this country."

"Yes, but that doesn't mean you can ignore the one that comes begging for help. Where's your heart, Janjic?"

"My heart's where it should be: with Karen."

"That's not what I meant. This has nothing to do with her. I'm talking about Helen."

"And Helen's an adult. It was her decision to leave."

124

Jan had battled conflicting emotions from the moment he'd heard of her disappearance. He'd come home to an answering machine stuffed with messages from a distraught Ivena. Helen had disappeared. At first a chill of concern had spread through his bones, but after collecting himself he realized that they should hardly have expected differently. Helen had come into their lives like a whirlwind and sent their minds reeling. So now she had gone as quickly and it was just as well, he thought.

And the vision he'd had upon their touch? He had responded already. Just because his eyes had been opened for her didn't mean he now carried a responsibility for her. Besides, the day with Karen had all but washed the vision from his mind.

"What did you expect?" he continued. "You can't adopt her."

Ivena stiffened beside him. "And why not? Is it so unwise to take in a wounded soul?"

"She's twenty-nine, Ivena. A full-grown woman, not some child. You don't just spend a thousand dollars on a full-grown woman and expect her to change."

The reference to the money fell on deaf ears. "Twenty-nine. Nadia would have turned twenty-nine this year, Janjic. Did you know that?" Her eyes misted.

"No. I'm sorry, Ivena, I had forgotten."

"Well, *I* have not forgotten my daughter."

"That's not what I meant."

Ivena turned to face the pool outside. "She could be her, you know. Blond hair, blue eyes, so frail. Like a child."

So, Ivena had seen her own child in Helen. "I am so sorry, Ivena. I wasn't thinking about—"

"You are not remembering so well these days, Janjic. You speak of it all the time, to so many men all puffed up in their white shirts, feeling so important. But do you *remember?*" She turned to him. "Do you remember what it *felt* like to see Nadia die?"

He stared at her, blinking. "But Helen is not Nadia."

"No, she isn't. But then she is, isn't she? It's why you wrote your book, isn't it? So that others could feel Father Micheal's and Nadia's love the way you felt it twenty years ago? So that they could show that love, not for Nadia or Father Micheal, but for others. For people desperately needing a touch from God. For street girls like Helen. Isn't that why you wrote your book? Or have you forgotten that as well?"

"Don't patronize me, Ivena. I may not have lost my daughter, but I did lose my innocence and five years of my life. I was there as well."

"Then perhaps your memory isn't so sharp. Is Helen really so different from my Nadia?"

"Of course she is! Nadia sacrificed her life, like a lamb. She was pure and holy and she embraced death for the love of Christ. Helen . . . Helen doesn't know the *meaning* of sacrifice."

"No. But what about you, Janjic? You couldn't stop the slaying of my child, but can you stop the destruction of this child?"

Jan stood to his feet. "I tried to stop the slaying of Nadia. You shouldn't rub that in my face! You have no right to heap this burden on my head. It's one thing to suggest I look into my heart for the love of Christ, but it's another thing to suggest I lay down my life for every vagrant who crosses my door."

"And you have no right to assume that just because it is I who *speak* the truth, it is also I who *make* that truth. I can't change the fact that you were at the village when my daughter was killed, no more than I can change the fact that it was *you* who showed up on my doorstep yesterday with a stray girl who was in desperate need. So I'm simply telling you, we all know about the love of Nadia—the whole world knows about the love of Nadia; you have written of it well. But what about the love of Jan?"

He wanted to tear into her; to tell her to hold her tongue. She was consumed with this resurgent focus on love. And now, because he'd made the mistake of bringing Helen to her, she had in her hands a tangible example of that love. He collapsed on the overstuffed chair and stared out at the swimming pool without seeing it. "You think that lowly of my capacity to love?"

She sighed. "I don't know what I think, Janjic. I'm simply struck by a deep desire to help Helen. Because she reminds me of Nadia? Perhaps. Because we spent a day and a night together and I grew to like the child? Yes. But also because she's desperate for love, yet she does not even know it. What good is our love if we do not *use* it?"

She was right. So very right! This wasn't some vagrant who'd waltzed across his doorstep. Helen was a woman; a grown Nadia, suffering and lost.

Ivena spoke quietly now. "You felt something, Janjic. Both times in my house with her you felt some things. Tell me what you saw."

The request took him off balance. Thinking of it now, his objections over the past hours seemed absurd. He had felt God's heart for Helen, hadn't he? And if Ivena knew how clearly . . .

He sighed. "I told you, it was strange."

"Yes, you did. So then, tell me what strange looks like."

"Sorrow. I looked at her and I felt the pain of sorrow. And I heard crying.

White light and weeping." Yes indeed, she would tell him straight now. And he deserved it. He shook his head. "It was so vivid at the time. Goodness."

They sat in silence for a moment. "So, you feel this breath of God on your heart and still you argue with me about whether Helen needs our help?"

He closed his eyes and sighed. Yes, she was right about that too, wasn't she? And yet he didn't necessarily *want* to feel the breath of God when it came to Helen.

"Why do you resist?" she asked.

"Maybe the idea of playing nursemaid to this street girl scares me."

"Scares you? And what you saw in her presence does not scare you?"

"Yes, Ivena. It all scares me! I'm not saying it's right, I'm simply telling you how I feel. I have a full plate already and I don't need a tramp camping out on my doorstep right now. I have a trip to New York in a couple days, I have wedding details to work out with Karen; I have the movie—"

"Oh yes, the movie. I had forgotten. How silly of me! You have a movie to make about what love really looks like. God forbid you take time out to try loving a poor soul yourself."

She is right, you know.

"Ivena!"

"No, you are right. It all makes perfect sense now. Christ has already died for the world's pain; there is no need for the rest of us to suffer unduly. A small girl here, perhaps. A priest there. But certainly not we who live in our fancy palaces here in God's backyard."

She is right! She is so right.

"Ivena, stop it!"

They sat in silence again. It was a thing with them; they either spoke with meaning or they did not speak.

"You know, Janjic, there are very few who have witnessed the unconditional love Father Micheal taught in the years before his death. He spoke of it often, about the hope of glory as if it were a thing he could actually taste." She smiled reflectively. "He would speak and we would listen, imagining what it would be like, wanting to go there. American Christians may not have hope for anything beyond what they can put their fingers around in this life, but we hoped for the *afterlife*, I tell you. '*When you have a desperate love for God,*' Father Micheal would say, '*the comforts of this world feel like paper flowers. They are easily put aside. If you really have God's love.*'" She paused. "Have you thought about our discussion the other day, Janjic?"

"Yes," he said. "Yes, I have."

"Perhaps God brings people like young Helen into our lives to teach us something of his love."

Jan leaned back and closed his eyes. "You're right." He rubbed his face with his hands. How could he have been so callous? *Has my heart grown so callous? God, have mercy on me.* "I had the dream again last night. Same thing. If you're right and the dream's somehow of God, I wouldn't be upset if he would speed up his clock just a little."

But Ivena wasn't listening. "Father Micheal taught Nadia well, you know," Ivena said, her voice distant. "Sometimes I think he taught her too well."

Her mouth quivered to a frown despite her best efforts to stay strong. He slipped from his chair and knelt beside her. She began to cry and he placed his arm around her shoulders. "No, Ivena. Not too well."

It happened very rarely, this free flow of sorrows, and neither tried to stop it. Tears slid from Ivena's clenched eyes and quickly ran in streams. Jan pulled her to his chest and let her cry, choking on his own emotion. "Shhh, it's okay. She waits for you, Ivena," he said. "Shhhh."

For several long minutes they held each other like that and then Jan brought her a drink of water and sat in his own seat again. She sniffed and commented about how soft she was getting in her old age and he insisted that her tender heart had nothing to do with age.

"So then," he said after some time. "If it's true that God has brought Helen into our lives to teach us of his love, who's taken her *out* of our lives?"

"She has taken herself out," Ivena responded.

"And how do you propose we find her?"

"We don't. If it is indeed God's will, he will lead her back to us."

Jan nodded. "You know, for all of my complaining about her, I must say that I did enjoy her company. She was something, wasn't she?"

"Yes. Just watch yourself, my young Serb. You are, after all, engaged to be married."

Jan blushed. "Don't be ridiculous!"

"If *I* suspected a *pitter* in your heart, do you think she did not?"

"Please. Not everyone's as thorough a romantic as you!"

"Me? A romantic? Ha! Not too many would accuse me of that."

"That's because few know you as well as I, dear."

"I'm not judging, Janjic. I'm only telling you what I see."

"And maybe it's why I'm not so eager to have Helen walk back into our lives," he said plainly. "I'm at a delicate stage of my life, you know. I have responsibilities; I have a ministry; I'm going to be married. All of this love talk is making me dizzy."

"Never mind the responsibilities Roald and the other church leaders place on you. Just guard your love for Christ and your other affections will follow."

He nodded. "You're truly a romantic at heart, aren't you, Ivena? All this talk of love is your cup of tea."

"And yours, my dear. And yours."

JAN PARKED the Cadillac and rode the elevator to the eighth floor at nine the following morning. He was back in crisp form—a starched white shirt, trim black slacks, and a narrow black satin tie.

Nicki chirped a bright-eyed *Good morning!* and brought him coffee. He should get his own coffee, he thought. Drive his own car, get his own coffee, and love as Christ had loved. What would Karen say to that?

Karen came in half an hour later, wearing a bright blue dress and a brilliant smile. "Good morning, Jan." She leaned against his doorframe and folded her arms. "You sleep well?"

"I slept well." The glint in her eyes brought a surge of adrenaline to his blood.

"Good. I did too. So, I hear you're driving yourself these days."

"Yes."

"You really think that's a good idea?"

"Yes."

She nodded and smiled. "Okay." But he knew she didn't really mean okay.

They held each other's gaze for a full second before she slipped out of his sight toward her own office.

What was it with the heart? What madness that a simple look from a woman could prove so distracting? Jan cleared his throat. He had a decent stack of calls to return, but suddenly the thought of making them seemed so utterly mundane that he pushed them aside and stood from the desk. He could return to them later. He needed to talk to Karen.

Jan walked into her office and sat across from her.

She lifted an eyebrow. "Well now. What's on your mind?"

That feeling swept through him again. A few words from her and his stomach was floating. "So, we leave for New York tomorrow. Everything's set?"

"It's all set up. But you know that from our meeting yesterday."

"Yes. I also know that with you things happen so quickly that I can't rest on yesterday's news," he said with a gentle smile.

"Nothing has changed. We fly at nine, meet Roald in New York at one, and sign the deal the following day. God willing."

"Yes, God willing."

They talked then of details already covered, but worth another pass considering the gravity of the deal they were about to sign. They also talked wedding plans. It would be a Christmas wedding—they had decided that much last night. A big wedding with a thousand guests. She would plan it, of course. She'd been born to plan this wedding. It would have to be in a park—a Southern belle affair—with enough glamour to attract national coverage. She thought she might be able to talk Billy Graham into doing the honors.

Jan finally excused himself to make some calls, he said. By the stack of messages on her own desk, Karen needed to make many more calls than he.

She came into his office late morning with some updates. Delmont Pictures was definitely on track, she said. They wanted to launch a fresh round of book interviews within the month, with a broader audience.

"So how does it feel, Jan?" Karen asked with a smile.

"How does what feel?"

"Please, don't pretend you don't know. You're going to become a star, my dearest."

He grinned slightly. "Oh? And here I thought I was already a star."

"Not like this, you aren't. Strap in, Jan, because you're going to be a household name. Just don't forget that your lovely wife played a part in it when they're scrambling for your autograph."

He laughed. "Ha! *My* autograph? Never. Even if they wanted it, I would have to sign Father Micheal's name. Or Nadia's."

"Hmmm," she said. "You'll see. We're entering brand-new territory here. I don't think you have a clue."

"Maybe. But we can never forget the price paid."

And paid for what, Jan? Your wealth and honor?

He looked away from her, sobered by the thought.

"What is it, Jan?"

"Do you ever wonder if the story has changed people, Karen? I mean really *changed* them?"

"Of course it has! Don't be ridiculous, it's changed thousands of lives."

"And how?"

She paused. "Jan, I know what you're thinking, and it's the prerogative of every artist to want to know that his work has somehow made a difference in the world. But believe me, your work, like none other I've known, has made an impact on the hearts of men. I came here because I believed in the book, and I've known from the beginning that it was the right choice."

He nodded. "Yes. And I'm not saying you're wrong, but tell me how it has changed a man's heart. Tell me about *one* man."

Karen eased around the desk and sat in the guest chair next to him. She placed a hand on his shoulder. "Jan, look at me."

He did and her eyes were round and gentle.

She lifted a finger to his cheek and stroked it very lightly. "You have no reason to feel this way," she said. "We're impacting hundreds of thousands with this ministry. You can't reach into the hearts of men and personally change them, but you can tell them the truth. And you have. You've done it well. And trust me, Jan, the movie will do even more."

What part was she playing now? The comforting agent, talking to her client, protecting her investment? Or the loving fiancée? Perhaps both. Yes, both. But why did he even question her motives?

"Look at me," she said. "I had no intention of loving God before meeting you. You think I haven't changed?" She smiled and winked. "And it's touched my heart in other ways as well."

"Yes?"

"Yes. It's not every day you'll find my hand on a man's cheek."

His face grew red beneath her touch—he couldn't see it, but he could feel the heat sweep over his skin. He lifted his hand and took hers. "And it's not every day that you'll find me holding such a delicate hand as yours."

She blushed pink. They sat silenced by their own admissions for a moment.

"And you . . . we can't forget you, Jan. The story has transformed your life."

"Has it?" he asked. "I wonder at times if my love for myself isn't greater than my love for others." He paused and shifted his gaze to the far window facing a blue sky. "Just two days ago, for example, I met this woman . . . a tramp really. A junkie. Her name was Helen." The memory of the vision he'd had at her touch suddenly skipped through his mind. *Choose your words carefully, Janjic.*

"Yes?"

Jan told Karen about rescuing Helen and taking her to Ivena's. And then he told her about how she'd disappeared. He left out the strange emotions he'd felt in her presence, but explained his fear of caring for such a wayward soul. How it might taint his perfect world. Somewhere in there Karen removed her hand from his and sat back to listen.

"So you see, if I've changed so much, why does the thought of showing compassion to this simple desperate girl scare me? Even repel me?"

"I don't know. You tell me." It struck him that her tone was not completely friendly.

"I'm not talking about any kind of romantic attraction, Karen. Helen's a poor lost soul. What would Father Micheal say? He would say that I should give her what is mine. That if she asked for my shirt, I should give her my coat as well. That if she wanted a lift for one mile, I should offer to take her two."

"Yes, he might. And you've done that, haven't you? A thousand dollars of clothes? What did the woman think she needed?"

"Well, that was actually Ivena's doing. They had differing ideas of what to buy so they evidently bought everything, just to be sure."

Ordinarily Karen would have laughed, but now she only smiled, and thinly at that. "So then you've done what you should have and she's gone. If you're concerned about not doing enough, I would think you're going a bit far." She said it and waited a moment before adding, "Don't you think?"

"Maybe." He nodded. Karen seemed impatient with the conversation and he could see that she wasn't the one to discuss Helen with. "Yes, you may be right." He smiled and turned the discussion to the coming trip. It took Karen a few minutes but she seemed to forget about Helen, and after a few minutes the twinkle in her eye returned.

Or so Jan thought, until he stood to leave for the night.

"Jan."

He turned back. "Yes?"

She stood and put her hand on his arm. "I think you were right about Helen. Okay? It's easy to lose sight of what love means these days, but I didn't mean to discourage you."

"No, and you didn't. But thank you, Karen. Thank you."

"So then, New York tomorrow?"

He lifted her hand and kissed it gently. "New York tomorrow."

CHAPTER FIFTEEN

GLENN LUTZ was back in his game. He conducted business over lunch—a shipment of hash from Jamaica—and by his rough count, the deal would put over five hundred thousand dollars in his bank over the next month. He would have to shove that morsel up Beatrice's nose.

The limousine took him back to the Twin Towers where he took the elevator up to his perch atop the East Tower. Memories of his reunion with Helen brought a smirk to his face. They were made for each other, he thought. Carved from the same stone as children and presented to each other only now, when they were old enough to play properly. Helen had gone sky-high last night and he'd joined her there. He had left her at two in the morning, curled semicomatose on the bed, gone to the house, showered, and regained his desire for her.

It had been a good morning, he thought. Everything was back in its place. He'd even seen the wife and kids, although he hadn't spoken to the kids—they were off to school by the time he emerged from the shower. His wife on the other hand had sulked about the kitchen, asking every question except the one he knew blared in her mind: *Where have you been for the past three days, Glenn?*

Never mind where I've been, meat brains. I own this house, don't I? Mind your own business or you'll be out on the street before you have the time to blink. And your kids with you. She was really no longer much of a wife anyway. A live-in mother, taken care of nicely enough, and they both knew it.

He spent the rest of the afternoon catching up on phone calls, slowly building an appetite for the woman. It wasn't the same kind of desire as when she left him—no, nothing could be so strong. It was a desire that came and went with the day's passing and now it was coming.

Glenn left his empty, mirrored office at six o'clock and entered the enclosed walkway that spanned the eighty-foot gap to the West Tower. Only he used the private passage. It was one of the Tower's features that had attracted him in the first place. He did not own the entire building, but he did own a twenty-year lease on the stories that mattered, including the walkway that conveniently separated his two lives.

He entered the Palace. "Helen?" The room lay in the dim late-day light. "Helen?" She was here, of course. He had called just an hour ago, received no answer, and sent Beatrice in to check. She had come back to the phone and informed him that she was still sprawled on the bed, dead to the world.

"Helen!" He strode for her door and shoved it open.

At first he thought she was in the shower because the bed sat empty; a tangle of sheets half torn from the mattress. He grinned and tiptoed across to the bathroom. It too was empty. Steamy from a recent shower, but vacant. The kitchen, maybe.

Unless . . . The thought that she might have fled again first crossed his mind then. A flash of panic ripped up his spine. He grunted, whirled from the bathroom and lumbered across the floor to the third room in the small apartment. He grabbed the corner and spun onto the kitchen floor. It was empty!

Impossible! The witch had just checked!

Glenn turned back to the main room and fixed his gaze on the wastebasket where he'd thrown her pink dress, muttering obscenities. But the basket gaped empty. The dress was gone. He knew it then with certainty; Helen had fled.

Unless she really hadn't fled but was hiding somewhere, to play. "Helen!" He ran back to the main room, screaming her name. "Helen! Listen you dope, this is *not* funny! You get yourself out here right now or I swear I'm gonna tan you good, you hear?"

The room's silence seemed to thicken around him; he wheezed, pulling at the air as if it would run out at any minute. "Helen!" He ran to the double doors and yanked on the handles, only to discover they were locked as he'd instructed. Then how? He bounded for the drawer under the bar, pulled it open and grabbed at the contents.

But the key was missing! The wench had taken the key and fled!

A red cloud filled Glenn's vision. He would kill her! The next time he laid hands on that puke he would skin her alive! Nobody . . . *nobody* did this and survived. His limbs were shaking and he grabbed the bar to steady himself.

Easy, boy, you're gonna pop your cork here.

As if it had heard, his heart seemed to stutter. A small shaft of pain spiked across his chest and he clutched at his left breast. *Easy, boy.* He breathed steadily and tried to calm himself. The pain did not repeat.

134

Glenn staggered over to the wall phone, wiping the sweat from his brow. He punched the witch's number. She picked up the interoffice line on the tenth ring.

"Mr. Lutz has gone home for the day. Please call back—"

"Beatrice, it's me, you idiot! And what were you doing while our little pigeon was busy flying the coop?"

"She . . . she's gone?" she stammered in response.

"Now you listen to me, you fat witch. You get me Buck now. Not in five minutes, not in three minutes, but now! You hear? And tell me you ran that reverse trace I told you to yesterday."

"I have the address."

"You'd better hope she shows up there. Now get over here and unlock this cursed door!" He slammed the phone into its cradle. This time he'd make sure things got done right, if he had to do them himself.

Glenn lifted his hands and covered his face. *Helen, Helen. What have you done?* The ungrateful dope would learn her lesson this time. He would not bear this nonsense any longer.

Could not.

THE STRANGE vine in Ivena's greenhouse had grown wild, adding a foot to its length in each of the last two days. She'd continued thinking it might be a weed of some kind, overtaking the rosebush in Amazonian fashion. But today she knew that something had changed.

It was the smell that greeted her when she first cracked the door to the greenhouse. The poignant aroma of rose blossoms, but sweeter than any of her flowers had ever offered.

She pushed the door open and looked in. To the right, the tall orchids glistened yellow after their misting. Three rows of pink roses lined the opposite wall. The red tulips were nearing full maturity along the kitchen wall. But these all registered with the vagueness of a gray backdrop.

It was the bush at the center of the left wall that captured Ivena's attention. Nadia's rosebush, which was hardly a rosebush at all now. A single flower perched above the green vines. A flower the size of a grapefruit and Ivena knew that the sweet scent came from this one bloom.

She stepped into the greenhouse and walked halfway to the plant before stopping. "My, my." The sight before her was an impossibility. She swallowed and searched her memory for a flower that resembled this one. A white flower with each petal edged in red, round like a rose but large like a trumpet lily.

"My, my." *Dear God, what have we here?*

The aroma was strong enough to have been distilled from flowers, as in a perfume. Too strong to be natural. Ivena stepped lightly forward and bent over to view the vines beneath the flower. They hadn't grown so much since yesterday, but they had yielded this stunning flower.

Ivena turned and hurried from the room, retrieved a thick book of horticulture from her living room and returned, flipping through the same pages she'd scanned three times already in as many days. She simply had to identify this fast-growing plant. And now that it had flowered it should not be so difficult. A flower was a plant's most striking signature.

She'd run through the pages of roses without a match. She turned the last page of roses without finding any similar. So, then, a lily. Perhaps even an orchid, or a tulip, somehow cross-pollinated from her own, which was impossible. Nevertheless, she was out of her realm of knowledge.

It took her three quarters of an hour to exhaust the reference book. In the end she could find nothing that even remotely resembled the strange flower.

She closed the book and leaned on the frame that housed the plant. "What are you, my dear flower?" she whispered. She would have to bring Joey in for a look. He would offer an explanation. You didn't become a master of botanical gardens without knowing your flowers.

Ivena lowered her nose to the petals. The aroma drew right into her lungs; she thought she could actually feel it. It was more than a scent—it was as if an aura was being emitted by the petals, something so sweet and delightful that she found herself not wanting to leave the room.

"My, my!"

She lingered for another ten minutes, mesmerized by the unlikely invasion into her world.

HELEN APPROACHED Ivena's house from the north, sprinting down the sidewalk in the dress, oblivious to her appearance. She had to get in that house; it was all that mattered now. Ivena and Jan would know what to do; she had spent the last few hours convincing herself so.

The plan, if she could call it a plan, had proceeded like clockwork. Of course the plan was only an hour old and it would end in less than thirty seconds when she knocked on Ivena's door. Beyond that she had no idea what to do. What she did know was that she had woken from her night of indulgence at 1:00 P.M. with the absolute knowledge that she had to leave Glenn's pigsty.

She had felt the same way before, of course, and she'd left. But this time . . . maybe this time it was for good. Images of Jan and Ivena wandered about her mind, calling to her. It had been good, hadn't it? Sitting like a real lady, eating sausage and kraut and discussing issues with such a real man. Such a sophisticated, kind man. And when had she ever spent a day with someone so wise as Ivena? Despite her ancient tastes, the woman had a mind books were written from.

Helen had spent four hours lying on the bed feeling sick and lonely and impossibly useless. She'd climbed out twice to throw up, once after allowing her mind to recall the way Glenn had slobbered over her during the night, and once from the drugs. She was in bed when the witch came to check her at five, and she decided to play dead. It was then, when Beatrice left, that she conceived of her plan. The trick was to throw herself together, get out using his key, and put as much distance as possible between herself and the Palace before the pig came back. She figured she would have an hour; Glenn wouldn't have sent Beatrice if he was on the way.

Helen had hit the street and boarded a bus before the possibility that Ivena might not welcome her with open arms even crossed her mind. Ivena did not strike her as the kind who would extend a second chance so easily. On the other hand, she and Jan were the kind who would forgive and forget. Or at least forgive.

She cast a quick look back down the street one last time, saw no cars, and ran up to the door. Breathing as steadily as possible, she lifted a trembling hand to the doorbell and pushed it. The bell's faint chime sounded beyond the door. She smoothed her dress—the dress Ivena had insisted she buy—and waited, wanting very badly to step into the warm safety of this house.

The door swung in and Ivena stood there, wearing a light blue dress. "Hello, Helen," she said as though nothing at all was strange about her reappearance. She might have continued with a question, like, *Did you get the milk I asked for?* Instead she stepped aside. "Come in, dear."

Helen moved past Ivena.

"Come into the kitchen; I'm making supper." Ivena strolled ahead. "You can help me, if you like."

"Ivena. I'm sorry. I just—"

"Nonsense, Helen. We can speak of it later. You're not hurt?"

Helen shook her head. "No. I'm fine."

"Well you do have a nasty bruise on your cheek. From this Glenn character, yes?"

"Yes."

"We should put some cream on it."

Helen looked at the older lady and felt a pleasure she had rarely known, an unconditional acceptance of sorts. It swept through her chest and clamped down on her heart for a moment. She couldn't help the dumb drop of her jaw. "So then, you aren't angry?"

"I was, child. But I released it last night. You were hoping for anger?"

"No! Of course not! I just . . . I'm not used to being . . ." She let her voice trail off, at a loss for words.

"You're not used to being loved? Yes, I know. Now, why don't you see how the stew is doing while I make a quick phone call."

"Sure." Ivena simply welcomed her back as if she *had* just run down to the corner for some milk. "You like?" Helen asked, curtseying in the dress.

Ivena grinned. "You wore the best for your little trip, I see. Yes, I like."

Helen let Ivena make her phone call while she peeked under the pot of simmering stew. The smell brought a rumble to her belly; she had not eaten since leaving yesterday. Ivena was speaking in excited tones now. To Jan! Meaning what? Meaning they were celebrating the return of their little project? Or meaning that Jan disapproved of Ivena's—

"Helen?" Ivena called.

"Yes."

"Did you use the phone yesterday?"

To call Glenn; she'd forgotten. "Yes," she said.

There was another moment of conversation before Ivena hung up and bustled into the kitchen, turning off the burner and placing the warm pot in the refrigerator. "Come along, dear. We must leave," Ivena said.

"Leave? Why?"

"Jan says that it's too risky. If Glenn is as powerful as you say, he may have traced your call. Do you know, would he do such a thing?"

Helen swallowed. "Yes."

"And there would be a problem if he came looking for you?"

"Yes. Good night, yes!" Helen spun around, panicked by the thought. It was true! He was probably on his way at this moment. "We have to get out, Ivena! If he finds me here . . ."

Ivena was already pushing her to the front. "Get in my car quickly." She snatched a ring of keys from the wall and gently nudged Helen out the door. They stopped and peered both ways before running across the lawn and piling into an old gray Volkswagen Bug with rusted quarter panels. Ivena didn't so much pile as climb and Helen urged her on. "Hurry, Ivena!"

"I am hurrying! I'm not a spring chicken."

Ivena fired the car up and pulled out with a squeal. "Thankfully I drive faster than I run," she said and roared down the street.

Helen chuckled, relieved. "Pedal to the metal, mama. So where to?"

"To Janjic's," Ivena said. "We will go to Janjic's mansion."

GLENN SAT in the town car's rear seat, fussing and fuming, screaming long strings of obscenities while Buck steered the car with his one good arm and used the other as a guide. Sparks hadn't been so lucky; it would be a month before the man would have use of his arm. But Buck's bullet had done nothing more than slice into his shoulder. A few inches lower and it would've drilled a hole through his heart; the fact hadn't been lost on him.

"Up ahead, sir," Buck said.

"Where?" Glenn leaned forward. The light was already failing.

"Should be one of these houses up on the left."

A car peeled from a driveway ahead; an old gray Bug. Some lowlife teenager showing off his new ride. They slowed and followed the numbers. 115 Benedict, Beatrice had said. 111 . . . 113 . . . 115. "Stop!" It was a small house surrounded by a hundred bushes blooming with white flowers. And if he was right, there would be one flower in that house ripe for the picking. Or squashing, depending on how it all came off.

"Isn't this the driveway that Bug came from?" Buck said.

Bug? The gray Bug! Glenn spun to the street. "Yes!" It couldn't be far. Had it turned left or right at the end? "Move, you fool! Don't just sit here, get after it!"

They squealed into pursuit and caught it thirty seconds later, cruising west. Glenn leaned over the seat, breathing heavy beside Buck and peering through the dusk. He recognized her head, immediately—that light blond head he had held just last night. If he could reach her now he would take a handful of that hair and shake her like a rag doll, he thought. And he would do that soon enough now, because he had *found* her! He'd found the tramp. Sweet, sweet Helen. It now made little difference whether she intended to hide back at the house of flowers or at the Bug's current destination. This time he would take care of things right. It would have to be a plan that lasted. One that took her completely off balance and thoroughly persuaded her to stay in her cage. Or better still, a plan that lured her back of her own choosing. Because she loved him. Yes, she did love him. *Here, kitty, kitty.*

It occurred to Glenn that his mouth hung open over the leather seat before him. A string of drool had fallen to the back of the seat. He swallowed and sat straight.

"Back off!" he snapped. "Back off and follow that car until it stops. You lose it and I swear I'll put a bullet through your other arm."

CHAPTER SIXTEEN

Q: "What does this kind of love feel like?"

A: "The love of the priest? Imagine mad desperation. Imagine a deep yearning that burns in your throat. Imagine begging to be with your lover in death. King Solomon characterized the feeling as a sickness in his songs. Shakespeare envisioned it as Romeo's death. But Christ . . . Christ actually died for his love. And the priest followed him gladly."

Q: "And why do so few Christians associate love with death?"

A: "Just because they're Christians does not mean they are necessarily followers of Christ. Followers of Christ would characterize love this way because Christ himself did."

Jan Jovic, author of bestseller The Dance of the Dead
Interview with New York Times, *1960*

JAN PACED the entryway and padded across the polished rust tile in stocking feet, feeling screwed into a knot without knowing exactly why. Ivena was on her way, bringing Helen with her. So the woman had come back after all. Ivena was right; they should show her Christian love. Christ had dined with the vagrants of his day; he had befriended the most unseemly characters; he'd even encouraged the prostitute to wash his feet.

So then, why was Jan reluctant to embrace Helen?

Father, what is happening here? You touch me with this woman; you give me this mad sorrow for her, but for what reason? Unless it was not you but me, conjuring those feelings in my own mind.

Perhaps it wasn't reluctance he felt at all, but fear. Fear for what the woman did to him both times he'd seen her. Karen's face flashed through his mind, smiling warmly. Even she had concluded that he ought to show friendship to Helen, although the conclusion had not come so easily.

Jan stopped his pacing and breathed deeply through his nose. The strong odor of vanilla from the three lit candles filled his nostrils. He'd turned the lights down, a habit ingrained during Sarajevo's siege. Turn the lights down and stay low. Of course, this wasn't Sarajevo and there was no siege. But this was Helen, and he had not imagined those two men chasing her in the park. She was in more danger than she let on.

The doorbell chimed and he started. Here already!

Jan stepped to the door and pulled it open. Ivena bustled in with Helen in tow. "Are you quite sure this is necessary, Janjic?" Ivena asked.

Jan closed the door, turned the deadbolt, and faced them. "Maybe not, but we can't take the chance of being wrong." He turned to Helen, who stood in the shadows. "Hello, Helen. So what do you think? Is this necessary?"

She stepped forward into the yellow light; the petite woman with short blond hair and deep blue eyes, dressed in a wrinkled pink dress. It was hard to imagine that she was the cause of all this commotion. She was just a junkie. She wore no shoes and her feet were dirty—that gave her away. On closer inspection so did the round bruise on her left cheek. She'd been hit very hard there. Jan's heart was suddenly thumping in his chest.

"It could be," she said.

"And what kind of danger are we talking about?" He swallowed, acutely aware that she was affecting him already; afraid that she might drown him with his own compassion. *Father, please.*

"I don't know . . . anything. You saw the men that chased us."

"Then we should call the police."

"No."

"Why not? This man has abused you. You're in danger."

"No. No police."

Ivena turned for the living room. "Standing here will do us no good. Come in, Helen, and tell us what has happened."

Helen kept her eyes on Jan for a moment before turning and following Ivena. Jan watched them go. Ivena had indeed adopted Helen, he thought. They sat in a triangle—Helen on the couch, Ivena on the love seat, and Jan in his customary leather armchair—and for a moment no one spoke. Then Helen twisted her hands together, pulled them close as if to hold herself, and smiled. "Boy, it smells good in here. Is that vanilla, Jan?"

Her voice played over his mind as if it possessed life. Goodness! It was happening again! And she had said what? *Is that vanilla, Jan?* Yet those words—the simple sound of her voice—and the image of her huddled on the couch played like fingers on the chords of his mind.

"Yes," he answered. "From the candle."

She was looking around. "So this is the mansion Ivena keeps talking about. It's nice."

"It's too much," Jan said.

"You live here alone?"

"Yes."

"Then you're right; it's too much."

Ivena *humphed.* "I've always told him the same. He needs a good woman to make this a home. Now tell us, Helen. Why did you leave yesterday?"

There it was; Ivena had opted for the direct approach, like a good mother.

And Helen did not seem to mind this time. "I don't know. I was lonely, I guess," she said.

"Lonely? Lonely for this fellow who put that bruise on your cheek?"

She shrugged and bit her lip.

Ivena glanced at Jan. "And why did you come back?" she asked.

Again Helen shrugged. She stared at one of the floor lamps, and Jan saw her eyes glisten in the amber light. She was as confused and desperate as they came, he thought. A child so categorically lost that she did not even know she was lost. A woman strung out by an impossible childhood and left to dangle by a single thread. In her case it might be a thread of pleasure. Give her pleasure, any form of pleasure, and she would cling to you. But give her love and she might fly away, confused by the foreign notions of trust and loyalty. Her leaving and coming were as much a matter of habit as desire.

Jan stared at her and felt his heart ache. *Helen, Helen. Sweet Helen.* He wiped a thin sheen of sweat from his palms. "You don't need to be afraid, Helen. You will be safe, here. I promise."

She lifted her blue eyes. "I hope so."

"But we should know more about Glenn, I think. We're involved now; we should know more."

Helen nodded slowly and then she told them about Glenn. The simple truth, from her own eyes, of course, but honesty hung in her voice. Slowly she unveiled the ugly truth about her relationship with the demented drug dealer. And slowly, as she talked, Jan felt his ache for her increase. He arose once to check the street, but came back reporting nothing unusual.

Glenn was a man who lived for control, and beneath the city's layers he pulled a lot of strings . . . Helen believed him. She'd heard him—seen him—manipulate men much more powerful in the public eye. But really it was Glenn who pulled the strings with his huge fistfuls of money. It was a power as intoxicating as the drugs. It was a give-and-take relationship—they both gave and they both took.

Her voice droned sweetly through Jan's mind, like an airborne drug—playing on his emotions as no voice had ever played. He listened to her and his heart seemed to physically swell. It grew and ached with every new sentence she spoke. So much so that toward the end of her story, he stopped hearing her altogether.

It wasn't the way she looked. It was more, far more. It was her voice; the look beyond her eyes. A fire deep in her pupils that mesmerized him. It was her sloppy English and her giggle and her plain way with the truth. There was not a shred of plastic about her.

But more even. It was the fact that her heart was beating. She was sitting there on his couch and her heart was beating and somehow his own heart was beating with it. The thought made his palms wet.

He imagined telling Karen about this. *Oh, Karen. This woman is so wounded. She's in such need of love. The love of God. Christ's love.*

Helen, sweet Helen, was no ordinary woman, he knew that now. And the realization began to soak the back of his shirt with sweat.

". . . will I stay?" Helen asked.

She had asked the question of him. "What? I'm sorry, what?"

"What do we do now? Have you been listening, Jan? Because you do look distracted. Doesn't he look distracted, Ivena?"

"Of course, I've been listening," he said and blushed. Helen was smiling slyly as if she'd caught him, and he suddenly felt very self-conscious. *She is beautiful,* he thought. *Wrinkled pink dress, scraggly blond hair and all. Quite beautiful. Stunning actually. Even with her bare feet. They are tender feet.*

Stop it, Jan! Stop it! This is absurd! You are nearly married and here you are ogling a young woman.

He faced Ivena and heard his voice as if at a distance. "What would you say, Ivena?"

She had lowered her head and was looking at him past her eyebrows. "I would say that I detect a *pitter*, Janjic."

She was referring to his heart! Good heavens, she was accusing him right here before Helen! "Good enough. You will stay the night then. It could be dangerous to return to your house alone. Use the apartment."

"Apartment?" Helen asked.

"There's a fully equipped suite in the basement. Old guest quarters. Actually no one's used it since Ivena occupied it for a few weeks while we found her house. It has its own entrance but it's well locked. Ivena knows the ropes."

Jan glanced at Ivena and saw that she held a raised eyebrow.

The shrill ring of the phone saved Jan from any further comment. He stood quickly and strode for the kitchen. Ivena had gone too far this time. He would speak to her about this *pitter* nonsense.

But she is right, Janjic.

He grabbed the receiver from the wall. "Hello." *She could not be right.*

"Jan Jovic?" a low voice asked.

"Yes?"

The man on the phone took a deep breath, but did not speak. Jan's heart spiked. "May I help you?"

"Listen to me, you little punk. You think you can keep her?" A few pulls of heavy breathing filled the receiver and Jan spun away from the women. A small strobe ignited in his mind and suddenly he was there, again. Facing Karadzic's venomous stare in a distant landscape.

"She's a dog in heat. You know how to keep other dogs away from a dog in heat?" It was Karadzic! It was him!

"You kill them," the voice said. "Now you've been warned, preacher pimp. If she's not back in her kennel within forty-eight hours you'll pray to God that you never laid eyes on her." Heavy breathing again.

Jan's mind spun, gripped by panic.

A soft click sounded. And a dial tone.

For a moment Jan could not move. Had he just been threatened? Of course he had! But it was not Karadzic, was it? It was Glenn Lutz.

He breathed deliberately and blinked several times to regain clear vision. The women had stopped talking. He forced the phone back onto its hook.

"Is there a problem, Janjic?" Ivena called.

"No," he said, and immediately thought, *That was a lie.* But what else could he say? *Don't mind me, I'm just losing my mind over here. I do that once a month. Helps me stay in touch with my past.*

Jan considered excusing himself and walking for the bedroom. Instead he opened the refrigerator and stared at the contents for a few moments. He reached for the pitcher of tea with a shaking hand, thought better of it and grabbed a small bottle of soda water instead. Slowly the tremble worked its way out of his limbs.

This was all far too much. He had a life to attend to, for heaven's sake. He was bound for New York in the morning. With Karen! His fiancée! He really should walk in there and tell Ivena that she should take Helen to a church shelter or another place properly staffed to help women in need. This was his home, not some church. And now his life was being threatened by her crazed lover!

But when he entered the room and saw Helen sitting on the couch, his heart swelled once again, despite the odd look she cast his way. His stomach hovered for a moment.

Dear God, this was madness!

Perhaps, but Jan knew then for the first time, looking at the young woman on his couch, that he did not *want* her to leave. In fact, the thought of her leaving brought a feeling not unlike panic to his chest.

Which was a problem, wasn't it? A very big problem.

JAN BARELY slept that night. He mumbled prayers to his Father, begging for understanding, but no understanding came. If God had indeed ignited his heart for this woman, what kind of switch had he thrown? And why? And what would Karen make of Ivena's *pitter*? Which was maybe more than a *pitter*.

She would never understand. Neither would Roald. How could they? *Jan* didn't even understand!

He rose half a dozen times and peeked through the windows for any sign of intruders, then finally drifted off near 3:00 A.M.

He left the house at six, before either Ivena or Helen had emerged from their rooms. They'd agreed that if anyone needed to leave the house, it would be Ivena, alone. Helen would not leave for any reason. And under no condition were they to open the door for a stranger. There was easily enough food in the icebox to tide them over. He would think things through and come back from New York with a plan, he promised.

Karen gave him several strange looks during their drive to the airport. "What?" he asked once.

"Nothing. You just seem distracted," she replied.

He almost told her about the crazy threat, but decided she didn't need the worry hanging over her.

"I have a lot on my mind," he told her with a smile. It seemed to satisfy her. An hour later the jet leveled off at thirty thousand feet. Slowly the images that had kept him awake during the night began to fade.

They sat side by side in the first-class cabin, fingers intertwined, talking of everything and nothing, flying high in their own private world. The musky perfume she wore smelled delicate and womanly, like Karen herself, he thought. Dinner was served: lobster tails with buttered potatoes and a red wine sauce he'd never tasted before—certainly not with lobster. It was heavenly. Although, Karen did advise the stewardess that the beans hadn't been properly stringed and Jan felt awkward for her saying it.

Roald had arranged to meet them with an entourage of Christian leaders and human rights activists who strongly supported the making of the movie. Some of Delmont's people would be there as well, Karen told him. They wanted to make an event out of the occasion. Trust Roald and Karen to come up with any excuse to publicize. He told her as much and she giggled, biting her tongue between her front teeth. She didn't laugh—that would have been expected. But she giggled like a little girl and she bit her tongue and she squinted her eyes as if she'd done something especially tricky, although they both knew it was nothing unusual at all. She did that because she was with him. She did that because she was in love.

Jan leaned back and smiled. *This is where you belong, Janjic.* "You know, it's amazing to consider God's faithfulness," he said.

"How so?"

"Look at me. What do you see?"

"I see a strong man on top of the world."

He tried not to blush. "I'm a boy who grew up in the slums of Sarajevo and who lost his family to war and illness. A young man who roamed Bosnia, killing along with the rest. And then once, in a small village I did something decent; something right. I stood up for the truth. I defended one of God's children and was immediately thrown into prison for five years. But now look at me, Karen. Now God has granted me this incredible blessing of living." He grinned with her. "Now I'm flying in first class, eating lobster with my wife to be. Wouldn't you say that God is faithful?"

"Yes. And that faithfulness is now in my favor," she said, smiling. "Because I'm seated next to you." She took his hand and kissed it gently. He looked at her and his desire surged. It was a mad moment; one in which he thought they should move the wedding up. December felt like another lifetime. *Let's elope, Karen.*

And why not?

"Do you love me, Jan?"

The question sent a ball of heat down his spine. "How could I not love you, Karen? You're brilliant, you're ravishing, and, yes, I love you."

She smiled at the words. "Fine. I'll settle for that."

Jan kissed her to seal the words. He needed the reassurance more than she, he thought.

When they landed in New York, a long white car took them to the downtown Hilton where they were ushered into the main reception room. A gathering of thirty or so waited under a huge crystal chandelier with Roald at their center. Frank and Barney stood by his side, both grinning wide—they must have come up from Dallas with him.

Karen turned him to her just inside the entrance and she quickly tightened his tie. "What would you do without me, huh? Remember to smile for the cameras. Not too big. Be confident. Remember, they pay for confidence."

He felt too awkward to respond, so he just cleared his throat.

The pattering of hands echoed through the hall and for a moment the hotel's bustle seemed to stall. Jan was suddenly aware that every eye watched him.

He nodded politely and let the applause die. Roald held up his hand. "Ladies and gentlemen, I'm proud to announce that we are entering into an agreement with Delmont Pictures to produce a movie of *The Dance of the Dead* for theatrical release." Immediately the room filled with applause. It was all unnecessary, of course, but Roald had his ways.

He wasn't finished. "This is Jan Jovic's story; a story that reaches out to all those suffering for the sake of the Cross; a film that will take a message of hope to millions who need to hear of God's love and of those still suffering throughout the world." Again they applauded. A TV camera caught the event on video. Jan dipped his head and they clapped yet again, beaming proudly at him. They had all gathered for their own causes; some for the sake of a profitable movie, others for amnesty groups, perhaps hoping to ride the coattails of this film to bolster their own coffers. Some for the church.

They wanted a word from Jan and he gave them a brief one, publicly thanking

Roald and Karen for their undying support and service to which they all owed this opportunity. Then it was a mingling affair with all present taking turns shaking his hand and discussing their particular appreciation or concern. He took a dozen questions from reporters holding bulging microphones. He was well practiced with the media, of course, and he gave them all their time while the rest talked in small groups, eating cheese and shrimp and sipping beverages. Karen made the rounds, pitching the deal as only she could. Several times he caught her eye. Once she winked and he lost the question just asked of him by a reporter.

Night had fallen by the time the last guest left. Roald and Karen insisted that they go out to dinner, the finest. An hour later they sat around a table at Delmonico's on Broadway, reviewing the day. Everything was set for the meeting with Delmont in the morning. It would be nothing more than a formality—that and the collecting of a check, of course. One million at execution, four million within thirty days. They lifted their glasses and toasted their success. It seemed appropriate.

"So," Roald said as they cut into their steaks. "Karen tells me that you ran into a drug addict the other day. She spent the night at Ivena's and then left with a thousand dollars from the ministry fund?"

Jan glanced at Karen. "Well no, she didn't actually take a thousand dollars. Ivena bought her some clothes on my suggestion."

"That's good, Jan." He smiled and Jan could not gauge the man's sincerity. "So somewhere there's a junkie wandering around wearing a mink coat and laughing about how she socked it to some sorry sucker."

Jan recoiled at the cynicism. "No. No mink coat. And she left the clothes, except for a pink dress."

"A pink dress?" Karen asked.

"It was one Ivena made her buy," Jan said with a grin. She didn't return the smile.

Roald stuffed another bite of meat into his mouth. "Well, she's gone. After tomorrow a thousand dollars will seem like loose change."

Jan dropped his eyes and sawed into his steak. "Actually, she's not gone," he said. "She came back last night."

Karen froze for a moment. "She's back?"

"Yes. She showed up at Ivena's house and I made them come to mine."

Roald looked at Karen and then back. "You mean this woman is in *your* house? Now?"

"Yes, with Ivena. Is that a problem?"

"Why your house?" Karen asked. A cube of steak remained poised on her fork. Her eyes were wide.

"She's being chased. I didn't think she'd be safe at Ivena's."

"So let me get this straight." It was Roald's turn again. They were not taking this so well, Jan thought. "A female drug addict comes to you on the run, runs off with a thousand bucks, comes back the next day with a flock of mobsters on her tail and you take her into your house? You don't take her to the cops or the shelter, but you leave her in your house while you take off for New York? Is that it?"

"Maybe I should've called the police, but—"

"You didn't even *call* the cops?"

"She insisted that I not. Look, she was in danger, okay? So maybe I should've called the police. But I couldn't just tell her to get lost, now, could I? You forget that I run a ministry that stands for embracing those who suffer. It's not only in Bosnia that people suffer."

The exchange left them silent for a moment. "We should watch *who* we embrace," Roald said. "This is the exact sort of thing we talked about at—"

"Why does it concern you?" Jan asked. "I help one woman desperate for her life and it's a problem?"

"No, Jan. But you have to understand—we're in sensitive times now. This movie deal depends on your reputation. Do you understand that?"

"And what does my helping one junkie have to do with my reputation?"

"She's in your *house*, Jan. You keep a young junkie in your house and that could definitely look off-color to some people."

"You can't be serious. You really think someone would question that?"

"That's exactly what I'm suggesting! You're in a new league now, my friend. Any sign of impropriety and the walls could come crashing down. To whom much is given, much is required. Remember? Or have you forgotten our discussion altogether? Frank would choke if he knew you were entertaining a young woman. Especially now that you're engaged."

"Stop it!" Karen said. "You've made your point, Roald. Don't be asinine about it. It's *my* engagement, not just Jan's you're talking so flippantly about. Have some decency."

Roald and Jan stared at their plates and went back to work on their steaks.

"Now, while it's true that a young woman staying with Jan could look off-color, we're talking about a fluid situation here. I doubt if even your most conservative partners would come unglued about Jan helping a drug addict for a few days, woman or not. Let's not make this more than it is."

"Thank you, Karen," Jan said. "I couldn't have said it better."

Roald didn't respond immediately. Jan caught Karen's eye and winked. "And don't worry, Roald. She won't be staying there long. As soon as I return I'll get her the help she needs."

"I'm sorry. Perhaps I spoke too quickly." Roald smiled. "You're right." He lifted his glass for a toast. "Just looking out for you, my friend. No offense intended."

Jan lifted his glass and clinked Roald's. "None taken." They drank.

"That's better," Karen said with a smile. "You do what needs to be done, Jan. Just remember that your big mansion there, as Ivena calls it, has room for only one woman." She winked and joined them in the toast. "You just make sure she's gone when we get back."

"Of course."

"Send her to the Presbyterian shelter on Crescent Avenue—give her to the Salvation Army—take your pick. But she can't stay at the house," she said.

"No. No of course not."

They looked at each other in silence for a few moments.

"Well, then," Roald cut in. "That's settled."

All three of them lifted bites to their mouths at the same time, and dinner resumed. It was a small caveat in an otherwise perfect trip, Jan thought. And Karen was right. He should settle the matter the minute he returned. He really should.

CHAPTER SEVENTEEN

WHILE JAN sat in the expensive atmosphere of Delmonico's in New York Friday night, Glenn Lutz sat alone at his own Palace bar, stewing. The room was mostly dark except the backlit bar itself. A half-empty bottle of rum stood next to his glass. It was his second for the day and it might not be his last. The bar had been carved from mahogany and stained a very dark brown. The decorator had wanted to paint it bright yellow, of all colors. That was before he'd fired her. He'd fired her, all right. Yes sir, he had fired that little freak, right after he'd bitten her lip. Now *that* had been a night.

Glenn remembered the occasion and tried to smile, but his face did not cooperate. The plan he'd settled on was a good plan, but it didn't feel good just now. It had come on the dawning notion that he could cage *any* woman. Women as pretty as Helen, women who wouldn't be missed. It wasn't the caging of Helen that he really wanted, was it? No, it was her free spirit that attracted him most. The very fact that she *did* resist him with a tenacity that most wouldn't dream of. Even the fact that she'd fled half a dozen times now. Each time his desire for her had swelled until now he could hardly stand it all.

So then, as much as he relished the idea of caging her or forcing her to return, he'd decided that he had to allow her to return on her own. He needed her to want him. It was the next step in this madness he'd given himself to.

The decision to let her free of her choosing was one he now doubted perhaps more than any he'd made in his life. Because there was always the chance that she would *not* come back, wasn't there? If that happened he would go out with a machine gun and cut her and anybody near her down in one long staccato burst. Or maybe he'd just revert to the caging approach.

The plan didn't prohibit him from removing obstacles that stood in the path between them, of course. Preacher-man, for instance. Good God, a *preacher* of all

152

things. The house Helen had entered belonged to a Jan Jovic, he learned from Charlie down at the precinct that same night. And Charlie had heard about the man. He'd seen a news story about the man sometime back—a preacher who'd escaped from prison or something. A preacher? A *preacher* was trying to steal his Helen? Glenn had thrown the phone across the room when Charlie had told him.

As it turned out he was one of those foreigners who'd written a book about the war and made a bundle. *The Dance of the Dead.* Glenn's first impulse was to make *him* dead. He'd learned all of this within thirty minutes of his return. It was then, after deciding that a preacher couldn't be a threat to him, that he'd settled on the plan. He'd made one phone call to the preacher, and then he'd drowned himself in several bottles of rum.

He had spent the entire day pacing and sweating and yelling, completely immobilized from conducting any business. He'd forced himself to keep a lunch appointment with Dan Burkhouse, his banker and friend of ten years. It was Dan who'd lent him his first million, in exchange for some muscle on a nonperforming loan. Well, he'd killed the nonperforming loan, thereby implicating Dan, and making him a confidant by necessity. Besides Beatrice, only Dan knew the dirty secrets that made Glenn Lutz the man that he was. Of course, not even they knew the truth about his youth.

He had gone still dressed in his smelly Hawaiian shirt and between bites of snapper at the Florentine told Dan about his decision to let Helen come and go. If not for the private dining room his agitated tone would've raised some eyebrows for sure. The banker had shaken his head. "You're losing perspective, Glenn. This is crazy."

"She's possessed me, Dan. I feel like I'm falling apart when she's not with me."

"Then you should get some help. The wrong woman can bring a man down, you know. You're going too far with this."

Glenn had not responded.

"How can one woman do this to you?" his friend pressed. "There's a hundred women waiting for you out there."

Glenn had glared at the man and effectively cut him off.

Now he lifted the bottle and chugged at its mouth. The liquid burned down his throat but he didn't flinch. He would suck it dry, he thought. Tilt it up and suck at the bottle until it imploded. Or just stuff the whole thing into his throat. No pain, no gain. And what was paining now? His chest was paining because Helen had driven a stake through his heart, and regardless of what that old witch

Beatrice told him, he did still have a heart. It was as big as the sky and it was burning like hell.

He yanked the bottle from his mouth and hurled it against the mirrored wall. It shattered with a splintering crash. *Don't be such a melodramatic lush, Lutz.*

The phone shrilled in the dead silence and he bolted upright. He scrambled for it, grasping for the tiniest thread that it might be Helen.

"Lutz."

"Glenn." It was the witch. Glenn slumped on the bar.

"I've got a phone call for you. You may want to take it."

"I'm not taking phone calls." The phone clicked in his ear before he could slam it in the witch's ear. She'd disconnected him. That was it! He was going to walk over there right now and—

"Hello?"

The voice spoke softly in the receiver and Glenn's heart slammed up into his throat. He jerked upright.

"Hello?"

His voice wavered. "Helen?"

"Hi, Glenn."

Helen! Glenn's heart was now kicking against the walls of his chest. Tears flooded his eyes. Oh, God, it was Helen! He wanted to scream at her. He wanted to beg for her.

"You're mad at me?" she said quietly.

Glenn squeezed his eyes and fought for control. "Mad? Why did you leave? Why do you keep leaving?"

"I don't know, Glenn." She paused. By the sound of her voice she was near tears. "Listen, I want some stuff."

"Who are you with?"

"No one. I'm staying in this man's house with the lady I told you about, but she went home to water some flowers or something. She'll be gone for a few hours."

"You think I don't know? You think I'm useless here, waiting for you to come crawling home!" *Easy, boy. Play her. Lure her.*

He took a deep breath and lowered his voice. "I miss you, Helen. I really miss you."

She remained silent.

"What did I do to make you leave? Just tell me," he begged.

"You hit me."

"You don't like that? You don't like being hit like that? I'm sorry. I swear, I'm sorry. I thought you liked it, Helen. Do you?"

"No." Her voice was very soft now.

"Then, I'm sorry. I swear I won't do it again. Please, Helen, you're killing me here. I miss you, sweety."

"I miss you too, Glenn."

Really? Dear Helen, really? Tears slipped down his cheek.

"I want to come, Glenn. But I want you to promise me some things, okay?"

"Yes, anything. I'll promise you anything, Helen. Please just come home."

"You have to promise me that you'll let me come whenever I want."

"Yes. Yes, I swear."

"And you've got to promise me that I can leave whenever I want. Promise that, Glenn. You can't force me to stay. I want to stay, but not if you force me."

He hesitated, finding the words difficult. On the other hand, she already had the power. And what was in a promise but words? "I promise. I swear you can leave whenever you wish."

"And I don't want you to hit me, Glenn. Anything else, but no hitting."

This time everything within him raged against the absurdity of her request. Letting her go was one thing, but she wanted to castrate him as well? He was slipping, he thought. "I promise, Helen."

"You promise all of those things, Glenn. Otherwise I don't think I can come."

"I said I promise! What else do you want? You want me to cut off my fingers?" *Easy, easy.* He lowered his voice. "Yes, I promise, Helen."

She hesitated and he wondered if he'd lost her on that last one. He felt panic swell in his chest.

"Can you send a car?" she asked.

"I'll have a car there in two minutes. I have one just down the street." She didn't respond. "Okay, Helen?"

"Okay."

"Okay. You won't be sorry, Helen. I swear you won't be sorry."

"Okay. Bye." The phone clicked off.

Glenn set the receiver in its cradle with a shaking hand. Exhilaration coursed through his veins and he gasped for breath. He uttered a small squeaking sound and skipped out to the middle of the room and back. When he went for the phone to call Buck, his hands were shaking so badly he could barely dial the number.

She would be here in fifteen minutes! Oh, so many preparations to make. So many, so many he could hardly stand it.

THERE WERE three flowers now, each the size of small melons, brilliant white and edged in red, twice as large as any other flower in the greenhouse. Joey inspected each part of the plant with delicate fingers. He'd always reminded Ivena of a jockey, very lean and short, hardly the type you might figure for a renowned horticulturist. He looked more the average gardener than the scientist with his frumpy slacks and cotton shirt.

"What do you make of them?" Ivena asked.

The small man pried through the petals and grunted. "Boy they sure do put off their aroma, don't they?"

"Yes. Have you seen anything like them?"

"And you're saying that you didn't make this graft? 'Cause this is definitely a graft."

"Not that I remember. Heavens, I'm not that forgetful."

"No, of course not. Has anybody else had access to this greenhouse?"

"No."

"Then, we'll assume that you made this graft."

"I'm telling you—"

"For the sake of argument, Ivena. It certainly didn't just appear on its own. Either way, I've never seen a graft like this. We're looking at several weeks' worth of growth here and—"

"No. Less than a week."

He dipped his head and looked at her over his wire-frame glasses. "This from the woman who doesn't even remember grafting the plant? I'm just telling you what my eyes see, Ivena. You decide what you want to believe."

She nodded. He was wrong, of course, but she let it go.

"Even with a few weeks' growth, these flowers are extraordinary. You see there the stamen reminds of the lily, but these white petals lined in red—I've never seen them."

"Could they be tropical?"

"We're in Atlanta, not the tropics. I did my thesis on tropical aberrations in subtropical zones, and I've never come across anything like this."

He touched and squeezed and *humphed* for a few minutes without offering any further comment. She let him examine the bush at his pace and searched her memory again for the grafting he'd insisted she must have done. But still she knew that he was wrong. She'd no more grafted the vine into the rosebush than she'd won the Pulitzer recently.

Joey finally straightened and pulled off his glasses. "Hmm. Incredible. Would you mind me taking one of these flowers to the Botanical Gardens Lab? It has to exist. I'm just not placing it here. But with some analysis I think we can. May take a couple weeks." He shook his head. "I've never even heard of a vine like this taking off from a rosebush."

"You want to cut one off?"

"Just one. You have plenty more coming along behind these. They are flowers, not children."

"No, of course they aren't. Yes, you may. Just one," she said.

CHAPTER EIGHTEEN

THE LONELINESS had struck Helen after two hours with Glenn while Ivena was off attending her flowers. Thing of it was, she was even high at the moment, but the emotion still swept through her bones like an unquenchable tide. Sorrow.

Somehow things had gotten turned around in her mind. This wasn't the Palace as Glenn liked to call it. This was feeling like a dungeon next to Jan's house. She had left the white palace for the dirty dungeon—that's how it felt and it was making her sick. Worse, she had left a prince for this monster.

She'd rolled on the bed and thought about that. The preacher wasn't her prince. He couldn't be. They were like dirt and vanilla pudding; you just don't mix the two. And it was clear who was who.

Not that Jan wasn't a prince—he was; just not her prince. He could never be her lover. Imagine that. What would they say to that? Helen winning the heart of a famous writer who drove around in a white Cadillac. A shy, handsome man with hazel eyes and wavy hair and a real brain under those curls. A real man.

Given just the two of them without all this mess around them, she might even have a shot with him. She might not be Miss Socialite, but she was a woman, and one who had no problem reading the look in a man's eyes. Jan's looks were not the roving kind she was used to, but there was light there, wasn't there? At times she thought it might be pain. Empathy. But at other times it had made her heart beat a little faster. Either way, each time they had been together his looks had come often and long. That much was enough, wasn't it?

He likes you, Helen.

He's married.

No, he's not. He's engaged.

Goodness, just imagine having a man like that on your arm! Or imagine

158

someone like that actually loving you. That last thought felt absurd, like the drugs were talking, and she pushed the nonsense from her mind.

But the sorrow wouldn't budge, and the thoughts returned five minutes later. *But what if, Helen.*

What if? I would die for a man like that! I'd be happy to just sit with him and hold his hand and cry on his shoulder. And I would love him until the day I died, that's what if. And not just a man like that, but Jan.

But then again, she was the dirt and he was the vanilla. She'd never deserve a man like that. There was no mixing the two.

She'd stayed another hour and then left the big pig facedown on the floor, passed out next to a small pool of his own vomit.

She'd returned still intoxicated, and to her relief Ivena was still gone. She climbed under clean sheets and passed out without removing her clothes.

Ivena was upstairs cooking breakfast when she awoke. It gave her time to shower and change before presenting herself with as much confidence as she could muster. If Ivena knew anything about her little escapade to the dungeon, she didn't show it.

Helen spent most of the day walking around the house in a daze and for the most part Ivena let her be. Jan's home really did feel like a palace, and in a strange way she felt like dirt on its floor. But she could clean up, couldn't she? The notion brought a buzz to her mind. *What if?*

And Jan was coming home tonight.

JAN PARKED the Cadillac on the street and walked up the path to his home two days later, on Sunday evening. Darkness had quieted the city, bringing with it a cool breeze. The cicadas were in full chorus, chirping without pause, ever-present but invisible in the night. The oak cross hung undisturbed above his door. *In living we die; In dying we live.*

The trip to New York had come off as well as they had planned in most regards and better than they had imagined in others. They'd signed the deal on Saturday, deposited the million dollars with some fanfare, and decided to stay in the Big Apple through Sunday. Jan had called Ivena and been informed that nothing had happened. At least nothing that he should concern himself about. Ivena had not elaborated. She'd made some flower deliveries on Friday evening—a few late customers to catch before the weekend—but otherwise she and Helen had mostly sat around talking and growing tired of remaining in a house that was not her own.

He withdrew his key and opened the front door. Dim light glowed from the far hall leading to the bedrooms, but the rest of the house lay in darkness. He flipped the switch that controlled the entryway lights. They stuttered to life.

"Hello."

Silence.

"Ivena!"

Jan walked into the living room, still holding his overnight bag. Had they left? He flipped another switch and the room stuttered to life. No sign of the women. "Ivena!"

"Hello, Jan."

He whirled to the voice. Helen stood, arms crossed, leaning on the wall in the hall's soft light with one leg cocked like a stork. Immediately his knees felt weak, as if she'd injected him with a drug that had gone for his joints.

"Good night! You scared me," he said.

"I'm sorry," Helen returned. But she was smiling.

"Where . . . where's Ivena?"

"She left an hour ago. Said she couldn't spend the rest of her life here while her flowers died at home. She's pretty excited about some flowers that she says are going nuts over there. We haven't heard a peep from anyone so we figured it would be safe enough."

"She just left? Is she coming back?" Helen lowered her arms and walked into the light. He saw the difference immediately and his heart jumped. She wore a strapless white evening dress with a sheen, and it flowed with her small frame like a fluid cream. She wore sandals and a pearl necklace that sparkled in the kitchen light. But it was her face that had pricked his heart. She was smiling and staring at him. The bruises had vanished, either under the hand of God or with the careful application of makeup, and honestly he thought it must have been the hand of God, because her complexion appeared as smooth as new ivory. Her hair lay just below her ears, bending in delicate curls.

Jan's hand released the travel bag he'd carried in. It landed with a distant *thump*. Goodness, he'd all but forgotten about the madness.

Helen stared at him with those impossibly blue eyes, smiling. She turned for the kitchen but her eyes lingered on him for a moment. She swayed naturally as if born to wear that dress. Jan's mind began to scramble. *You dropped your bag, you big oaf. You stood here like an idiot, gaping at her, and you dropped your bag!*

"Yep, she left," Helen said. "She wants you to call her when you get back, which I guess is now." She picked an apple out of the fruit bowl and took a small bite from it.

"So she said nothing about coming back?" Jan asked, opening the icebox.

"She said she didn't think that was necessary."

"No?"

"No." Helen looked at him from behind the apple and she winked. "She said you should take us out for dinner."

"She said that? Take you and Ivena out?"

"Yes. What do you say, Jan? Want to take me out to dinner? I didn't get all dressed up for nothin', you know." She took another bite, her teeth crunching through the brittle fruit.

There now, he was cornered. Cornered with a pounding heart and weak knees, like a teenager on his first date. The icebox was open and he'd retrieved nothing from it. He closed the door.

"Well, I guess that would be—"

"I knew it!" She tossed the apple into the sink and rushed over to him. Before he could move, she had her hands around his own, pulling him back down the hall. "I want to show you something," she said. Jan stumbled after her, too stunned to speak, very aware of her hands on his.

"What about Ivena?"

"I'll call her while you get ready."

She led him to his own bedroom. "I hope you aren't mad, but I just couldn't resist," she said, glancing back with a smile. His door was open and she pulled him through. On his bed lay his best black suit. A white shirt and his red tie were arranged neatly with the jacket. The slacks draped to the floor and his shoes rested at their cuffs. "Will you wear this?"

She had been in here. Helen had done this.

"I found them in your closet. They're perfect."

"You found these in my closet?"

"Yes. They're yours. Don't you recognize them?"

"Yes, of course I do. I just . . ." He chuckled. "It's not every day that I have my clothes laid out for me."

"You're upset?"

"No. No. So you want me to wear this suit and take you to dinner, right?"

She stared at him without responding.

He laughed. "Okay, madam." He dipped his head. "Your wish is my command. If you will please step outside, I'll get dressed and we'll be off. Did Ivena suggest where we dine?"

"The Orchid."

"The Orchid, then."

She tilted her head, as if surprised that he'd taken her up so suddenly. A mischievous grin lit her face and she curtsied in return. "I will be waiting." She left and pulled the door closed behind her.

Jan showered quickly, his mind busily scolding himself for playing along. It wasn't that he didn't want to take her to dinner, or even that he shouldn't take her to dinner. It was that his knees had gone weak at the sight of her. It was that he *did* want to take her to dinner. It was the madness of it all. It was the voice that had started speaking to him while the hot water cascaded over his skull. *You like her, Jan. You really like her, don't you?*

Yes, I like Helen. She's a refreshing person with charm and . . .

No, you really like her, don't you? You like her so much you can hardly stand it.

Don't be absurd! I'm engaged to Karen. What of Karen? Oh, dear Karen!

He forced his mind to a new line of thought. They were going to the Orchid, the finest restaurant in town. A romantic . . .

Stop it! He shook his head and stepped from the shower. Goodness, he was not an undisciplined schoolboy. These matters of the heart were best left to careful thought.

Jan grunted and dressed quickly.

You aren't married. Ivena will be there, of course. It's only dinner. A farewell dinner—you will tell her that she must leave at dinner.

A tremble had taken to his fingers and he had some trouble with the buttons, but he managed after a few more lines of scolding. He examined himself one last time in the mirror. His wavy hair lay combed back and wet, darker than Helen's but still blond. His eyes were nearly as bright, hazel not blue, but as bright. Now his jaw, it was square and strong while hers was so . . . delicate. He smacked his cheek lightly with his right hand. *Stop it!*

She was waiting in his chair, one leg folded over the other, a copy of *The Dance of the Dead* spread open in her hands. Her eyes looked up as she closed the book.

"My, we are quite handsome." She set the book on the coffee table and walked toward him with an extended hand, sliding gracefully in that dress.

"What about Ivena?"

"She's going to meet us there. Shall we, then?"

"Yes," he said, and he took her elbow and led her from the house.

Dear God, help me, he prayed.

JAN SLAMMED through the men's room door and stepped inside. Ivena was late! And her absence was becoming a very big problem.

The bathroom was empty. He slumped against the wash counter and leaned on his hands. His mind spun in crazy circles, confused, buzzing. His breath came in short pulls. It was as if he'd ingested some hallucinogenic drug that now raged through his blood stream. But he hadn't, he was sure of it. He had done nothing but bring her here, order his food, and engage her in small talk. *Get a grip, Janjic. Control yourself.*

He twisted the faucet and splashed cold water on his face. It was the girl. It was Helen. She had bewitched him. Her voice was the drug, her breath an intoxicant that made straight for his spine and spread like a fire through his bones. It was why he had excused himself and come here not five minutes into the meal—because he was losing his mind out there, watching her bite into her salmon and drink her water. Watching her jaw move with each word.

Jan patted his face with a towel and straightened to stare at his image in the mirror. "My God, what are you doing to me?" he muttered, and he said it as a prayer. "What's the meaning of this?"

You are falling for her, Janjic.

He didn't answer the charge. It just sat in his mind, awkward and misguided, like a belch in the middle of careful speech.

If you're not careful, you'll have fallen for this girl.

But why? Why, why, why? I don't want to fall for her! There's no reason to it.

He had to find some control somewhere, because he simply could not afford to give his heart to someone as unlikely as this woman sitting wide-eyed and so very delicate and . . .

Oh, God . . . it was the most ridiculous thing he could imagine. Ask him to tell a fanciful tale and his imagination would not wander this far. He'd just asked Karen for her hand in marriage before the entire world, just a few days ago. Now he was in Atlanta's most extravagant restaurant, sharing dinner with another woman. With Helen.

With such a beautiful, sweet, genuine woman who seemed to have the power to melt his heart with a single innocent look.

Karen's face wandered through his mind and Jan moaned. He fell back to the counter. *Karen, dear Karen! What am I doing. Rescue me!* If she could only see him now, playing teenager with the sexy little hippie. He ground his teeth and struck the side of his head with his palm.

"Stop it, Janjic! Just stop this nonsense!" he said aloud. And then to himself, *Coming here was a terrible mistake, and now you're going to have to go out there and straighten this mess out. You've gone over the edge on this.*

"Excuse me."

Jan spun around. A stranger stood by the door looking at him curiously. "Are you all right?"

Jan blinked. "Yes." How long had the man watched him? "Yes, I'm fine." He straightened his coat and hurried from the room. *You're losing it, Jan.*

Jan walked back to the table on weak legs. He saw her when he was still twenty paces off, sitting frail and alone against the Orchid's twenty-story view of Atlanta's skyline. A tall white candle cast a yellow hue across her neck. She was looking away from him, at the city lights below. Her left hand was cocked delicately over her glass; she drew circles around its rim with her forefinger. Her hair rested delicately against her cheek, touching her silky skin.

It was details such as these that screamed out at him. And he wasn't seeing them because they were exceptional; he was seeing them because *she* was exceptional. She could be scraping the mud from her soles over there and his knees would go weak.

A tingle ran up Jan's spine and flared at the base of his neck. The air thickened about him, forcing him to pull at it deliberately in order to breathe. He pulled up behind the salad bar.

You're acting like a schoolboy, Jan. Control yourself!

He straightened his tie and walked on. Then he was there, and he slid into his chair. Actually, he *attempted* to slide into his chair; it came off more like a collapse. *Collect yourself, you oaf.*

"Oh, hi. You're back."

"Yes." *Now, Janjic. You must tell her now that this has all been a terrible mistake and that you should leave immediately.*

"I was just thinking about how wonderful you've been to me," she said. He looked up and saw that she was innocently forking a piece of pink salmon into her mouth. Innocent because it didn't seem as though she was deliberately tempting him or intoxicating him or any such thing. She was simply eating a piece of fresh salmon. But it wasn't looking so innocent to him. It flooded him with a dizzying shower of images. Images that set off crazy vibrations in his bones.

She lifted her eyes and the candle's flame flickered in her pupils. "I can't remember anyone being so kind to me."

"It's nothing, really," he said. "You're a person who should be . . . that it is good to be kind to."

"Why?"

"Why?"

"Why am I a person who should be loved? That is what you meant, isn't it?"

Good God! Heaven help me! "Yes. Everybody should be loved."

"You're very kind."

"Thank you. I try to be kind."

"I read some of your book this afternoon. You had a tough time when you were a kid."

"Not unlike you," he said. *You are delaying, Janjic.* He cut into his own salmon and took a bite. The meat was tender and sweet. "Did you read about the village?" he asked.

"Yes."

"And what did you think?"

She shrugged. "It seemed . . ." She hesitated.

"Say what you like. It seemed what?"

"Well, it just seemed a bit, I'm not sure . . . crazy maybe. What Ivena's daughter did—what was her name?"

"Nadia."

"That was crazy. I can't imagine anyone dying like that. Or the priest for that matter. Really, I could never do anything so dumb. Don't get me wrong, I'm sure it was hard for Ivena to see her girl killed. I just don't really understand how she could do something so pointless. Does that make sense?"

"And what would you have done?"

"I would have told them whatever they wanted to hear. Why die over a few words?"

Jan stared at her, struck at her lack of comprehension in the matter. She really didn't understand love, did she? *And do you, Jan?* More than she. Far more than she.

"Then you've never felt the kind of love that Nadia or the priest felt," Jan said.

"I guess not. And have you?"

"Yes," he said. "I think so."

Jan went for another bite. *There you have it, Romeo. How many times have you asked that same question of yourself? How many times has Ivena asked? And now it comes from Helen.*

She said nothing. Her fork clinked on the china; her lips made a very soft popping sound as they took in another bite.

"You write very well, Jan," she said in a soft voice. He looked up. She was throwing her magic at him again. Her eyes, her voice, her hair, her smile—it all smothered him and made his heart feel as though it were trying to beat in molasses.

"Thank you. I started writing when I was a boy."

"Your words are very beautiful. The way you describe things."

"And you are very beautiful," he said.

Goodness, what had he just said?

His first instinct was to take it back. To beg insanity and tell her that they should leave now because he had just flown in from New York and was very tired. Tired enough to say that she was beautiful, which, although true enough—so very, *very* true—had no business coming from his mouth. He was engaged to another woman. Did she know that? Of course she knew that.

He ignored the impulse entirely.

"You know that, don't you? You are very beautiful, Helen. Not just in the way you look, but in your spirit. You. Helen. You're a beautiful person."

She blinked slowly, as if caught in a surrealistic dream. Her eyes drifted for a moment, as if sheltering something, and then she gazed at him. "Thank you, Jan. And I think you're very handsome."

Jan felt his hands go numb. They were staring at each other, locked in a visual embrace. Everything inside of him wanted to reach across the table and stroke her chin. To leap from his seat and take her in his arms and hold her and kiss her lips. He managed to find some deep reservoir of control and remain seated.

Please, Father! Why do I feel so strongly? These are new feelings.

Heat rushed through his ears. It was madness, still. But for the time he embraced the madness and it raged through his body like a ferocious lion. *This cannot be of my own doing*, he thought. *It is beyond me.* There was a physical bond between them now, like a chord of electricity.

"Is it warm in here, or is it just me?" she said softly.

"Perhaps it's just us," he said, and he knew that later he would regret saying that. Complimenting someone for their beauty was one thing. Telling a woman that she was making you warm was another matter altogether. But the moment demanded it, he thought. Absolutely demanded it.

"Yes, maybe," she said, and she smiled.

Jan broke off and took up his water glass. He drank quickly, suddenly feeling panic biting at his mind. What was he doing? What in God's name did he think he was doing?

"I have a confession to make," Helen said. "I lied. Ivena didn't say a word about you taking us to dinner. I made that up."

He set the glass down. "You did?"

"I wanted to be alone with you."

"She's not coming?"

"No. I didn't call her."

He began to shovel salad into his mouth, acutely aware of the heat that flushed his face. But it wasn't anger.

She followed his lead and picked at her own salad. They ate in silence for a full minute, pondering the exchange. It did Jan very little good—his mind had ceased to function with any meaning. Something had happened to him, and he couldn't corner it with any understanding. First the vision and now this.

"What about Glenn?" he asked. The question sounded like something an adolescent might ask in a state of hurt jealousy. Jan shoveled the salad quickly.

Helen shifted her eyes. "I told you, we're through."

"Yes, but you did return to him after saying that. And he's quite obsessive, isn't he? He may not be through with *you*."

"Yeah well, I *am* through with him. And he may be obsessive, but it cuts both ways. If I leave, it's over. It was stupid of me to go back, but I hardly knew you then, you know."

Jan lost his focus on the line of questioning and went back to his salad. He'd said enough already.

Helen shifted the topic by talking about the book again. Asking him questions about what Serbian prison was like. It was a welcome segue and Jan plunged after it. Anything to distract him from the madness. But there was a twinkle in her eye from that moment—one that told him she'd seen his heart. One he feared was flashing in his own eye as well. It didn't matter, he was powerless to change it.

They sat at the table for another hour, talking of their pasts and staying away from the present. After all, the present had already done a fine job of presenting itself.

Jan took Helen home, to Ivena's. She would stay with her at least for the night, until they developed a more adequate plan. Like what? she asked. Like he didn't know. Maybe Ivena had some ideas. But he couldn't go in and talk to Ivena now. No, horrors no! It was too late. He should really get to bed.

Jan left Helen at the curb, watched her walk to the door, and left without looking back to see how Ivena might react. His palms were wet, his shirt was sticky, and his mind felt as though a blender had made a pass or two while he was busy fighting off the butterflies with Helen.

He cried out to God then, in the silence of the car. *Father, you have created me, but have you created me to feel this? What kind of emotions are these running through my heart? And for whom? This woman I hardly know? Please, I beg you, possess my spirit! I am feeling undone.*

And what of Karen. Oh, dear God, what of Karen?

Jan no longer held the presence of mind to pray. He just drove home and slowly shut down.

CHAPTER NINETEEN

KAREN HAD been scheduled to fly to Hollywood at ten on Monday morning. Jan didn't come in until ten-thirty. For starters, his sleep had been interrupted by the dream again. The encounter with Helen hadn't helped his sleep either. But in all honesty, his coming late was as much motivated by Karen's schedule as his sleeping habits. He was certainly in no condition to look Karen in the eye, much less explain the rings under his own. To his relief she'd departed on time. Appointments with a dozen contacts would keep her tied up for three days. He would not see her until Thursday, which was fine by him. He needed to clear the voices that ran circles through his head.

He sauntered in, determined to return his mind to a semblance of reason. Billy Jenkins, a skinny mailroom clerk, congratulated him in the elevator. "Boy, Mr. Jovic. It's really cool about the movie, huh?"

Jan mumbled an awkward, "Uh-huh," and smiled as best he could. But his heart was not well.

All hope for a clear head disappeared at eleven, while Jan sat at his desk, feet propped on the writing surface. Because that was when Ivena called him and told him of her idea. She had seen some car loitering on her street and she didn't feel Helen was safe in her little cottage. So she and Helen would stay in Janjic's basement suite for a few more days. That was her idea. There were no other alternatives. They would be safe in that huge apartment under Janjic's house; God knew that security system he'd gotten was useful for something.

"What?"

"It's either that or send her to a shelter, and you know very well that sending her to a shelter would be no better than cutting her loose on the street. She would be back in that beast's hands by nightfall. And we can't have that."

Jan didn't respond.

169

"Janjic? Did you hear me?"

"She can't stay at my place, Ivena."

"Nonsense, dear. I will be there." She paused. "And there is something strange going on at my house, Janjic."

"She's acting strange?"

"No, no. Nadia's rosebush has died."

"Please, Ivena. Forgive me for sounding uncaring, but there's more at stake here than your garden. She can't stay at my house."

Ivena exhaled into the phone. "Janjic, please now. Think beyond yourself. It's not only about you this time. You'll hardly be aware of us."

He wanted to tell her some things. Like the fact that he was quite sure he would hardly be aware of anything *but* them. Like the fact that the little *pitter* she'd detected had now grown to a steady *thump*.

But he didn't. And she was right, he thought; this was more than just himself. Sweat broke from his brow. He knew Ivena sensed his heart already. And yet she suggested this? What was she plotting?

"Anyway, you don't mind us. Now I must leave; we have some shopping to do."

"More shopping?"

"Food. Your selection is quite dreadful. Good-bye, Janjic."

"Good-bye, Ivena."

She had not asked about the previous night, and Jan hadn't offered any details. But surely she knew that something was up.

And what *was* up? His heart was up. Unless he was sorely mistaken, his heart had attached itself to her. To Helen. Every cell of gray matter objected with vigor, of course, but it seemed to have little impact on the emotions that ran through his veins.

He spent a good portion of the day arguing with himself. Telling himself that he'd been a fool for taking her to dinner. For allowing himself to even look at such a young woman.

On the other hand, she was only nine years younger than him. And she was a woman. An unmarried woman. And he an unmarried man.

But you are engaged, Janjic! You've made a promise!

But I am not married. And I've done nothing to betray Karen. Can I help this madness? Did I ask for it?

You're in love with her, Jan.

He was no longer arguing so strenuously against that voice. It had repeated itself a dozen times, and he'd been unable to persuade it differently. He could only spin through all the reasons why he should not love her—at least not love her in *that* way. Reasons such as the fact that she was a junkie, for heaven's sake! Or like the fact that she was another man's lover. This madman Glenn's lover. Or had been. Goodness, what was he thinking? Karen was perfect in every respect, and she too made his heart beat with a steady rhythm.

Yes, but not like Helen, Jan. You're in love with Helen, Jan.

Nonsense! And what about Roald and *The Dance of the Dead*? What of Frank Malter and Barney Givens and Bob Story? The church leaders' ears would likely steam if they knew what was broiling here. They'd warned against the appearance of evil—this madness with Helen would be nothing less.

And the movie deal—what would Hollywood care what he did? They weren't the most moral lot, those movie people. They wouldn't have any problems.

See now, the very fact that he thought in terms of Hollywood's lack of morality in connection with this Helen business proved that she had to go!

It was Karen who was being trampled on with this foolishness. This betrayal in his heart.

By the end of that first day Jan had managed maybe an hour's work. Ivena called him at four and informed him that she and Helen were concocting supper. At his place.

"What?" he stammered, leaping to his feet.

She hesitated. "There is a problem, Janjic? I'll pay for the groceries if—"

"No, no, no." Pay for the groceries? What was she talking about? He proceeded to insist that in the wake of the big movie deal he had to work late. Go on without him. She reluctantly agreed, and Jan breathed a sigh of relief. Not that he didn't want to see Helen. Not that he did not want to sit across from her and look into those deep blue pools of love. In fact, the very thought of sitting under her spell made his palms break out in sweat. But he could not! Not with Ivena there! Not *without* Ivena there! Not until he made some sense of this madness.

When Jan drove up to the house at ten, Ivena's Bug sat on the street. He left the Cadillac on the front apron, careful not to alert them by opening the garage door. He peeked through the mail slot and saw that the lights had been turned down. If Helen was here, she had retreated to the basement suite. Unless she was waiting for him in the hall again. He wouldn't put it past her. The thought sent a chill down his spine and suddenly he hoped desperately that she'd done just that. He fumbled with the key and let himself in quietly.

But Helen wasn't in the hall tonight. In fact, he couldn't be sure that she was even in the house. And he wasn't about to go knocking on her door. He tiptoed down the hall, set the alarm for 5:00 A.M., and fell into bed.

Tuesday ended up being a mixed day. On one hand it was busy, which was good. On the other hand, he discovered that his little secret was not such a secret.

Lorna and John both came by his office and asked him if everything was all right, to which he answered, of course, and promptly steered the conversation to operational details.

But Betty was not so easily put off. She was concerned; he was not himself these days.

"Nonsense."

"This wouldn't have anything to do with the girl, would it?"

"What girl?"

"The one you rescued in the park."

He felt the blood leave his face.

"Oh, come on, Jan, everyone's whispering about it. They say that this girl stayed in your apartment for a few days."

"Who told you that?"

"I heard it from John. Is it true, then?"

"Yes. Just for a few days. With Ivena, of course."

"And what about you, Jan? What do you make of this girl?"

"Wha . . . Nothing. What do you mean? I'm just giving her a place to stay while this blows over. What do you mean?" It occurred to him that he might have given himself away with that delivery.

"You can't hide your feelings from me, Jan," she said with a tilted head, her eyes fixed on his. "And what would Karen make of this?"

"Karen knows. Helen's a mess, for crying out loud. We can't throw her out on the street for the sake of appearances."

"Maybe. I'm not judging you; I'm only asking. Someone needs to keep you in line. Anyway, I just wanted you to know that there's some talk—you know how these things go."

"Well, kindly tell all the chatterboxes that I don't take kindly to their prying."

Her eyebrow arched. "No one's accused you of anything. Karen's such a lovely lady, you can understand how she has the employees' sympathies."

"That's absurd! There's nothing to sympathize about!"

"I didn't say I disapproved, Jan. I'm only advising you that others might."

"What are they doing down there? Placing bets over the matter? This is ridiculous. Helen's just a woman, for heaven's sake. Just because she's using my flat doesn't mean I have any feelings for her."

"Do you?"

"Of course not. As a person, yes, but . . . Please, Betty. It's been a very difficult day."

"Then I will pray for you, Jan. We certainly can't have our movie star falling apart at the seams on us, now can we?" She winked at him and then left.

Jan spent the next half-hour trying desperately to dismiss the revelation that he'd become a walking wager. Was his insanity that obvious?

Roald called at ten and wanted Jan to meet the director of Amnesty International, Tom Jameson, who was flying in to Atlanta at noon. Jan spent three hours with the man and eagerly agreed to meet him for dinner at seven. By four that afternoon, he'd recaptured a semblance of reason, he thought.

He called Ivena at five and informed her that he would not be joining them for dinner again. She did not object. In fact she seemed distracted.

"Is everything okay, Ivena?"

"Yes, of course. It could not be better."

"You heard me then; I won't be home until late tonight. Please don't wait up for me."

"Something is happening, Janjic." She sounded eager. Even excited.

"Meaning what? Helen has done something?"

"No. But I feel it in my bones. Something very unique is going on, don't you feel it? The sky seems brighter, my feet feel lighter. My garden is in full bloom."

"I thought Nadia's rosebush was dead."

"Yes."

"Hmm. Well, you sound in good spirits. That's good. Just don't leave her alone too much."

"Helen? She's fine, Janjic."

"Yes, but it's still my house. We can't have a stranger just wandering around all alone."

"She's not a stranger. Let go, Janjic."

Let go?

He wasn't sure he'd heard right. "What?"

"You must relax, Janjic. Something is happening."

"Of course something's happening. I'm getting married. We're making a movie."

"Much more, I think."

"And I have no idea what you're talking about."

Silence settled between them for a few moments. She wasn't telling him everything, but he wasn't sure he wanted to hear everything right now.

"Has she seen a counselor?" Jan asked.

"She saw Father Stevens this afternoon. She liked him."

"Good. That's good. Maybe he can find her new accommodations."

"Perhaps."

They left it at that, and Jan spent the next two hours shaking the conversation from his head.

Let go. Something is up, Janjic.

The dinner with Tom Jameson was a welcome distraction. The man's enthusiasm for the movie deal and its possibilities dwarfed this Helen business. By eleven that night, Jan had recovered himself sufficiently to whistle lightheartedly as he drove himself home. The madness had left him.

But that all changed on Wednesday.

He rose at five and showered, thinking about the conference call Nicki had arranged between him, Roald, and Karen at nine. Karen had some news she wanted to share with both of them.

Only when he left his room dressed and ready for the office did he once again think of Helen, sleeping in the suite below. Butterflies lifted his stomach. He rounded the corner for the kitchen and stopped mid-stride.

Suddenly those butterflies were huge and monstrous and doing backflips, because suddenly she was there, leaning over the coffeepot, dressed in an oversize white shirt that hung to her knees.

Jan took one step back on the chance she had not seen him.

"Morning, Jan."

He swallowed, replaced his foot and walked in. "Morning, Helen." She had not looked up at him yet. "Where's Ivena?"

"She's still in bed. Sleep well?" she asked, and now she turned her head, still fiddling with the coffee machine.

"Yes," he thought he said, but he couldn't be sure with all the commotion streaming through his head. He said it again, just to be sure. "Yes." She was looking at him with those blue eyes, smiling innocently. Nothing more; he could see that.

But he *did* see more. She was throwing her magic at him. His knees felt weak and his breathing stopped. Waves of heat washed down his back. He instinctively reached a hand to the refrigerator to steady himself.

You are in love with her.

"I can't seem to get the water . . . Do you know how this thing works?"

"Yes."

She waited for him to say more. But he just stood there stupidly. He wasn't thinking so quickly. "Could you show me how?" she prompted.

"Yes." He walked over to her and bent over the coffee maker, absolutely clueless as to what she wanted him to do. She moved over a foot maybe, certainly no more. Not beyond the reach of his elbow, which bumped up against her stomach. The touch sent a wave of hot air through his mind and he lost what little concentration he'd had.

You are in love with her, Jan.

He almost straightened and told the voice to shut up. But the thought of doing even that swam away with the rest of his reason. Instead he just fumbled cluelessly with the buttons and the pot and the plug, still wondering what he was supposed to do here.

She stood beside him, looking over his shoulder, her hot, sweet breath playing with the hairs on his neck. Or maybe not; maybe that was a breeze from the window. But it lifted the hairs on his neck just the same, and he was struck by a sudden panic that she might notice her effect on him.

Jan straightened, but too quickly and without aim; his head hit the cupboard above the counter. *Thump.*

Helen giggled. "Are you okay? Actually, I just need it turned on."

"On?" He bent over the machine. Maybe she hadn't noticed his stiffness. The power button was suddenly there, big and bold on the right and he wondered how she could have missed it. He pressed it, heard a soft hiss, and extracted himself from the workspace. "There."

"Thank you, Jan."

"Sure. No problem." He backed away and took a banana from the fruit basket. "So everything's working for you downstairs?" he asked.

"Perfect. The television doesn't work but at least the coffee maker is a simple affair." She smiled, and he laughed as if it were a truly humorous comment.

"Well, if there's anything you need, please let me know."

"Jan?"

"Yes." He took a bite from the banana.

"How long can I stay here?"

"Well, how long do you think you need to stay?"

"I think that depends on you." Her eyes! Dear God, her eyes were drowning him! *Look away. Look away, Jan!*

"You think?"

She nodded, not moving her eyes from his. "It *is* your house."

"Yes, I guess it is that." He took another bite from the banana. "Well, let's just say that you can stay until you need to go," he said.

"Really?"

"How long are you thinking?" he asked.

"I don't know." She smiled and he thought she might have winked, but he quickly decided she had not. "Like I said, that's up to you."

"Okay." For an impossible moment they held eye contact, and then he turned. "Well, I have to get to the office for a conference call." Jan started for the front door, still gripping the banana in his right hand.

"Jan."

He reached for the door with a sweaty palm and turned to face her.

"Maybe we could have dinner tonight," she said.

His knees would not stay still. She stood there smiling at him, and every fiber in his body cried to run over there and fall to his knees and beg for her forgiveness for even considering that she was anything less than an angel.

You are in love with her, Jan. You are hopelessly in love with her.

He didn't bother putting up a defense this time.

"Yes. I would like that," he said. His voice wavered but he didn't try to steady it. "I would like that very much."

Jan opened the door and walked out into the fresh morning air, barely able to breathe. He'd already made the turn down the sidewalk that paralleled the street when he remembered the car and turned back. It occurred to him that he had a half-eaten banana in his hand when he tried to open the car door. He hated bananas with a passion. Ivena must have bought them. He grunted and laid it in the flower bed, thinking to throw it away when he returned.

When he returned to take Helen to dinner.

GLENN LUTZ sat at his desk at a quarter to four that same afternoon, sweating profusely. He'd taken the last five impossible days without Helen as well as any sane man could. But what sanity he still possessed was wearing unbearably thin.

She'd come last Friday night, snorted a fistful of his drugs and then teased him the way only Helen could tease. She'd played cat and mouse with him for an hour, running and laughing hysterically, before he could finally take it no longer and broke his promise not to hit her. It had been a blow with his fist, on top of her head, and it had dropped her like a sack of potatoes. When she'd come around fifteen minutes later, she proved much more cooperative.

He had let her go as promised, swearing the blow to her head had been a mistake. When would she be back? Soon, she'd said. The next day? Maybe. But only if he promised not to hit her.

But she hadn't come back the next day. Or the next, or the next, or the next. And now Glenn knew that he wouldn't be able to keep his promise to give her the freedom she demanded. He'd initially persuaded himself that going without would only elevate the pleasure when it did come. Like crossing a desert without water and then plunging into a pool at an oasis. Well, that was fine for a day or two, but now the desert was killing him and it was time to call in the marines. Either that or lie down and die.

Glenn glanced at the clock in his office. It was now 5:00 P.M. He hadn't been home in four days. It was a new vow he'd fallen into: He would only go home to shower on days after seeing Helen. The rest of the time he could conduct business on his terms, caking on the deodorants if a meeting necessitated, but otherwise staying pure until her return. It occurred to him in moments of clarity that he had become a demented man over time; that any man on the street who knew how Glenn Lutz lived his life would go white as a sheet. But they were not him, were they? They didn't possess the power he did, the self-control. They did not have his past with Helen. And so they could go drown themselves in their holy water, for all he cared. There was a time to conquer the world and there was a time to conquer a woman. He'd had his fill of conquering the world; it was a woman who begged to be conquered now. Truth be told, a far nobler task.

It was time to fetch Helen. He wouldn't break into the preacher's house, of course. Breaking and entering involved neighbors and alarms and physical evidence that proved risky. It was always better to snatch a person outside of their home.

Glenn stood, wiped the sweat from his face and flung his fingers out, dotting his desk with droplets of moisture. This time . . . this time he would have to deposit a greater reservoir of motivation in her. If she expected him to sit and wait in death, then she would have to give a little of her life to sustain him. He smiled at the thought. Clever. Very clever.

A knock sounded on the door and he started. That would be either Buck or Beatrice. No one else would dare, even if they could get to the top floor. "Come."

Beatrice walked in. She'd stacked her hair a foot high and it looked absurd, exaggerating her sloping forehead. She was clearly a witch.

"What?" he asked.

"I have a surprise for you." Her teeth seemed large for her mouth, but that too could've been an illusion cast by the hairdo.

"What?"

"She's in the Palace."

"She . . ." The meaning of her words hit him then and he lost his voice.

"Helen's in the Palace," she said.

"Helen?" His voice came out scratchy. Impossible! He spun to the door that led across to the West Tower. "She . . . Helen?"

The witch refused to smile. "She's waiting."

The relief washed over him like a wave of warm water. Immediately his entire body began to tremble. *Helen!* His flower had returned!

Glenn was breathing heavily already. His face drained and his lips quivered. He broke from his stance and lumbered for the door that would lead him to her.

HELEN SAT on the edge of the dance floor in the Palace, fidgeting with her hands, terrified for having come. After nearly five days without him she'd come back, powerless to stop herself, it seemed. And powerless because her legs were trembling and her body was convulsing from withdrawals. It made her stomach float and her mouth salivate. If she wasn't physically addicted, then she was addicted in a worse way, from the soul up.

But she had to return by five-thirty. Yes, she had to get back to Jan, she couldn't go crazy here—it would ruin her. She'd spent the day a nervous wreck, fighting desperately for control until she finally decided that one hit would not hurt. One dip back into the waters. She was, after all, still a fish, and fish could not stay up on the shore forever. One taste of . . . this.

That priest Ivena had sent her to had talked about stability in terms of loyalty and trust. But what could he possibly know of her? *This* was her loyalty and trust; the drugs. And Glenn. The beast. Beauty and the Beast.

The door to her right slammed open and she leaped to her feet. He stood there with his arms spread like a gunslinger, panting and sweating.

Helen stood. "Glenn." She should go now, she thought. Or she should run to him and throw her arms around him. Helen smiled, partly with seduction, partly in amusement at herself. "I missed you, Glenn."

He dropped to his knees and started to cry. "Oh, I missed you too, baby. I missed you so much."

She felt an odd blend of empathy and disgust, but it did not stop her. She went for him, and when she reached him, knelt down and kissed his forehead. He smelled of sick flesh, but she was growing accustomed to his peculiarities.

Then Helen put her arms around his huge frame and together they toppled over backward.

CHAPTER TWENTY

"The love that I saw in the priest and in Nadia was a sentiment that
destroyed desire for anything less than union with Christ. If you say
you love Christ, but are not driven to throw away everything for that
pearl of great price, you deceive yourself. This is what Christ said."

The Dance of the Dead, 1959

JAN THREW safety to the wind and roared toward Ivena's house. Put a man
who'd relied too heavily on a chauffeur for most of his driving career behind the
wheel and stir his heart into panic and you'd better warn the public. A car blared
its horn to his right, and Jan punched the accelerator. The Cadillac shot through
the intersection safely. He'd just run a stop sign. He braked hard and heard a
squeal; those were *his* tires! *Settle down, Janjic!* Ivena's was just around the corner.

It was jealousy that raged through his blood, he thought. And he really had no
business courting jealousy. Especially over Helen. Not so soon. Not ever! Goodness,
listen to him.

But there it was: jealousy. An irrational fear of loss that had sent him into this
tailspin. Because Helen was missing. Helen was gone.

It had been a good day, too. The conference call with Karen could have been
awkward, but Roald's ever-present booming voice had preempted any opportunity
for private talk. Karen announced her news: In light of the movie deal, their publisher, Bracken and Holmes, had agreed to publish another edition of *The Dance
of the Dead*, with updates that tied into the movie. And they were underwriting a
twenty-city tour! What does this mean? Jan wanted to know. "It means, dear Jan,
more money, I'd say," Roald had boomed. Karen then told them that the publisher
had arranged a dinner with Delmont Pictures Saturday evening. They wanted Jan

there. Where? New York, of course. New York again? Yes, New York again. It would be huge, better than anything she could have wished for.

Jan had joined them in their enthusiasm and then hung up, feeling stretched at the seams. His mind had become a rope, pulled at by two women. Karen the lovely one, deserving of his love; Helen the unseemly one, suffocating him with her spells of passion. The craziness was enough to send any man to a psychiatrist's couch, he thought.

But that had been the least of it.

Jan had rushed home at five-thirty, found Helen gone and a note from Ivena on his fridge. She would be back in a couple of hours. But there was no word of Helen. He quickly showered while he waited for her return.

He'd dressed in the same black suit he'd worn on their last outing, but with a yellow tie this time. An hour had ticked by. Then two, while he paced the floor. And then he knew that she would not return, and his world began to crumble. He'd called Ivena, swallowing back the tears so that she couldn't hear.

Helen was missing. Helen was gone.

He brought the Cadillac to a halt in front of her house and climbed out. He still wore the black suit, less the tie. His shiny leather shoes crunched up Ivena's sidewalk, loud in the night. He would have to tell her everything—he could no longer walk around carrying these absurd emotions alone.

She greeted him quietly. "Hello, Jan. Please come in."

He stepped past her, sat on the sofa, crossed his legs and lowered his head into his hands. A strong scent of flowers filled the room—perfume or potpourri perhaps. It was nearly suffocating.

"Ivena—"

"Why don't I get us some tea, Janjic. Make yourself comfortable."

Ivena walked straight for the kitchen and returned with two cups of steaming tea. She put his on the lamp table at his elbow and sat in her favorite chair.

He looked white in the face and he ignored his tea. "Thank you. Ivena, there is something that I have to tell you. I really—"

"So, Janjic, I was not wrong about the *pitter?*"

He looked up, surprised. "No, you weren't." He stood and paced three steps and then returned to his chair. "I don't know what's happening to me. This crazy idea for Helen to stay in my house wasn't the best."

"You're upset, I can see. But don't take your frustration out on me. And if you must know, I approve."

"You approve?"

"I do approve. I didn't at first, of course, when I first saw you looking at her, I thought you must be mad, being engaged to Karen as you are."

He stared at her, unbelieving.

"But no, you weren't mad. You were simply falling for a woman and doing so rather hard." She sipped her tea and set the saucer on the table. "So now you are in love with Helen."

"I can't believe you're talking this way. It's not that simple, Ivena. I'm not just *in love* with Helen. How can I suddenly be *in love* with a woman? Much less this . . . this . . ."

"This improper woman? This tramp?"

"How could this possibly happen to me? I'm engaged to Karen!"

"I've been asking myself that same question, Janjic. For three days now I've asked it. But I believe it's beyond you. Not entirely, of course. But it is more than your making. You care for Karen, but do you love her?"

"Yes! Yes, I love Karen!"

"But do you love her the way you love Helen?"

"I'm not even sure I *do* love Helen. And what do you mean 'the way'? Now there are different ways to love?" He immediately lifted a hand. "Don't bother answering. Yes, of course there are. But I'm no judge between them."

Ivena sat quietly.

"You should be outraged," he said, and truly *he* felt outraged. Outraged at his confusion and angry at Helen's disappearance. "And how do you suppose that I love Helen?"

"With passion, Janjic. She takes your breath away, no?"

The words sounded absurd, spoken out loud like that. It was the first time the matter had been presented so plainly. But there was no doubting the matter. "Yes. Yes, that's right. And what kind of love is that?"

Ivena smiled. "Well, she's quite a stunning woman, under all the dirt. It's not so confusing really."

He just looked at her for a minute. "I'm saying things that I shouldn't be saying, and you are counseling me as if this were a high school crush."

Ivena didn't respond.

"She had an impossible grip on my heart from the first, you know. I didn't look for it," Jan said.

Ivena only nodded, as if to say, *I know, Janjic. I know.*

"And there's something else you should know. I took her out. Before I brought her here on Sunday night we went to the Orchid for dinner. I didn't ask, mind you. She asked *me!* She'd laid out my suit—this suit." He jabbed his breast, suddenly grinning at the memory. "It was incredible. I could hardly eat."

"I know."

"You know?"

"She told me," Ivena said with a slight smile.

"She did? She told you that I could hardly eat?"

Ivena nodded. "And she said that you excused yourself to the rest room to gather yourself because you were—how did she put it—coming apart at the seams, I think."

"She told you *that?*"

"It's true?" she asked with a raised brow.

"Maybe, but I can't believe she would tell you that. She picked that up?"

"She's a woman. You're a man. The love between you carries its own language. Love is impossible to hide, Janjic. And Helen is far more intelligent than you seem to realize."

"You're right, she is." Jan sat back and cradled his face with both hands. "So you know everything then. You know that I'm madly in love with her." He said it and it felt good to say. He lowered his hands and leaned forward. "That I've never loved another creature with so much passion. That I can hardly think of anything but her. That every time I look into her eyes, my knees grow weak and my tongue feels thick. I can't breathe properly when she's in the room, Ivena." He suddenly felt that way now, he thought. "My heart aches and fills my chest. I am—"

"I think I get the point, my young Serb."

"And now she's gone back to him."

Ivena lifted her porcelain cup and drank slowly, as if tasting her tea for the first time. She set the cup in her lap. "Yes. And it's not the first time."

"What do you mean?"

"She went back the night you left for New York. Only for a few hours, but I could see it in her eyes."

What was she saying? "You could see *what* in her eyes?"

"I could *smell* it. And she held her head in pain the next morning. I'm not an idiot, Janjic."

Rage mushroomed in Jan's skull. He stood from his chair. "I swear if I ever . . . I'll kill that devil!"

"Sit, Janjic."

"He's beating her, isn't he?" His face flushed with blood. "He's abusing her! How could she go back to him!"

"Sit, Janjic. Please sit down. I am not the enemy."

He sat and buried his head in his hands. It was madness. It was more than madness now. It was horror. "And who *is* the enemy?" he asked.

"The thief who comes to steal and destroy," she said.

Yes, of course. He knew that, but it made nothing easier.

"Do you think Father Micheal's love came out of his own heart?" Ivena asked.

"No."

"Of course you don't, Janjic. You've told the whole world the same. Do you forget your own words?"

Jan looked at her. "No, I don't forget my own words. We're speaking of Helen here, not the priest. This isn't about fighting for our lives against some madman named Karadzic. This is about ridiculous emotions that are driving *me* insane!"

"And these emotions that are driving you insane, they are the same sentiments that put Father Micheal on the cross. They are the same that Christ himself showed. For God so loved the world, Janjic. Is this the love with which you love Helen?"

He stared at her stupidly.

"I swear, Janjic, you can be thickheaded at times. You are feeling the love of the priest; the love of Christ. It's not coming from your own heart. Have you ever considered the likelihood that you aren't meant to marry Karen? Then I'll tell you now, you can't marry Karen."

"Because of this minor inconsistency with Helen? Don't be—"

"No! Because God wouldn't want you to marry Karen. It's better to break off now before you have a covenant with her. Or do you consider an engagement the same as a covenant marriage?"

"No."

"Well then. You must follow this love God has placed in your heart for Helen. And you must do so without any offense to Karen."

"How on earth can I pursue a relationship with an unbeliever?"

"Did God command Hosea to take Gomar? I'm not suggesting you marry the girl, anyway. But there is more here than meets the eye, Janjic. Consider it a word from God."

It struck him as clearly as the mountain air in that moment. Could it be? He'd seen that brief vision of the flowered field and heard the weeping. Perhaps it was more than a casual act of God's grace to reveal it. Perhaps it was God's *intent* that he love Helen! And not just as a poor lost soul, but as someone his heart ached for.

The notion flooded Jan with a sudden sense of ease. It took the craziness out of his turmoil, lent him validity. Ivena must have seen the change in him because she was smiling.

"You think Helen is *meant* to be loved by me," he said. "It's why you approve."

"In as much as Christ loves the church, I think so."

"And Christ loves the church with this mad, passionate emotion?"

Ivena stood and walked to the bookcase on the opposite wall. "Would you like to see something, Janjic?"

A blue vase holding a single flower rested on the third shelf. A brilliant white bloom with red-trimmed petals, the span of Jan's hand. She pulled the flower from the base and faced him like a schoolgirl presenting her carnation.

"Do you smell it?"

It was the strong fragrance he'd smelled walking in. "I smell something. Your perfume, I thought."

"But I'm not wearing any perfume, Janjic."

Jan stood and walked toward the flower. Immediately the scent strengthened in his nostrils.

"Now you smell it," she said, smiling.

"That's impossible."

"But true. It is a lovely scent, isn't it?"

"And it all comes from the one flower? Naturally?"

"Yes."

Jan studied the petals. They seemed oddly familiar. She handed it to him and he held it up to the light.

"Where did you find this?"

"I'm growing them, actually. You like it?"

"It's stunning."

"Yes. I think I may have stumbled across a new species. I've already given Joey one for analysis."

"You don't know the name?" he asked, turning the flower in his hand. The petals were like satin. The scent reminded him of a very strong rose.

"No. They're the result of a rose graft."

"Amazing."

Ivena smiled wide, like a proud child. "Yes. The aroma is like love, Janjic. Unless a seed dies and falls to the ground it cannot bear fruit. But look at where it all leads. It's a sweet scent begging to be taken in. Not something you can just ignore, is it?"

Jan placed his nose near a petal and sniffed again. The flower's fragrance was so strong it brought water to his eyes. He returned it to the vase and retreated to his chair.

"So you think I should love Helen?"

He shook his head. "They'll blow their tops."

"Who will?"

"Karen, for one. Roald, the leaders, the employees—everyone."

"But you can't pretend. That would be worse."

Then he remembered why he'd come here in the first place. "She's gone."

Ivena turned. "She'll come back."

"You're sure? How can you know that?"

"I can't. But she's a woman and I'm telling you, she'll be back."

They sat and talked about what they should do then. Should they call the police? And tell them what? Jan said. That this girl named Helen had returned to her lover, which was not a good thing because Jan Jovic—yes, the famous author Jan Jovic—had a crush on her. But it wasn't a crush because it was God's love, which both was and wasn't like a crush. The same but different. Maybe. Yes, that would go over nicely.

In the end they agreed that they could do nothing else themselves. Not tonight at least. They would pray that God would protect Helen and reveal his love to her. And that Jan would hear God's voice and not run amok in his own emotions. Actually that last prayer was Ivena's, but Jan found himself agreeing with it. God knew that he was walking on new ground here. The grounds of love.

JAN NEARLY called in sick Thursday morning. Helen hadn't returned and he'd slept only three hours, half of it on the couch. In all honesty, he was sick, but it wasn't the kind of illness Karen would understand. At least not while it was directed at another woman. He finally dragged himself in at ten, if for no other reason than to save himself the agony of waiting.

The employees were looking at him with questioning eyes, he thought. They knew, they all knew. Their soft smiles and gentle frowns were saying so. The frowns he may have imagined, but then again maybe not. According to Betty's admission—which he was still trying to dismiss—they were practically laying odds on his sanity.

Karen bounded into his office within five minutes of his arrival, humming and moving to her tune. Thank goodness she was not so well connected with the gossip on the lower floors. He smiled with her as best he could, and listened patiently as she talked about her trip.

It had been a smashing success, by her telling; one to put in her portfolio. It was not only the reprint agreement with the publisher, it was eight—count them, eight—television appearances in the next two months and that was not including the tour to kick off the new edition. Jan was happy for her, and the news did distract him slightly. He found enough resolve to keep Karen in a state of general ambivalence about him, he thought.

But his thinking proved incorrect.

She flashed two tickets in her hand. "It's all set, Jan. We have first-class tickets to New York on the five-thirty flight tomorrow."

New York! He'd forgotten. "I thought the dinner was Saturday."

"It is, but I thought we could make a weekend of it. Roald won't be there, you know."

Suddenly it was all too much. He did smile; he did do that, but evidently not with enough muster to fool her. In fact, he couldn't be sure it didn't come off as a frown, if his heart was any judge. Karen dropped the hand holding the tickets to her side, and he knew that she'd seen through his facade.

She closed the door and slid into one of the guest chairs. "Okay, Jan Jovic. What's wrong?"

"What do you mean?" *She means why is your face sagging, dummkopf.*

"Something's up," she said, staring straight at him. "All day you've been wearing this plastic smile. I could walk in here and tell you that Martians have just landed on Peachtree Street and you'd smile and tell me how nice that was. You are as distracted as I've seen you. So what's up?"

Jan looked out the window and sighed. *Father, what am I doing? I do not want this.* He faced her again. She looked at him with her head tilted, beautiful in the morning rays that streamed through the window. Karen was a treasure. He could not imagine a woman as lovely as her. Except Helen. But that was absurd! Helen was off with another man! For that matter she might not even return. And if she did return, how could he possibly entertain thoughts of love for such a woman?

Father, I beg you! Deliver me from this madness.

"Jan, tell me." Karen was pleading with a woman's knowing voice now. She knew something already, by intuition.

He looked into her eyes, and suddenly he wanted to cry. For her, for him, for love. For all it was said to be, love had turned him into a worm this week. His eyes stung, but he refused to cry in front of her. Not now.

"Helen's gone again," he said.

She sat back and crossed her legs. "Sure, we agreed she would go. And that's a problem?"

"Yes. Actually it is." He could not look at her directly.

"Jan . . . She's just one girl." Her voice was soft and soothing. "Lost, wandering, hurt, sure. I can understand that. But our ministry goes way beyond this one person." She leaned forward and put her open palm on the desk for his hand. He took it. "It'll be okay, I promise."

He could not carry on any longer. He could not. "She's not just one girl, Karen."

The room fell to a terrible silence. "And what does that mean?"

He looked into her eyes and tried to tell her. "She means more to me. She . . ."

Karen removed her hand and sat straight. "You've fallen for her, haven't you?" Her eyes misted over.

"I . . . Yes."

"I knew it!"

"Karen, I . . ."

Now she was red. "How *dare* you?" She said it trembling and Jan recoiled. "How could you slobber all over a tramp like that?"

"I'm not slob—"

"How dare you do this to me!"

"Karen, I—"

"I *love* you, you big oaf! I've loved you for three years!" Now she had slipped into rage and he knew he'd made a very big mistake in telling her. "We're engaged, for God's sake! We went on television and promised our love in front of half the world and now you're telling me that you've fallen for the first bimbo that struts in front of you? Is that it?"

"No, Karen! That's not it! It was beyond me."

"Oh, yes, of course. How silly of me. You couldn't help it, could you? Did she crawl up at the bottom of your bed to keep you company at night?" Tears ran from her eyes now. "And what do you suppose this means for our engagement?" she demanded.

"I had to tell you the truth."

"What am I supposed to tell the studio? Did you even think of that before inviting this pathetic bimbo into your house? What should I tell them, Jan? Oh, yes, well Jan is no longer speaking on the martyrs. He's writing a new book; a personal guide to live-in bimbos. In fact, he's living with one now. *That* will go over huge, I can assure you! Roald will fry you!"

Jan was too stunned for clear thoughts, much less words. He only felt like curling up and dying. *I do not mean to harm you, Karen! I am so very sorry. Karen, please . . .*

"You think you can make this movie without me? You're a fool to throw it all away!"

She suddenly stood. Her hand came across the desk and landed with a loud *smack* on his cheek. His head jerked to the side. Without saying another word Karen spun around, pulled the door open, and walked from the office.

"Karen! Please, I . . ." Nothing else came. *You love her, tell her that. You do love her! Don't you?*

He heard the loud slam of the suite's front door.

For a full ten seconds Jan could not move. Nicki ran in, glared at him, and then ran out after Karen. To tell the world.

His face stung, but he barely felt it. He just sat there in a daze, looking with a blank, watery stare. Then he lowered his head to the desk and let the tears come. He was dying, he thought. Life could not be worse. Nothing, absolutely nothing could possibly feel as sickening.

But he was wrong.

CHAPTER TWENTY-ONE

"We all have some of Karadzic swimming under the surface.
We have all spit on the face of our Creator. Thinking that we have not
is self-righteous arrogance—which is itself a form of spitting."

The Dance of the Dead, 1959

JAN PULLED into his driveway at seven, just as dusk darkened the sky over Atlanta. Helen had been gone for one day now and his world had caved in on itself.

He'd already shut the car door when it occurred to him that he could have pulled into the garage. There was no longer anyone to sneak past. He turned and walked for the front door.

He saw the white paper pegged to his door when he rounded the corner and it made him stop. A note? His heart bolted in his chest. A note!

Jan dropped his briefcase, bounded up and ripped the paper from the tack that had been shoved into the post. It was a full sheet with faint lines, the kind found in any full-size notebook. He tilted the sheet into the moonlight and dropped his eyes to the bottom.

Helen.

It was signed by Helen! His fingers trembled.

Help me please.
I'm so sorry. Please come. I need you.
The top of the west tower. Hurry, please.

Helen.

A drum took to Jan's chest. Dear God! Helen! He ran for the car, threw the door open, and fired the engine.

It took Jan ten minutes to reach the Towers—enough time for him to wet his steering wheel with sweat and spin through a dozen reasons why coming here was a bad idea, not the least of which was Glenn Lutz. The man had threatened Jan directly on the phone, and there was no guarantee that the note hadn't been written by him rather than Helen.

But she was almost certainly in trouble. He could have taken the note to the police, but he'd never quite lost his skepticism of the authorities, not since Bosnia. And going to the police would make this a public affair; he was quite sure he wasn't ready for that. Not with Helen.

In the end it was his heart that kept his foot on the pedal. He *wanted* to go. He had to go. Helen was there, and the thought of it made him throw reason to the wind.

Jan pulled the Cadillac under the first towering building—the West Tower—and inched to a stop in a space adjacent to the elevators. The underground structure was nearly vacant in the after hours.

A tall man dressed in black stood with his hands clasped behind his back near the elevator. Jan sat still for a moment. Maybe going to the police would have been a better idea after all. He climbed out and walked for the stranger.

The man ignored Jan until the doors had slid open and he'd stepped into the car. Then the Mafia type dropped his arms, walked in, turned around, and punched a code into a small panel. The doors slid closed.

Jan searched for the top floor button and was about to push the highest number on the panel when the man held out his hand. Message clear. The man was his escort.

A trail of sweat crept over Jan's temple. Helen hadn't arranged this. He couldn't shake the notion that he'd just stepped off a cliff. The elevator car rose past the last lighted number and jerked to a halt. It opened to a hallway and after hesitating, Jan followed the man down the passage and then to a set of massive copper doors. His host nodded and Jan pushed past them, swallowing at a knot that had risen to his throat.

He stepped into what appeared to be a plush penthouse suite, complete with a bar to his left and a dance floor to his left. But it was the large man standing next to a white pillar at the room's center that arrested his attention.

The doors shut behind him.

He was huge and pale, nearly albino in the dim light. His hair was blond, almost platinum, and his eyes were black. He wore a Hawaiian shirt and booted feet poked out from white cotton slacks. The man's lips twisted into a smile and Jan knew that this freak before him was Glenn Lutz.

"Well, well, well. The lover boy has come to force my hand," Glenn said. He lowered his head and peered at Jan past his eyebrows. "You do realize that you are trespassing on my ground, don't you? You do realize what that means, don't you?"

Jan quickly scanned the room for Helen. She wasn't here. This was not good. Jan took an involuntary step backward.

Glenn chuckled. "You'd like to kill me, wouldn't you, Preacher? That's why you came. But we can't have that. I have a surprise for you."

A shadow suddenly shifted to Jan's right. He'd only just begun to turn when the side of his head exploded.

A flashback.

But it wasn't feeling like a flashback. His world swam in darkness. He staggered to his right and instinctively threw out his arms for balance. And then finding it, he grabbed at his head, half expecting to feel a great hole there. His fingers felt a full head of hair, wet above his left ear, but intact.

The pain struck him as he tried to straighten, a deep ache that throbbed over his skull. He'd been hit on the head. Then a blow landed on the other side.

Thirty years of life in Bosnia roared to the surface. He was a writer and lecturer, but he was a survivor first, albeit a survivor who hadn't practiced surviving for a long time. Either way, his mind knew the drill well.

He staggered back two steps, groping for consciousness, blind to the world from that last blow. He nearly fainted then. If he didn't move quickly he might not move again. Jan gathered every last reserve of strength and he rushed straight forward, right past his attackers and out onto the floor. Grunts of objection sounded behind him and he lumbered forward, like a bull struck by a sledge.

He couldn't fight—not in this state—that much screamed through his mind. But it was all that screamed through his mind, because the rest of it had shut down, cowering from those two cracks to the head. He could not see; he could only run. The condition proved unfortunate.

Jan had covered less than ten yards when his knees smacked into a piece of furniture. He cried out and pitched headfirst onto a cushioned object. A couch. His head swam and he rolled off, landing on his side with a dull *thump* that took his breath away.

They were on him then, like two hyenas pouncing for the kill. Hands jerked him to his knees and held him still. It was as if they carefully lined up the last blow;

one, two, three . . . Crack! It landed on the crown of his skull, and he collapsed in a sea of black.

TWILIGHT LAPPED the edges of Jan's mind, tempting him to awaken, but he thought he would sleep a while longer. An annoying bell had crashed through his ears one too many times already, like a huge mallet swung for a gong.

The sound invaded his dead sleep relentlessly and he rolled . . .

But that was where the gong show ended. Because he couldn't roll.

His eye cracked and he saw nothing but black. A monster pounded on his skull, sending shafts of pain right down his spine. He tried to lift his head, but it refused to budge. Slowly his focus returned.

He knew then that he wasn't in his bed. He lay on his side in a corner, with his back to a wall. He was naked except for his underwear. Dark stains ran down his belly and dyed his white briefs red. Blood.

He'd been beaten badly by those two shadows. Jan tried to lift his head again, and this time it came up for a full second before falling back down to the carpet with a dull thump. He paid for the effort with a spike through the brain, and he clenched his eyes against the pain.

He was still in the nightclub, he'd seen that much. Mirrored walls and a dark dance floor. Colored lights cast eerie hues of red and green and yellow across the black carpet.

A voice sounded to his left. "He's waking, sir."

Hands grabbed his arm and pulled him into a sitting position. He wavered there for a moment and then lifted his head. This time he got it all the way up and rested it on the wall behind him. A figure stood by the bar to his right, replacing a phone in its cradle. The man had a bandage around his shoulder. Jan hadn't done that, had he? Not that he could remember.

The black-suited man seated himself in a folding chair and looked at him without expression. Jan's reflection stared back at him from the mirrored wall. Blood ran in long fingers down his neck and chest from red-matted hair. *What are you doing here, Jan? And where in the devil are you?*

He answered his own question. *You are in a place owned by Glenn Lutz because Helen asked you to come.*

A door to his left smacked open and he turned only his eyes, favoring his aching head. It was Glenn. The man seemed to glide more than walk. His hands hung huge with thick fingers that curled like stubby roots. Jan looked into his eyes. They were nothing more than black holes, he thought. A chill spiked down his spine. The man was smiling and his crooked teeth looked too large for his mouth.

"Well, well. So the preacher has decided to join us again. You've been here for nearly a day and finally you have the courtesy to show your face." He stared at Jan, obviously relishing the moment. "I apologize for the blood, but I wasn't sure you'd want to cooperate without the right persuasion. And stripping you . . . I hate to humiliate you but . . ." He paused. "Actually, that's not true. None of that's true. I love the blood. Even if you'd agreed to everything up front I'd have beat you bloody."

Helen was right. This man was evil. Possessed maybe. Jan uttered a silent prayer. *Heavenly Father, please save me.*

"But you know that already, don't you, Preacher?" Glenn tilted his head forward and grinned like a jack-o'-lantern. "You've touched our tender flower, haven't you? Hmm? Felt her bruises?"

"No," Jan said hoarsely.

Glenn stepped forward and swung his arm in a wide arc. His hand crashed against Jan's head like a club. If he hadn't already been sitting, the blow would have taken him from his feet. As it was, it nearly broke his neck. A white ball of pain swallowed him and sent him over a cliff of blackness.

HE DIDN'T even know he'd passed out until he struggled back into consciousness. It must've been some time, because Glenn was leaning over the bar with a drink in one hand. His belly hung low, bared like an albino watermelon beneath his Hawaiian shirt hitched up by the bar. He looked back, saw that Jan had stirred, pushed himself off and strode across the floor

"Back again? Thoughtful of you."

Hands jerked Jan to a seated position. He let his head slip and closed his eyes. A finger rested under his nose and pushed it back. "You look at me when I'm talking to you." Lutz stepped back and Jan steadied his head.

"That's better. Now we're going to do this once, Preacher. Only once. Because you know I don't have all day, right? You do know that I'm Satan, don't you? To you I'm Satan. I would just as soon cut your tongue off as listen to you talk. But you caught me on a good day. I have my precious flower back, and that makes me feel generous, so we're going to do it differently. But we're only going to do it once; I want you to be very clear about that. Are you understanding this?"

Jan's head slowly cleared. He gave the man a shallow nod.

"Speak to me when I ask you a question, Preacher."

"Yeth," Jan said around a swollen tongue. That last blow had done some damage to his mouth.

"Okay." He turned and nodded to the man sitting in the folding chair by the bar. "Bring her."

The man walked to a door and knocked. Two came from the other room; another thug first, and then a woman.

Helen.

It was an odd moment. Jan wasn't even fully conscious; he was still in a fog; his life hung over a cliff, suspended by a thin thread it seemed. And all of this *because* of Helen.

Yet when his eyes focused and he became certain that it was her, everything else became useless information. Because she was here and he was here, and he was watching her wide blue eyes emerge from the shadows, flowers of delicate beauty. His pulse surged and his knees suddenly felt weak. He wanted to beg for her forgiveness and that terrified him. She should be begging for *his* forgiveness. And how could his knees feel weak at the sight of her? They'd been cut from under him already.

His body was too weak to show any of this—too weak to move. He sat like a side of beef against the wall, unmoving, but his heart began to do backflips when Helen looked at him.

"Thank you, my dear, for joining us," Glenn said. "Come, stand in front of him."

She walked to a point five feet from Jan, all the while looking at him with those fawn eyes. *Listen to me, Helen. Listen to me, it's all right. I love you, my dear. I love you madly.* His mind spoke it, but he knew she couldn't possibly gather any such thing from his sagging face.

"Stand him up!" Glenn said.

The two men walked over, each took an arm, and they hoisted Jan to his feet. His head throbbed and he could not support his own weight. They held him under the arms.

"Now we have the two lovers together." Glenn stood to one side, like a minister wedding a bride and groom. "It is a lovely sight, isn't it? What do you make of him, my dear?" This to Helen.

She stood frozen with her mouth slightly agape. Perhaps he'd doped her. Or perhaps she'd doped herself.

"Helen?" Glenn said.

"Yes?" she responded, breathy and quiet.

"I asked you what you thought of him."

"He looks hurt."

Glenn chuckled. "Good. That's good. Doesn't it make you want to spit on him?"

She didn't respond.

"Helen, remember our little chat earlier? Hmm? Do you remember that, honey?"

"Yes."

"Good. Now, I know that it may not feel natural at first, but it will later. So I want you to do what we talked about. Okay?"

The room seemed vacated of air. Nobody moved. Jan hung limp. Helen looked as if she were in another world altogether. A moment of reckoning. But Jan didn't know what was being reckoned.

Glenn spoke very softly now. "Helen."

Nothing.

"Helen, if you don't do what we talked about I'll break some of your bones. Do you hear me, princess?"

Helen hesitated and then took a step forward. She swallowed hard and closed her eyes. The sound of her shallow breaths worked like billows in the room. But she made no other move.

Glenn's threat came very quietly. "Helen, I swear I will break some bones, dear."

Her nostrils flared and she pursed her lips. Then she leaned forward and spit into Jan's face.

Jan blinked, shocked, staring at her wounded expression, hardly aware of the spittle on his cheek.

"Good," Glenn cooed. "Good. Now hit him, Helen. Hit him and tell him that he makes you sick."

Helen shifted on her feet, and Jan saw the terror in her eyes. She stood still.

Glenn took one long stride toward Jan and swung his fist like a mallet from his hip. "Hit him!" he screamed. The knuckles struck the left side of Jan's chest and a pain stabbed through his heart. The room swam, and for a moment Jan thought he might pass out again.

Glenn stepped back and looked at Helen. Sweat glistened on his face. He smiled. "You hit him or I hit you. That's the game, Helen."

It struck Jan then that Glenn meant to ruin him. This was all about Helen, not him. He was only the prop. Jan felt the first real shafts of fear run through his mind.

Don't do it, Helen! Don't do it! This is madness!

This couldn't be happening. At any moment the police would crash through the door with drawn weapons. He was a well-known man. He was on the verge of becoming a household name, and here he was in some absurd lovers' quarrel between two twisted souls. He had no business being here!

Karen's face flashed through his mind. *Dear, God! What have I done?*

Helen's body began to tremble—Jan saw it and he wondered if Glenn saw it. She looked small and puny standing next to him. Ugly. Jan blinked.

She's my enemy, he thought. A small wave of revulsion swept through Jan's gut. He felt inhuman in that moment. Like a pile of waste stepped on by a passing parade. Not the celebrity writer at all.

Oh Karen, dear Karen, what have I done?

Helen's face began to wrinkle. Tears ran down her cheek. Her hands began to quake badly, and Jan thought she was building her rage. But Glenn's face was suddenly white; he'd seen something else in her.

"You do it, you pig!" he growled. "You do it or I'll pound you to a pulp, you hear me?"

Her mouth suddenly cracked to a frown and a high, squeaking sound escaped her throat. Her eyes closed and her hand balled into a fist. Her cry wasn't a wail of rage. It was a cry of anguish. She was being torn to shreds.

Helen suddenly moaned loudly and she swung her hand in a wide arc.

The blow may have landed, Jan didn't know, because in that moment the nightclub vanished.

With a brilliant flash of light, it was gone.

He wasn't in the colored light, propped up like a side of beef. He was standing on the edge of an endless flowered field. The same white desert he'd seen once before, when he'd first touched Helen.

And then suddenly he knew that he'd seen this scene more than just once. He'd seen it a thousand times! This was the scene from his dreams! The white field that flashed into his dreams! How had he not recognized it?

It lay absolutely still.

Still except for the weeping.

He noticed her then. There was more than the field of flowers before him: There was a figure wearing a pink dress, lying on the petals not fifteen feet from him, looking at him. It was Helen.

Helen!

Only Helen hardly looked like Helen because her face was as white as cotton and her eyes were gray. She looked as though she'd been in a grave for a while before they'd dug her out and placed her here, on the bed of strange flowers.

Her chest rose and fell slowly, and she stared at him. But if she recognized him her blank look did not show it.

The weeping was for her.

He knew that because it came sweeping out of the sky on the lips of invisible mourners. Like a Requiem Mass for the dead. Such sadness, such anguish over Helen.

Still she gazed at him with flat, pale lips and dead eyes, breathing slowly while the sky filled with a million baying voices. Then the voices suddenly descended upon him, drowning him in their sorrow.

He was weeping immediately. Without warning. The pressure of grief fell so strongly on his chest that he couldn't breathe. He could only expel his breath in a long moan. He began to panic under the pain. He was dying! This was surely death flowing through his veins. He fell forward, unable to stand.

Jan collapsed among the white petals, prone at her feet. At Helen's feet. He gasped and rolled onto his back. The sky sustained a long howl; the mourners' undying grief. And Jan wept bitterly with them. He held himself tight to keep from falling apart and he wept.

Jan's eyes were closed when the sky went black and silent. Only his own weeping sounded. His eyes snapped open. He was back in the nightclub, hanging limp between the two men and blubbering like a baby.

Glenn was yelling. ". . . you hear me, you piece of trash!" He was towering over Helen, who had fallen to her knees, cowering and sobbing. "You make me sick!" Glenn spat at her. "Sick!"

Jan strained against the hands that held him, but succeeded only in inviting a new surge of pain through his head. *Helen, dear Helen!* His face twisted in empathy. *Oh, God, please save her! I love her.*

Tell her that, Jan. Tell her!

She sagged on the floor, heaving with sobs, her face white and her lips peeled back in desperation. Jan spoke to her. "Helen." It came out more like a moan, but he didn't care now. "Helen, I love you."

She heard and opened her eyes. They were blue. Deep blue. Swimming in tears and red around the edges and stricken with grief, but blue.

"Helen." They were both crying hard then. Looking at each other with twisted faces and weeping without words.

Glenn took a step back and glanced between them. For a moment his eyes widened. Then his face flashed red and screwed to a knot. He leaped forward and swung his foot like a place-kicker. The black boot struck Jan in his ribs. Something snapped and Jan's world began to fade.

Helen had stretched her arms out to him; her fingers spread and taut, like desperate claws. Glenn whirled and swung his foot at her. The blow knocked her to her side and she quieted to a quivering lump, but her eyes did not leave Jan's.

The brutes dropped him and he collapsed onto his face. Another blow landed on his back. And another.

He lost consciousness then, thinking the world was ending.

THEY LEFT Jan tied in the corner for another day, alone and without water. During that time he saw no one. He drifted in and out, through fields of white flowers and chambers that echoed with the sound of weeping. Heaven was weeping. Heaven was weeping for Helen.

He could only guess what the beast had done to her. But he could hardly bear to guess and so mostly he didn't. New wounds on his chest had soaked the carpet at his feet with blood before finally coagulating. Glenn had kicked him twice; he remembered that. But the aches and bruises were all over. They had beat him after he'd passed out.

They came for him at night—two thugs and Glenn. The monster was wearing a grin and he looked freshly showered. If Jan had been in working order he might have thrown himself at the man and choked him.

"Dump him in his backyard," Glenn said with satisfaction. "And tell him the next time he messes with my woman, he won't be so lucky." He chuckled and the men hoisted Jan to his feet. His world faded with the pain.

When he awoke he was in his backyard by the pool, staring at the stars.

CHAPTER TWENTY-TWO

"If you were to put all of the world's pain in one fifty-five-gallon drum,
it would look silly next to the mountains of gold and silver found in each
moment with God. Our problem is that we rarely see past the drum."

The Dance of the Dead, 1959

SUNDAY PULLED Jan along a hazy road of reawakening with fits and starts.

Evidently he'd pulled himself into the house and passed out on the carpet by the
couch. It was light out when an incessant ringing had awakened him again. He
remembered thinking that he must get to that phone; he needed help. He hauled
himself to his feet and answered. It was Ivena. The sound of her voice brought tears
to his eyes. Ivena had been trying to reach him for two days now, and what in the
world did he think he was doing not answering his phone? "I don't care if you have
woman problems or not, you don't ignore me! I nearly called Roald looking for you."

"I was beaten, Ivena," he'd said. And she was at his door five minutes later.

She took one look at him, appalled, all that dried blood from head to foot,
and she was immediately the war mother. No time to bemoan the injustice of it
all; this one needed attending. He actually thought he was feeling much better and
insisted that he could shower and eat and everything would be fine. But she would
have none of it. They were going to the hospital and that was final.

In the end, he acquiesced. He hobbled out to the Cadillac, his arm over Ivena's
shoulder, and she drove him to St. Joseph's Hospital. Everything started going
blurry again when they turned the first corner.

When he awoke again, an IV tube snaked out of his arm, chilling it to the
shoulder. A doctor hovered over him and pulled at his chest with strings. They
were stitching up some cuts there. This time consciousness came and stayed; the

IV's hydrating solution was primarily responsible, the doctor told him. He was as dry as a cracked riverbed. Another day and he would've been dead. And how did all this happen anyway?

Jan told him and an hour later there was a cop standing by the hospital bed, asking questions and taking notes. Ivena heard it all then for the first time as well, sitting in the corner, his concerned mother. They asked her to leave once but she wouldn't, and Jan insisted that she stay. The policeman seemed to hurry the interview along just a bit when he learned that this was all supposedly done at the hands of Glenn Lutz. *The* Glenn Lutz? he'd asked. Jan presumed so, although he'd never met *the* Glenn Lutz before. The description certainly fit. The cop left soon after, assuring Jan that the proper authorities would pursue the matter.

All told, Jan had a mild concussion, two deep cuts—one above his right ear and one on his chest—two broken ribs, a half dozen smaller cuts and bruises, and a severe case of dehydration. By early afternoon they had him fully rehydrated, sewn up, and adequately medicated to get about. He asked to be released and the doctor agreed only after Ivena assured him in the strongest terms that she would care for him. She had cared for worse. Anyway, his concussion was already three days old, his cuts had been bandaged and his veins flooded; what else could they do but observe? She could observe.

Once home, it took Ivena an hour to arrange him on the couch and satisfy herself that he was settled. She would make supper, she announced. It didn't matter that it was only four o'clock, he needed some real food in his system, not some hospital Jell-O. So they ate a meaty cabbage soup with fresh bread and they talked about what had happened.

"I know what you told the police, Janjic, but what else happened?" Ivena asked.

He remained quiet for a few moments, looking out the window now. Yes indeed, what did really happen? And where was Helen now?

"This is beyond me, Ivena."

"Of course it is."

"I told Karen."

"Hmm."

"She wasn't happy."

"You broke your engagement?"

"No."

They sat quietly for a moment.

"I had another vision."

"Yes?"

He watched the swaying willow beyond the pool. "I was tied there waiting for Helen to strike me. He forced her to hit me, you know. I didn't tell the policeman that, but he did. He made her spit on me . . ." A lump rose to Jan's throat and he swallowed. "She didn't want to, I know she didn't want to. And when she swung, I went into a vision."

They had stopped eating for the moment. "Tell me," Ivena said. "Tell me the vision."

Jan told her what he remembered, every detail. And as he told her, the emotions of it came back. Heaven was weeping for Helen. He too was there for Helen, weeping at her feet. It was so vivid! So very vivid, paling the beating in comparison. By the end, Ivena had set her bowl aside and was wiping tears from her eyes.

"Describe the flowers on the field again."

He did. "And there's something else, Ivena. It's the same field that I've seen in my dreams for twenty years now. I saw that."

"You're sure? The same field?"

"Yes, without question. Not the dungeon, just the very end of the dream. The white field."

"Hmm. My goodness. And where is Helen now, Janjic?"

"She's with him." He sat up and pushed the pillows aside, wincing. "Dear God, she's with him and I can't stand it! We should go up there and throw the man out!"

"You're in no shape to play soldier. Besides, you've told the police everything. This is America, not Bosnia. They don't tolerate kidnapping and beating so easily here. They'll arrest the man."

"Maybe, but I did go there on my own. He made a point of mentioning that. Said I was trespassing." Jan stood and paced to the window. "I'm telling you, Ivena, there's more here; I can feel it."

"And I agree, my dear. But this battle is not yours to pursue. It's one to receive."

"Meaning exactly what? Just let things happen? It wouldn't surprise me if she were dead already."

"You mustn't speak like that! Don't speak that way!"

"And yet you're suggesting that we just sit by and allow the police to deal with Glenn? When they do launch their investigation, you think a powerful man like this will have nothing to say in his defense? I'm telling you he will say it was me who went to threaten him. At the very least it will be days, weeks before anything is done."

She scrunched her brow. "I'm not saying we should do nothing. Simply that the police will do something, and we should wait until we see what they do. And I'm saying that you're in no condition to run around."

She took up her bowl and dipped into it again, but her soup must have been cold because she set it down. "Then again, I may be wrong. I could easily be wrong. I wouldn't have suggested that Nadia do what she did, and yet it was the right thing. It was beyond her."

"It *was* the right thing. And if this madman were to kill Helen, I think I would kill him."

Ivena sat in her armchair, glassy-eyed. Neither of them was seeing things too clearly, Jan thought. Yes, he had seen the vision clearly enough, but it gave him no clues how to save Helen. And that was the one thing they both did see: Helen *did* need saving. Not just from the monster, but from her own prison.

"I wanted to, you know," Ivena said.

"You wanted to what?"

"I wanted to kill Karadzic." A tear left its wet trail down her cheek. "I tried, I think."

"And so did I."

"But Nadia didn't. She didn't even *want* to kill him. And neither did the priest. They chose to die instead."

Jan turned back to the fading light. What could he say to that? His head was hurting. "Yes, they did." He returned to the couch, suddenly exhausted.

Ivena stood and took their dishes to the kitchen and just like that the conversation was over. They did not return to the subject until late that night. "So I guess we just sit tight and see what the police do for now?" Jan asked after Ivena had announced her intentions to retire.

"Yes, I guess so."

"And we'll deal with the ministry tomorrow. The employees will be concerned about my absence."

"Fine."

And that was that. She made sure that he was in good shape, fed him a painkiller, and left him to sleep.

JAN DIDN'T sleep quickly. He'd spent half the day in sleep and it didn't return so easily now. Instead he began to think about what the others would say to this. Or at least what they would say to what *he* would tell them about this, because he wasn't sure he could tell Roald and Karen all the details.

In fact, he wasn't sure he would be telling Karen *anything* soon. He didn't even know if she was still working for him. Did she know what had happened to him? He hadn't shown up for work Friday, but that was not unheard of. And the dinner! He'd missed the dinner in New York!

Suddenly Jan was wide awake. He tried to put the concerns out of his mind. Tomorrow was Monday; he would find out then. But the thoughts chased about his mind like a rat on a running wheel. Karen's face—her sweet smiling face—and then her angry slap. Perhaps he'd been a fool to tell her about Helen. He could hardly even imagine what would become of his relationship with Helen. They would . . .

He didn't know what they would do. If indeed she came out of this in one piece. And yet he had sacrificed his relationship with Karen already. Hadn't he?

Jan finally threw the sheets from his legs in a fit of frustration and walked for the phone.

He called Roald. The man's gruff voice filled the phone on the tenth ring. "Hello."

"Roald, this is Jan."

"Jan. What time is it?"

"It's late, I know. I'm sorry—"

"Everything okay?"

So. The man had not heard. "Yes. Have you talked to Karen?"

"Not since our conference call. Why? Weren't you with her in New York yesterday?"

"No, we had a problem with that. Listen I have something I need to talk to you about. Can you come by my house tomorrow?"

"Your *house?* I suppose I could. What's up?"

"It's nothing, really. Just something I'd like your input on."

They agreed to meet at ten.

It took Jan another hour to shake the mental mice and drift into sleep.

THE MORNING came quickly, to the sound of Ivena's singing in the kitchen— "Jesus, Lover of My Soul." She was in there cooking something that flooded the house with a delicious smell. "Let me to Thy bosom fly," her voice warbled.

Jan lifted himself to his elbows and fell back with the aches of stiff sleep. By the time he'd loosened enough to walk out to the kitchen, she was already setting the table. She saw him, still dressed in his pajamas, and she chuckled. "Oh my, my, look at yourself."

He glanced at his reflection in the chrome oven-hood and saw that she referred to his hair; it stood straight up past the white bandages. He flattened it. "I am a sick man, Ivena. Don't cross me."

"Not sick enough to stay in bed, I see."

"And did you expect less?" he asked, motioning to the two place settings.

"No, I have had a wonderful sleep, Janjic."

He hobbled for the chair. "That's more than I can say. I feel like a steamroller ran over me." He then told Ivena about his call to Roald. "They don't know. Karen doesn't know. I don't know if she's even on board any longer."

"No?"

"How can she work for me? This isn't good."

"You'll be fine."

"She's the backbone of the ministry."

"No, the testimony's the backbone, Janjic. *The Dance of the Dead.* The martyr's song. The testimony you've been waving about like a flag for five years; *that* is the backbone of the ministry."

"Yes, and it's been Karen who's done most of the waving. I'm nothing but the flagpole. Without her . . . I can't imagine what it would be."

She chuckled. "So then choose your women carefully, Janjic. They all want my handsome Serb. So many women . . ."

"Stop your nonsense. It's more serious than you think," he said, and ordinarily he would have grinned, but his heart was sick. "Do you know that I missed a dinner engagement in New York on Saturday night?"

She cast him a side glance. "Am I hearing some anger in this voice of yours, Janjic?"

He sipped at the steaming coffee. "Maybe. I'm not sure I've done the right thing with Karen. I feel like I've cut off one leg to save the other and now I may lose both."

"Don't worry, you will find your way. And I'm sure that missing one meal with Karen won't have any bearing on the path you end up taking."

"The dinner was with the movie people."

"Yes, and I'm not sure about this movie business anyway."

"Well, it's too late. It's finished."

"What is finished? Your life is finished, so now they will make a movie of it? I don't think so. We will see what happens to your movie deal, Janjic."

"That's ridiculous."

"Still, we will see." She said it smiling. "Roald will be here soon enough. It's already nine-thirty."

Nine-thirty! He hadn't realized it was so late. Jan excused himself and hurried off to dress.

Roald arrived fifteen minutes later while Jan was still in his room, struggling to get his socks on without ripping his stitches. "Where is he?" the elder statesman's voice boomed.

"Take a breath, my friend. May I get you something to drink?" Ivena returned.

Jan shook his head at her condescending tone. He entered the living room behind Roald, who'd taken a seat. The man was wearing a black tailored double-breasted suit familiar to Jan. "Good morning, Roald."

The man did not turn. "Jan I hope you have more sense than I think you have, partner. What in tarnation did you do to Karen?"

Roald turned, saw Jan's head, and came out of his chair. "What on earth happened to you?"

"Nothing," Jan said, sitting. He wore a navy shirt that covered his chest wounds. "Sit. So, I take it you talked to Karen."

"Doesn't look like nothing. Goodness, what happened? Are you okay? You look like you've been trampled by a herd." He sat.

"Not quite. Tell me about Karen first."

"Karen? Well, Karen's in New York, did you know that?"

"We had a dinner engagement there Saturday night. I couldn't make it."

"And you didn't have the decency to at least call? They had the dinner without you, you know."

"Honestly, Roald. I was quite tied up." He said it without humor. "So Karen attended?"

"No. And frankly that's a problem. What happened to you?" he asked for the third time.

Ivena interrupted them when she brought drinks, and then excused herself. She had some flowers that needed tending, she said. They would have to conquer the world on their own. She gave Jan a wink and left.

"So, *no one* from the ministry attended the dinner, then?" Jan asked.

"No one. It was a handful of executives from Delmont Pictures and the publisher."

"Goodness, what a mess. I'm sure Karen's upset about that."

Roald leaned back and picked up the coffee Ivena had placed by his chair. "Actually, she seems to care less about all that. She's directed her anger to you, my friend."

"Me?"

"You. She seems to think there may be a problem. There are greater concerns at hand now, and I told her as much. We're on the verge of breaking new ground; you realize that, don't you? No one's ever done what we'll do with this film. It's unprecedented. Already the whole evangelical community is talking about it. I'm out there talking you two up to the world—speaking about how the 'Jan and Karen show' will change the way Christianity is seen in the broader realms of arts and entertainment—and unbeknownst to me, the two of you are home having a world-class spat. It's embarrassing to say the least."

"And you shouldn't be embarrassed. You're mistaken—we're not having a fight. We had a talk. Karen took it badly. That's all." That was not all, of course, and Jan knew it well.

"Then maybe you can explain to me why she's talking about moving her things out of the office."

"She's leaving?"

"Not yet. But she seems to think the engagement's in some sort of jeopardy, and I told her that was nonsense. There's far too much at stake."

Jan cringed. "I didn't break off the engagement."

Roald nodded. "I told her that you cared for her, you know. She went on about this Helen character that you've helped, and I told her there was no way on God's green earth that you—after all that you've been through and with all that lies ahead of you—would do something so foolish as fall for a hooker. The church would throw you out on your ear! I think Karen somehow got the idea that you were actually losing interest in her, Jan. You have to watch your words, my friend. Women'll take what you say farther than you intend."

"Helen's not a hooker." He could see a glint cross the man's eyes.

"Hooker, junkie, tramp . . . what's the difference? She's not the kind of woman you can be seen with. It would be a problem. Especially with Karen in your life. You do see that, don't you? We warned you as much."

Jan nodded. This was not going as planned. Roald was somehow moving him along a path of reason he didn't want to travel.

"Do you know what a rare woman Karen is?" Roald asked. "Yes, of course you do. That's what I told her just an hour ago. And do you know what she told me?"

"No."

"She told me that matters of the heart have nothing to do with what's rare or common, or right or wrong. The heart follows its own leading. And you know she's right. So I guess I have to ask you, Jan, where is your heart leading you?"

Jan swallowed. "I don't know. I mean I do know. But the direction seems to change."

Roald blinked a few times. "It does, does it? In case you hadn't realized it, Jan, my boy, you're not some adolescent teenager; you're a full-grown man with the trust of the church. And you're engaged to be married, for heaven's sake! Don't you think sticking your nose in the air to sniff out where the winds of love are blowing on any particular day is a bit preposterous for a man of your standing?"

"Don't lecture me, Roald. Did I say that I was sticking my nose in the air? Not that I can remember. You asked about my heart, not my will. If you want me to be straight with you, then give me some respect."

Roald took a deep breath. "Fine. I only hope that your will doesn't flip-flop like your heart. You do know if you don't find a way to reconcile with Karen, we stand to lose everything. Millions."

Jan stared at him, angry now. "Millions? This isn't about money!"

"No, but it is about a whole lot of basic issues that seem to have escaped your reason more frequently lately. We're changing the world with this, Jan! We're moving the church forward." He grasped his hand to a fist as he said it. "And you want to throw that all away over a woman?" Roald leaned forward. "Never! If you were to jeopardize this project by taking to this tramp of yours, the board would undoubtedly remove its endorsement of you. I can hardly imagine Bob's or Barney's reaction. Frank Malter would do backflips. I would have to consider leaving myself."

Jan leaned back, stunned by the statement. He sat speechless.

Roald tilted his head. "I know that's not going to happen, because I know you're not that stupid. But I want to be absolutely clear here: I will tie neither my name nor my goodwill to a man who betrays the trust of the church by taking up with a freak."

"She's not—"

"I don't care what she is, she's out!" he thundered. "You hear? She's out, or I'm out! And without Karen and me, your world'll come crashing down around your ears, my friend. I can promise you that."

This couldn't be happening! Roald was gambling, of course, positive that Jan had no real intention of continuing any relationship with Helen.

Roald sat back and crossed his legs and let his breath out slowly. "Now, I'm not saying that you have to resolve this all by day's end. I'm not saying you have to kick her out on the street, but there are places that care for women like her. Where is she anyway?"

"She's not here."

"Good. That's a start." Roald paused. "Jan, I know this may sound rather harsh, but you have to understand that I'm protecting a much larger interest. An interest which has bearing on not only you and me and Karen, but on the whole church. *The Dance of the Dead* has and must continue to impact the church at large."

"But not at the expense of its own message," Jan said thickly.

"No, of course not."

"And yet you are meddling with God's love."

"God's love. What's God's love without purity? I'm rescuing you from dipping into deception, my friend."

For a while they sat in silence—Jan because he had nothing to say; Roald probably for effect. "You agree then?" Roald said.

"I'll think on it," Jan said.

"And you'll give Karen a call?"

Jan didn't answer that one. His head was still spinning. Spinning and aching.

Roald evidently took his silence for a positive sign. "Now, tell me how you managed to bump your head. My goodness, it looks horrible."

He wasn't about to tell Roald the grim details now. "It was nothing. Rather embarrassing really. I was jumped by a couple of hoodlums," he said.

"Hoodlums? You were robbed? Good night! You filed a report?"

"Yes."

"Good. When will the bandage come off?"

"It'll be off in a few days, I guess. It happened Friday, and I ended up in the hospital. That's why I missed the New York trip."

"You were in the hospital? I had no idea! Well that explains a lot. Karen's due back today." He patted Jan's knee and gave him a wink. "You let me handle this,

Jan. I'll call her for you. You know how women love to care for the wounded. She'll be doting on you before you know it."

Jan wanted to slug him then. It was the first time he'd felt quite so offended by the man's audacity, and it swept over him with a vengeance.

Roald stood and set down his glass. "I'm just looking out for you, buddy." He stretched out his hand and Jan took it. "I'll see you soon. Call me when you have things straightened out." He started for the door and paused.

"By the way, Betty wanted me to tell you that she would call this afternoon. They are concerned, naturally. And she said she's praying. And that all bets are off—she said you'd know what that meant." He lifted an eyebrow.

Jan nodded.

Roald left then and Jan steamed through his house, tending to his errands, which amounted to little more than getting himself another drink and finishing some cold breakfast. The visit had made a bad day impossible, he thought. Not only was he sick about Helen, he was now forced to feel sick about feeling sick. Roald was robbing him of his true purpose. He was a thief. One who pulled many strings in the evangelical church, and one who made some pretty compelling arguments, but a thief just the same.

And Helen? *Father, rescue me from this pit,* he prayed. *Lead me out.*

CHAPTER TWENTY-THREE

IVENA STOOD in the greenhouse, blinking at the sight, breathing, but barely. There was a new feel in the air.

To her left Nadia's rosebush had died, but you would never know it without digging through the swarming green vines to the dried branches beneath. No fewer than fifty vines now ran from the bush along the wall, reaching at least twenty feet toward the rose beds along the adjacent wall. Bright green leaves dominated the heavy foliage, but they paled under the dozens of large flowers that flourished along each vine, each as crisp and white as the day they first bloomed.

And all of this in two weeks.

Joey hadn't finished his analysis, but Ivena hardly cared. She knew now that he'd find nothing. This was a new species.

She stepped forward and stopped. The strong, sweet scent flooded her lungs like a medicinal balm. The orchids to her right were looking soft due to her neglect. So be it; she'd lost her interest in any but these new flowers. And today there was something new in here; she just couldn't put her mind to it.

A strand of her hair tickled Ivena's cheek and she brushed it aside. She glanced at the window, expecting to see it open. But it wasn't. The door then. No. The kitchen door? No. But there was movement of air in here, wasn't there?

The flowers' aroma seemed to sweep into her nostrils. And her hair whispered ever so gently along her neck. She'd put a swamp cooler in two years ago precisely because of the room's complete lack of ventilation, but it sat quietly on the far wall.

She walked to the vines and touched some of the flowers. *What are you doing, Father? Am I going mad? Janjic knows, doesn't he? You showed him that vision.* But she wasn't sure he did.

She waited, numb in the silence. But very much alive; she always felt thoroughly awake with these flowers. A very faint sound drifted through her ears. The sound of a chime off in the distance. The neighbors, perhaps.

Ivena stood still for another twenty minutes, swimming in the impossible notion that something significant had changed in the room but unable to understand what, or even verify if anything was different. It would be her secret. Other than Joey, she had decided to share the greenhouse itself with no one until she herself fully understood what was happening here. And something was definitely happening.

HELEN CRAWLED out of bed late afternoon on Tuesday. She had been in the Palace since Thursday evening, when she'd come for the quick visit before her big date with Jan. Funny, it didn't feel like five days. And five days of her own choosing, for the most part. She would have left when Glenn had first told her about his plans with Jan. Oh yeah, she would've flown the coop then, but he'd drugged her and swore to break every finger on both hands if she didn't do precisely what he asked. And then they'd brought her out and there Jan was, crumpled on the floor, beaten to a pulp. She was still partly drugged at the time or she might have bolted then. Instead she'd done it. She had actually done it.

The moment her hand first struck his flesh, she knew she couldn't continue. She could not because she *did* love this man she'd just spit on. And although she had not attacked Jan as Glenn had insisted, she *had* technically fulfilled his demands: She'd spat on him and she'd hit him. Glenn stopped short of breaking her fingers, and she'd stayed there with him, hiding in the drugs, feeling sick of herself. She could have gone at any time, but to where? Definitely not back to Jan.

She could never go back to Jan.

Tears came to her eyes every time she thought about him. She'd never known the meaning of shame as she knew it now. The thought of Jan made her feel small and puny—he was too good for her. And not just too good, but beautiful and lovely, and she was sick and ugly in front of him, leaning forward and spitting in his face.

Helen showered slowly, washing three days of grime from her skin, letting the hot water soak deep into her bones. She pulled that dress on, the white one she'd worn for Jan when they went to dinner, the one that made her look beautiful. She cried as it came over her shoulders. She just could not stop these tears.

Helen tore the dress off, threw it in the corner and fell onto the bed, weeping. She was a fool. That much was an inescapable fact. A useless piece of flesh walking around pretending to be alive. Dead meat. Her tears wet the sheets. And that was how it was meant to be because she was a fish who belonged in water. This pool of tears was her home. Never mind that she could not manage more than a few days in the environment before disgust overtook her—it was no better on dry land. There she was only a fish *out* of water.

Thirty minutes later, she pushed herself from the bed, plodded over to the corner, and picked up the dress. She pulled it on without thinking now, afraid that if she did think, she would end up in a pool of tears again. And what if Glenn walked through those doors right now? He might break her fingers anyway, just for wearing this thing. She'd snuck it in, intending to change into it for her big date with Jan that night . . .

Stop it, Helen! Please. Just go.

She didn't bother with the makeup. She combed her hair and left the Palace the back way, looking like an overdressed tramp, she thought. But she did not know what else to wear. Not for this.

The westbound bus lumbered up ten minutes later, and she climbed aboard, avoiding eye contact with the dozen other passengers who were undoubtedly gawking at her. Undoubtedly.

The bus motored through the city, stopping every block to exchange riders with the street, and Helen took the ride staring blankly out the window. She couldn't afford to break down right here in front of strangers. It was only when she stepped off at Blaylock Street and started the one-block trek to the house that she started fighting misgivings again.

She plowed on, most definitely feeling like a fish out of water now. She had no business doing this. None at all. For one thing, Glenn *would* break her fingers despite his guarantee that she could go as she liked. For another, she had hit him. She had spat in his face.

Then Helen was there, standing in front of the door. She read the sign above: *In living we die; In dying we live. I am dying,* she thought. She stood swaying on her feet for a full minute before walking forward. She tapped lightly and then stepped back.

The door opened. Jan stood there, a white bandage around his head. He looked at her, dumbfounded, eyes growing. He was not speaking. It was a terrible moment, Helen thought. Her gut was twisting and her chest felt like it might explode. She wanted to turn around and run. She had no business being here. None at all! Her fingers trembled at her side.

"Helen?"

She spoke, but no words came. She meant to say, "Yes," but only a breathy rasp came out.

"Oh, dear God!" He suddenly leaped into motion and waved her forward. "Come in! Come in!"

Helen hesitated and then stepped across the door's threshold, compelled by his hand. Her skin was burning. She hung her head and looked at the floor while he closed the door and locked it. From her peripheral vision she saw him hurry over to the window, pull the curtain aside, and peer outside. Satisfied, he quickly crossed the room, looked out another window and pulled the drape tight. Then he hurried back and stopped in front of her. She could hear his breathing, hear him swallow. She almost expected his hand to swing for her face. She'd already decided to expect some measure of displeasure. Some harsh words at the very least.

"Helen." His voice wavered. "Helen." His hand reached for her face. He touched her chin. Helen closed her eyes and lifted her head slowly, thinking that she should flee now, before it was too late. She opened her eyes.

The skin around his misted eyes wrinkled with grief. "Helen." He lifted his other hand and took her face in both hands. Oh, the pain in those eyes! Tears slid down his cheeks as he held hers tenderly.

Then suddenly, without warning, his arms were around her neck, and he stepped forward, pulling her to him. He rested his hand behind her head. "Oh, thank you, Father! Oh, my dear, you are safe!" he sobbed. Her nose pressed into his shoulder and she stood there, stunned.

He swayed back and forth, heaving with sobs and blubbering about her coming home. He was not angry? Her mind screamed foul. It couldn't be! She should be punished! It was a trick—at any moment he would throw her against the wall and glare at her.

But he didn't. He just held her tight, lost in his own tears, and he told her that he loved her. He was moaning that now. That she was beautiful and that he loved her.

Helen lifted her hands and placed them slowly around his waist.

The sorrow and relief came like a flood, rising right through her chest and rushing out of her eyes. "I'm so sorry!" she cried. "I'm sorry, Jan." She kept repeating that and she cinched her arms around his waist.

They held each other for a long time there on the entry tile.

Then they stepped back and her eyes widened at the sight of his shirt. "Oh, my goodness!" she said, lifting a hand to her lips. "You're bleeding!"

He wiped his eyes and looked at his white T-shirt, now stained with red streaks. "So I am." Then he chuckled and spread his hands as if they were wet, still looking down. "I was just changing my bandages when you came."

She didn't see the humor but she chuckled with him. It seemed to fuel his own humor and he started laughing. Then they were laughing together. Looking at his bloodstained shirt and laughing together, out of pure, sweet relief.

Helen looked at his face—at his dark skin wrinkled around laughing hazel eyes; his teeth white in his delight, his hair swept back to his collar—and she knew she did not deserve him. Not this wildly handsome man giddy with joy at her return. She swallowed a lump that had gathered in her throat.

She helped him into the bathroom where together they finished changing his bandages. She winced at seeing the cuts and felt tears coming again. They slipped down her cheeks like a cleansing oil and he let her cry softly.

They didn't talk about Glenn that night. They did not talk about what had happened or about what they would do. They each had their own problems, that much needed no voicing. Instead they talked about the fact that the pool needed to be cleaned, and about Ivena's roses, and about why Cadillacs were really no better than Fords, a subject about which both were undeniably clueless.

And they laughed. They laughed until Jan insisted that he would split a stitch if they didn't control themselves.

THE NEXT morning drifted by like a dream for Helen. She'd slept in the suite downstairs and risen to the smell of bacon. Ivena was busy over the stove, smiling and humming her song. That song she'd said was the priest's favorite. Ivena had placed three settings about the table.

"Hello, Ivena," she said, coming up behind.

Ivena whirled around, incidentally flinging grease across the kitchen. "Helen! Oh, come here, child!" She waved her forward. "It is so good to have you home."

Helen stepped forward, unable to suppress a wide grin. "Good to be home," she said. They hugged each other and Helen helped by mixing up some orange juice. They ate breakfast together and laughed about things Helen could not remember, but they were certainly funny at the time.

She wandered about most of the morning, slowly disconnecting herself from the past, spending time with Jan and Ivena, pinching herself from time to time to make sure this was not some long hallucinogenic trip she'd taken. But it was not.

It was all real. The rose Ivena had brought smelled like a real rose, the ice clinked in the afternoon stillness, the tea tasted sweet to her tongue, the leather furniture felt cool to the touch, and the light sparkled in Jan's hazel eyes whenever he looked at her, which was at every possible opportunity. In all respects it proved to be a perfect morning.

They ate lunch together, the three of them, suspended by an air of unbelief at being together. And Jan could not seem to keep his eyes from her. When she finally excused herself for a nap, a shadow passed across his face, as if it were a great disappointment. She was falling in love with him, she thought. Not just loving, but falling. She couldn't remember feeling so strongly for one man. It was a good emotion.

HELEN'S RETURN came like a breath of life to Jan. He thought of it as her homecoming, even though this was obviously not her home. Actually, it felt like it should be her home. He had spent the night in peaceful sleep, wondering at the effect this one woman had on him. She had gone back to Lutz, yes. And she had spit on Jan, but none of that seemed to bear any weight in his mind. Instead he found himself dizzy over her choice to return here. She had chosen to come back!

Helen was now in *his* house, wandering around on those bare feet, shy, yet curious, spreading an air of expectancy wherever she stepped. And he was wondering why he should be so lucky to have her in his house. *Father, Father, what are you doing? What on earth have you done with this meddling of yours?*

They talked only once of Glenn Lutz, and then only in the context of the danger he might pose. Jan wanted to call for police protection, but Helen would still have none of it. Glenn would not be a problem, she insisted. She'd come to tears when Jan had pressed for her reasoning and left it at that. Poor Helen! Poor, poor dear! Ivena held her for a few minutes and brought comfort. It would be all right— the police already knew of the attack and not even Lutz would be so mad as to try a repeat. So Jan told himself. But he did check the window every hour just to be sure.

Thoughts of the movie deal came only sporadically. He had talked to Roald midday and the man seemed pleased with himself. Everything was back on track. Just get better, Jan. We miss you.

After lunch Helen excused herself to the apartment for a nap. Ivena announced that she too must leave for a few hours. Her flowers needed her touch. Jan found himself alone in the house, reading through parts of *The Dance of the Dead*, trying to guess what Helen thought as she read.

The doorbell suddenly echoed through the house, startling Jan. A salesman, perhaps. He set the book down, walked to the door, and pulled it open. Karen stood there. Karen! Dressed in a pure white blouse and a navy skirt, stunning and more beautiful than ever.

Jan felt his jaw drop and he barely had the presence of mind to close it before speaking. "Karen!"

"Hi, Jan. May I come in?"

Come in? Jan glanced back into the house instinctively. "Are you okay? Is there a problem?" she asked.

"No. No, of course you can come in." He stepped aside. "You just . . . I just . . . Come in, please."

She held his eyes for a moment and then stepped past the threshold and into the living room. Jan closed the door. "Roald told me what happened. I'm so sorry. Are you okay?"

"I'm fine, really."

She reached up and touched the head wrap very gently. "How bad is it? Shouldn't you be lying down?"

"Just a surface wound. I'll be fine, really."

"You sure?" She searched his eyes, genuinely caring, he thought.

"Yes. Would you like a drink?"

"Yes, that would be nice."

Yes, that would be nice, she said, and her voice carried sweet and lovely and terrible to Jan. He cut straight for the kitchen and pulled out a glass. *Yes, that would be nice.* Four years of affection were carried by that voice. He poured her a drink of iced tea and returned to the living room.

"Here you are," he said, handing the glass to her. They sat—he on his chair, she on the adjacent couch. Her brown hair rested on her shoulders, curling delicately around soft cheeks. Her eyes avoided him in the silence, but they were speaking already, saying that she wanted to make amends. That she was sorry for her outburst and that her life was miserable without him.

Then they were looking at each other, frozen in the heaviness. *She's thinking that I'm fixed by her beauty,* Jan thought. *She's thinking that I'm speechless because of my deep love for her.* Her perfume was musky and strong.

"Jan." Her eyes were moist. "Jan, I'm sorry. I am so sorry."

"No, Karen. No, it's I who should be sorry. I had no right. I don't know what to say—"

"Shhh." She put a finger to her lips and smiled. "Not now. And just know that if my imagination went wild it was because of my love for you. I would never hurt you. I don't want to hurt you."

Jan sat still, immobilized by her words. What had Roald told her? That Jan had sent Helen away? Yes, that's what he'd told her. Anything less and Karen would be demanding to know where Helen was. She was not a weak woman.

But he could see that she'd been deceived yet again. And she deserved far more. He had to tell her now. But the words were not flowing so easily.

"You were being mugged and here I was imagining that you were off with this woman." She laughed. "I should've known you better—forgive me. You were in the hospital and I was off steaming like a silly schoolgirl."

Roald had made the situation impossible. Now she was making it unbearable. And to make matters worse, Jan just smiled. He should have frowned and told her some things. Instead, he was sitting there smiling like a gimp. *Yuk, yuk, how silly of you, Karen.*

"I called the studio and explained what happened to you. They extend their best wishes."

He nodded. "Thank you. I . . . Thank you." *Now, Jan! Now.* "Maybe you should tell that to Roald. I'm not sure he's so understanding."

"Oh, I don't know. He's just concerned for you. The logical one, you know. For him it's a simple matter of mathematics. Deals like this come to the church only once every decade or so—you can't blame him for overreacting when something looks like it might interfere."

"He threatened to withdraw his support," Jan said.

"He did, did he? You see, he is overreacting. And maybe I had something to do with that. I think I convinced him that you had gone off the deep end with this woman." She smiled apologetically. "It was plain silly."

Now, Jan. You must tell her now! "Yes, but it still concerns me. Am I supposed to think that every time Roald doesn't agree with something, he'll threaten to withhold his support?"

"No."

"So then why would he make such a statement?"

"I'll talk to him about it." She paused. "But he *was* faced with this nonsense that I fed him. You shouldn't be so hard on him."

"Perhaps. But I don't see his right to threaten me. What if it were true? What if I had fallen for . . . well, for a woman like Helen, for example? Am I to assume that if I step over the wrong line I will be punished like a child?"

"No." Karen had tightened slightly. Or maybe it was just his imagination. "No, you're right. Like I said, I'll talk to him." She lifted her glass and let the liquid flow past her lips. She was lovely; he could not deny the fact. And she was a strong woman, though not strong enough to let his comment about Helen pass, hypothetical or not.

She spoke, smoothing her skirt, looking down. "It isn't true though, is it, Jan?"

"What isn't true?" he asked. He knew of course, and his heart was hammering in his chest.

"You're not in love with this woman." She looked at him. "With this Helen."

He would have answered. Sure he would have. What he would have said he'd never know, because suddenly it was neither his voice nor Karen's speaking in the stillness. It was another.

"Hello."

They looked toward the basement entrance together. She stood there with her blond hair in tangles, smiling innocently. Helen.

Helen! Heat washed down Jan's back. He shot a quick glance at Karen, who was staring, stunned. She'd never met Helen so she could not know . . .

Then Helen changed that as well. She walked forward and extended her hand to Karen. "Hi, I'm Helen."

Karen stood and mechanically reached out her hand. "This is Karen," Jan said. "Hi, Karen."

"Hello, Helen," Karen returned. But she wasn't smiling. Jan rose from his seat and they stood there awkwardly, Karen to his right and Helen to his left, staring at each other in very different ways. Helen as if wondering what the big deal was, and Karen as if she'd just been stabbed in the back with a ten-inch bowie. It was an impossible moment, but Jan knew that there was no chance of rescuing it.

And then he knew something else, staring at these two women side by side. He knew that he loved the woman on the left. He loved Helen. Somehow seeing them side by side, there was simply no question of it. It was the first time that he'd held both in his mind and seen their places in his heart. To Helen he was even now giving his love, and to Karen his empathy.

He cleared his throat. "Helen's staying with me for a few days while she gets back on her feet. I'm sorry, I should have told you."

Karen glared at him. "Back on her feet? And here I thought it was you who was receiving all the attention. Or is that bandage something you picked up at the dime store?"

"Karen . . ." He shook his head. "No, it's not like that—"

"Then what is it like, Jan? You take me for a fool?" The daggers from her eyes tore at his heart. *No, Karen! It's not like that! I do care for you!*

But you love Helen.

"Please—"

"Save your breath." She was already walking for the front door. "If you need me, do us both a favor and call Roald." Then, with a slam of the door, she was gone.

For a long moment Jan and Helen just stared at that closed door in silence. "Maybe I should go," Helen finally said.

"No! No, please don't leave me."

"She seemed so . . . hurt."

"But it's not you. It's me. It's my love for you."

She thought about that for a few moments, and then she came to him and put her head on his chest. "I'm sorry," she said.

"No, don't be." He stroked her hair. "Please don't be."

NEVER BEFORE had Helen felt so chosen. It was how she came to see the meeting with Karen. She'd been chosen by Jan. Not chosen as Jan's girl, necessarily, or even as the woman who belonged in this crazy scenario. Just . . . chosen. To think of it beyond that led only to confusion. And whom had *she* chosen? Glenn or Jan?

Jan.

On Thursday, Jan emerged without the head wrap. It had been a week since his attack; four days since his hospital visit; three days since Helen's return. The two-inch cut above his right ear was healing remarkably well. He carried himself like someone who'd just discovered a great secret, and Helen caught him looking at her strangely on occasion, as if there was something in her eyes that threw him for a loop. At times he seemed to have difficulty keeping his gaze from her. Not that she minded. Goodness, no! She didn't know what to do with it, but she certainly didn't mind.

He made mention of a man named Roald a few times, a man associated with his work. Something about the fact that Roald would just have to adjust. They seemed busier that day, eager for the day to run its course. Several times she heard Jan and Ivena talking in soft tones, and she let them have their space. If the talk concerned her, she didn't care. Actually, it probably did concern her—what else would they be discussing concerning the police and Glenn? But hearing this she wanted to interfere even less.

She continued her reading of *The Dance of the Dead*, and it struck her that the central character in the book was perhaps the most profound person she'd heard of or read about. The fact that his name was Jan Jovic and that he was in the next room talking to Ivena, the mother of the daughter, Nadia, was difficult to believe. The fact that he had winked at her no less than three times that very day was mind numbing. She had winked back, of course, and he'd turned red each time.

Ivena left at five o'clock, after a long talk with Jan in the backyard. They were up to no good, those two. "I will see you tomorrow, Helen," she announced wearing a grand grin. "Behave yourself and don't let Janjic out of your sight. He is trouble-prone, you know." She winked.

"I wouldn't dream of it, Ivena."

Jan walked up behind her. "We're not children, Ivena."

"I know. And this is supposed to comfort me?"

They laughed and Ivena was off in her little gray Bug.

She'd been gone for less than ten minutes before Jan entered the living room and made his grand announcement. "Helen, I think that you owe me a date. Am I right?"

She laughed nervously. "I guess."

"You guess? Either I am right or I'm not, my dear. Which is it?"

"You're right. I did stand you up, didn't I?"

"Well then, shall we?"

"Now?"

"Yes, now."

"To where?"

"Ah, but that would ruin my surprise."

"Wearing this?" she asked, indicating her jeans and T-shirt.

"You look lovely."

She stood, smiling nervously. "You're saying that you want to take me on a date now? Right now?"

"Yes. That's what I'm saying."

"You're sure?"

"I insist. Have I given you any other impression since you first came back?"

"No."

He smiled very wide. "Okay, then." He stretched out his hand.

Helen touched it . . . then took it. "Okay, then."

CHAPTER TWENTY-FOUR

IT HAD been a bad week for Glenn Lutz. A very bad week indeed.

Homicide detective Charlie Wilks and another cop, Parsons, sat across from him in black suede guest chairs, the only furniture in the office other than his desk. They sat with crossed legs, their hands in their laps, avoiding his direct glare, isolated in the top story of the East Tower. They, like the Atlanta sky beyond the great glass wall to their left, wore a gray pallor of death.

Glenn was losing his patience with them. In fact, he'd lost his patience long before their arrival, when Beatrice had first informed him that Charlie needed to see him. It meant that the slime-ball preacher had whined like some two-bit hooker.

"So you receive one call from some lowlife preacher and you come whimpering to me? Is that all the esteemed Atlanta police force is good for these days? Can't you go find yourselves a cat to haul from a tree or something?"

"If we were talking about one call from some lowlife preacher, we wouldn't be here and you know it, Glenn," Charlie returned. "We interviewed him in the hospital and we checked the guy out. He's one of the most popular religious figures in America." The detective nodded to a copy of *The Dance of the Dead* sitting on Glenn's desk. "A fact you seem to have familiarized yourself with already."

"Yeah, so the guy's a writer. Does that make his word better than mine? I thought we had an understanding."

"We do have an understanding. You keep your habits out of the public, and I won't throw any fits. This Jan character is definitely a public man."

"Actually, as I recall, the understanding was you keep your hands off and I get you elected."

Wilks smiled uneasily and turned pink around the collar. "Come on, Glenn. I'm not a magician. You can't expect me to keep my hands in my pockets every time you haul some upstanding citizen in and beat him up. Who's next, the mayor?"

"This punk's not the mayor, and I'm not saying that I did beat him. And as far as Mayor Burkhouse is concerned, he may be the mayor today, but you just remind him that he *is* up for re-election in nine months."

Charlie scowled briefly. "Come on, Glenn. Come on, man, we all go way back. All I'm saying is that there are ways and there are ways, you know what I mean? Not everyone's attention is best arrested by a club to the head. I don't need you upsetting the balance we have by making a public display of people like this Jan fellow."

Glenn looked at the detective and thought about reaching into the desk drawer for his revolver. Put a hole in that forehead. That was absurd, of course. He might have this city by the short hairs, but that was *because of,* not in spite of, men like Charlie here.

He glanced at the book on his desk. Jan Jovic was no louse. He'd been through more than most; had to hand him credit there. There was as of yet no conclusive evidence that Helen had gone back to him, but if it surfaced that she had, Glenn would have to kill the preacher, that much he knew with certainty. It was one thing for a man to stumble onto your possession and mistakenly think it his for a time. It was another thing for that man to be schooled in the matter for a couple of days and then still have the gall to take what was not his.

Glenn placed his hand on the book and tapped its red cover lightly. "This man isn't doing me any favors, Charlie. If he touches my girl, I'm gonna have to kill him. She's been gone for two days now, and if it turns out that she even went near him, I'm gonna have to put a slug in his head. You know that, don't you?"

Charlie lifted his hands in resignation. "No, I don't know that, Glenn. This guy made a complaint, for crying out loud! He turns up dead and I'm supposed to say what? 'Oh, well, let's never mind that one'?"

"He came here to threaten me. I defended myself. That's the story. And you watch your tone in my office! Do something useful—go find Helen. You should be turning this punk's house inside out but instead you're here telling me how to run my business."

Charlie shook his head slowly. "I can't cover up everything. Some things have a life of their own, and I'm telling you this is one of them."

The man needed a lesson in respect, Glenn thought bitterly.

"Did you know that Delmont Pictures just announced a movie deal with this guy?" Charlie asked. "That book there is slated to be on the silver screen soon, and you're sitting here talking about taking out its main character. You think I can cover that up?"

Glenn squinted. "Delmont Pictures? Delmont Pictures is making a film about *this* guy?"

"That's right. News to you, I take it. Maybe if you took a bath and got your head out of that powder now and then, you'd know what—"

"Shut up!" Glenn shoved a huge hand toward the door. "Get out!"

They stood to their feet. Detective Parsons was wide-eyed, but Charlie was not as easily influenced as he once was. He'd seen this all before—one too many times, it appeared.

"Out, out, out!" Glenn jabbed his forefinger at the door.

"We're getting out, Glenn. But you remember what I said. I can only do so much. Don't cut your own throat."

"Out!" Glenn thundered.

They left.

It had been a bad week. A very bad week indeed.

JAN DROVE the Cadillac in silence, his stomach floating with anticipation, exchanging amused glances with Helen and generally ignoring her questions as to their destination.

She had brought the magic into his house with those blue eyes, Jan thought. She had appeared at his doorstep dressed in her wrinkled dress, trying so hard to find acceptance, feeling despondent and puny, when all the while it was *she* who carried the power. *She!* It was a power to intoxicate with a single look. The magic to send him to the ground, weak-kneed, with a casual glance. The ability to squeeze his heart with the delicate shift of her hand. She could move her chin, just so, to ask for some more bacon or another glass of tea, and his breathing might thicken right there at the table. It was a raw power, maddening and exhilarating at once. And it was she who possessed it. *Helen.*

If she only knew this—if she could only grasp her hold over his thoughts, if she too could feel, actually *feel* this same love for him—they could rule the world together. Never mind that she was from the street, it was nothing in the face of these emotions that swept through him.

But she didn't know her own power, he thought. Not the way he knew it. Well, tonight that might change. And the thought of it made Jan's stomach rise to his chest as he pulled the Cadillac along the deserted drive, toward the dead end.

"This is it?" Helen asked.

"What time is it?"

"Almost seven."

"Let's hope we are not late."

A round white moon cast a perpetual twilight over a wall directly ahead, perhaps twelve feet in height, extending each way as far as Jan could see. Vines covered the barrier, thick and dark but still green by the bright moonlight. No other structures were in sight, only this tall fence. Jan stopped the car and turned off the ignition.

"This is it?"

He looked at her and winked. "Follow me, my dear."

They climbed out. "This way." He led her to a small gate buried in vines, cut from the wall, no more than five feet tall. Jan looked back and saw that she stepped lightly, her eyes wide and casting their spell without even looking at him. His heart was bucking already. *Father, this is what you mean. Yes?*

He rapped on a section of wood bared from vines. He glanced back and winked. "Jan Jovic is not a man without friends, my dear."

A muffled call answered and the gate swung in. Jan stooped and walked through the entrance, followed by a hesitant Helen. The man who'd opened the gate stood to Jan's shoulder and wore a smile that could have been stolen from a happy-face sticker. "Thank you, my friend. I won't forget this." He turned to Helen. "Helen, meet Joey, Atlanta's premier expert on botany. He's the gardener here. A friend of mine."

She took his hand and gazed about. "Where *are* we?"

They stood at the edge of a sprawling garden—a botanical garden with flowering trees and rosebushes and perfectly groomed hedges as far as they could see. Flagstones surrounded by tiny white flowers led deeper and then branched in three directions within twenty paces. Tall shaped trees stood like guardians over the prize below them; gazebos spotted the paths, each laden with red and blue and yellow flowers glowing by moonlight. It was a paradise.

"You ever hear of the Garden of Eden?" Joey asked. "This is the closest you'll find on earth today. Welcome to the Twelve Oaks Botanical Gardens, my friends. A gift from God with a little help from the taxpayers."

They looked about without responding. They could not respond, Jan thought. It was a breathtaking sight in the moon's surreal hue.

"You kids enjoy," Joey said with a wink. "Lock up when you leave." He walked down the path, around a bush and disappeared from their sight.

Jan stood there in the quiet and suddenly his heart was sounding loud in his ears. This was it. He prayed a silent prayer—*Father, if it is your desire, make it so.*

Then he grabbed her hand and ran onto the path. "Come on!" he cried breathlessly.

Giggling, she ran behind him. Her hand felt cool and soft in his. He was feeling everything. The breeze against his face, the flagstone underfoot, the sweet smell of flowers lifting through his nostrils. He released her hand and ran between two tall trees shaped like rockets poised for launch. A thick lawn opened before him and he veered to the right.

She chased him, squealing with delight now. "Jan! Don't lose me. Where are we going?"

"Come on!" he cried. "Come on!"

They raced through the garden; he without direction, only acutely aware of her breathing just behind and to his left; she gaining on him and that was good. *Catch me, my darling. Catch me and touch me.*

Then she did. She reached out and touched his side, still giggling. Her finger sent a chill through his skin. Jan pulled up and swung to her. Helen ran full into his arms. He held her and twirled around as if they were on a dance floor and this was an embrace in motion. She laughed and threw her head back.

It was the first time he had held her without tears and he thought his heart would burst from the joy of it. He wanted to say something—something smart or romantic, but he forgot how to speak in that moment. The moon shone on her neck, and her small Adam's apple bobbed barely as she laughed—it was this he saw and he couldn't stand its power over him.

It is only a whisper of what I feel, Jan.

The voice spoke in his mind and he nearly stumbled, mid-twirl. So then Ivena was right. It was beyond him. But then he knew that already. *I love you, Father.*

Jan broke away, laughing with Helen now, feeling more alive than he thought possible. He jumped into the air like a child. *I love you, Father! I love you, I love you, I love you!* Then he faced Helen and his love for her and the Father were nearly the same.

He winked at her and ran farther into the garden.

She flew after him; they were two birds frolicking in flight. They tore through the garden, falling into a sort of hide-and-seek on the run. It was the finding that attracted them, and they did it as frequently as possible, at nearly every bush large enough to conceal whoever led the chase until the other caught up for an embrace.

Jan plucked a yellow flower and placed it in her hair above her ear. She found it funny and picked another for his hair. Time was lost. Man had been created for this. It was the kind of thing a man might sell everything he owned for, Jan thought. But it could not be bought.

Spare me, Father, or I will die looking at her. You've put a fire in my heart and I cannot tame it. But no, don't quench it! Feed it. Feed it until it consumes me.

Robbed of breath from the run and aware for the first time that his wounds sent a slight ache through his chest, Jan swung into a gazebo and crashed back into a bench. She hopped into the seat opposite him and they sat sprawled, panting and laughing and looking at each other.

This is it, Jan thought. *This is what I have waited my whole life for. This madness called love.* He put his head back on the latticework, looked to the sky and groaned. "Oh, my dear God, it's too much."

He looked back at Helen. She was staring at him with a wide smile, catching her breath. "This is what I call a date, Jan Jovic."

"You like?" he asked, mimicking her customary verbiage.

"I like. I most definitely like."

"I couldn't think of a place more suited for you."

She sat up and leaned on both arms. "Meaning what, Wordsmith?"

"The flowers, the smell of sweet honey, the rich green grass, the moon—they're nearly as beautiful as you."

She blushed and turned to face the lawn. Goodness, that had been rather forward, hadn't it! He followed her gaze. He had not noticed before, but the lawn sloped to a fountain, surrounded by a glimmering pool. It was a warm night and a breeze drifted over the water to cool them. The rich smell of a thousand musky flowers lining the gazebo filled the air. In this very private garden they had found a secret place, hidden from the bright moon's direct glare but washed in its light.

"We're not so different, you and I," Jan said.

"We are very different. I could never measure up to you." She had grown sober.

"Nor I you."

"Don't be silly. You're a rich man," she said. "A good man."

"And your grace could not be bought with the wealth of kings."

She turned to him, grinning. "My, we *are* a wordsmith, aren't we?"

"There aren't words for you, Helen. Not ones which tell with any clarity what should be told."

Helen was staring at him now, her blue eyes swimming in the moonlight. She held him in her gaze for a long time before standing and walking to the gazebo's arching entrance to face the moon with her back to him. "This can't happen," she said softly. "We're from different worlds, Jan. You've got no idea who I am."

"But I do. You're a woman. A precious woman for whom all of heaven weeps. And my heart has joined them."

"Don't be crazy! It's too much. I have no business being here with you." The strain of tears had entered her voice. "I'm a drug addict."

He stood and approached her from behind. "And I am desperate for you." He couldn't help himself. He could not bear to hear her speak like this. His heart was pounding in his chest and he wanted only to hold her. The madness was so very heavy.

"I'm sick," she bit off bitterly. "I . . ."

And then she ran. She ran from the gazebo and around a row of short pines, crying in the night.

Oh, dear Father, no! This can't happen! Jan bolted after her. "Helen!" His voice rang in the night, desperate, as if braying in death.

"Helen, please!" He caught sight of her fleeing around a bush ahead and he tore after her. "Helen, I beg you, stop! You must stop, I beg you. Please!" He was near panic. How could she have swung in his arms one moment and now fled so quickly?

He saw her ahead, running fast in the moonlight and then disappearing around a billowing hydrangea. "Helen!"

Jan reached the bush, but she was not in sight. He ran on, looking in all directions for her, but she had vanished. "Helen! Please, Helen!"

The night echoed his call and fell silent. Jan pulled up, panting hard. He clutched his gut against a sharp pain that had speared him there. His vision blurred with tears, and he mumbled, "Oh, God, my God, my God, what have you done?"

The sound of a soft cry drifted to him and he spun to a row of gardenia bushes. He released his stomach, the pain forgotten, and he stumbled forward. The sound carried on the night, a soft gulping sob.

He rounded the flowers and stopped. She sat on a bench, head planted in her hands, crying. Jan walked to the bench on shaking legs. He sat and swallowed.

"I am so sorry for your pain, Helen. I am so very sorry."

"You don't understand. I'm no good for you," she said softly.

"I will decide what is good for me. *You* are good for me. You are perfect for me!" He placed a hand on her shoulder.

She pulled back. "I'm dirty. I'm—"

"You are clean and you have stolen my heart!" he blurted. "Helen, please look at me. Look into my eyes." He shifted around and lifted a hand to her chin.

She looked up, her face wrinkled in shame, her eyes swimming in tears.

"What do you see, Helen?"

For a moment she didn't speak.

"What do you see?"

She spoke very softly. "I see your eyes."

"And what do they say to you?"

She wiped her face, breathing steadily, catching her breath. "They say you're hurting."

"And why? Why am I hurting?"

She hesitated. "Because your heart aches."

He held her eyes in his stare, begging her to say more. To see more. A knot rose to his throat. *My poor Helen, you are so wounded.*

She had settled and she blinked. "Your heart aches for me," she said.

Jan nodded. "Put your hand on mine," he said, reaching his right hand out, palm up. She did so gently, without removing her gaze from his. Her touch seemed to run right up his bones and lock itself around his heart.

"Do you feel that?"

She didn't respond, but she moved her hand slightly. Their breathing sounded loud in the night.

"What do you feel?"

She swallowed and he noted that both of their hands were trembling with the touch. Her eyes were pooling with tears again.

"How does it feel?"

"It feels nice."

"And when I speak to you, when I say, '*I am mad about you,*' what do you feel, Helen?" He was having difficulty speaking for the pounding of his own heart.

"I feel mad about you," she said. He couldn't be certain, but he thought she might have leaned forward slightly, and that made him dizzy.

Jan reached his free hand to her cheek and stroked it gently. He slid his other hand up her arm now, and every nerve in his body screamed out for her love. She *was* leaning forward! She was leaning forward and the tears were slipping silently down her cheek.

Jan could not hold himself any longer. He slid his arms around her shoulders and drew her against him. The tears flooded his eyes then. She pushed him back and for one terrible moment he wondered what she was doing. But her lips found his and they kissed. They held each other tenderly and they kissed deep.

It was as though he had been created for this moment, he thought. As though he were a man parched bone-dry in a desert, and now he had fallen upon a pool of sweet water. He drank deep from that pool, from her lips. From this deep reservoir of love. The moments stretched, but time had lost itself in their passion.

It is only a whisper of how I feel, Jan.

The voice again. Softly. Gently.

Jan released her and they played with each other's fingers, lightheaded, shy. "It feels too good to be true," Helen said. "I've never felt this kind of love."

He did not respond but reached for her and kissed her lightly on her lips again. His heart was kicking madly against his chest; if he wasn't careful he might fall over dead right here in Joey's Garden of Eden.

Jan rose to his feet and pulled her up. "Come."

They walked through the hedges, hand in hand, lovers numb from each other's touch. Everything they saw now had a heavenly glow. The flowers seemed unnaturally bright by the moon's light. Their senses ran sharp edges, feeling and tasting and smelling the air as if it were laden with a potion concocted to squeeze their hearts.

They walked laughing and giggling, stunned that such care had been taken for their benefit. Anyone watching might very well see them and think them drunk. And truth be told they *were* drunk. They had sipped from each other's lips and were inebriated beyond their reason. It was a consuming love that swept them through the garden. They might have tried walking on the pond had it come to mind.

And yet for Jan, it was all just beginning. He had not brought her to the garden for this alone. Not at all. They reached a white metal pillar at the end of a long flowered archway and he knew it was time. If it was not now it might be never, and it definitely could not be never.

He gripped the pole and swung himself around to face her. She pulled up, surprised, with not an inch to spare between them. Her musky breath covered his nostrils. Her eyes flashed blue, and her lips impulsively reached forward and touched his. "I love you, Jan Jovic," she whispered. "I love you."

"Then marry me," he said.

She froze and pulled back. Their eyes held each other, round and glazed. Jan pushed a strand of hair from her cheek with his thumb. "Marry me, Helen. We are meant to be one."

Her mouth opened in shock, but she could not hide the smile. "Are you serious?"

"I'm madly in love with you. I've been madly in love with you from the time you walked up to me at the park. I can't imagine spending my days without you. I am meant to be with you. Anything less would destroy me."

She blinked and looked into his eyes. "I . . . I don't know what to say."

"Say yes."

"Yes."

He kissed her. His world began to explode then, and he knew he could not contain the passion that racked his bones. He had to do something, so he stepped back and leaped into the air. He whooped and beat the air with his fist. Helen laughed and hopped on his back. He cried out in surprise and not a little pain, and then collapsed to the sod. They lay there panting, smiling up at the stars and then at each other.

It was the end of a long journey, Jan thought. A very long journey that began with the priest's departure to heaven and now deposited him here, in a heaven of his own.

But it was also just the beginning. He knew that too, and a fleeting terror sliced through his mind. But the intoxicating lips of his new bride-to-be smothered him with a kiss, and the terror was lost.

For now, the terror was lost.

THE PHONE rang five times before Ivena picked it up. "Hello."

"Morning, Ivena."

"Good morning, Joey."

"How's the garden?"

"Good. Very good."

"And the flowers?"

"Growing."

"The tests came back today, Ivena."

She didn't respond.

"It's an unknown species."

"Yes."

"They're . . . extraordinary, you know." He cleared his throat. "I mean very unusual."

"Yes, I know."

"My flower has taken root."

Silence filled the phone.

"Ivena?"

"Then guard it well, Joey. It's not for everyone to see."

"Yes, I think you're right. Do you want to hear what I found?"

She hesitated. "Not now. Come over and explain it to me sometime. I have to go now, Joey."

"You okay, Ivena?"

"I've never been better. Never."

BOOK THREE

THE LOVER

"As a bridegroom rejoices over his bride,
so will your God rejoice over you."

ISAIAH 62:5 NIV

"I remember the devotion of your youth,
how as a bride you loved me . . ."

JEREMIAH 2:2 NIV

CHAPTER TWENTY-FIVE

Three Months later

GLENN LUTZ stormed through the walkway between the Twin Towers like a bull, panting from the exertion, his hands red with blood. The passage was not air-conditioned and Atlanta's late-day heat pressed through his skin. He was slipping into the boiling waters of madness and there was no life preserver in sight. Even the violence he periodically delivered to some unsuspecting soul who crossed him no longer eased his fury. Detective Charlie Wilks had approached him three times in the last month, begging him to ease up. Well now he could expect another call, just as soon as the detective learned of the whipping he'd just administered. Beating the mayor's third cousin to a pulp had a ring of absurdity to it, which was perhaps why Glenn had not been able to resist.

Maybe one day he would take his whip to old Charlie—now there would be a smart move. His relationship with the man wasn't as cozy as it once had been. One of these days Charlie might forget their past altogether and send in a hit squad. Which was why Glenn *had* gone easy. Which was why he had left the preacher alone. Which was why he hadn't gone out with a Tommy gun and sawed through Jan.

Glenn slammed through the door to his office. "Beatrice!" She wasn't here. He swore, crossed to his desk and punched the intercom. "Beatrice, get in here. Bring a towel."

He held his hands up, careful not to make too much of a mess. His knuckles glistened red; half of the blood was probably his own.

Beatrice walked in, took one look at his hands, and *tsked.* "You really should stop this nonsense, you know. Let her go." She tossed him the white towel. "You have a luncheon tomorrow; you think people won't notice skinned knuckles?"

He wiped his hands without answering her. Beatrice was growing as bold as Charlie. She sat in one of the guest chairs across from his desk and studied him condescendingly, as if she were his mother. He slid into his chair. It was an odd relationship, this depending so completely on someone you detested so much. And in truth, besides Helen, she was his dearest friend. It was a horrible thought.

"But I take it you aren't going to let her go her way, are you?" Beatrice said.

"Her way is my way."

"On occasion, obviously, or she wouldn't keep coming. But she is married to another man now. She's been married to him for two months, and I don't see divorce papers floating around anywhere. She's chosen him."

Glenn crashed his fist on the desk. "She has *not* chosen him! He's a witch!"

"He's a religious man," she corrected. "And I thought I was the witch."

"Same thing. No one could have swept her off her feet like that."

"Maybe it would be best if she was faithful to him. Best for you, that is."

He stared at her and scowled.

They sat in silence for a few moments, she swinging one leg over the other with hands folded; he mulling over a mental image of his fists smashing into that long face.

"You should find yourself another woman, Glenn," Beatrice said.

"And you should find yourself some sense, Beatrice. There is no replacement for Helen. You know that."

"Why? Because of something that happened twenty years ago? Because you were called Peter then and were possessed by an adolescent obsession for her? You're no longer fifteen, Glenn. And Helen is no longer the prom queen. I could find you a dozen girls far better than her."

"Uhhh!" He grunted and slammed both fists on the desk top once. Then twice. He frowned at her. "Do you know why I make in a single day what you'll never make in your entire life, Beatrice? I'll tell you why. Because I know how to get what I want, and you don't even *know* what you want! Because I *am* obsessed! And you are possessed. *I* own you. You remember that."

She blinked at the reprimand.

He leaned back and closed his eyes, furious with her. In fact he did feel possessed at times, unable to function for the voices in his head. But it had been the same for as long as he could remember. When he first caught sight of Helen across the hall in junior high, for example, wearing her navy skirt and sucking on a lollipop.

Her image danced over the rope in his mind's eyes, blue skirt flapping in slow motion. *One, two, buckle my shoe; three, four, close the door; five, six, peek-a-boo, guess who I am; that's right, and you ain't seen nothing yet.*

"I'm going to help her out," Glenn said, shifting his eyes toward the glass wall on his left. It had been two months coming and now it was time. Charlie could go suck on a tailpipe. He'd played by the fool's rules long enough.

"You're going to help her out? And how are you going to help Helen out?"

Glenn did not look at her. "I'm going to give her a little motivation."

"The movie deal?"

"Yes. But . . . more."

He could hear her breathing in the stillness now. It was the way he said *more*, he thought. As in, much more. As in terribly much more. He faced Beatrice now, pleased that she had kept silent.

"They say that the path to some women's hearts runs through the skull," he said quietly.

"They say that?"

"I say that."

"Charlie won't sit by if you hurt the preacher."

"Who said anything about the preacher?"

She shifted in her seat, all two hundred pounds of her, squirming. Glenn smiled and spoke softly before she could ask another question. "I'm telling you this so that you'll quit flapping your jaw, Beatrice. Soon this'll all be over. I'm going to force the issue. So you can shut your hole, and be a good witch."

She stared him down, but not with her usual backbone. His power had softened her some, he thought. She still wasn't speaking.

"But yes, the movie deal. I want the movie deal done this week. Can we do that?"

"Maybe. Yes," she said.

"I don't care what it takes, Beatrice. Anything, you understand?"

"Yes. This does not sound especially smart, Glenn."

His hands trembled on the desk, but he said nothing.

"Does she know who you really are?"

Shut up, Beatrice! Shut up, you fat weasel! Glenn bit his tongue to keep the thoughts from blurting out. "No. No, she doesn't know anything. And in truth, neither do you. Not even close."

Beatrice stared at him for a full five seconds and then stood and left the room, waddling like a black duck.

Glenn exhaled slowly and rested his head back on the chair, thoughts of Beatrice already dismissed. It was Helen who filled his mind again. Helen, who had evaded him for so long. Helen, who was about to learn who her lover really was. Helen, that two-timing sick worm. Helen, sweet, sweet Helen.

HELEN SET the breakfast table carefully, humming absently. Outside, the morning birds chirped and skittered about the large willow's branches. It had rained in the night, leaving the air cool and the shrubs glistening, washed of the summer dust. A scattering of leaves drifted on the pool's glassy surface. *I'm home,* Helen thought. *This is my home.*

It struck her that the tune she'd been humming was the old hymn Ivena often sang: "Jesus, Lover of My Soul." Antique lyrics but a rather catchy tune once you let it set in. To think that two months ago she'd never even heard the tune. And now here she was, bouncing around Jan's kitchen—her kitchen—wearing a pink house robe, arranging place settings and orange juice for two.

She had heard of whirlwind romances before but hers and Jan's had been a tornado. A storybook affair, scripted perfectly with everything except the glass slippers. Even the wedding had been fanciful, under a bright sun in that very garden—Joey's Garden of Eden—with a minister and thirty or so witnesses, exactly four weeks to the day after Jan had asked for her hand. And these first seven weeks had drifted by in a hazy bliss. Nearly perfect.

Nearly.

"Good morning, dear." Helen started and spun to his voice. Jan stood less than a step from her, smiling warmly, dressed to kill in a crisp white shirt and a red tie. A dusting of gray swept along the sides of his wavy dark blond hair, disheveled above those bright hazel eyes. Her handsome Serb.

He stepped forward and kissed her forehead. "How's my peach tree?"

She chuckled and kissed his chest without answering. He was like this always—loving and warm and saturated with passion for her. His love leaked from every pore of his body. And she was not worthy of it. Not she.

"Good morning. Sleep well?"

"Like a baby. You know I still haven't had the dream—not once in three months. Twenty years like clockwork, and then you walk into my life and the dreams end. Now tell me you're not a gift from God himself."

"What can I say? Some of us have it and some of us don't. I made us some breakfast," she said, grinning. He slid onto his chair at the table's head and lifted his glass of orange juice with a wink. "And you most definitely have it." He took a long drink and set the glass down with obvious ceremony and a long sigh.

"Perfect," he said. "It's the perfect drink for the occasion."

"Occasion? What occasion?"

"It's been seven weeks. Seven. The number of perfection, you know. They say that if your first seven weeks go without a hitch, you're in for another seven years without a single conflict."

She smiled. "I've never heard any such thing," she said.

"Hmm. Maybe because I made it up. But it's a good saying, don't you think?"

She joined him, laughing now despite herself. "You see things too simplistically, honey." *Honey.* She was calling this man such an endearing term and it suddenly struck her as odd, in light of what he did not know. But he was that and more. Far more. A perfect man. He was looking at her now, across the table as he often did, obviously pleased at the sight of her. She tried not to notice, but failed with a blush.

She directed the conversation to more rote matters. "So what do you have on your plate today?"

"Today. Today it's business as usual, but I have to fly to New York on Friday."

Helen blinked. "Again? You were just there three days ago." Her heart quickened at the revelation.

"Yes, I was. And I'm sorry to leave you alone in the house again so soon. But Delmont Pictures called last night and insisted we make this meeting. I'm sure it's nothing. You know these movie people; everything's always urgent." He grinned as if she should find some amusement in that. But her mind was already nibbling at the notion of having another weekend alone.

"Perhaps Ivena could come and stay the weekend with you," Jan suggested, biting into his cereal.

"No. No, I'll be okay." Helen returned his smile. "I might as well get used to it. It comes with marrying a star, I suppose," she teased.

He tossed his head back and laughed. "Nonsense. And if you married a star, then I married a queen."

She giggled with him and picked at her breakfast. *Oh, dear Jan, please do not leave me alone!*

"Besides," she said, "I'm not sure Ivena would cotton to being torn away from her garden for a whole weekend. Is it just me or is she obsessive?"

Jan chuckled. "She is taken with it, isn't she? You know, since our marriage I don't think I've even been in her greenhouse. In fact I've only been in her house once or twice. We really should visit her more often."

"She visits us all the time. I think she likes it that way. But still, she seems to have changed."

"In what way?"

"I don't know. She always seems to be in a hurry to get home. Preoccupied."

"I haven't noticed. But then my mind's been on another woman these past few months."

"Well, at least you've got that right." They laughed and picked at their breakfast.

"You're all right when I leave you, aren't you, Helen?" Jan asked.

"Yes, of course. Sure, of course. Why wouldn't I be?"

He grinned. "A beautiful woman like you? If another man even glances in your direction while passing on the street, you tell me. I will discipline him, I promise. With my belt or a paddle."

"Don't be silly. You'll do no such thing." He was such a lovely man. In moments like this he could take her breath away with those crazy comments.

"Still, you are a beautiful woman. Please be careful."

"Don't worry, my ever-protective lover. I will behave." Helen said it and then diverted the discourse again. "Roald will be there?"

"In New York? Roald and Karen both."

"Karen?"

"Yes, Karen."

"So you'll see her again."

"In a matter of speaking. At a meeting. She *is* still the agent of record on this picture, and she stands to gain or lose a tremendous amount of money, depending on how well it does. Not that money was ever Karen's primary motivation."

"No, you were," Helen said with a smile. "Or maybe your status was."

"Perhaps. Betty tells me that she's seeing someone in New York. A producer. It was just as well she moved back."

"Well, you don't need her in the office anyway. You have Betty and the others."

"It's still a bit quiet. Roald's been to the office only twice since . . ."

"Since you married the tramp," Helen filled in.

"Nonsense!"

"You know that's how he feels. Don't worry, I'm used to it."

"And you shouldn't be used to it." His face was suddenly red. "Ever!"

"Okay, Jan." She couldn't help her smile.

He exhaled and continued. "Anyway, you're right: the others have been very supportive. It's nearly like the old days, only without Roald and Karen. And actually, you'd never know anything had changed by the flow of money. I'll tell you, Helen, I've never seen so much money. When you deal in millions, the world changes. Speaking of which, your Mustang is due in at the dealership today. Should I have it picked up?"

"Serious?"

"It is what you asked for, isn't it? A red convertible?"

"Yes."

"Then it's in. I'll have Steve pick it up."

She looked at him with a sense of wonder. It was hard to believe that she actually owned half of what he did, which was a lot now. And it wasn't bothering him one bit. The Mustang was the least of it. They had spent the first week in Jamaica and there Jan had begun with the gifts, each given as if it were but a small token of his love. A diamond necklace over a candlelight lobster dinner, a pair of sparkling emerald earrings on a moonlit beach, impossibly expensive perfume under her pillow. A dozen others. But it was the new home he had conceived for her—the castle, he liked to call it—that often lit his eyes. A home twice the size of this meager cottage. One fit for his bride, nothing less would do. He'd already purchased the forty acres on which construction was slated to begin in one week. Two months ago the expense would have been unthinkable. But to hear Jan speak of it, now anything less would be beneath them. It consumed most of his energies these days. The book, the movie, the money; they were the fruits of love. And there seemed to be no reasonable limits to his desire to express his love. She was his obsession.

And not his alone.

Jan looked out the window. "You know, if it wasn't for all this money, I wonder if Roald would have carried out his threats. I think he and his boys are still fuming under their collars, but the money has silenced them. Not that I'm complaining; they've done well to keep the matter private. Karen too. But I wonder where they would be without the money."

"You question their belief in you?"

"I never would have thought so, but I don't know now. Not everyone is as understanding or noble as you, my dear."

Noble? *No, Jan. I may have captured your heart, but I am not noble.*

"Money is the glue that holds us all together now," he said. "The ministry, the movie, the book—it all seems to have boiled down to a few million dollars."

"Wars have been fought for less," she said.

"True enough. But I think that when this movie is over, both Roald and Karen will be out of our lives. Of course, we won't need them, will we? We have enough now to live our lives out in comfort in our new home. I will be free to travel at leisure, speaking as I like. Not even their rumors will affect us."

"Sounds good to me." She stopped. "What rumors?"

He blinked. "Rumors. They're nothing."

"They're about me?"

He hesitated.

"They're about me. Tell me."

He sighed. "An article was written in a leading evangelical periodical, casting suspicion on any religious leader that would marry a woman with . . . how did they say it . . . questionable morals. You see, that is what they say. But they don't know you. And they certainly don't know me. And besides, like I said, as soon as the movie is made, it won't matter."

Heat washed over Helen's face. They were asinine! Hypocrites! When had one of them ever reached out to her with Christ's love? Even after she'd publicly prayed for forgiveness in Jan's church. And she had done it with complete sincerity, yet now these leaders were turning on her, openly questioning her morals? Men were such pigs. Churched or unchurched, they were evidently all the same. Except Jan, of course. Guilt nipped at her.

And if he were to discover the truth she might have to slit her wrists!

"You're right," Jan said to her silence. "It's absurd. It means nothing. Helen, look at me."

She did, feeling small and dumb at his table, but she did look at him. His eyes were sad and his mouth held a slight smile. "You must know one thing, my dear Helen. You are more precious to me than anything I could possibly imagine. Do you understand? You are everything to me."

She nodded. "Yes, I know that. But the world obviously doesn't share your feelings. It's a bit awkward being the hated half of a celebrity known for his love."

"No, no, no. Don't say that. Some love my book; some hate my book. It's not me they love or hate. And just because a few religious men take exception to you doesn't mean the whole world hates you." He grinned mischievously. "In fact, sometimes I think my own staff prefers you to me."

"Yeah, well that's Betty and John and Steve. But I swear, the church people . . ." She shook her head.

"And the church leaders are not the church, Helen. We are all the church. You and I. The bride of Christ. And you, my dear, are my bride."

His smile was infectious and she returned it. Jan threw his napkin on the table. "I have to go." He rounded the table and took her face in both of his hands. They were large, tender hands that had been brutalized by war and now took nothing for granted. "I love you, Helen," he said.

"I love you, Jan."

"More than words," he said, and he bent down.

She closed her eyes and let him kiss her lightly on her lips.

If you only knew, Jan.

He released her face and when she opened her eyes, he was already at the front door. He turned there. "Helen, when I am gone, be careful. Guard your heart. I could not bear to lose it," he said. Then he smiled and left without waiting for a response.

Helen was not so accustomed to praying, but she prayed now. "Oh, dear God, help us. Please, please, help us. Please help me."

CHAPTER TWENTY-SIX

IVENA STEPPED from her home Friday evening and took a long pull of fresh air into her lungs. The heat had been tempered by rains over the past few days, and looking at the boiling skies, she thought it would rain again tonight. Janjic had gone off to some meeting in New York again. Perhaps she would call Helen and ask her if she would like to come for a visit later. She was a bottle of heaven, Janjic's girl. And in some ways she was Ivena's girl too.

Ivena locked the door and stepped past her rosebushes onto the sidewalk. A black car rolled by slowly, headed in the same direction as she, toward the park three blocks west. A man looked absently at her from the side window. Thunder rumbled on the far horizon. The breeze swept through a row of huge leafy spruce trees across the street, like a green wave. Yes, it would rain soon but she wanted to walk for at least a few minutes.

Her mind buzzed with the awareness that he was near. That God was near. In fact, not since the days following Nadia's death so many years ago had God been so close. And when God was near, the human heart did not fare so well, she thought. It tended to turn to mush.

Ivena looked back to her small house with its greenhouse hidden behind the tall white fence. He was certainly in there, crawling all over his jungle of love. She stopped and faced the house, tempted to return to the garden. To the flowers and the aroma that could no longer be contained by the glass walls. The green vines had taken over not only the garden but her own heart, she thought. To step into the room was like entering the inner court, the bosom of God. She'd smelled the flowers a block from home once and feared someone had broken in. She'd run all the way only to find them swaying in the light breeze that sometimes moved through the room. She never had found its source.

Ivena turned and continued on her walk; she needed the exercise.

She could not be gone from the garden too long without being overcome by a yearning to return. And she had noticed something else. She was remembering things very clearly for some reason. Remembering the expression on her daughter's face when that beast Karadzic had pulled the trigger. Remembering the even drawing of Nadia's breath. And the slight smile. "I heard the laughter," Nadia had said.

"Oh, Father, show me your laughter," she mumbled quietly, walking with her arms wrapped around herself now.

Boom!

Ivena flinched. It was thunder, but it might as well have been the bullet to Nadia's head.

She sighed. "You know that I love you, Father. It still does not seem right that you've taken Nadia before me. Why must I wait?"

One day she would join her daughter and that day could not possibly come quickly enough. But it would not be today. For one thing, her body was showing no signs of slowing down. It might be another fifty years before natural causes took her. For another thing, she had a part to play in this drama about her. This passion play. She knew that like she knew that blood flowed through her veins, unseen but surging with life.

Nadia had heard the laughter of heaven, and the priest had *laughed* the laughter of heaven, right there on the cross, begging to go. Now Janjic had heard the heavens weeping.

And then Christ had planted his love for Helen in Janjic's heart.

Once Ivena understood that, she'd known that she was in a passion play. They were walking through Solomon's Song. Solomon's garden, more likely. A sprinkling of love from heaven, for the benefit of the mortals who wandered about, oblivious to the desperate longing of their Creator.

"And what of me, Father? When will I hear so clearly?"

Nothing but distant rumbles answered her. She reached the park's entrance and decided to walk once around before returning home, hopefully before the rain.

This drama unfolding behind man's eyes was a great thing. Much greater than the building of grand cities or towering pyramids. Greater than the winning of wars. It had a feel of far loftier purpose. As if the destiny of a million souls hung in the balance of these few lives. Of Janjic's story, *The Dance of the Dead.* Father Micheal, Nadia, Ivena, Janjic, Helen, Glenn Lutz—they were the main players here on earth. And the masses lived in ignorance of the struggle, while their own future was being decided.

The how and why were lost on Ivena. Only this vivid sense of purpose. But one thing she did know: This passion play was not over. Janjic may make his movie, but the story was not yet complete. And now she was being called to play a larger role. She did have the benefit of the garden, but as astounding as that was, she yearned for more. For a glimpse of heaven itself.

"Show me, Father. You cannot show me? You showed Nadia and Father Micheal and Janjic. Now show me. Don't leave me out here in the wind by myself."

The park was vacant except for her, she saw. That car she'd seen drive by sat parked near the outbuildings to her right, but she saw no people. It was a warm wind that blew through her hair, carrying the smell of freshly mowed grass. It reminded her of the smells from the garden in which Janjic and Helen were wed. A smile bunched her cheeks at the memory. Janjic had invited some of his closest friends and all of his employees to a dinner party, explained his heart and then presented his fiancée.

They were a conservative lot for the most part, and they had gawked at dear Helen as if she were from a newly discovered culture. But Betty, the motherly one, had given a rousing speech in the defense of love. It had quelled their doubts, she thought. At least some of their doubts. The rest had slowly faded in the weeks following. It was not every day that a man as respectable as Janjic reversed his engagement for another woman. Especially after only two weeks.

The ceremony had been simple and stunning. The setting was idyllic, yes, with all those flowers and perfectly manicured bushes, but it was the sight of Janjic and Helen together that turned the event into an unforgettable day. Her dear Serb simply could not keep his eyes from his bride. He stumbled through the day grinning from ear to ear, responding slowly when spoken to, terribly shy and thoroughly smitten. It was enough to keep the entire party in a perpetual blush. If only they knew the truth—that this display was nothing less than a clumsy mortal's attempt to contain a few cells from God's heart in his own.

Their love hadn't stopped there, of course. The two were inseparable. Yet, regardless of Janjic's love, he was still human. As human as ever and sometimes more, Ivena thought.

And Helen . . . Helen was categorically human.

A shadow shifted to her left and Ivena turned. Two men approached her, large men dressed in black cotton pants, looking past her at something. They had appeared rather suddenly, she thought. A moment ago the park was empty, and now these two strode toward her, now less then ten feet off. How was that possible?

She continued to walk and turned to her right to see what had caught their attention. But there was nothing.

Ivena had just started to turn back when a hand clamped around her face. They had come right to her! "Hey!" Her cry was stifled by a piece of cloth. The man was suffocating her! *Oh, dear God, these men are attacking me!*

"Hey!" she cried again, both arms flailing. Her voice was completely muffled by the hand this time, but she did manage to hit something soft and she heard a grunt.

A sharp metallic smell stung her nostrils, right through her sinuses. They were drugging her! Ivena's mind began to swim. Thunder rolled again, louder this time, unless that was how it felt to be drugged. Black clouds obscured her vision. She screamed at them then, but she knew that nothing was coming out. It was a wail in her own dim world.

Am I dying? Am I dying? she asked.

But Ivena did not know, because her question stopped in a pool of darkness. She slumped in her attacker's arms.

THE RAIN crashed down in sheets, bringing twilight an hour early to Atlanta. Helen stood by the sliding door to the backyard and watched droplets dance furiously on the pool's surface. Behind her the house lay in dim shadows, silent except for the dull roar of rain. She should really turn on the lights, but she lacked the motivation to move just now.

Jan had left for New York. He would be up to his eyeballs in meetings right now, being important. Being the star. *I need you, Jan. I need . . .*

You need what, Helen? Jan? Or the feelings he will bring you? Call Ivena.

She ground her teeth. The urges had started at noon, a muddled mix of desire and horror stuffed in her chest. She wasn't physically addicted, she knew that because she'd broken her addiction in those first four weeks of abstinence, with the help of a drug counselor, as Jan called him. Still, her mind was craving; her *heart* seemed hooked. She didn't understand how all of that worked, but she did know that her mind was hooked. She couldn't break the mad desperation that raged through her veins. Physical dependence would've been easier, she thought. At least with it, she would have an excuse people might understand.

But this craving was maybe worse. It was through her whole being.

Yet it was more than just the drug. Helen wanted the Palace. That horrible, terrible, evil place. That wonderful place. It was this realization that made her cringe.

You should call Ivena, Helen.

No! Helen spun from the door. She made her decision in that moment, and the shackles of her desperation fell away. She ran for the phone and snatched it from the wall. Now it was only desire that flooded her mind, and it felt good. God, she had missed that feeling. No, not God . . . She sealed the thought from her mind.

The witch answered the phone. "Beatrice. It's Helen."

Glenn's assistant drew a breath. "Yes?"

"Can you send a car?"

"The wench wants to return, is that it? And what if Glenn's not here?"

"Is he?"

Silence. The woman obviously wanted to say no. But her silence had answered already. "You don't know what you're messing with, honey."

"Shut up, you old witch. Just get me a car. And don't take all day."

She heard a few mumbled expletives. The phone went dead.

Helen hung up and retreated to the window, biting at her nails. Her heart thumped in anticipation now. The rain pelted in sheets, covering the concrete in a thick mist of its own splatter. It was like a shield, this dark rain. What happened now would be gone when the sun came out.

She ran about the house, turning on lights with trembling hands. She changed quickly into jeans and a yellow T-shirt. When the car pulled up fifteen minutes later, Helen bolted from the house, yanked the rear car door open, and plowed in. The driver was Buck. She leaned back in the safety of the dark cabin and breathed deep. The rich smell of cigarette smoke filled the car.

"Got a cigarette I can bum, Buck?"

He handed a pack of Camels back without answering. She lit one and drew on the tobacco. Rain thundered on the roof. The smoke filled her lungs and she smiled. She was going home, she thought. Just for a visit, but she was definitely going home.

They parked in the Tower's garage ten minutes later and rode the private elevator. It clanged to a stop at the top floor, and Helen stepped in the causeway that led to the Palace. "Go on in," Buck said. "He's waiting for you."

He was waiting? Of course he was waiting! Glenn would be waiting on his knees. And Jan . . . She snuffed out the thought.

She crept down the empty hall, expecting to see the witch at any time. But Beatrice wasn't here to greet her. Helen stopped at the entry door and tried to calm herself. But her pulse was having none of it. *This is insane, Helen. This is death.* It was the last thought before the door swung in under the pressure of her hand.

Helen entered the Palace.

Music greeted her. A soft rhythmic saxophone; the sound of Bert Kampfort, Glenn's choice of sensual tunes. The lights glowed in hues of red and yellow. It was hard to believe that she'd been here just last weekend and still the atmosphere was crashing in on her like a long-lost wave of pleasure. The dance floor reflected slowly turning pinpoints of light from the overhead mirrored ball.

"Helen."

Glenn! She spun toward the voice. He stood by the couch under the lion's head.

"Hi, Glenn." Helen stepped onto the floor. He wore his white polyester slacks, barefoot on the thick carpet. A yellow Hawaiian shirt hung loosely on his torso. His sweaty lips were peeled back in a wide grin, revealing his crooked teeth. This part of him—this dirty smelly part—had not stayed in her memory so well, but it came raging to the surface now. She needed the drugs. They would dull the edges.

Helen stopped three paces from him and saw for the first time the wet streaks on his cheeks. He had been crying. And it was not a grin but a grimace that twisted his face. His legs were shaking.

"Glenn? What's wrong? Are you okay?"

He sat heavily to the couch, crying openly now.

"Why are you crying?"

"You're killing me, Helen," he growled through clenched teeth. And then like a lost boy, "I can't stand it when you're gone. I miss you so much."

He was sick, she thought, and she wasn't sure whether to feel sorrow or revulsion for him. Large sweat stains darkened the pits of his shirt and she smelled the stench from his underarms. "I'm sorry, Glenn . . ."

He grunted like a hog and shot out of the seat in a blur of rage. His fist slammed into her solar plexus and she folded over his arm. Pain speared through her stomach. His fist crashed down on the crown of her head and she fell flat to the floor.

"You are killing me!" he screamed. "Don't you know that, Helen? You're killing me here!"

She curled into a ball, trying desperately to breathe.

"Helen? Do you hear me? Answer me." He knelt over her, breathing hard.

"Are you okay, dear?" He leaned close, so that his breath washed over her face. She caught a snatch of air and moaned.

A hot wet tongue slid up her cheek. He was licking her. Licking her face. She squelched a sudden urge to turn and bite his tongue off. It would be her death.

"Helen, my dear, I missed you so much."

She could breathe now and she feigned a giggle. "Glenn, dear. Give me some dope. Please."

"You want some dope, honey?" he asked, as if she were his baby.

"Yes."

"Beg."

"Please, Glenn." She kissed him.

He leaped from the floor like a child now. "I have a surprise for you, Helen. What do you want first, the dope or the surprise?" She pushed herself to her knees. His eyes glinted with delight.

She ran a finger along his arm seductively. "You have to ask? You know how much I like to fly, honey."

He threw his head back and howled with laughter. He was mad, she thought. He had actually lost his senses. Glenn led her to the bar where he produced a pile of powder and within the minute Helen was feeling better.

"Now the surprise," he insisted with a crackerjack grin.

"Yes, the surprise," Helen cried, raising her fist. She was feeling so much better. "Lead me on, my king."

His eyes flashed mischievously and he loped for the apartment. She followed, giggling now. "What is it? What is it, Glenn?"

"You'll see! You're gonna love it!"

He crashed through the door and pulled up. She stumbled in and peered about the apartment. "Where? What is it?"

Glenn's eyes glistened, round, eager. He kept his eyes on her and crept to the bathroom door. "Is it here?" he asked in play, and opened the door. She looked in. Nothing.

"No. Stop playing, you big oaf."

"Is it here?" he asked, lifting the bedspread.

"Come on, Glenn, you're driving me crazy. Show me."

He stepped to the closet, eyes wide, a gaping smile splitting his face. "Is it here?" he asked.

"What are you playing at, you silly—"

Her words caught in her throat. The closet was open. A person stood, bound like a mummy and propped in the corner. A woman.

Ivena!

At first Helen did not comprehend what she was seeing. Why was Ivena here? And wasn't it odd that she was tied up like that? The woman's eyes were open, looking at her, crying tears that wet the gag in her mouth.

Realization crept over Helen like a hot lava flow, searing her mind despite its state of numbness. Glenn had brought Ivena to the Palace! And he had hurt her, badly enough to produce a bloody nose and a bruised face.

Those soft brown eyes stared at Helen, and she felt her heart begin to break. "Ivena?" she croaked.

"Do you like my surprise, Helen?" Glenn asked. He was no longer smiling.

"Oh, Ivena. Oh, God, Ivena!" Helen sank to her knees. Her world began to swim. Maybe this was one of those bad trips.

Glenn was laughing now. He was enjoying this. His whole body shook like a bowl of jelly and that struck Helen as odd. The door to the closet was shut now, and she wondered what she had seen in there. She'd dreamed that Glenn had bound and gagged Ivena, of all people, and propped her up in the closet. Goodness, she was hallucinating badly.

Helen giggled with Glenn, testing the waters at first. But when he howled with humor, she let restraint fly out the window and joined him, laughing until she could hardly kneel, much less stand.

The world drifted into a safe place of fuzzy edges and warm feelings. She was home, wasn't she? Hands hauled her up onto the bed.

Yes, Helen had come home.

CHAPTER TWENTY-SEVEN

THE MASSIVE storm that pounded Atlanta stretched right up the eastern coast and dumped rain on New York that dark night as well. But in the delicate ambiance of Brazario's Fine Dining, the party from Delmont Pictures was oblivious to it. Here the light was soft, the smell of coffee rich, and the laughter gentle. Jan picked at his soft-shell crab and nodded at Tony Berhart's assertion that if a movie could make the women cry, it was destined for success. Well, *The Dance of the Dead* would make most men cry as well, he said, and that would make it unstoppable. The studio's VP of acquisitions lifted a toast to accent his point.

"Here, here," agreed Roald, who lifted his own glass in acknowledgment. They had arrived on different planes, he, Karen and Roald, all from separate states, brought together by the good folks at Delmont Pictures.

Karen sat across the table to Jan's right. Three tall red candles burned between them, casting an orange glow over her face. She laughed with Roald. She had perfected the art of socializing like few Jan knew, laughing at precisely the right moment but knowing when to stand up and be heard as well.

Jan thought back to their encounter just an hour earlier. The wind was blowing when he reached the restaurant, and he held the door for a woman approaching to his left. She was less than five feet away before they recognized each other.

Karen.

She pulled up as if slapped.

"Hello, Karen."

She recovered quickly. "Hello, Jan." She walked past him and he entered behind her.

"So, here we are then," he said. "We meet after all."

"Yes." She cast him a quick glance, then scanned the foyer for a sign of their hosts. "They should be here. Have you seen Roald?"

"No. No, I just arrived. Are you okay, Karen?"

"What do you mean?"

"You know what I mean."

"I'm fine, Jan. Let's just get this movie out of the way. We can do that, can't we?"

"Yes . . . I heard you were seeing someone. I'm glad."

"And so am I. Let's not talk about it. You do what you need to do, and let me do what I need to do. Okay? Where's Roald?" She crooked her neck for view.

"I really had no choice, Karen. You do realize that, don't you?"

"I don't know, Jan. Did you?"

"I don't know what you've heard, and I don't expect you to understand, but what happened between Helen and me, it was beyond us. God is not finished with this story."

"And what happens to the rest of us poor sad sacks while God finishes your story? We just get trampled for the greater good, is that it?"

"No. But this love for Helen, it did come from him. The attraction between you and me was somewhat misplaced. Surely you see that now."

"Oh come on, Jan. Don't cast this off on God. You know how pathetic that sounds? You dumped me for another woman because God told you to?"

"Then forget how it happened. Were we really right for each other? You're already with another man. And I'm with another woman."

She stopped her searching and looked into Jan's eyes without responding.

"We were caught up in the momentum of it," Jan said. "Perhaps you were as interested in *The Dance of the Dead*—in the Jan Jovic franchise—as in me."

Finally she responded. "Maybe. And what would that make your attraction to me?"

"A strong infatuation with the woman who made me a star." He smiled.

They held stares. "A month ago I would've slapped you for saying that."

Roald had walked in then and effectively ended the conversation.

Now she looked at him from across the table, and smiled, proud of her pet project. Professionally delighted to be with the author of *The Dance of the Dead* if not his fiancée.

"Well, I'm sure you're wondering why we called you all here so suddenly," Tony said. "We appreciate your understanding."

The table grew quiet. The Delmont executive glanced around at them and settled his eyes on Jan. "I'm sure Karen has told you there's been a change." He smiled. "This is how we in the world of entertainment like to introduce changes. We entertain first, and then we discuss business." A few chuckles. "But let me assure you, you'll be pleased with what I have to say. Your contract with Delmont Pictures allows for the studio to sell the movie rights at our discretion as long as it does not materially affect you. It's something we would do only if it were clear that the sale would make fiscal sense for all parties. We have received and accepted such an offer."

Meaning what? Jan glanced at Karen.

"You're selling the movie. Why?" she asked.

"Yes, we're selling the movie. The deal both guarantees us a good profit and offers you higher payment. An additional three million upon completion."

They sat stunned. It was Karen again who pressed for details. "Forgive my ignorance here, Tony. But why?"

"They're an upstart studio, you've heard of them, I'm sure. Dreamscape Pictures?"

She nodded. "They have that kind of money?"

"Yes. Point is, they want full assurances that you will fulfill your contract, so they threw in the three-million incentive. They're obviously extending themselves on this deal and they can't afford any missteps. And, if you want to know, I think it was a smart move on their part. This movie will make a bundle. A new company like Dreamscape could use that."

"And why not you?" Jan asked.

"Because ten million in the bank is always going to trump a hundred million on the table." Tony shrugged. "If it means anything to you, I voted against the deal."

Roald spoke up for the first time. "So bottom line is, we lose nothing. And all things remaining equal, we gain three million dollars. What about production and distribution? These guys know their business?"

"They have solid partners. And with the amount of money they're putting on the deal, you can bet they won't settle for a home movie. You'll get what you want."

"What kind of contract?" Karen asked.

"Virtually identical to the existing one. Like I said, they're just interested in protecting their investment."

Karen nodded. "Well. Then I guess congratulations are in order, Tony. You've done us well."

The executive looked at Jan. "What do you think, Jan?"

"I think Karen's right. If they want to pay us three million dollars for what we would've done anyway, I won't turn down their money. So we're now at an eight-million-dollar deal? Isn't that rather much?"

"That, Jan," Roald said, "is exceptional. And Karen's right: Tony, you have done us very well. I think this calls for celebration."

Tony laughed. "We are celebrating, Roald. Can't you tell?"

It did become a celebration then, for another two hours, drinking and laughing and enjoying the benefits of wealth. In many ways the evening was like a mountain peak for Jan. Not only had God given him Helen, he had returned Jan's favor with the world, it seemed. With Karen and Roald and *The Dance of the Dead*. Everything was going to return to normal now. And normal as a millionaire was something he was getting to like. Very much.

HELEN PRIED her eyes open and stared at the clock by the bed. It was 10:00 A.M. Hazy memories from the night drifted through her mind. She'd called Glenn . . .

Helen jerked up. She was in the Palace! And Jan . . . Jan was in New York. She collapsed, flooded with relief. But the sentiment left her within the minute.

She rolled to her back and groaned. Rain still splattered on the window. Jan wasn't scheduled to return until the next day, Sunday, but he would have called, no doubt. She would have to concoct a reasonable story for not answering the phone.

Oh, dear Jan! What have I done? What have I gone and done? Helen put a hand over her eyes and fought the waves of desperation crashing through her chest. One of these days she would have to end this madness. Or maybe Glenn would do it for her. A notion to call out to God crossed her mind, but she dismissed it. This wasn't some fanciful world filled with visions and martyrs and a God who spoke in the darkness. This was not Jan's *Dance of the Dead*. This was the real world. Glenn's world. Jan had grown up in a different land altogether. Jan and Ivena both—her husband and her mother. Mother Ivena . . .

Ivena.

Ivena!

A chill spiked through her spine. Helen scrambled from the bed, squinting against a throbbing headache. She had imagined seeing the dear woman bound and gagged. Helen threw the closet door open.

It was empty. *Oh, thank you, God! Thank you!* So then she had imagined it all. Drugs could do that easily enough. She wandered into the bathroom, splashed water on her face and brushed her teeth. She had to get home—to Jan's home. To her home. It was crazy coming here! *This is the last time.*

She stopped her brushing and stared at the mirror, her mouth foaming white. *This is the last time, you understand? You understand that, Helen? Never again.* She suddenly spit at the mirror, spraying it with toothpaste.

"You make me sick!" she muttered and rinsed her mouth.

Helen pulled on a pair of blue jeans and slunk from the apartment, headed for the bar and a cigarette. Maybe a drink. The large room lay in shadows, light-less except for the foreboding gray that made its way through the far windows. The room's pillars stood like ghosts in the silence. She veered to her right and made for the bar.

Helen had reached the counter and was bending over it when she heard the sound. A soft grunt. Or a moan of wind. No, a soft grunt!

She spun around and faced the shadows.

A form sat there, its white eyes staring at her from the gloom.

Helen jumped, terrified. The form was human, bound to a chair, gagged. Helen could not move. She could only stare for the moment while her heart pounded in her ears and the woman drilled her with those white eyes.

It was Ivena. Of course, it was Ivena, and that hadn't been a dream last night. Glenn had taken the woman and . . .

The horror of it brought a sudden nausea to Helen's gut. She brought her hand to her mouth and fought for her composure. The injustice of it, the sick-ness of it—how could any human do this? And then in that moment Helen knew that she was staring at a mirror. Not a real mirror, because that was Ivena bound to the chair twenty feet off. But a mirror because she was no less bound than Ivena. Helen was looking at herself and the sight was making her nauseous. But unlike Ivena, she came here willingly. With desire, like a dog to its own vomit.

A groan broke from Helen's mouth and she stumbled forward, gripping her stomach with one hand. She couldn't read Ivena's expression because of the gag, but her eyes were wide. The ropes pressed into her flesh—the pink dress she wore was torn, Helen could see that as she neared. And yes, her face was badly bruised.

A knot wedged in Helen's throat, allowing only a soft moan. Tears blurred her vision. She had to get that gag off. Panicked, she rushed right up to Ivena and tore at the strip of sheet wrapped around her mouth. It took some wrenching, and Ivena winced in pain, but the gag came free, exposing Ivena's face. The woman was crying with an open mouth and quivering lips.

Helen grasped for the knots that held Ivena. She found one at her waist and tugged at it, whimpering in panic. "Are you hurt? Did he hurt you?"

Of course she was hurt.

"Leave them, Helen," Ivena said softly. "He'll only hurt me more."

Helen yanked at the ropes, desperate to free her.

"Helen, please. Please don't."

Helen grunted in frustration and hit the chair with her palm. She sank to her knees, lowered her head to Ivena's shoulder, and wept bitterly.

For a full minute they did not speak. They shook with sobs and wet their faces with tears, Ivena bound to the chair and Helen kneeling beside her. Ivena was right: she couldn't untie her; Glenn would kill them both.

"Shshshshshsh . . . ," Ivena whispered, gathering herself. "Be still, child."

"I'm sorry, Ivena! I'm so sorry." There were no words for this.

"I know, Helen. It will be all right."

Helen straightened and looked at the older woman. The gag made of sheet was still in her hand and she gently wiped Ivena's face with it. "He's a monster, Ivena." Then she was crying again.

"I know. He's a beast."

"How long have you been here?"

"Yesterday, I was attacked . . ." Ivena turned her face away.

If I had called her to spend the weekend as Jan suggested, she would be safe, Helen thought. *I've done this to her!*

Ivena seemed to gain some resolve. She set her chin and swallowed. "And why are you here, Helen?"

Ivena didn't know? She had not suspected! Helen lifted both hands to her face and hid her face, utterly shamed. She turned away and wept silently.

"Come here, child."

Helen stood frozen.

"Yes, it's a terrible thing. But it's done. Now you will be forgiven."

Helen turned to her. "How can you say that? How can anyone say that? Look at you. You're tied to a chair, beaten and bloody, and you're talking to me about forgiveness? That's not right!"

"No dear, you are wrong. Forgiveness is love; love takes us past the death. You must know something, Helen. You must listen to me and remember what I now tell you. Are you listening?"

Helen nodded.

"Blood is at the very center of man's history. The shedding of blood, the giving of blood, the taking of blood. Without the shedding of blood there is no forgiveness. Without the shedding of blood there is no *need* for forgiveness. It's all about life and death, but the path to life runs through death. Does this make any sense?"

"I don't know."

"Whoever will find his life must lose his life. If you want to live, you must die. It was what Christ did. He shed his blood. It sounds absurd, I know. But it's only when you decide to give up yourself—to die—that you yourself will understand love. Hear this, Helen. You will never understand the love of Christ; you will never return Janjic's love until you die."

"That doesn't make sense."

"No. Trying to love without dying doesn't make sense."

Helen looked at Ivena's body, still bound like a hog. She fought to hold back the tears.

"I've heard the laughter, Helen."

The door to their right suddenly thumped open and they stared at it as one. It was Glenn, standing in the light, hands on hips, grinning. He walked toward them, still dressed in those white polyester slacks, now smudged with dirt.

"I see you've found your gift, Helen? You didn't seem too interested last night so I wrapped her for you here."

Helen fought to contain her rage, but it boiled over. She shrieked and swung her right fist at Glenn. He caught her wrist easily. "Easy, princess."

"I hate this! I hate this, you pig!"

Glenn twisted her arm until she winced with pain. "You watch your tongue, you filthy slug!"

"She means nothing to you!"

"She means everything to me. She's going to work some magic for me, aren't you, old woman?" He shoved Helen off and she held her arm, still glaring at him.

"Yes, she is," Glenn said.

"What can you hope to gain by this?" Helen asked.

"I hope to gain a little cooperation, princess." His upper lip bunched up, revealing his large crooked teeth. "This bag of bones here will provide some motivation for you and your preacher."

Helen tensed. "Meaning what?"

"It means that since you've had difficulty with your loyalty, I'm going to help you out a little, that's what it means. That's my gift to you. You might even think of it as a wedding present."

He was headed into dangerous waters with this tone of his, and Helen decided not to push him.

"Don't you want to know how it works, dear? Hmm? Operating instructions? Okay, let me tell you. First, you let this bag of bones free on the street. Let it wander back home or go shopping or whatever it does. Maybe clean it up a little first." He took a deep breath and paced theatrically.

"The point is to try to keep the bag of bones alive. A game really. If you and your preacher friend agree to separate, the bag of bones lives. If not, she dies. That's the only rule. You like it?"

Separate? Glenn was demanding that she and Jan separate?

"Oh, and one more thing. You've got three days. Sort of like a resurrection thing. If you do the right thing, the tomb will be empty in three days. The tomb being the preacher's house. Empty of you, Helen."

He couldn't be serious, of course. It was insane! "Come on, Glenn. Don't fool around. She's not—"

"I'm *not* fooling around!" he screamed.

Helen jumped. Glenn's face scowled, red.

"I'm as serious as a heart attack, baby! You have three days, and if you want this bag of bones here to live through our little game, you'd better do some thinking."

Helen's knees suddenly felt weak. He was insane! She spun her head to Ivena. The woman was looking at Glenn, her eyes still soft, absent of fear. Maybe smiling.

"Now cut her ropes and turn her loose," Glenn said. He flashed a smile. "Time to play."

With that he turned on his heels and strode from the room

CHAPTER TWENTY-EIGHT

"Suffering is an oxymoron. There is unfathomable peace and satisfaction
in suffering for Christ. It is as though you have searched endlessly for
your purpose in life, and now found it in the most unexpected place:
in the death of your flesh. It is certainly a moment worthy of laughter
and dance. And in the end it is not suffering at all. The apostle Paul
recommended that we find joy in it. Was he mad?"

The Dance of the Dead, 1959

JAN APPROACHED his home's entryway midafternoon Monday with a sense of
déjà vu raging through his mind. He'd been here before: walking up to the sign
that read *In living we die; In dying we live*, on a hot summer afternoon, surrounded
by stifling silence, wondering what waited behind those doors.

Helen had not answered his calls from New York.

Father, you must save her, he prayed for the hundredth time since leaving her
on Friday. *You must protect her.* He prayed it because she was slipping—he could
feel it more than deduce it. Helen was in a fight for her life and the fact that he'd
left her for three days now played like a horn in his mind. It was killing him.

Jan unlocked the door and stepped in. The lights were off; the house appeared
vacant. "Helen! Helen, dear, I'm home!"

He set down his garment bag and tossed the keys on the entry table. "Helen!"
Jan hurried into the kitchen. "Helen, are you here?" Only the ringing of silence
answered his call. Where was she? Ivena! She would be with Ivena.

"Hi, Jan."

He whirled to the hall. Helen stood by the basement stairs, dressed in jeans
and a white T-shirt, trying to smile and managing barely. Jan's pulse spiked. He

reached her and took her into his arms. There was something wrong here, but at least it was *here*, not there; not in some place of wickedness.

"I missed you, Helen." Her musky smell filled his senses and he closed his eyes. "Are you okay? I tried to call."

"Yes," she said thinly. "Yes, I'm all right. How was your trip?"

Jan stepped back. "Terrific. Correction, the meeting was terrific, the trip itself was dreadful. These trips are getting more difficult every time I take them. Maybe you should come with me next time."

"Jan, there's been a . . . a problem." If she'd even heard his last comment she didn't show it. "Something's happened."

"What is it? What problem?"

She turned and walked into the living room, not responding. It was serious then. Serious enough to make Helen balk, which was not so easily accomplished

"Helen, tell me."

"It's Ivena." She turned and her eyes glistened wet. "She's . . . she's not so good."

"What do you mean? What happened?" His tone was panicked and he swallowed. "What happened to Ivena, Helen?"

She lowered her head into her hands and started to cry. Jan stepped up to her and smoothed her hair. "Shhh, it's okay, dear. Everything will be okay. You're more precious to me than anything I know. You remember that, don't you?"

The comment only added to her tears, he thought. "Tell me, Helen. Just tell me what's happened."

"She's hurt, Jan."

Now he stepped back in alarm. "Hurt? Where? Where is she?"

"At home."

"Well . . . How did she get hurt?" he demanded, aware that he'd taken a harsh tone now. "Did she have a car accident?" A picture of that crazy gray Bug stuttered through his mind. He'd told her a hundred times to get something larger.

"No. She was hurt."

"Yes, but how? How was she hurt?"

"I think you should ask her that."

"You can't tell me?" Now Jan was worried. She was making no sense. This was more than an accident. "Okay, then, if you won't tell me, we'll go there."

"No, Jan. You go."

"Don't be ridiculous! You'll come with me. I'm not leaving here without you."

She shook her head and the tears were flowing free now. "No. I can't. You have to go alone."

"Why? You're my wife. How can I—"

"Go, Jan! Just go," she said. Then, with closed eyes, "I'll be here when you return, I promise. Just go."

He stared at her, stunned. Something very bad had happened to Ivena. That much was now obvious. Not as clear was Helen's behavior.

"I'll be right back," he said. He kissed her on the cheek and ran for his car.

JAN FOUND Ivena's house unlocked and he stormed in, not thinking to knock. His imagination had already pushed him past such formalities.

"Ivena . . ." He pulled up.

She sat in her brown overstuffed chair, humming and smiling and slowly rocking. The heavy scent of her roses filled the room; she must have strewn them everywhere. The distant sound of children laughing carried on the air.

"Hello, Jan." Her head rested on the cushion—making no effort to look at him.

Jan shoved the door closed behind him. At first he didn't see the bruising. But the discoloration beneath her makeup became obvious—black and blue at the base of her nose and on her right cheek.

"Did you have a good trip?" she asked.

"What happened?"

She straightened her head. "My, we are demanding. Did you speak to Helen?"

"Yes."

"And? She told you what?"

"That you'd been hurt. That's all. She refused to come. What's going on?"

She leaned her head back. "Sit, Janjic." He sat opposite her. "First you tell me how your trip was, and then I'll tell you why my head hurts."

"My trip was fine. They're paying us more money. Now stop this nonsense and tell me what's going on."

"More money? Goodness, you will be floating in the stuff."

"Ivena!"

Ivena's body ached, but her spirit was light. She might not be floating in money like Janjic, but she was still floating. "Okay, my dear Serb. Calm your voice; it hurts my head."

"Then tell me why your head hurts and why my wife will not come here with me."

Ivena took a deep breath and told him. Not everything, not yet. She told him how the big oaf, Glenn . . . how his men had taken her in the park, using chloroform, she thought. When she'd awoken she'd met the man behind Helen's fears. Nothing less than a monster, ugly and smelly and no less brutal than the worst in Bosnia. He had bound her and spit on her and clubbed her with his huge fist.

Janjic was out of his chair then, red in his face. "That's . . . insane! We should call the police! Did you call the police?"

"Yes, Janjic. Please sit."

He sat. "And what did they say?"

"They asked me if I wanted to press charges."

"And?"

"I said I would have to think about it. I wanted to talk to you first."

"That's absurd! Of course you want to press charges. This man's not someone to play with!"

"You think I do not know? You weren't the only one who spent some time in his chambers. But there's more to this than what the eye sees."

Jan shoved a hand toward her. "Of course there is! There's a monster who first tried to destroy Helen and who's now trying to destroy my . . ." He swallowed. "My mother."

It was the first time he'd called her that. "I am flattered, Janjic. And if I had a son, I could only hope for one as kind as you. But there's still more. You're not asking *why* Glenn took me."

"Why?" he asked.

"As a threat." Ivena pushed herself slowly from her chair and hobbled for the kitchen. "Do you want a drink, Janjic?"

He followed her, but did not answer her question. "This has to do with Helen." His voice had stiffened. "Look at you. You can hardly walk and yet you're playing this as if it were some kind of game. What does Helen have to do with this?" he demanded.

She stopped in the middle of the kitchen and faced him. "But it *is* a game, you see? And it seems that Helen is the prize." She left him staring and retrieved two glasses.

"What game?"

"What game? It is the game of life, a testing to see where the player's loyalties really do lie. Like Christ's temptation in the desert—bow to me and I will give you the world. But with Glenn it is, 'come to me and I will extend my mercy.'" She poured the lemonade, knowing Jan couldn't understand yet.

"Ivena—"

"Leave Jan, Glenn told Helen, and I will allow this bag of bones to live." She handed him the drink.

For a long moment, the kitchen was quiet except for the sound of those children laughing down the street. Ivena took a sip of her drink and then walked for the living room again, smiling. She had nearly reached the chair when he spoke.

"He said that? Glenn said that if Helen didn't leave me he would kill you? He actually threatened your life?"

"Yes, Janjic. He said that."

He marched into the room and set his glass down without drinking from it. "He can't do that! He can't just threaten like that and hope to get away with it! We have to call the police immediately!"

She eased into her chair and sighed.

"Ivena! Listen to me! This is madness! He's not one to fool with!"

"You know, I have had an incredible peace these last few weeks. And do you know what has accompanied that peace?"

Jan sat down without answering.

"A desire to join Christ. To join Nadia. To see, with my own eyes, my Father in heaven."

"But you're not saying that you want to die! That's why you haven't called the police? Because you actually want this creep to end your life? That's suicide!"

"Please!" she chided. He blinked. "I have no death wish. I said that I wish to join Christ. I did not say that I wish to die. There is a difference. Even Paul the apostle saw joining Christ as gain. Do not mock my sentiment!"

"I'm sorry. But you seem to take this all too lightly. Goodness, your life has been threatened and you've been beaten up! Did he give a time frame?"

"Three days."

"He said that if Helen does not leave me in three days, he will kill you?"

"Am I not speaking clearly, Janjic?"

"It's impossible! Who does he think he is?"

"He is a man obsessed with destroying your union with Helen. With stealing her love. And he's doing it by threatening death. Love and death. They seem to intersect often, have you noticed?"

"Perhaps too often. I'm going to call the police." He started to walk for the phone. "This is utter nonsense."

"There is more, Janjic." She guessed it was her tone that stopped him.

He hesitated and then turned to face her.

She looked at him, unable to hide a smile, wanting him to ask her. He only stared at her, still distracted.

"I saw the field."

"The field?"

"The vision."

His eyes widened and he blinked. "Of Helen? You heard heaven weeping?"

Her face took on a wide grin. "Not the weeping. But I heard the laughter."

"You saw the field of flowers?" Jan asked.

She nodded. "Tell me again what the flowers in your vision looked like, Janjic."

"White."

"Yes, but describe them."

"Well, I wasn't looking too closely . . . they were large . . . I don't know."

Ivena stood and walked for the bookcase behind him. She pulled the single red-rimmed flower from a crystal vase and turned to him. "Were they like this?"

He stepped toward her. "Maybe. Yes, as a matter of fact I think they were. It's the same flower you showed me before. What is it?"

"I'll show you." She took his hand and pulled him through the kitchen, excited now. "You will like this, Janjic. I promise you."

"Ivena—"

"Hush now. You will see. I know you will like this."

She reached the greenhouse door and paused, thinking that such an occasion needed an introduction. But there was nothing that could prepare him. She turned the knob and shoved the door open.

A soft breeze greeted their faces, pushing the hair from their foreheads. Ivena stepped in and spread her arms in the wind, drawing the air into her lungs. The delicate aroma rose through her nostrils, stinging but sweet. Oh, so very sweet. She faced the rosebushes and for a moment she forgot about Janjic stepping in behind her. Hundreds of vines covered the walls and ceiling in emerald green. A thousand brilliant white flowers trimmed in red swayed gently, bowing with the breeze. The vine's leaves rustled delicately against each other, filling the room with a cacophony of soft rustling. It all swept over Ivena's senses like a drug. She could almost taste honey on the air.

The door shut behind her, and Ivena turned to see Janjic standing wide-eyed, mouth agape.

"They came from Nadia's rosebush," she said. She ran for the bush and rustled her hand through the leaves. "You see it was a graft, but I didn't make it."

"A graft?" He stepped gingerly, as though anything less might break something. "What . . . ? This is amazing, Ivena! How did you grow this?"

"I didn't. It's beyond me. It began the day Helen came into our lives."

He shot her a glance, and then looked about, blinking.

"And there is more," Ivena said. "I can't find a source for the breeze. I think it comes from the flowers themselves."

"'Let your wind blow through my garden,'" he quoted from the Song of Solomon. "It's impossible!" He spun around to face her. "Who else have you told?"

"Only Joey."

Jan couldn't stop his turning and staring. "And you knew about this all along? Why didn't you tell me? How did it grow?"

He looked closer at the graft and then she retraced the plant's growth for him, first along one wall, then another and another until the whole greenhouse was covered with vines and leaves and flowers.

She watched him walk around the small garden for thirty minutes, amazed.

"I should go to Helen," he finally said.

"Yes. And now you know the truth."

He shook his head. "I'll do anything to keep her love. Anything."

"Then promise me one thing. Promise me that no matter what happens in the days to come you won't become distracted by hate or revenge or any other notion that seizes your heart."

They'd stepped into the kitchen and he looked back at her, surprised. "Of course. You say that as if you know something I don't. And you'll still press charges. This changes nothing. We should call the police immediately."

"Yes, I will press charges, but know that this could all become very public."

"Public? We're talking about your safety, for heaven's sake! What do you mean?"

"She's been back to him, Jan. More than once," Ivena said.

He was halfway across her living room and he froze mid-stride. "What?"

"She has been to Glenn four times already. All in the last month."

His face drained white. "That can't be! How's that possible? I've been with her constantly! We've just been wed! How can you say this?"

"Glenn told me."

"And he's a liar!"

"Helen was there, Janjic. She came to Glenn the same night he took me."

He's stopped breathing, Ivena thought.

"She saw me bound and gagged, and she removed my gag. We talked and she was very sorry. But she was there, Janjic. By her own choice."

He started to shake his head and then stopped. Slowly his face filled with blood; his neck bulged with fury. A tremble took to his lips and he stood enraged.

He spoke in a low, bitter voice. "How dare she? I have given her everything! How can she even think of wallowing back to that pig!?"

A chill of fear swept through Ivena's back at his tone. "It's no different than what most men do with Christ," she said. "No different from Israel turning her back on God. Helen is no different than the church, worshiping at the altar one day and blundering back into sin the next. She's doing nothing more than what you yourself have done."

His eyes were glazed. "I don't care! I'll kill him!"

"Janjic—"

"No!" The muscles in his jaw flexed. "No man will do this to my wife! No man! I can't sit by while he plays his games."

"You must. Janjic—"

He whirled for the door.

"Where are you going?"

He didn't answer.

She knew then that she might not see him again. Not if he was going to the Towers. "Janjic! Please!"

The door slammed shut and he was gone.

Ivena rose from her chair and watched him through her front window. He pulled the Cadillac out of her driveway and roared down the road. A single tear snaked from the corner of her eye.

Father, you will protect him, won't you? You must. It is not finished for him. His story is not yet complete.

And what about your story, Ivena? Is it complete?

She answered aloud. "Yes, I am finished now. If you give me a choice I will join the laughter up there."

Ivena sighed again and walked to the telephone. She should call the police. Yes, she would do that.

CHAPTER TWENTY-NINE

JAN DROVE straight for the Towers, his vision clouded red with fury. He knew that he had snapped back there. The fact loitered in his mind like a fly, slightly annoying but small enough to disregard for the moment.

It was the image of Helen slinking back to that pig, lying on his bed, that drove Jan mad. Or it was three months of images, all hidden in a reservoir deep in his mind, building to this day when they had broken past their dam and now drove him like a lunatic toward the pig's house. Toward Atlanta's Twin Towers, visible from five miles out, rising tall against the blue sky.

He had no plan; no idea what he would do when he arrived or how he would get to Glenn. He only knew that he had to face that beast now.

And what about Helen, Janjic? Will you knock some sense into her as well?

Yes.

No! Oh dear God, no! The image of the garden flooded his mind. No, he could never harm her. He loved Helen desperately.

She would not be this way if it weren't for Glenn. The man's evil touch was still running through her veins. And now the madman had taken his fight to Ivena. Dear Ivena was the innocent bystander in this, as she'd been twenty years ago. Nadia had died then; there was no way he would allow any harm to come to Ivena now.

The thoughts battered his mind, occupying what space he should have given to reason. To a plan. It occurred to Jan that he was stopped at a red light not two blocks from the Towers, and he had better start thinking about what he was going to do here. He was going to ride to the top floor and he was going to take a tire iron with him. That's what he was going to do.

A horn blared and he saw that other cars had already crossed the intersection. He punched the accelerator and shot through. Helen had said that Glenn's office was in the second tower—the East Tower. He sped past the first building with which he was already familiar and approached the second.

Jan whipped the Cadillac into the underground parking and screeched to a stop in a restricted space beside the elevators. It had been twenty years since he had set his mind on harming another man, but the memory of it came to him now with a surge of adrenaline.

He grunted, popped the trunk and jumped from the car. He yanked the car's tire iron from the repair kit, slammed the trunk and slid the rod up his shirt. A parking attendant walked toward him from the entry gate. Jan ran to the elevators without acknowledging the man. One of three elevator doors slid open and he entered quickly. Thank God for small favors. *God?*

Jan stabbed the top floor button and rode the humming car to its peak without stopping. Maybe he should have called the police before leaving Ivena's. But then she would. Either way, the police didn't seem too interested in bringing this powerful man under their thumb. These Karadzics of the world seemed to have their way too often. But not with his wife!

The arrival bell clanged and he entered the thirtieth floor, his nerves strung tight. A receptionist looked up at him from her station behind a counter that hid all but her head. A huge brass sculpture of the Twin Towers hung on the wall behind her.

"May I help you?"

Jan walked for the counter. "Yes, I'm here to see Glenn Lutz."

"Do you have an appointment?"

"Yes. Yes, of course I have an appointment."

The receptionist glanced to Jan's right, toward a tall cherry door, and picked up the telephone.

Jan turned and strode for the door without waiting for her to let him in. "Excuse me, sir. Sir!" He ignored the call and pushed through, gripping the iron under his shirt.

A black-haired woman looked up from her desk sharply. Jan took in the room with a glance. Beyond her, wide-paneled doors led to what would be the man's office. This would be his secretary, then. An ugly wench with a hooked nose. He had to move while she was still off balance.

She stood as he moved forward. "Excuse me."

"Not now, miss," he snapped.

Her eyes widened suddenly, as if she recognized him. As well she might—he'd been here before. She stepped out from her desk quickly, blocking his way with lifted hands. "Where do you think you're going?"

"Out of my way," he grunted. And he slapped her hands aside. She made a high squeaking sound, protesting like a mother hen. But Jan wasn't interested in this woman. His mind was now thoroughly taken by getting through the door. He didn't stop to think clearly about what might be waiting behind the doors; he simply barged ahead.

The woman charged him from behind. She dived onto his back with a wild shriek. Janjic dropped instinctively. It had been twenty years since his special forces training, but his reflexes had not forgotten. He dropped to one knee and threw his right shoulder down. The wench's momentum carried her over his back and she sailed through the air, landing with a loud crash against the wall. Her black bun had unraveled in the flight and now drooped past white cheeks.

Jan sprang for the doors and yanked them open, his heart now slamming into his throat. *You want a war, baby? You want to threaten my family? You will feel a touch of Bosnia today.*

Glenn's bulky frame stood across the room, by a windowed wall, hands on hips, gazing to the city beyond. He spun around, snarling at the sudden intrusion. But when he saw that it was Jan, the snarl vanished. He gawked for a moment.

Jan whipped out the iron, slammed the door shut behind him, locked it, and angled for the desk to his right.

Isolate and minimize. The training came like a haunting memory now, dulling the edge of fear. Isolate the man from any potential weapon and minimize his ability to take the offensive.

Glenn had regrouped already and now a wicked grin split his face. "So the preacher wants to get serious. Is that—"

"Shut up!" Jan yelled. Glenn blinked. "Just shut up!"

The millionaire's face turned red.

Jan held the iron out and felt the desk at the back of his knees. He reached for the drawers behind him, found the one closest and pulled it open. An assortment of pens and notepads crashed to the floor.

"You still think of me as a preacher? But you know me better now, don't you? I'm the man Helen loves. That's me. But before I became that man; before I came to your land I was what? I was a killer. How many men have you killed with your own hands, Glenn Lutz? Ten? Twenty? You're a novice."

He glanced back, found another drawer and ripped it out. More junk, but not the weapon he looked for. *Keep speaking, Jan. Keep him distracted.*

"You think you can throw terror around as if you own it?" He yanked another drawer out and papers spilled to the black tile floor. "Have you ever felt terror, Glenn Lutz?"

The man stood there huge and ugly, his arms spread like a gunslinger. But the smile had gone, replaced by flat lips. From this distance his eyes looked like black holes. The man was large enough to crush Janjic. Surely a man like this would have a weapon of some kind in his desk. Jan jerked a fourth drawer open, keeping his eyes on the man.

"No, you have not felt terror!" Jan's breathing came heavily now. Seeing the monster's thick face filled his gut with revulsion. He wanted only to kill the pig.

Glenn's eyes shifted to the drawer Jan had just opened. Suddenly the man snapped out of his trance. His lips pulled back and he bolted forward like a charging bull.

For a fleeting second, Jan knew that coming here had been a very bad idea. Panicked, he blindly snatched at the drawer behind him. His hand closed around cold steel.

Glenn came in, roaring now, his face bulging. Fury rose through Jan's veins and he whipped what he now knew was a gun around to face the charging man.

Glenn thundered forward, undaunted.

Jan sprang to his left at the last moment, narrowly avoiding the huge body. He spun around and swung the tire iron down on the man's blond skull. Glenn grunted and slammed into his desk, facedown on the polished wood grain. It was the first time Jan had struck a man in twenty years, and now the horror of it seeped through his bones.

A fleeting image of himself standing over the priest with a bloodied rifle filled his mind.

Still, this was the man who had molested his wife! Who now threatened to kill Ivena! He begged for a beating!

Jan jerked the iron back and swung again, this time hitting the man's back. Glenn grunted. Jan swung again, this time with all of his weight. The blow landed on his shoulder with a sick crunch. It should have immobilized the monster.

It did not.

Glenn growled, rolled to his back and stood. He faced Jan, his eyes flashing red, his neck bulging with veins. His right arm hung limply, but Glenn didn't seem to notice. His eyes glared, bloodshot above twisted lips. He growled and took a step forward. Jan knew then that if he did not stop the man, it would be his own death.

He jerked the gun up and pulled the trigger.

Boom! The report thundered in the enclosed room.

Glenn's right arm flew back, like a tether ball on a string. The room fell to a surreal slowness. Glenn seemed oblivious to his pain, but his eyes snapped wide in shock.

Yes, that's it, you pig. Yes, I do have your gun and it is loaded isn't it? That one was through your hand, the next will be through your head!

"Don't move!" Jan screamed.

Glenn's arm dropped to his side. The right corner of the man's mouth twitched. They stood rooted to the floor, facing each other down, Jan with the extended pistol and Glenn with a sick grin.

"You've just signed your own death warrant. You know that, don't you?" Glenn said. His right shoulder had broken under the tire iron, Jan saw, and the bullet had torn a gaping hole through his hand.

Glenn looked at it slowly. He measured the damage and then seemed to accept it with a blink. He looked up at Jan and closed his eyes. "You will die along with the old hag now."

"I don't think you understand the situation here," Jan snapped back. "You see, I have the gun. One small pull from my finger and you will die. If you don't at least pretend to understand that, then I will be forced to demonstrate my resolve. Are we clear?"

Glenn opened his eyes. "You talk big for a preacher."

Pounding sounded on the locked door.

"Pick up the phone and tell your friend out there to leave us alone," Jan instructed.

Glenn snarled angrily. "You're dead meat!"

A wave of heat washed over Jan's back. He wanted to shoot the man in his bulging belly. He trembled in restraint. "You really should have more respect, but obviously you don't know the meaning of the word, do you?" He was a pig who wouldn't think twice about smashing those big fists over Helen's ears. How could she come to this man! Jan's gun hand shook.

"You aren't going to do anything I ask?"

Glenn only stared at him.

"Lift your left hand," Jan ordered.

Glenn did not move.

"Lift your hand!" Jan screamed. "Now!"

The man had the audacity to stand there without flinching. Jan lowered the gun, lined up its sight on Glenn's left hand, and pulled the trigger. *Boom!* The slug took off the end of his index finger. The pounding on the door intensified.

Glenn's face drained white and then immediately flushed red. He gaped at his finger and began to roar in pain. He fumbled with his shirt in an attempt to stop the flow of blood but succeeded only in drenching it.

"Next time it will be your knee and you will use a crutch the rest of your life," Jan said. "Do you understand? Take your shirt off."

"What?"

"I said take your shirt off, you oaf. Take it off and wrap it around your hand. The flow of blood will distract me."

This time Glenn followed the suggestion quickly. He eased his flabby torso out of the shirt and crudely wrapped it around both hands. Sweat glistened on his white flesh.

"Tell them to shut up," Jan ordered, waving the gun toward the door.

"Shut up!" Glenn screamed at the door.

The pounding stopped.

"Good. Now I want you to listen and listen very carefully. You may be a wealthy man with the power to squash weak women, but today this power will not extend to my world. Not to me or to Ivena or to Helen. Helen has chosen to accept my love and now you will let her have her choice. You will not bully her. Do you understand?"

"I didn't bully her into coming back," Glenn said. "We all make our own choices."

"And you'll stop manipulating hers," Jan shouted.

"Manipulating? How? By providing a little motivation? That's nothing less than what you did when you took her away. You show her a carrot. I show her a stick. In the end she makes the choice."

"You think I keep her caged in my house? She's free to come and go as she wants and I don't see her running to you every day. She would stay with me except for your drugs. And if you think this pointless game with Ivena will somehow persuade her to come crawling back against her own will, then you're wrong. Even if she did, what would you have? Someone you pressured against their will?"

"We all apply pressure. Even your God applies pressure. It's either the carrot or the stick. Heaven or hell."

Jan blinked at the man's logic. It was an odd place to argue these matters, Jan holding the gun and Glenn bleeding into his shirt. "But love can't be bought with heaven or hell. It's given freely. Did she ever *love* you? No. She loves me."

Glenn's lips twisted to a grin. "She loves you but she comes begging to me, is that it? You're as stupid as she is. Call it what you like, when she's here she's loving me!"

"With your threats and your violence you'll gain nothing."

"I will gain Helen!" Glenn growled.

"No, you have already *lost* Helen."

"She'll come crawling back, don't kid yourself. We both know it. You'll lose her. *And* the old bag of bones."

"Silence! This is all nonsense! Helen will *not* come back to you! Never!"

"And that choice is hers," Glenn said. "You said so yourself." He shuddered. "I need a doctor."

"Yes, and so did I when I last left this building," Jan said. "Do you think the police will just stand by and let you threaten whoever you like? You have no sense of yourself."

"The police? You walk into my property and assault me and you think you can run to the police? You are naive, Preacher. You don't even know the truth about your precious wife."

For the first time Jan saw the true mistake in coming here. The police. "She loves me, it's all the truth I need," Jan said. There was something about the man's tone, though. "What truth?"

"I knew your precious lover when she was a child, you know," Glenn said, still smiling.

What was he talking about? He knew *Helen?*

"Only I wasn't Glenn back then. I was Peter. She tell you about Peter?"

Peter! The boy who'd trailed Helen home from school and supplied her mother with drugs! The revelation whirled about in Jan's mind. Glenn wasn't confessing; he was twisting the knife. Jan suddenly felt sick, standing here in this man's tower, playing his game. He was beyond this. And what had he gained by coming here? An image of the garden swept through Jan's mind and he suddenly wanted out. *Oh Helen! Dear Helen, if you only knew.* But she didn't know and he would not tell her.

"You're a sick man," Jan said.

"You think I'm sick?" Glenn licked his lips. "Then what will you think when I tell you that the reason Helen's mother got sick in the first place was because I poisoned her?" He grinned wide, showing his crooked teeth.

"You poisoned her?"

"That's right. I made Mommy sick and then I eased her pain with drugs." Glenn began to giggle. He stood there with bloodied hands, thrilled with himself, giggling insanely.

Jan backed up, revolted. Evil possessed this man's soul to the very core. Glenn Lutz was no less than Karadzic, but in a new skin.

It was time to leave.

"Pick up the phone and tell your men to give me safe passage out," Jan said.

Glenn just smiled with parted lips.

Jan waved the gun. "Do it!"

"What's the matter, Preacher? I'm not quite what you bargained for, am I?"

"You just leave us alone, do you understand? You hurt a single hair on Ivena's head and your world will crumble around you. I promise you that much. Now tell your men, before you bleed to death."

Glenn hesitated, but he went for the phone after glancing at his blood-soaked shirt.

Jan left then, keeping his gun trained on Glenn. He stepped past the glaring assistant he'd sent flying and ran for the elevator. Behind him he could hear Glenn cursing at her. If he took the man's roaring as any indication, this wasn't over. Coming here might have been a terrible mistake. He had just blown a man's hand off.

Jan roared from the parking structure, his hands trembling on the steering wheel. Yes indeed, this hadn't been such a bright idea. Not at all.

GLENN SLUMPED in his chair and held his hands up as best he could to keep the blood flow in check. It was the first time anyone had marched into his own building and demanded anything, much less waved a gun at him and uttered vile threats. Jan Jovic had shifted the balance in the game.

Of course, the preacher had also just handed him the leverage he needed with Charlie. He had been assaulted. This meant open war.

"Where's that doctor?" Glenn demanded.

"On his way," Beatrice returned, pulling loose strands of hair behind her ears. "So is Charlie."

Glenn hardly heard her for the pain in his arms. He couldn't keep them from shaking.

Buck appeared in the door. "You called, sir?" His eyes shifted to the wrapped hand and widened. "Are you okay?"

"No, I'm not okay. I've been shot!"

"The preacher shot you?"

Glenn didn't answer and Buck just stared at him.

"I want the old bag dead," Glenn said matter-of-factly.

He refused to look at Beatrice, who was no doubt glaring at him. It wasn't often he conducted business of this nature in front of her. She liked to pretend that it was beneath her, although they both knew differently.

Buck glanced at her. "Yes, sir." He dipped his head without expression and left.

"You have a problem with that, Beatrice?"

She hesitated. "No. But you'll lose your advantage."

"My leverage is with Dreamscape Pictures. I own him! And now he's just handed his life over to me. Our preacher's about to get more than he bargained for."

Glenn's shoulder ached. His hands burned with pain and a shiver worked its way through his bones.

"Find the old man. Roald. It's time I introduced myself."

CHAPTER THIRTY

IT WAS 5:00 P.M. when Jan swung the Cadillac into his driveway and turned off the ignition. The drive through the city had cleared his mind some, enough for him to know that he'd slipped back into his war skin back there and it hadn't paid any dividends.

He had shot Glenn Lutz. Goodness, he'd just shot a man through the hands! Jan shoved the door open and stepped out of the car.

A surge of anger rose through his chest. But now it was directed toward Helen, not Glenn. It had been flaring at the base of his spine from the moment Ivena had told him about Helen's infidelity. And now Helen waited for him past that door and Jan wasn't sure he could walk through it.

In living we die; In dying we live, the sign above the door read. *You are killing me, Father.* How could anyone betray him as Helen had? He had loved her in every way he knew how, and still she'd betrayed him! Ivena's suggestion that her rejection of him was no different from his own rejection of Christ was well and fine, but it did not ease the whirlwind of emotions whipping through his mind.

Jan felt a tremor take to his bones. He stood on the sidewalk and balled his hands into tight fists. "Why?" he muttered through clenched teeth. There could be no pain worse than this ache of rejection, he thought. It was a living death.

A sudden image of Helen standing, smiling innocently, came to him. In his mind's eye he snatched the image by the throat and strangled her. The image struggled briefly in terror and then fell limp in his hands. He grunted and dropped her.

Jan shut his eyes and shook his head. "Father, please! Please help me." Ivena's words strung through his mind. *She is no different than you, Jan.* The rage and the sorrow and the horror all rolled into a searing ball of emotion. He dropped to one knee and stared up at the sky. "Forgive me, Father. Forgive me, I have sinned."

Another thought filled his mind. *The police will come for you, Jan.*

The tears came freely now, streaming down his cheeks. He lifted both fists above his head and opened his hands. "Oh, God, forgive me. If you have grafted this love of yours into my heart, then let it possess me."

He didn't know how long he remained on his knees facing the house before standing and making sense of himself. He had just leaped off a cliff back at the Towers, he thought, and he had no business loitering around for the impact. But there was Helen —it was all about Helen. He could not continue without resolving this madness.

In living we die; In dying we live. He was living and he was dying and he was not entirely sure which was which.

JAN'S GOING, even for these two hours, had dumped Helen back into a deep pool of depression. It was a strange brew of shame and sorrow and a desperate longing to be held in someone's strong arms. In Jan's strong arms. She'd distilled the emotions to one: loneliness. The kind that felt like a living death.

She imagined throwing herself at him when he returned, but her shame dismissed the image. Instead she paced away the minutes, making the trip to the front window to peek for his return a hundred times, while a terrible agony gripped her heart. It was a pain that overshadowed all the pleasure of a thousand nights in the Palace. Dear God, she was a pig!

The sound of the latch froze her to the carpet on the far side of the room. She was gripped by the sudden impulse to hide. *God, help me!*

"Helen."

Oh, the sound of his voice! *Forgive me, please forgive me!* A lump rose to her throat and she swallowed it quickly.

"Yes?"

He closed the door and walked across through the shadows toward her. She shivered once. He emerged from the darkness, his eyes soft and lost. But there was no anger in them.

Helen sat on the couch. *You see, Helen? He loves you deeply! Look at his eyes, swimming in love.*

How could anyone dare to love her with such intensity, knowing what he now surely knew? Surely Ivena had told him everything. Helen felt the tears rising but was powerless to stop them. She dropped her head into her arms and began to weep.

He stepped forward, dropped to his knees and gently placed both arms around her shoulders. His hands were trembling. "It's okay, Helen. Please, don't cry." His voice was strained. She dissolved now, gushing with sorrow that had welled up in her chest.

"I'm so sorry!" She wept, shaking her head. "I'm so sorry."

"I know you are." So he did know. "Please, Helen. Please stop crying. I can't bear it!" And then he was crying with her. Not just sniffling, but crying hard and shaking.

She draped one arm over his shoulder and they buried their faces in each other's necks and wept. Neither spoke for a long time. For Helen the relief of his love came like water to a bone-dry soul, parched by his absence. By her own folly. *Forgive me! You've given me this man, this love, and I've rejected it! Oh, God, forgive me!* She squeezed Jan tighter. *I'll never let him go! Forgive me, I beg you!*

Jan lifted her face with gentle hands and wiped at her tears with his thumbs. "I love you, Helen. You know that, don't you? I would never reject you. Never. I could not; you are my life. I would die without you."

"I'm sorry."

"Yes. But no more. No more tears. We are together, that's all that matters."

"I don't know why I go back, Jan. I . . ."

He pulled her into his shoulder and shook with another sob. "No, no! It's okay." He held her tight, like a vise. It was the first time she fully understood his pain—that he was screaming inside, fighting to hold his sorrow from crushing her.

The realization was numbing, shocking her into a dumb stare as he fought for control. *Oh, God, what have I done? What have I done?*

And she knew then that her own tears—her loneliness and her heartache—it was all for herself. Not for Jan. *She* missed him. *She* felt lonely. *She* wanted to be forgiven.

But this man in her arms, his emotions were directed toward her. He wanted to comfort *her*. He wanted to forgive *her*. It was the difference between them, she thought. A gulf as wide as the Grand Canyon. Her selfish love and his selflessness. That was the message of his book, *The Dance of the Dead.* He had died to a piece of himself for her. Even now in her arms he was dying to a piece of himself for her sake.

And what death was she willing to give for him? Not even the death of her own self-gratifying pleasures. She clenched her jaw and swore to herself then that she would never, never go back to Glenn. Never!

Helen kissed Jan's mouth, and she wiped his tears away. He returned the kiss and they held each other for a long minute.

"Helen, listen to me," Jan finally said.

"I'm so sorry—"

"No, no. Not that. We have another problem. I've made a mistake. I think we might have to leave." He suddenly stood and strode quickly for the kitchen.

Helen sat up. "Jan? What mistake?"

"I went to the Towers," he said with his back to her. "I shot Glenn Lutz."

She sprang to her feet. "You shot him? You killed Glenn?"

"No. I shot his hands." He lifted the receiver from the wall and faced her. "I'll explain in the car, but right now I think we should get Ivena and find a safe place while we work this out."

Helen stared at him, stunned. "A safe place?"

"Yes." He quickly dialed Ivena's number. "You could grab a few items, but we need to leave."

"How long?"

"I don't know. A day. Two." He leaned into the phone. "Ivena? Thank God you're safe."

Jan had shot Glenn's hands? The truth of it struck her as she stood in the living room, staring dumbly at Jan's back while he talked to Ivena. Heat suddenly rushed over her skull. She spun to the front door, half expecting to see Buck or Stark in the frame. But the door rested shut. Either way, Glenn would've undoubtedly dispatched them by now.

Helen ran for the bedroom, panicked. She stuffed a toothbrush and a tube of toothpaste along with a few other toiletries and some underwear into Jan's overnight bag. Where could they possibly go?

Jan had shot Glenn. Did he know what that meant?

She ran out to the living room. Jan was locking the sliding door to the backyard. "We've gotta move, Jan. Do you have any idea where we're going?"

"To safety," he said.

"And where will you be safe from Glenn? He has ears—"

"I know, Helen. And I'm not a stranger to danger. I've seen my share."

Jan quickly pulled the drapes. He shot her a fleeting smile, grabbed her hand, and hurried for the door. "If there is danger it will likely be at Ivena's house, not here."

"He said three days," Helen said. The street was clear and they walked briskly for the car.

"That was while he still had two good hands. I may have changed his mind."

Helen uttered a small nervous laugh and climbed into the Cadillac. But there was no humor in her voice. They sped from the house and Helen demanded Jan tell her exactly what had happened at the Towers.

He did.

Helen knew then that someone would die. That much was now a certainty. The only question was who.

CHARLIE WILKS stood in Glenn's office, stunned by the bloodied floor before him. Glenn sat limply in his chair, weakened by the ordeal. It was an unusual sight to be sure; not because Charlie was unaccustomed to bullet wounds or puddles of blood, but because it was Glenn's blood. The strong man had been visited by his match.

A doctor Glenn called Klowawski had already fixed his shoulder in a temporary sling and bound his hands in white strips of gauze like a boxer. The repair work would be done in the clinic, but not until Glenn had had his say with Charlie.

"You're sure it was Jan Jovic who did this?" Charlie asked. "Not someone who looks—"

"It was the preacher, you idiot! He stood here for ten minutes waving my own gun at me. You think I imagined the whole thing?"

Charlie glanced at the bloodied shirt glistening in a heap on the floor. "Of course not." Someone had tried to mop some of the blood from the floor with the white cotton shirt and succeeded only in smearing circles on the tile. Glenn had this coming to him, and for that Charlie felt no sympathy. But the law did prohibit citizens from storming into other people's offices and blowing holes in their hands. Jan Jovic had just found himself a heap of trouble and Glenn would play it to his advantage.

"This gives me what I need," Glenn said. "You do realize that."

"Yes it does. It gives you the right to have Mr. Jovic apprehended. But nothing more."

"That's not what I'm talking about."

"And what are you talking about, Glenn?" Charlie knew, of course.

"This muddies the waters. It gives you a good cover."

"Gives me cover? And why would I need cover? I'll get your man, throw him in the slammer for a few days, prosecute him like the law requires—"

"That's not what I want. It's not enough."

"What then? You want him dead?"

"No." Glenn wore a small smirk. "Not him—he's too valuable alive. I just paid ten million for his backside. I need him alive but I also need him willing. The old hag, on the other hand . . ."

"The woman?"

"I'm going to kill the old woman and I want you to stay out of my way. Help me if I need it."

Charlie took a breath and let it out slowly. It wasn't the first time, of course. But Glenn was messing with decent people, not the regular scum he mixed with.

"I'll make it worth your while, of course."

Charlie sat in a guest chair. "So let me get this straight. You want to kill an old defenseless woman who's known by half the country as an icon for motherly love and you want me to cover up the murder? That about it?"

Glenn's lips flattened. "Yes. That's exactly what I want. You haul the preacher in and let me deal with him up close, and you use the distraction of this whole mess as a smoke screen when they find the old woman's body."

"They are two different people—"

"I don't care if they're ten different people!" Glenn yelled, red in the face. "I'm going to kill the old hag, and you're going to see that no one looks my way! Is that too much to ask? He's a criminal, for crying out loud. He shot an unarmed man."

Charlie drummed his fingers on the chair's armrests and pursed his lips. It could be done, this cover-up of Glenn's. But it could also blow up.

"There's fifty thousand in it for you," Glenn said. "One hundred if we need your help."

Charlie felt his pulse quicken. "Fifty? Five-O?"

"Fifty."

"Help in what way?"

"Setting her up." He waved a bandaged hand in a dismissal. "It won't come to that."

"You'll make it look like an accident?" Charlie said.

"Of course."

"Okay. But if this goes sour, this discussion never happened. You remember that." Charlie stood. "I'll put out an APB on the preacher; you go ahead and create your little accident. But for God's sake, keep it clean."

Glenn smiled past crooked teeth. "It's already done, my friend. It's already done."

CHAPTER THIRTY-ONE

JAN SAW the black Lincoln parked across the street from Ivena's house the moment he entered her block. He jerked the Cadillac's steering wheel and plowed into the curb sixty yards from the house.

"What are you doing?" Helen demanded. "You just drove off—"

She saw the car and froze.

Jan clawed at the handle and shoved the door open. "Stay here."

"Jan, wait . . ."

But he didn't hear the rest because he was already sprinting for the house. The black Lincoln had been in the Towers' parking garage. It had no business here. He muttered under his breath and veered for Ivena's backyard.

A tall wooden fence bordered Ivena's heavily vegetated yard. Purple hydrangea and white gardenia flowers spilled over the white pickets. Jan slid to a stop at the fence, peered through two slats, and seeing nothing but an empty lawn past the vines, clambered over. He dropped to a crouch, his heart now pounding in his ears. Behind him, a car door thumped shut—Helen was following. Too late to stop her now.

The greenhouse's glass walls were too crowded with vines to see past at this distance. A steady breeze whispered through the leaves overhead, but otherwise the air lay quiet. Jan rushed for the back door.

Images of Ivena's body, crumpled and bleeding, filled his mind. If he was right she would be in the greenhouse with the flowers. It was a preoccupation for her.

Jan grabbed the knob and threw the door open.

Ivena stood there in the middle of the room, her face raised to the ceiling, her eyes closed. The breeze swept her hair back from her neck. If she'd heard him, she did not show any sign of it.

Jan scanned the room. The doorway to the house gaped to a dim interior. The assailant, if there was one, would be in there, waiting.

"Ivena," he whispered, keeping his eyes on the kitchen doorway.

"Hello, Janjic. You are back, I see," she said loudly.

He started and snatched his finger to his mouth, but she hadn't moved her head to him.

"Come in, Janjic."

"Ivena!" he whispered harshly. "Shhh. Quickly! You must come!"

She faced him. "What's wrong?"

"Come now! Shhhh!"

He looked through the door to the house and Ivena followed his gaze. She hurried over to him, wide-eyed. "What is it?"

Jan didn't respond. He grabbed her hand and yanked her through the door. Such a relief swept through his bones at her stumbling safely into the backyard, that he hardly noticed the tall man materialize in the inner door's shadows.

But then he did notice, and his heart lodged firmly in his throat. His muscles locked up. The man stepped from the shadows, a gun leveled. Behind Jan, Ivena crowded his back. "Janjic Jovic, you tell me the meaning of this immediately or I will—"

Jan threw himself backward, into Ivena.

She cried out, but managed to stay upright.

Boom!

The gun's detonation sounded obscenely loud in the small room. Ivena needed no further encouragement. Jan snatched her hand and they ran together nearly step for step toward the back fence.

Helen had one leg draped on each side of the pickets. "Back, Helen!" Jan shouted. "Get back!" He spun around, grabbed Ivena around the waist, and hoisted her the full height of the fence with a grunt. "Pull her over!"

Helen complied and Ivena disappeared. Jan threw himself over without waiting. He glanced back in time to see the black-clad gunman slide to a stop at the corner of the greenhouse. The man was no idiot; he was powerless outside with a noisy gun.

Jan dropped to the ground. Helen had Ivena's hand and they were running for the car already.

Winded and panting like billows in chorus they piled into the Cadillac. Jan fired the engine and threw the car into drive. Jan squealed through a U-turn and sped down the street.

JAN SWERVED through suburban Atlanta a good five minutes before easing his foot from the accelerator and slowing the Cadillac to the posted speed limit. It took a full ten minutes for the flood of questions and explanations to subside into silence. Ivena seemed more horrified with Jan's attack at the Towers than with the fact that a gunman had nearly put a bullet through her skull in her own home.

"It was foolish, Janjic. Now you've endangered yourself."

"And I wasn't endangered before? He's a beast. I couldn't just stand by while an animal rampages through our lives."

"And now he will rampage less? I don't think so."

Jan ground his teeth but didn't respond directly.

"Where are we going?" Helen asked beside him.

"To Joey's cottage," Jan said.

"The gardener?" Helen asked.

"Yes. He lives in a small house on the property, bordering the gardens."

"You think it's safe there? What makes you think Glenn's men aren't already there waiting?"

"Glenn may be a monster, but he's not omniscient. No one knows of the place. It's pretty secluded."

Ivena spoke from the backseat. "My, my, I see we are in a pickle, Janjic. What are you up to now?" This from a woman who'd been kidnapped and beaten not forty-eight hours earlier.

They sped toward Joey's Garden of Eden rehashing their predicament. Ivena was right, Jan thought: They were in a pickle. Jan took a deep breath and breathed a prayer. *I beg you to see us out of this madness, Father. It was your meddling that started it.*

But it was not God who'd blown holes through Lutz's hands, was it? No. On the contrary, not so long ago someone had driven holes through *God's* hands. So what did that make Jan? The devil? Now there was a thought.

They approached Joey's cottage unseen as far as Jan could tell. Overgrowth crowded the dirt driveway that snaked along the property's bordering twelve-foot hedge. Tall oaks surrounded the small wooden structure, foreboding in the failing light. A yellow Ford Pinto sat on a gravel bed beside a house shrouded in foliage. The shades were pulled, but light glowed beyond them. It was six o'clock; Joey would be home from his day in the garden.

They climbed from the car, unspeaking. Vines crawled over the red brick. Green vines with large white flowers. They stood still and gazed at the sight. Ivena's flowers covered the side of the house; Jan could not mistake them.

Ivena walked for them without a word. She touched a blossom and turned back, her eyes round. Jan led Helen up the steps. Joey opened the door before their first knock. "Jan? Well, my goodness. I wasn't expecting company."

"Forgive me, Joey. We—"

"Come in, come in." The short man swept a thin arm into his home. "I didn't say I didn't *want* company. Only that I wasn't expecting it."

They walked in and Joey closed the door.

"Can I get you something to drink?"

"Actually, Joey, this isn't exactly a social visit. I mean it is, but not like you might expect. I'm afraid we're in a bit of trouble."

"The flowers have done well, I see," Ivena said.

Joey smiled. "Yes. Yes they have." They looked at each other but said no more.

Joey turned back to Jan and Helen. "Well, well, please sit down." He hurried around the small living room, straightening rust-colored cushions on a green rattan couch and a matching chair. A stone fireplace ate up half the floor space, but the decor was surprisingly colorful and cozy. Then again, Joey was a gardener—he would favor beauty.

He sat on the washed stone mantel. "So you are in some trouble. Tell me."

He listened while they spun their story, hearing it from beginning to end in one sitting, Saying it aloud, Jan was struck by its absurdity. This tale of love and horror, it sounded impossible in this land of peace. And to think, not four miles away construction was already in progress on the castle he was building for his bride. He looked at Helen—at the amber light shining in her glassy eyes—and a hand seemed to squeeze his heart. God's hand, he thought.

Joey kept looking at him as if checking to make sure it was really him, the author he knew. He could only nod. But in the end Joey insisted that they would be safe here. At least for a day while they decided what to do. Although they would have to manage with two bedrooms. Joey would take the couch.

He offered them bowls of a beef stew and they talked over a dozen options, none of which made any sense to Jan. The situation seemed impossible. Walking into a man's place of business and shooting him wasn't exactly self-defense. At the very least Jan needed to contact an attorney. In fact, why not drive to the police station right then and turn himself in? Yes indeed, why not? It seemed their only option.

Jan finally set his bowl on the coffee table and sighed. "I think there's only one thing that makes sense. But it's not Helen who's angered Glenn now. It's me. And he's made a direct threat against you, Ivena. There's only one way to ensure your safety."

"And what of you?"

"Please hear me out. If I were to contact the police and demand protective custody for you I believe they'd give it. You've already lodged a complaint. They can't ignore you now."

"So you want them to put *me* in jail?"

"You've done nothing wrong; they wouldn't put you in jail."

"But you have, Janjic. You have assaulted this man. They will put *you* in jail for that."

"Maybe. But then a prison may be the safest place for me. Until they unravel the truth."

"The truth is you shot a man," Helen said. "Regardless of what Glenn has done, they won't let that slide."

They looked at each other. "Either way I'll face consequences. If I can bring a detective here to hear our story we'll at least buy protection for Ivena. Do you have any doubt that Glenn will hurt Ivena?"

"No. But you're putting a lot of confidence in the police, aren't you? We're safe from him here."

"And how long do you think we can stay here? I have business expected of me. By midday tomorrow they'll be scouring the country for my whereabouts. I see no alternative. In the morning I'll call the detective who took Ivena's statement. What was his name?"

"Mr. Wilks," Ivena said. "Charlie Wilks."

"I wouldn't trust a soul," Helen said. "I'm telling you, if you think turning yourself in to the police is the way to go on this, then you don't know Glenn. He's got connections. You should call an attorney."

"I will. But first I will use my own contacts," Jan said. He stood and walked to the black telephone that hung on the wall.

"Who?"

He picked up the receiver. "Roald. Perhaps my estranged friend can pull a trick from his hat yet."

DETECTIVE CHARLIE Wilks was at his office desk at nine o'clock Tuesday morning when the third light on his phone lit to an annoying buzz. He punched the flashing cube. "Wilks."

"Detective Wilks, this is Jan Jovic."

Charlie sat up. "Jovic?" He glanced through the open door of his office. A dozen desks filled the gap, occupied by other detectives with lessor seniority.

"Yes. I have something—"

"Hold on. Could you hold on?"

"Yes."

Charlie rose from his desk, closed the door and returned. "Sorry about that. Where are you, Mr. Jovic?"

"I'm safe, if that's what you mean."

The man's voice carried a foreign accent. *Safe?* "You do realize that I have a citywide APB on you as we speak. I'm not sure what the laws are like back in your country, but here in America shooting a man's hands off is a crime. Are the others with you?"

The man hesitated a moment. "Others?"

"We have Helen and this Ivena who are also missing. I'm assuming they're with you."

"Yes. And Ivena reported her complaint to you yesterday, is that right?"

"Of course. But surely you understand that until I've had a chance to examine her claims, my hands are tied. In the meantime, I have seen Mr. Lutz's hands with my own eyes."

"All in good time, my friend. I want you to guarantee Ivena and Helen protective custody. When you hear their stories you will see that it is Glenn Lutz, not I, you should be searching for."

"I know where Glenn Lutz is. In fact I spoke to him this morning. You, on the other hand, I do not. You're only making things worse for yourself. Just tell me where you are and I'll hear you out."

"I will. But not until tomorrow morning. Until then, please do not make more of this than is absolutely necessary. I'm not a man without influence, Mr. Wilks. You may expect a call tomorrow."

The phone went abruptly dead.

Charlie's pulse spiked. He immediately punched up another line and dialed a string of numbers. Who would've guessed that a man with the backbone to shoot Glenn Lutz would cave so easily. Then again, Jovic had no reason to mistrust the police.

His friend's familiar voice spoke over the receiver. "Yes?"

"Hello, Glenn. I have some news."

"You do, do you? For your sake, Charlie, it better be good."

"See now, why are you always so hostile?" Charlie leaned back in his chair, confident. "He called."

Glenn's heavy breathing cut short. "The preacher called?"

"He wants to meet with me tomorrow morning. Ivena and Helen are with him."

"Where?"

"He wouldn't tell me. But he will."

The sound of Lutz's breathing filled the earpiece again. "And you'll tell me, won't you?" A few more loud breaths. "Won't you, Charlie?"

The man was clearly sick. "A hundred grand? That's what you said you'd pay if you need my help, right? I'd call this helping."

"That's what I said."

"You'll be my first call," Charlie said, grinning. "I'll even give you an hour head start."

"You just call me."

CHAPTER THIRTY-TWO

THE SKIES boiled black over Atlanta that evening, threatening rain before the traffic ended its rush. Jan parked the Cadillac in an alley two blocks from the ministry and climbed out. He was counting on his call to Detective Wilks buying him some time. If there was a police car watching the building for his return, this visit might backfire.

Jan scanned the street, saw no sign of the police, and stepped onto the sidewalk. He buried his hands in his pockets and walked with his head lowered. The employees should all have gone home by now, but there was always a chance that someone from the neighborhood would recognize him.

Jan had left Helen and Ivena at Joey's cottage nearly three hours ago. He'd made a pass by his street, hoping to retrieve a fresh change of clothes for he and Helen, but the police cruiser parked across the road had changed his mind. Ivena's house was also being watched. He'd opted for Woolworth's instead. Helen would have to live with the white dress he'd selected. It was a size five and the salesclerk had assured him that five was a good size for a small woman. He bought himself nothing.

He glanced up. The street was clear of cars. Evidently the police were more concerned with the houses than the ministry. Or perhaps it was the late hour.

Jan veered into the alley adjacent to the ministry building and walked for a steel fire door. "Don't let me down, Roald," he muttered. "Please not now."

He pulled the handle and the door swung out. A chill of relief washed down his back. He entered the dark hall, felt his way to the stairwell, and took the stairs two at a time. Red exit signs showed the way, but eight floors winded him and he paused at the top landing to catch his breath.

He pushed his way into the familiar office suite. He heard the voices immediately and knew that Roald had come through. He had not seen their cars, which meant they'd parked on the back street as he'd requested.

The conference room door was open and Jan walked in.

They were all there, and they looked at him as one. Roald, Karen, and Betty. Frank and Barney Givens, as well. He'd asked Roald for the council's attendance if possible; whether Frank and Barney had flown in or happened to be in the city, Jan did not know. Two of the four were here. And Betty was here as a representative from the ministry. The employees would want to know the truth once it hit the street, and he intended they receive it through Betty.

"Good evening, my friends," Jan said with a slight smile.

Roald sat at the head of the long table, frowning, his glasses riding the end of his nose. Beside him Karen leaned back with folded arms. Frank and Barney sat stolcally to the left and Betty smiled warmly on his right.

"You'd better sit, Jan," Roald said.

"Hello, Roald. It's a pleasure to see you as well." A voice of caution whispered through Jan's mind. They were not reacting with the concern he'd imagined. Betty was smiling, but the others were not even cordial. "I was under the impression that I called this meeting. Why do I feel like I've walked into a snake pit here?" Jan asked, still standing.

"Oh, no, Jan," Betty said. She glanced around nervously. "How could you say—"

"You have something to say, say your piece," Roald interrupted.

Jan glared at him. "Thanks, Betty. Okay, Roald, I will." He pulled a chair out on Betty's side and sat. "Thank you for coming, Frank and Barney. Karen." They nodded in turn but offered no formal greeting.

"By your stiff lips I gather you've heard about the incident yesterday."

No reaction.

"I'll take that as a yes. I also know that from the beginning you haven't understood my relationship with Helen. No, let me rephrase that—from the beginning most of you have detested my relationship with Helen. Well, now the balance has shifted, because now I've been forced to do some things I'm not proud of. Something you may think will tarnish my image. But if you will just open your minds for a few minutes, I sincerely believe that you'll see things differently."

They sat and stared at him without responding.

Jan shifted his eyes from Roald. "Frank, three months ago you and Barney and the others from the council warned me about the delicate nature of my image as a church spokesman, and I will say that I questioned your judgment at the time. But I see some truth in your assessment now. 'To whom much is given, much is required,' I believe that was your quote. There were greater concerns at stake besides my own issues, you said. Concerns of the church. The ministry, for example. *The Dance of the Dead.* An opportunity to reach millions with a message of God's love. You wanted me to subordinate my own needs to the greater good of the church, isn't that right?"

Frank's eyes flickered and Jan spoke on.

"Well now perhaps there is an opportunity for you, all of you"—he glanced about the table—"to subordinate your own issues to the greater concerns of the church. To *The Dance of the Dead.* Perhaps now it's time for you to support me and my ministry, because, believe me, no one else will. What you've heard is true. I shot this madman Glenn Lutz in his hands, with his own gun, but only because he threatened to kill Ivena. Only because he's a monster of unearthly magnitude. And if you really knew—"

"We know more than you think we know," Roald interrupted.

"Meaning what?" A spike of anger rode Jan's spine.

"Are you finished?"

This was not going as planned. He had intended on laying out the whole scenario as he knew it to be. He'd come confident that they would hear him out and rally to his defense. But Roald did not seem to possess a soft bone in his body. Which seemed beyond even Jan. Karen had hardly moved since his entrance. Not that he expected any huge favors from her. Betty was the only one who showed a sympathetic spirit, but Betty did not possess the power these others did.

"No, I'm not finished. But you're obviously not understanding my point here, so why don't you go ahead and tell me what's on your mind, Roald." He bit down hard and suppressed an urge to walk over there and knock his head against the wall.

"Fine, I will. While you've been busy hiding from the police, which is the most ridiculous thing I've ever heard of, we've been busy trying to salvage your career. This goes much deeper than you realize, my naive friend. You have some problems, and now by association we have some problems."

"You think I don't know this? What—"

"The contract we signed with Dreamscape has some problems."

"The contract? What does the contract have to do with this? I thought they said it was virtually identical to the old one."

"Virtually, yes. But not exactly. It has a clause relating to morality that has come to our attention."

"Morality. And how does morality affect us in this contract?"

"That depends. It contains a clause that gives Dreamscape the right to pull the plug in the event that the moral character of the story's subject comes under question at any time before the movie's release date. The subject of the picture is you, Jan."

The statement dropped in Jan's mind like a small bomb. He blinked. "*My* moral integrity? What does that mean? They're already taking exception to my mistake yesterday? Or is it you, who are making more—"

"Not the shooting, you idiot! Stupid as that was—"

"Please don't interrupt me, Roald!" Jan said. "At least give me that courtesy."

"Of course."

"And if it's not the shooting, then what?"

Roald didn't respond. Frank did. "It's the woman, Jan. You were warned about her, weren't you?"

Jan's mind swam, too stunned to piece their reason together.

"I told you she was a risk," Roald snapped. Karen still hadn't spoken. She simply rocked back in her chair, arms still folded. Roald continued. "The studio is putting millions on the table, producing a picture that views the world through an exceptional lens—the eye of Jan Jovic, a man who has learned of love through the brutal lessons of war. And now they discover their *hero* is living with a . . . an unseemly woman. I told you she was a bad idea, didn't I? I sat right here and told you that this junkie of yours could ruin everything. And did you listen? No. Instead you go off and marry her, of all things!"

"And you know nothing, Roald!"

"No, of course I don't. That's why you ignored my advice to begin with. Because I know nothing. And you, the white crusader, know everything."

"Okay, guys," Karen said. "We're still on the same side here."

"Are we?" Roald shot back. "I'm on the side of getting this movie made, of getting this message out. And frankly I don't know what side Jan's on anymore."

"I'm on the side of love," Jan said. "The same side you were on at one time. It's the heart and soul of my story."

"Well, now your love is going to get *The Dance of the Dead* canceled. Your relationship with Helen undermines your moral authority."

The notion felt like a sick joke to Jan. "We're married, for heaven's sake! How could morality be an issue in marriage?"

Roald shook his head. "You really should have listened to me. It's the appearance of evil that matters, Jan. How are they going to sell a movie about one man's discovery of God and morality when his morals are in question? Isn't that what I told you?"

"And I'm asking you how my morality is in question!"

"Because appearances do matter, Jan. And your . . . *wife* does not give off the best appearances!"

Jan wanted to strike the man with his fist. He rose and stood against the conference table, shaking with rage.

"Now you want to shoot me like you did Mr. Lutz?" Roald asked.

"Okay, Roald," Karen said. "You've made your point." She turned to Jan and her eyes were emotionless. "Sit down, Jan."

Jan forced himself back into his chair. Frank and Barney sat side by side, like a jury studying the cross-examination.

"Dreamscape has given us a condition for continuance," she said. "They won't make the movie with a questionable moral dilemma hanging over your head."

"That's utterly ridiculous! And what's 'questionable' supposed to mean anyway?"

"It means," Roald said, "that either the woman goes or the movie goes. That's what it means."

"That's absurd! They want me to divorce? And they see that as moral? No studio could be so stupid! Someone else will buy the movie rights!"

"No they won't. Dreamscape has already made it clear that they won't sell the rights. Not as long as there's an adulterous relationship in the mix."

"I am *not* in an adulterous relationship! Who would make such a claim?"

Karen spoke. "They didn't say you were committing adultery—they claim that Helen's still seeing Glenn Lutz."

The room fell to silence. A sweat broke out on Jan's forehead. "The movie is about me, not Helen. And how would Dreamscape know of Glenn?"

"You are married to Helen. It looks bad," Roald answered, holding his eyes on Jan. "And Dreamscape would know about Glenn because for all practical purposes, Dreamscape is Glenn."

Dreamscape was Glenn? But how?

Then Jan knew how. Glenn had set this up for one purpose and one purpose only. The man would stop at nothing to get Helen back!

"So, Glenn acquires *The Dance of the Dead* through Dreamscape and he tells you that unless I end my relationship with Helen, *his* lover, then he won't make the picture. Is that about it?" Jan knew that a tremble accompanied his words, but he no longer cared. "And that doesn't sound odd to you? This pig is the devil himself and you don't see it, do you? It seems that I have grounds to sue him for manipulating the terms of the contract!"

"It doesn't matter how it sounds to us, Jan," Karen said. "He paid for the rights to the movie and we signed a contract that gives him the technical right to cancel the movie on these grounds. And now that you've assaulted him, he no doubt has other grounds."

"And he assaulted me. When the world discovers that, Glenn won't have a leg to stand on."

"So you say, but he has a voice as well. And either way he'll probably sue for all moneys already paid. Am I right, Roald?"

"Yes. That's right."

Jan faced the man. "So you talked to him yourself, Roald? You plotted behind my back with this devil?"

"Yes, I spoke to him. He called me. What did you want me to do? Refuse a call from the man behind our futures?"

"Your future, perhaps, but not mine. I'll *never* give in to a monster like Glenn."

"You will refuse, then? You'll kiss off seven million dollars and this entire ministry and everything you've lived for? Over this one lousy woman?"

Jan slammed his hand on the table and they all jumped. "She is *not* one lousy woman! She is everything! I have lived my life preparing to love her. And nothing—not seven million dollars, not a hundred million dollars—nothing will come between us! Do you understand this, or do I need to stamp it on your forehead?"

Roald's face flushed red. "You're throwing everything away! Everything!"

"Not Helen. I will not throw Helen away. *She* is everything! Nothing else matters!" Jan sat back and breathed heavily. "How can you sit there and suggest that I divorce my wife so that you can line your pockets with gold?"

Roald's face turned red and for a moment Jan thought he might leap over the table and attempt to remove his head.

"I don't think that's what Roald had in mind," Karen said with an apologetic smile. "I think he's genuinely concerned with the bigger picture here—"

"Is that what you think?" Jan interrupted. "And what did you have in mind, Karen? That somehow in this mess you would be vindicated?"

She appeared to have been slapped. Karen pulled herself up to the table. "Now you listen to me, you meathead. First of all, you must know that if this deal falls through it will be the end of the ministry. You ever think of that? The book will be canceled, the tours, everything will go away without the movie. A million lives will be impacted. You must see that. And the fact that you're living with—or married to—a woman who's in an adulterous affair with another man does give you right of divorce, doesn't it? In many circles it would be the only moral thing to do. What Roald's suggesting isn't that unreasonable."

Jan stared at Karen, wondering what other motive lay behind her sudden plea for reason. "Then, you don't understand either, Karen. The world doesn't turn on reason alone. It's a matter of love. I love her. Desperately. Surely *you*, of all people, can understand that."

He saw a flicker of surprise in her eyes. She did not answer.

Barney cleared his throat and spoke for the first time. "You can't always follow your heart," he said. "Not when it defies reason. God's given man a mind for good reason. We all know the pull of love. Love is blind and full of passion and, yes, reason hardly stands a chance. But it must, don't you see? All that is good and decent depends on it. You cannot just leave your mind to follow your heart's whims. There are greater issues at stake."

Jan felt anger rise again. "Such pretty words from a great lover, I am sure. But let me tell you, Father Micheal's love for God was not born of his mind alone. No, it came first from his heart. He was desperate for God and glad to die for him. Your words of reason will drain the heart of its power."

He turned to the others, leaning forward now. "I'll tell you, I've been given a very small slice of God's love for Helen and it makes my knees weak in her presence. You're suggesting I face God and tell him to keep his heart? Because a leader in the church said it was *unreasonable?* That's your position on this matter?"

"Of course not!" Frank said. "We're telling you to do what is right! But I can see that you're too selfish with this love of yours to consider what consequences your decision might have on the rest of the church. This is not simply about you and your feelings for one woman. The greater good of the church must be considered."

"The greater good of the church, you say. And the church is the Bride of Christ. So what is the greatest good for the Bride?"

"You're twisting my words to suit your own means! The Bride is not this one woman. The Bride is the church, millions strong. It is she you must consider."

"Love for the masses outweighs love for the few, is that it? Then let me suggest that God would quickly choose the true love—the unbridled, passionate love—of one soul over the acknowledgment of his deity from a hundred million churchgoing souls!"

"You demean the church?" Roald challenged.

"No, Roald, *you* demean the church. You mock the Bride. You undermine the value of love. The universe was created in the hopes of distilling a portion of genuine love. And now you suggest ignoring such love in favor of creating a moving picture for a profit. Nothing will ever compare to love, brother. Not all the devices man's mind can conceive, not a hundred thousand bulls slaughtered on the Day of Atonement. Nothing!"

Roald frowned. "And you have the spiritual pride to assume that you alone now possess God's love in your own heart? This love for an adulterous woman?"

"No, not me alone. But it's no different than God's love for an adulterous nation. For Israel. No different than his deep love for the church. His bride. You."

The leader found nothing to say. For a moment Jan thought he might see the light. But after blinking a few times, Roald set his jaw and pushed his chair back. "This is crazy. I can't believe we're even thinking of throwing this away because of one . . . The way you speak smells of heresy." He stood. "Well, Jan Jovic, I told you this once, but I'll tell you now for the last time. If the woman stays, then we go." As if on cue Frank and Barney stood with Roald.

"We've had enough of this nonsense. I assume you called us here to ask for our support. And now you have our conditions. I only hope that God speaks some sense to your heart."

"Yes, well you may pray for me, Roald. You do remember how to do that, don't you?"

Roald glared at Jan then huffed from the room with Frank and Barney.

Karen blew out some air and crossed her legs. "Well, *that* was quite a speech."

"Perhaps I expressed myself too strongly."

Betty spoke quietly. "I don't think so. I think you said what you needed to say. I've never heard such wonderful words." Her kind eyes smiled, and Jan thought that asking for her attendance was perhaps the only part of the meeting that had come off as planned.

"Thank you, Betty. You're very kind."

Karen grinned. "You certainly left no doubt as to where you stand. You're really going out on a limb this time, aren't you, Jan?"

He sighed and closed his eyes. What was happening? *Father, what have you done to me? You're stripping me of all you've given me.*

And now Glenn was threatening worse. How had he managed this impossible turn of events? He pictured the heavy man standing with bloodied hands in his office just yesterday, and now seeing the man's twisted smile, fear lapped at Jan's mind. The man was capable of anything.

"Jan."

He opened his eyes. Karen studied him. "You know on one level I can understand what you're doing."

"Yes? What am I doing, Karen? *I* don't even know what I'm doing."

"You're staying by the side of an unfaithful woman, that's what you're doing. And in staying by her side, you're throwing away the kind of life that most people can only dream about."

"Maybe." Jan looked at the chalkboard to their left. The figures of the new edition's intended distribution sprawled in white numbers, still vivid from the planning meeting during which they'd been drawn three weeks ago. "Or perhaps I've found the kind of love that most people only dream about. Anything less would be meaningless."

"Perhaps. That's the level I can understand. I look at you, and I find it hard to believe that you actually love her that way. It tears me up, you know. That could have been me you were speaking about." She shifted her gaze. "It's your sticking by her when she doesn't deserve you that I can't understand. That you love an unfaithful woman so much."

It was the first time they had spoken so candidly of Helen. Betty's eyes shone with understanding. Jan looked at Karen. "I'm sorry, Karen. I didn't mean to hurt you. Please tell me you know that."

"Maybe," she said. She was barely smiling and that was a good thing.

"I swear, Karen. I'm not sure I even understand it myself."

"This could change your life, you know? You could lose everything."

"The studio won't back down?"

"I don't know. It does seem crazy, doesn't it?" She shook her head. "This is all happening too quickly. You don't actually think Lutz would hurt Ivena, do you?"

"Of course he would! You don't know the man."

"Then you should go to the police," Betty said. "You hurt a man who threatened you. It may not be the act of a saint, but it's not the end of the world."

"She's right," Karen agreed. "That may be your only hope now. *Our* only hope; you're not the only one who stands to lose on this."

"I came here hoping that Roald could pull some strings. Either way, I've already arranged to meet the police in the morning."

"Good." Karen stood and Betty followed suit.

"And what if Glenn isn't bluffing?" Jan asked.

Karen walked to the door and shrugged. She faced him. "I think you're doing the right thing, Jan. I want you to know that. Your love for her is a good thing. I see that now."

"Thank you, Karen."

She smiled. "We've pulled through some bad times before."

"None this bad," he said.

"No, none this bad."

Then she left.

Betty patted him lightly on the shoulder. "I will pray for you, son. And in the end, you'll see. This will all make sense."

"Thank you, Betty."

She too left him, now all alone.

Jan lowered his head to the table and he cried.

CHAPTER THIRTY-THREE

"The day of death [is] better than the day of birth.
It is better to go to a house of mourning than
to go to a house of feasting."

Ecclesiastes 7:1–2 NIV

JAN PULLED the Cadillac onto the overrun driveway leading to Joey's cottage. He drove slowly, listening to the crunch of gravel under the car's tires. *Father, you have abandoned me. You have given me everything only to strip it away.*

Joey's Pinto was missing. Perhaps the gardener had gone for supplies.

Jan parked the Cadillac and walked to the house. He'd reached the first step up to the porch when the door flew open. It was Ivena. She stared at him with wide eyes.

"Hello, Ivena."

Suddenly Joey pushed past her.

"Hello, Joey. I—"

A buzz erupted in his mind. He instinctively turned to where the Pinto should have been. But of course it was not there.

"Where's Helen?"

"Janjic. Janjic, please come in. We were worried."

He spun to her. "Where is Helen?" he shouted.

"We think she took the car," Joey said.

Jan closed his mouth and swallowed. He stared at Ivena and she looked back, her eyes misted with anguish. He wanted to ask her how long Helen had been gone, but that didn't matter, did it?

No, nothing really mattered. Not anymore. She had gone back. His bride had gone back.

300

Jan suddenly felt such a shame that he thought he might break into a wail right there on the front step. He whirled from them and fled down the path leading into the garden. Overhead, thunder boomed and he stumbled forward, through the hedge, and now a growling sound escaped his throat. It was a moan that he felt powerless to stop. His chest was exploding and he could not contain himself.

He plunged through the garden without thinking of where his feet carried him; he only wanted to leave this place. It was a place of treachery and mockery and the worst kind of pain. It was not what he wanted. Now he only wanted death.

"SHOULD WE go after him?" Joey asked.

"No. It is something he must face on his own," Ivena said. Tears glistened on her cheeks.

"Are you sure he'll be okay?"

"He is walking through hell, my friend. He is dying inside. I don't know what will happen. All I know is that we are witnessing something the world has rarely seen in such a plain way. It makes you want to throw yourself at the foot of the cross and beg for forgiveness."

Joey looked at her, a puzzled look on his face.

She turned to him and smiled. "You will understand soon enough. Now we should pray that our Father will visit Janjic." Then she walked into the cottage.

HELEN TOLD herself that her decision to go was for Jan's sake. She told herself that a hundred times.

As a matter of fact, it had been her first thought. That first seed that had taken root in her mind. *Maybe you can talk some sense into him. Maybe Glenn will listen to you.* That had been around noon, before she really had time to mull the possibilities through her mind.

By midafternoon her thoughts had become as stormy as the skies rumbling overhead. No matter how strenuously she tried to convince herself otherwise, she knew then that she actually wanted to go back. That she *had* to go back. And not just to tell Glenn that he was being a baby about this whole mess, but

because butterflies were flapping wildly in her stomach and her throat was craving a taste.

By late afternoon a perpetual tremor rode her bones. The possibility of pleasure had taken up residence and was growing at an obscene rate. Her reason began
to leave her at four. Questions like, *How could you even think of doing this again?*
or *Who in God's name would stoop so low?* became vague oddities, worth noting, but
hardly worth considering. At five her reason was totally gone. She stopped trying
to convince herself of anything and began planning her escape.

The fact that Joey left the keys in the yellow Pinto made leaving that much
easier. She would have the car back before they knew it was missing. Ivena was off
talking to Joey in the garden about some new species of rose; they wouldn't know
if a meteor struck the house.

By the time Helen pulled into the underground parking structure at the
Towers, she was sweating. She very nearly turned the car around then in a last-
minute flash of sense. But she didn't. She stepped onto the concrete and suddenly
she was desperate to be upstairs, high on the thirtieth floor.

To tell Glenn what a baby he was being about this whole mess, of course.

Just that. Just to step in for Jan and call the pig off Ivena and save the day. And
to take a tiny snort. Or maybe two snorts.

JAN CLIPPED his foot on a small shrub rounding a corner and sprawled face
first to the cool sod. He lay there numb for a few moments. Then it all gushed
out of him in uncontrollable sobs. He lay there and shook and wet the grass with
his tears.

Time seemed to lose itself, but at some point Jan hauled himself from the
ground and settled into a heavily flowered gazebo. Thunder continued to rumble,
but farther away now.

Jan slumped on the gazebo bench and stared at the black shapes of bushes lining the lawn before him like tombstones. Slowly his mind pieced together his
predicament. He was hiding from the police, but that was the least of it. The price
his imprudence would extract from him would be relatively small compared to
what he'd lost with Helen's leaving.

The rug was being pulled from beneath his feet, he thought. *The Dance of the
Dead* was finding its death. And not mercifully, but with savage brutality. Karen

was right: Everything would change if they canceled the movie. The ministry, his notoriety, the castle he was building for his bride. It would all be snatched away—leaving him with what?

His bride.

Ha!

His bride! Jan trembled with fury in the small shelter. For the first time since entering the garden he spoke aloud.

"Father, I want you to take this from me. I cannot live with this!" His voice came in a soft growl and then grew in volume. "You hear me? I hate this! Take her from me. I beg you. You have given me a curse. She's a curse."

"Good evening."

Jan jerked upright at the voice. A man stood in the moonlight, leaning against the gazebo's arch.

"Beautiful night, isn't it?"

Jan ran a hand across his eyes to clear his vision. Here was a man, tall and blond, smiling as if meeting another person after dark in this garden was an everyday occurrence.

"Who . . . who are you?" Jan asked. "The garden's closed."

"No. I mean yes, the garden is closed. But I'm not anyone to be afraid of. And if you don't mind my asking, how did you get in?"

"My friend is the gardener. He let me in."

"Joey?" The man chuckled. "Good old Joey. So what brings you here so late at night? And looking so forlorn."

Jan stood. Who did this man think he was, questioning him like this? "I guess I could ask the same of you. Do you have permission to be here?"

"But of course. I have come to speak with you."

"You have?"

"Do you still love her, Jan?"

Jan's heart quickened. "How do you know my name? Who sent you?"

"Please. Who I am isn't important. My question is, Do you still love her?"

"Who?"

"Helen."

There it was then. Helen. "And what do you know about Helen?"

"I know that she is no more extraordinary and no less ordinary than every man. Every woman," the man said.

The answer sounded absurd and it made Jan wonder again who he could be, knowing Helen and Joey and speaking so craftily. "Then you don't know Helen. Nothing could be farther from the truth."

"Tell me why she is so different."

"Why should I tell you anything?" Jan paused. Then he gave the man his answer. "She's stolen my heart."

The man smiled. "Well, then that would make her extraordinary. And what makes her less?"

"She has broken my heart."

"Does she love you?"

"Well, now that's the big question, isn't it? Yes, she loves me. No, she hates me. Which side of her mouth would you like the answer to come from? The side that whispers in my ear late at night or the side that licks from Glenn's hand?"

The man suddenly grew very still. The smile that had curved his lips flattened. "Yes, it hurts, doesn't it?" He swallowed—Jan saw it because the moon had broken through the clouds and now lighted one side of a chiseled face. His Adam's apple bobbed. The man turned to face the shadows, and lifted a finger to his chin. The anger in Jan's heart faded.

The stranger cleared his throat. "It does hurt. I won't dispute you." He faced Jan again and spoke with some force. "That doesn't make her more or less extraordinary, my friend. She is predictably common in her treachery. So utterly predictable."

Jan blinked, unable to respond.

"But how you respond to her, now that could be far less common." The man's words hung on a delicate string. "You could love her."

"I do love her."

"You do love her, do you? Really love her?"

"Yes. You have no idea how I have loved her."

"No? She is desperate for your love."

"She cannot even *accept* my love!"

"No, she can't. Not yet. And that's why she's so desperate for it."

Jan paused, removing his gaze from the man. "This is absurd, I don't even know you. Now you expect to engage me about this madness without telling me who you are? What gives you that right?"

"Ivena once said that God has grafted his love for Helen into your heart. Do you believe that?"

"And how do you know what Ivena has told me?"

"I know Ivena well. Do you believe what she said?"

"I don't know, honestly. I no longer know."

"Still, you must have an opinion on the matter. Was Ivena mistaken?"

"No. No, she was not mistaken. It started that way, but it doesn't mean I still have any part of God's heart. A man can only live with so much."

"A man can only *live* with so much. True enough. At some point he will have to *die* for something. If not now, then for an eternity."

Jan stilled at the words, surprised. How much truth was in those few words? *At some point he will have to die for something.* They could easily be from his own book, and yet spoken here by this stranger they sounded . . . magical.

"I love her, yes," Jan said, and a lump rose to his throat. "But she does not love me. And I'm afraid she will never love me. It's too much. Now I feel nothing but regret."

The stranger did not move. "Do you know that even the Creator was filled with regret? It's not such an unusual sentiment. He was sorry he'd ever made man, and in fact he sent a flood to destroy them. A million men and women and children suffocated under water. Your frustration is not so unique. Perhaps you are feeling what he felt."

"You're saying that God felt this anger? It certainly doesn't seem to fit with this love he gave me."

"You are made in his image, aren't you? You think he's beyond anger? The emotions of rejection are a powerful sentiment, Jan. God or man. And yet still he died willingly, despite the rejection. As did the priest and Nadia. As will others. So perhaps it's time for you to die."

"Die? How would I die?"

"Forgive. Love her without condition. Climb up on your cross, my friend. Unless a seed fall to the ground and die, it cannot bear fruit. Somehow the church has forgotten the Master's teachings."

A buzz droned through Jan's mind. They were his own words thrown back into his face. "The teaching's figurative," he argued.

"Is the death of the will any less painful than the death of the body? Call it figurative if it makes you comfortable, but in reality the death of the will is far more traumatic than the death of the body."

"Yes. Yes, you are right. In the death of the body the nerve endings soon stop feeling. In the death of the will the heart doesn't stop its bleeding so quickly. Those were my own words."

"Perhaps you've forgotten," the man said. "Now you're tasting that same death."

"*She* is causing my death. Helen is forcing me to die," Jan said.

"No more than you have caused the death of Christ. Yet he loved you no less." A wide smile spread across the stranger's face and the moonlight glinted off his eyes. "But the fruits of love are worth death, my friend. A thousand deaths."

"The fruits?"

"Joy. But for the joy set before him, Christ endured the Cross. Unspeakable joy. A million angels kissing one's feet could not compare to the rapture found in the tender words of one human."

Jan swallowed. This stranger would know, he thought, although he wasn't sure why. He stood and paced the floor of the gazebo, thinking of these words. He turned his back to the man and stared out at the round white moon. The man was no ordinary friend of Ivena, surely. Not with this insight.

The edge is gone from my pain already, he thought. *I have spoken to this man for no more than a few minutes and my heart is feeling hope again.*

"And what of Helen?" Jan asked without looking back. "How will she learn to love? She must *die?*"

It was a backward way of looking at the universe, he thought. He'd always understood the place of death, as it related to life. A seed must fall to the ground and die before giving life to the tree. But he'd never associated death with *love.* Yet it was in love—in the death of self required by love—that it made the clearest sense. The man hadn't answered his question.

"You're saying that she too"—he turned to the man—"must find—"

He caught himself mid-sentence. The man was gone. Jan spun around, found no one and stepped from the gazebo. The stranger was not in sight! He had said his piece and then left.

Jan called into the night, "Hello. Is anybody there? Hello." But the garden remained still except for his own voice.

The stranger's words echoed through his mind. *She is desperate for your love.*

What was he doing? His whole life—all of eternity—seemed to be in the balance for this one woman. For Helen. And he had all but cursed her. *Oh, dear Helen. Forgive me!*

Jan tore for the path and angled for the east wall that hid Joey's cottage. A panic fluttered through his stomach.

Oh, Father, forgive me!

THE PINTO was still missing when Jan burst through the hedge. He slid to a stop on the gravel, his heart thumping in his chest. She had come back and left already, perhaps.

He bounded up the cottage steps and flung the door open. A dim lamp glowed by the single rattan chair, casting light over Ivena's face.

"She hasn't come yet, Janjic." She'd been crying, he could hear it in her voice. Ivena walked toward him without waiting for him to close the door. She placed her arms around him and laid her head against his chest. "I am sorry, dear. I am very sorry."

Jan put his hand on her head. "So am I, Ivena. But we aren't finished. There's more to this story. Isn't that what you've been saying?"

"Yes." Ivena stepped back and sniffed. "I have been praying for your understanding, Janjic."

He stepped into the cottage and closed the door. "And God has answered your prayer."

She smiled. "Then I will retire now."

"And I will wait for her."

Ivena and Joey each slept in the bedrooms, leaving the living room to Jan, a gracious gesture considering the circumstances. The night rested eerily quiet. Crickets chirped in the forest, but no traffic sounds reached the cottage. Jan suddenly felt a return of the pain that had flooded his bones earlier. He sank to his knees by the amber lamp, feeling destitute.

What if Helen did not return? Silence rang in his ears, high-pitched and piercing. He gripped his hands into fists. How could the stranger in the garden possibly know of this dread that rushed through his veins? It was death. His heart was being torn to shreds by a death no less real than Father Micheal's. At least the priest had gone to the grave with a smile.

He gritted his teeth, biting back a shaft of fury.

No, Janjic. If you die, it will be for love.

I am dying for love and it is killing me. He should brand that on his forehead. He slumped to his haunches, overcome by grief. The night blurred in his vision.

For a long time Jan knelt like a lump of clay, feeling lifeless. He got up once and poured himself a glass of tea, but he left it full on the counter after a single sip. He walked to the fireplace and slid along the wall to his seat.

The noise came to his ears then. It was a slight grating and it was at the front door. He had not heard a car approach.

He looked up, thinking it was the wind—it would cease any moment. But it didn't. In fact, if he wasn't mistaken, it was the front latch and it was being poked and scratched. Jan came halfway to his feet, his heart pounding.

And then the door swung in, open to the night, and Jan froze. She stood there. Helen stood there, wavering on her feet, taking in the room as if she were trying to understand it.

It occurred to Jan in that moment that he should scream at her. He should slap her and send her packing, because she was standing in the doorway, obviously stoned, slinking back from that beast.

But he could do no such thing. Never.

Helen took two steps forward and stopped again in a wedge of light from the moon, orienting herself in the darkness.

Jan stood up in the darkness and she faced him, perhaps not even knowing precisely who he was. "Helen?"

She looked at him with blank eyes glistening in the dim light.

Jan stepped toward her. "Helen, are you okay?"

She stood still, unresponsive.

"Helen, I'm so sorry!" He reached her and saw that she was trembling. He swept her from her feet, and she felt like a rag doll. A limp doll shaking and now whimpering with tears. "Oh, my dear. I'm so sorry," he said.

You are sorry for precisely what, Janjic? It is she, not you, who has betrayed.

But it is I who love, he answered himself.

Jan took her to the couch and laid her down. "Sleep, darling. Sleep." He pulled an afghan over her body. "It's okay. I'm here now." He knelt beside her and tucked the blanket around her carefully. Tears were streaming down her face, he saw. And his. His heart was breaking for her. Weeping. Like heaven, his heart was weeping for Helen.

She didn't speak to him for a long time, but he knew from her drooping eyes and sweet mouth, wrinkled with anguish, that she felt so much shame. So much that she could not speak it. It was this as much as any lingering intoxication that immobilized her.

Jan laid his head on her breast and he held her gently. They wept together for long minutes. Then she pushed herself up and buried her wet face in his neck.

"I'm sorry . . . ," she whispered. A sob choked her off.

"Shhhh." He pulled her tight.

She groaned. "No. I'm so sorry. Oh, God, I'm sorry. I'm so sorry . . ." Her words were loud enough to wake the house.

But Jan couldn't speak for the fist in his throat. He only wept with her and she kept groaning her remorse. It was a union of their spirits and it was sweet. The fruit of love. The stranger was right; his death in forgiveness was nothing compared to this joy.

Slowly she quieted, and he held her against his chest. Her body eventually stopped its shaking and then her breathing fell into a deep steady rhythm. She was asleep. His wife was asleep.

CHAPTER THIRTY-FOUR

HELEN KEPT to herself the following morning, nursing a cup of coffee and looking as if she would have chosen to remain hidden under the covers given a choice. Fortunately the hours leading up to Jan's phone call to the police were too mixed with speculation about their futures to give any space to the previous evening's debacle. Now more than ever, it seemed that a meeting with Detective Charlie Wilks was their only hope to save Jan and keep Ivena safe. One thing they all agreed on: Lutz had to be stopped. Regardless of how they felt about it, he quite literally held their lives in his hands. And now that Roald and the council had refused to help, there was no one but the authorities to whom they could appeal.

Jan put an overdue call in to Bill Waldon, an attorney the ministry had used on occasion, but Bill was no defense counsel. He put Jan in touch with a Mike Nortrop who was. Nortrop heard the short version of the story and then announced that there was nothing he could really do until the police charged Jan with a crime. The minute they did, Nortrop would be at the station. In the meantime, *Yes!* Jan must absolutely turn himself in. Running had been a "cockamamie" idea in the first place, he said. He hung up with the insistence Jan call him the minute they had any word.

Helen still didn't like the idea, but Jan saw no alternatives.

He made the call.

"Detective Wilks, please."

"One moment."

Ivena, Helen, and Joey all sat around the table, watching Jan in silence.

"Wilks here."

Jan took a breath and spoke calmly. "Good morning, Mr. Wilks. This is Jan Jovic."

"Jan. Well, Jan, it's good that you called. We were getting worried down here. Is everything all right?"

"Everything's fine. You're ready to meet?"

"Yes, of course we are," Wilks said. "I've been waiting for your phone call. Just tell me where you are."

Helen suddenly leaned forward and waved her hand frantically, whispering words Jan could not understand.

"Hold the phone a second." He covered the mouthpiece with his palm. "What?"

"Tell him to meet you alone, first. Not here."

"I thought our point was to secure protection for Ivena," he whispered.

"Just ask him. Please, it can't hurt."

Jan lifted the phone. "Hello?"

"I'm waiting, Jovic."

"I would like to meet you alone," he said. "Without Ivena."

"Alone? That wasn't the deal."

The detective's voice had tightened, and it triggered an alarm in Jan's spine. Why would the man care? He glanced at Helen. "It's me you want."

"We had a deal, Mr. Jovic. Now you're backing out of that deal, is that it?"

"Why are you interested in seeing Ivena? She's done nothing."

"That was *your* deal, mister."

"Yes, and now I'm changing it. Do you have a problem with that?"

"Yes, I have a problem . . ." He heard the man take a deep breath. Jan knew then that Helen was right. He could not trust the police. Heat washed over his shoulders.

"Look, Mr. Jovic, let's be reasonable—"

"I am trying to be reasonable. But I don't understand *your* reason. What crime has Ivena committed that you need to see her?"

"Please, Jan. Okay to call you Jan?"

"Sure."

"Okay, Jan. You've broken the law, do you understand that? I can book you on a dozen counts as we speak. Now you don't turn yourself in like we agreed and I swear I'll put you away as a felon, you hear me?"

"Yes, but why *Ivena?*"

"Because that was the deal! I need to verify her story," the detective snapped. "And don't think I can protect you if you don't play ball, buster. Glenn may be the victim on this one, but believe me, he knows how to play both sides."

"That sounds like a threat."

"You just tell me where you are."

"I will call you back, Detective Wilks. Good-bye."

Jan dropped the phone in its cradle, his head buzzing from the exchange.

"What did he say?" Helen blurted. "He went weird on you, didn't he? I told you he was in Glenn's hands. I knew it!"

Jan shook his head, unbelieving.

"The police are corrupted by Glenn, then?" Ivena asked.

"And I'll tell you something else," Helen said. "We won't be safe here forever."

They all turned to her. "Why?" Joey asked.

"They know we're north of town. They followed me that far before I lost them."

Silence settled around Joey's kitchen table. No one knew quite how to deal with the revelation.

"Which basically means we've got a problem," Jan said. "A very big problem. We have no one to turn to."

"Karen?" Ivena asked.

"She has no political clout. She might be help in a courtroom, as a witness, but not with the police now. What does it matter if we're in the right if Glenn kills Ivena? What we need is protection now." He shook his head. "I can hardly believe it's come to this. It's a free country, for heaven's sake!"

"Can the ministry help?"

"No."

"What about other friends? Surely you have well-placed friends," Joey said.

"I've been in the country for five years. Apart from Roald and Karen and their circle I'm only a passing face. And what does it matter? Glenn owns the rights to the movie. He owns me!"

"No one owns you, Janjic. What is this movie? I told you—"

"The movie is the future of the ministry, Ivena. Say what you like, but it's the gateway to a million hearts. And it's a livelihood."

"Not if Glenn Lutz owns it."

She was right. She could not be more right.

"Then what?" Joey asked. "I'm not hearing too many options that make sense."

No one responded.

"It's not safe here. What do we do?" Joey asked quietly, his eyes wide.

Jan knew then what they had to do. He'd known deep inside from the moment Roald walked out of the conference room last night. But it was suddenly very clear. He glanced at Helen and wondered how she would respond.

He snatched up the phone and punched in a number. The others only stared at him. It rang four times before someone picked up.

"Hello?"

"Betty?"

"Jan! Jan what on earth's happening? The police are—"

"Thank God you're there. Listen to me carefully, Betty. I need you to hear me very carefully. Is anyone else in the room?"

"No."

"Good. Please don't tell anyone that I called. It's very important, do you understand? What I'm going to say to you has to remain absolutely confidential. You can't tell the police anything. Can you do that?"

"Yes. I think so."

"No, you need to be certain. My life may depend on it."

"Yes, Jan. I can do that."

"Good. I need you to do a couple things for me. First you must go to my house. It'll be watched by the police, but ignore them. If they question you, tell them that you're retrieving mail as you always do when I'm absent on trips. If they ask where I am, you tell them that I'm in New York, of course. You have that? New York."

"Yes."

"Under my bed you'll find a small metal box. It's locked. Take it with you. Can you do that? It should fit under your dress." Jan glanced at Ivena, who'd raised her eyebrows. He ignored her.

"Yes," Betty said.

"Good. And I need to meet with some of the employees tonight. John and Lorna and Nicki. Some of the group leaders. Not at the ministry."

"My place?"

Jan hesitated. Betty's house would be perfect. She lived on a small farm on the west side of town. "Yes, that would be good. Be sure that no one knows. I can't overstress the need for secrecy."

"I understand. Really. What about Karen?"

The question took Jan by surprise. "If she's still in town, perhaps. Yes. There's one more thing. I need ten thousand dollars in cash. You'll have to convince Lorna to cash a check, but do it discretely. She may give you some trouble, you know how she is—"

"I can handle Lorna. Are you okay, Jan? This isn't sounding good."

"We're fine, Betty. I'll see you at nine o'clock tonight. If there are any problems, please leave your porch light off. I'll know not to come then."

Betty told him that she'd pray for him, and not to worry, she hadn't been born yesterday. That much he knew. He wondered if sending her to the house to smuggle his safe out under the nose of the police had been so wise. He hung up and exhaled.

"And what was the meaning of that?" Ivena asked.

"That, Ivena, was our ticket out of this mess. Our only way now. And it's your dream come true."

JAN TURNED the Cadillac's headlamps off before entering the long dirt drive to Betty's house at nine that evening.

"Light's on," Helen said.

The porch light was on. "I see that." He flipped the car's lights back on and drove to the ranch house. A white picket fence bordered the small neat lawn. Jan recognized the cars parked along the drive, Karen's blue Fairlane among them, straddling the grass to their right. He turned off the ignition and they got out.

"You're sure about this, Jan?" Helen asked, standing before the white farmhouse.

Jan took her hand and kissed her knuckles. "It's the only way."

"He's right," Ivena said. "It feels right."

"You're not sure, Helen?" Jan asked.

"It's not me. I like the idea, but I'm not the one jumping off a cliff."

Jan pulled her hand and they walked up the sidewalk. "We eagles like the cliffs," he said with a grin.

Betty answered his tap on the door. "Jan. Come in." He ushered Helen and Ivena inside and they stood gazing at nearly a dozen familiar faces, now crowded in Betty's living room. Silence swallowed whatever speculation the staff harbored about the meeting's purpose.

Betty smiled and nodded at Jan. John sat beside Lorna, both intent on him. Steve wiggled nervously to their left. Karen stood at the back with folded arms.

"Good evening, my friends," Jan said, smiling.

"Good evening."

Helen and Ivena took seats that Betty had set out facing the couch. Jan stood behind his chair. "Thank you for coming on such short notice. And thank you, Betty, for getting everyone here."

He took a deep breath. "So then, I'll be as brief as possible." They hung on his words already. Such a devoted group, so many friends. "You've all met my wife, Helen." A string of acknowledgments. "Most, if not all of you, were at our wedding." He paused and looked at Helen. She'd agreed to his plan wholeheartedly, but now she blushed.

"Some of you know the circumstances surrounding our marriage. But today you will all become participants in a dilemma that is changing our lives." *Move on, Janjic. Tell them.* "What you hear may sound . . . unusual to some of you. It may even sound impossible, but please hear me out. For your own sakes, hear me out."

No one moved. He glanced at Betty and saw her head dip slightly. Not even she knew what he'd come to tell them.

"Twenty years ago a priest named Father Micheal discovered a love for God, and he died for that love. Little Nadia died for the same love; you all know the story well—it is *The Dance of the Dead.* That love changed my life. It introduced me to the Creator."

He cleared his throat and took a deep breath. "Today, it seems that love has been born in me as well. I who saw the martyr's death, I who saw the love of Nadia am myself learning their love. We all are, I suppose. But to feel the love of the Father, it is something that will undo a man."

Jan fell silent for a few moments, judging their response. But they just stared at him with round eyes, eager for him to continue.

"I tell you this to help you understand what I will say now. I am taking my bride back to Bosnia."

The room suddenly felt evacuated of air.

"I won't be returning to America. Ivena, Helen, and myself are leaving for Bosnia to live. In Sarajevo."

They sat like mannequins, unmoving. Perhaps they didn't understand what he was saying. "But . . . but what about the movie?" John asked.

"The movie is gone."

Now a gasp ran through the gathering. "What? Why? That's impossible!"

"No, I'm afraid it's not impossible, my friends. You see, I was given a choice. The producer doesn't think my marriage . . . benefits the movie."

"But that's ridiculous," John said. "What does your marriage have to do with the movie?"

Choose your words, Janjic. "Nothing. Nothing at all. And yet they disagree. They seem to think that my character is in question." He put his hand behind Helen's head and she blushed.

"I would like to wring their necks personally!" It was Betty again.

Jan did not laugh. "Believe me, I understand the sentiment."

"So they can do that?" John demanded. "They can insist that?"

"They can and they have."

Lorna spoke the question undoubtedly on all of their minds. "And what does that mean for the ministry?"

"I'm afraid we'll have to return what we've been paid to the movie studio. It means that we have no choice but to close the ministry."

The cry of outrage came immediately from every corner of the room. "No! They can't do that! Never!" Even Karen looked stunned. Yet surely she knew this was coming.

"Can't we fight this?" Steve demanded. "Can't we get a lawyer or something?"

Jan looked at the wiry old man. The ministry had become his life. Helen lowered her head as if she was beginning to understand the price being paid for her.

"We could, but I am told that technically the producers are within their rights. It comes down to a choice that I must make. And I've made that choice. The ministry must close its doors. I'm sorry. The time has come for me to return to my homeland."

"What about Roald?" John asked. "Can't he do something?"

"Actually, I'm afraid even the council is deserting us this time. Not everyone sees the church in the same way, and now they see it differently than I do."

"I never did like that stuffed shirt!" John said.

"Please understand me, my friends. I don't want to leave you. But it's the call God has put in my heart. My story isn't finished, as Ivena has insisted for some time now, and the next chapter does not occur on American soil."

"And what will happen in Bosnia?"

"We will be free to love each other." He glanced at Helen.

Jan stated it simply and firmly, but they did not swallow it so quickly or easily. They went back and forth for another full hour, the more outspoken employees speaking their minds repeatedly, some arguing that Jan was right, others questioning what they saw as a preposterous suggestion. How could a whole ministry just shut down because of one deal gone bad?

In the end it was Lorna, biding her time for most of the debate, who brought the room to stillness once again. She simply outlined the financial state of the ministry. Without the movie deal, they would be lucky to get out of their lease without legal action. They were flat broke. Payroll was out of the question—even the one coming this Friday. And Jan? Jan would have to give up his house and his car, not to mention possibly being forced into bankruptcy. They might all be losing their jobs, but Jan was losing his life.

That silenced them all.

They stared at Jan with sad eyes now, finally understanding the full purpose of the meeting. For five long years they had given their lives to *The Dance of the Dead*. And now the dance was over.

They cried and they hugged and in the end they smiled. Because Jan could not hide the glint in his eyes. He was sure that they finally did believe him: It was indeed God who had placed this new tune in his heart. So he would dance a new dance—a dance of life, a dance of love.

And now that he thought about it, Jan could hardly stand to remain on American soil a second longer. It was time to go home.

CHAPTER THIRTY-FIVE

GLENN SAT cross-legged like a brooding beast on top of his desk. A dull pain throbbed relentlessly under the sling that held his right arm. A single white bandage sufficed for the finger on his left hand, but at times its pain overshadowed that of his shoulder.

They had scoured the northern outskirts of Atlanta for nearly two days without finding a sign of Helen following her disappearance. She'd come to him, and that had been a slice of heaven. But she had also left, and then lost the tail he'd put on her. Worse, the preacher had not followed through with his promise to meet Charlie. Charlie had tipped his hand, and Glenn had nearly taken his head off telling him so.

But they couldn't hide forever. Now it would be better to kill them all. One way or another he would at least kill the preacher and the bag of bones. And the next time he laid hands on Helen, he would maim her. At least.

The door suddenly cracked and Beatrice stepped in. "Sir, I have some news."

"Well, give it to me. You don't have to be so theatrical," he growled.

She ignored him and made her way to the guest chair. Only when she'd seated herself and smoothed out her black skirt did she speak. "They've left the country," she said.

Glenn sat, speechless. What was the wench telling him? They had fled to Canada? Or Mexico?

"The preacher has signed ownership of everything over to a manager for liquidation and he's taken the women out of the country."

A panic washed over his back. *He's taken her? He's taken her for good?* Glenn shoved himself off his desk, hardly aware of the pain that shot through his bones. His phone crashed to the tile. "He can't do that! He can't do that, can he? Where? When?"

Beatrice shrank back. "To Yugoslavia. Yesterday."

"Yugoslavia? Bosnia?" Glenn strode quickly to his left and then doubled back to his right. The preacher had taken Helen back to Bosnia! It was impossible! "He can't just leave! He owes me over a million dollars. Don't they know that?" He was having difficulty breathing, and he stopped to pull air into his lungs. "Doesn't that imbecile Charlie have any control at all?" He swore. *Think. Think!* "We have to stop them."

"I'm not even sure Detective Wilks knows it's happened. I received a call from the man in charge of the liquidation. He told me not to bother suing; he's already been instructed to funnel all proceeds from the sale to satisfy your debt."

"But she went with him?"

"Relax, Glenn. It's not the end of the world. You stand to lose a lot of money on the movie deal. That should concern you more."

He whirled to her. "And you know nothing, you witch!" He spit savagely to his right. "I'm losing her!"

She did not respond.

Glenn suddenly pulled up. "They are in Bosnia?"

"That's what I—"

"Shut up! Maybe it's better this way. I'll have them killed in Bosnia! They can't touch me!" *But that was not true.* Nothing *could be better this way!*

Beatrice sat back. "Killed in Bosnia? All of them?"

"If I can't have her, I have no choice but to kill her. You know that."

A thin smile crossed her mouth. She stared at him over her horn-rimmed glasses. "Who do you know in Eastern Europe?" she asked.

Glenn closed his eyes and desperately tried to settle himself. How could this have possibly happened? He groaned and exhaled a lungful of stale breath. He walked to the desk and ran his hand along its high-gloss finish. He would see her again, he swore it to himself. Dead or alive he would see her again.

His hand came to rest beside a notepad. He lifted it. The preacher's book stared up at him, its red cover mocking him in full-throated laughter. *The Dance of the Dead.* He picked it up. To think that this maniac had actually made a fortune from his tale of death. They were not so different, he and the preacher. And the other pig, the one who had butchered—

Glenn froze. A chill snaked down his spine. The notion exploded in his mind like a white-hot strobe and he stood with a limp mouth.

"Glenn?"

"I want you to do something, Beatrice," he said softly and turned to face her. "I want you to find someone for me. Someone in Bosnia."

"Who? I have no idea how to find anyone in Bosnia," she said.

Glenn smiled as the idea set in. "You will, Beatrice. You will find him. And you will learn about him in this book." He held it toward her with a shaking hand.

"Who?" she asked again, taking the book.

"Karadzic," Glenn said. "His name is Karadzic."

BOOK FOUR

THE BELOVED

"Love is as strong as death,
its jealousy unyielding as the grave.
It burns like blazing fire,
like a mighty flame.
Many waters cannot quench love;
rivers cannot wash it away.
If one were to give all the wealth of his house for love
it would be utterly scorned."

SONG OF SONGS 8:6–7 NIV

CHAPTER THIRTY-SIX

Sarajevo, Bosnia
Four Weeks Later

IVENA STOOD at the graves where they'd buried Father Micheal's and Nadia's bodies. She stared up at the pitted concrete cross. It was her third visit in as many weeks since their return. Already the vine she'd brought from Joey's garden curled around the graves and wound up the lower half of the cross in a delicate embrace. The large white flowers seemed totally natural now, reacting as she had expected to the rain and the sun that spurred their growth.

The small village had faded over the years, now hardly more than a collection of vagrants who eked out an existence off the land and lived in the crumbling houses. The church's blackened spire stretched against the sky, a burned-out backdrop to the overgrown graveyard she stood in. Most towns had managed to recover after the war's atrocities. Most.

Some of the others who had been there that day still visited regularly, but they could not keep the grounds up. The locals couldn't care for the grave of an old dead priest, no matter how horrible the tale of his death. The country was simply littered with a hundred thousand stories as terrible.

Ivena sank to her knees and gripped the foot-high grass in both hands. The dirt felt cool under her knees. *Father, are you taking care of my beloved? Is she keeping you company?*

She looked up at the cross, still stained with the priest's faded blood. Their bones were under the dirt, but they themselves were laughing up there somewhere. Ivena let the images from that day string through her mind now, and they obliged with utmost clarity. The priest's face beaten to a bloody pulp by Janjic; her Nadia standing and staring into the commander's face without a trace of fear; the marching of women under their crosses; Karadzic's furious snarl; the boom of his gun; the priest hanging from this cross, begging to die. His laughter echoing through the cemetery and then his death.

A tear crawled down Ivena's cheek. "I miss you, Nadia. I miss you so much, my darling." She sniffed and closed her eyes. *Why did you take her and not me, Father? Why? I would go now. What kind of cruelty is it to leave me here while my daughter's allowed this frolic of hers? I beg you to take me.*

She'd nearly found her way there a month ago, in those Twin Towers of Lutz's. But it had not been God's timing, so it seemed. She wasn't finished in this desert yet. Still, she could not escape the hope that her time would come soon. If nothing else, that she would die of old age.

Now she lived with her brother on the very edge of Sarajevo, not so far away from her little village, really. She'd lost everything in Atlanta, but the quick departure felt more like a cleansing than a loss. In her mind it was more good riddance. Janjic and Helen had taken an apartment downtown where he had sequestered himself to write. Ivena saw them every few days now, when she went to visit. By all appearances God still had a firm grip on Janjic's heart. It seemed that the extraordinary play of God's wasn't over yet, and knowing it made Ivena long for heaven even more.

Ivena sat on her knees and began to hum. Americans did not understand death, she thought. They were not eager to follow the footsteps of Christ. In reality, joining Christ was a terrifying notion for most churchgoing Americans. Oh, they would quickly snatch up the trinkets he tossed down from heaven—the cars and the houses and such gifts. But talk to them about joining Christ beyond the grave and you would be rewarded by a furrowed brow or blank eyes at best.

Even Helen, after her incredible encounter with Christ's love, was still confused. Even after being on the receiving end of Jan's love she still did not know how to return that love for the simple reason that she wasn't yet willing to die to her own longings. *Love is found in death. Love is found only in death.*

They had come to Bosnia and all seemed well enough; Helen had not gone back to her ways. But she was not a transformed woman either. Not really. She had made it about as far at the average believer, Ivena supposed. But you would think that after such an overt display of love, she would be clambering for Jan. When else in history had Christ actually placed his love for the church in a man? When else had a woman been the recipient of that love in such a unique way?

Ivena sighed and opened her eyes. "Well, I will join you, Father. Call me home now and I will come gladly." She smiled. "I love you, Christ. I dearly love you. I love you more than life."

The sun was dipping in the west when she stood. "Good-bye, Nadia. I will visit next week."

She walked for her brother's old black Peugeot. The town lay in a dusky silence found only in the country. A dog was barking incessantly across the village. At a squawking chicken by the sound of it. "Ah, my Bosnia, it is good to be home."

Ivena climbed into the car, shut the door and reached for the key. The faint odor of petrol filled the cab. Half the cars in Bosnia were either parked on their axles or patched with twine and wire. Blasco's was no exception. At least it ran. Though with gas or whatever caused this terrible smell leaking it was a wonder it didn't blow sky—

A hand suddenly clamped over her mouth and yanked her head back into the seat. Her fingernail caught on the key ring and tore. She cried out but the sound was muffled by the rag the perpetrator was trying to jam past her teeth. She instinctively bit down hard and heard a grunt of pain.

The strong hand shoved the rag into her mouth and she felt she might gag. Another hand gripped her hair and pulled her head backward. She stared at the bare metal ceiling and screamed from her throat. Blackness covered her eyes—a blindfold, strapped tightly to her skull.

Hands shoved her onto her belly and then bound her wrists behind her back. It was only then, blinded and tied facedown, that Ivena stopped reacting and scrambled for some reason.

Her kidnapper had climbed over the seat and now he fired the car. The Peugeot lurched forward.

Suddenly the sentiments that had preoccupied her mind over the past hour were gone. Another took their place. The desire to live. The desperate hope that nothing would harm her. She cried out to God again, but this time the words were different.

Save me, my Father, she prayed. *Don't let me die, I beg you!*

HELEN WALKED over the concrete slab in bare feet, holding a cup of tea close to her chest. She approached the square window in the tenth-story flat and peered out to the sprawling city of Sarajevo, dimmed by the late-day overcast. Behind her, the living room clacked with Jan's incessant typing.

Clack, clack, clack . . .

Square houses bordered thin streets in the Novi Grad district in which she and Jan now lived. The frequent rains made the trees green enough, but the cold that accompanied them could hardly be in greater contrast to Atlanta's smothering heat. And it was not the only contrast. Her whole existence here was one giant contrast.

For starters, the flat. Janjic's uncle Ermin had offered the place to them for a pittance, a thousand dollars for the year, paid up-front of course. Jan had brought the ten thousand dollars in cash with them and given three thousand to Ivena. The remaining seven thousand was enough to live comfortably in Sarajevo for a year, he'd said. They had spent three thousand already, most of it on the rent and out-fitting the top-floor apartment with amenities that helped Helen feel more at home. A toaster oven, stuffed furniture, a real refrigerator, rugs to warm the floors. A typewriter, of course. Jan was a writer once again; they had to have the type-writer. By Sarajevo standards they had done well with the place.

But it wasn't America. Not at all. What was first-class in these hills would do well to pass for middle-class back home.

This is home, Helen. This is your new home.

She sipped at her hot tea. Behind her Jan sat at the kitchen table, a pair of old glasses hanging off his nose. He'd started working on his new book the very day they'd taken the apartment.

Clack, clack, clack . . .

They saw Ivena once, maybe twice a week now, but she had already fit back into her beloved homeland, with greater ease than Jan—no surprise considering what each had given up to come here. The days Ivena came were Helen's favorite. She was family now. Besides Jan, her only family.

Helen looked to the street below; the market across the way bustled with a late-day rush. Which reminded her, she needed some potatoes for dinner. Helen turned around and leaned on the window sill. "Jan?"

He smiled and pried his eyes over those silly black-rimmed glasses. "Yes, dear?"

"I think I'll go down and buy some potatoes for supper. I was going to try that potato soup again. Maybe this time I can get it right."

He chuckled. "It was fine last time. A bit crisp, perhaps, but in my mouth it was deliciously crisp."

"Stop it. Not only am I learning to cook, I'm learning to cook strange foods. Maybe you'd like to cook tonight."

"You're doing wonderfully, dear."

Helen drank the rest of her tea in one gulp and set the cup on the tile counter with a clink. Every surface seemed harsh to her. If it wasn't cement, it was tile. If it wasn't tile it was brick or hard wood. Carpet was hardly known on this side of the world. She didn't care how upscale this flat was in Sarajevo, it still reminded her of the projects back home.

Clack, clack, clack . . .

Jan was intent over the machine again.

"I'll be going then. Do you need anything?" *Listen to me, "I'll be going then."*
That's how a European would say, "I'm outta here." This land was changing her already.

"Not that I can think of," Jan said.

She walked over to him and kissed his forehead. "I'll be back."

"Make some friends," he said with a grin.

"Yes, of course. The whole world is my friend."

"I'm mad about you, you know?"

"And I love you too, Jan," she said smiling, and she slipped out the door.

The steep stairs were enough to discourage more than one or two ascents each
day, and the thought that she would be coming back up with a bag full of potatoes brought a frown to her face. They hadn't heard of elevators in this corner of
Europe yet.

Helen walked briskly for the market, keeping her head down. A bicycle
careened by, splashing water from the morning's shower onto the sidewalk just
ahead of her. Horns beeped on the street. They didn't *honk* here; they beeped, a
high tone expected of tiny cars. *Beep, Beep.*

Clack, clack, clack . . .

Jan could work for twelve hours straight without a break on that book. Well,
he did take breaks, every hour in fact. To smother her with kisses and words of
love. She smiled. But otherwise it was only the book. Her and the book.

It was really *The Dance of the Dead,* but written from a whole new point of
view. Ivena was right; the story wasn't finished, he said. It wasn't even that well
told. And so he was up there clacking away, engrossed in a world even more foreign than this wacky world below.

Helen entered the open marketplace and nodded at a woman she'd seen shopping here before. One of the neighbors, evidently. Some of them spoke English,
but she was growing tired of discovering which ones did not. A nod would have
to do. The tin roof over her head began to tick softly. It was sprinkling again.

The market was crowded for late in the day. Helen passed a shop brimming
with bolts of colored cloth. The owner was checking some plastic he'd strung
across the back where the tin gaped above. A small kiosk selling snacks made on
the spot filled her nostrils with the smell of frying pastries.

Helen made her way to the fresh vegetable stand and bought four large potatoes from a big man named Darko. He smiled wide and winked and Helen

thought she'd made herself a friend as Janjic suggested. Perhaps not what he'd imagined.

She left the market and crossed the street. It was then that the deep male voice spoke behind her, like a distant rumble of thunder that pricked her heart. "Excuse me, miss." Helen glanced back, saw the tall man keeping stride with her ten feet behind, but she immediately dismissed his comment as misdirected. She certainly did not know him.

"You are an American?"

Helen stopped. He was speaking to her. And then he was beside her, a very large man, square and wearing black cotton pants. His shirt was white with silver-and-pearl buttons, like those cowboy shirts she'd seen in the shops back home. She looked into his eyes. They were black, like his pants. Like Glenn's eyes.

"Yes?" she asked.

A crooked smile split the man's boxy jaw. "You are American, yes?"

He spoke with a heavy accent, but his English was good. "Yes. Can I help you?"

"Well, miss, actually I was going to ask you the same thing. I saw you in the market and I thought, now there is a pretty woman who looks like she could use some help."

"Thank you, but I think I can handle four potatoes. Really."

He tilted his head up and laughed. "An American with humor. So then humor me. What is your name?"

A bell of caution rang through Helen's bones. "My name? And who are you?" she asked.

"My name is Anton. You see, Anton? Is that such a bad name? And yours?"

"I'm not in the habit of giving my name to strangers, actually. I really should be going." She turned to go. But did she really want to go? She stunned herself by answering the question quickly. No.

"You don't want to do that," the man said. She looked at his face. White teeth flashed through his grin. "Really, you want to know me. I have what you're look-ing for."

Helen stared at him. "You do, do you? And what is it that I'm looking for?"

"For a destination. For a place to go. A place that feels like home; that swims in your mind the way you like."

She blinked. "I'm sorry, I need to leave."

"No. No you shouldn't do that. You're American. I know a part of Sarajevo that's very . . . what should I say? Friendly to Americans. Do you like to fly, American?"

What was he talking about?

You know what he's talking about, Helen. You know, you know.

"What's your name?" the man asked again. The sky was still spitting the odd raindrops. Pedestrians had cleared the streets for the most part. To Helen's left, an alley ran between two gray buildings, dark and dingy.

"Why are you talking so strangely to me? Do I look like I have 'fool' stamped on my forehead?"

He found the remark funny. "No. And that's precisely why I'm speaking strangely to you. Because you're not a fool. You know precisely what I'm talking about. You really should join us."

Helen's blood was pumping steadily now. A thousand days from her past screamed through her spine. She should leave this man now. He was the devil himself—she should know, she'd shared the devil's bed many a night.

But her feet were not moving. Instead they were tingling, and it had been a while since her feet had tingled like this. She wet her lips, and then immediately hoped he did not read her too clearly.

"There are other Americans here?"

"Did I say that? No. There are others like you."

She hesitated. Her breathing was coming harder now. *Run, Helen, Run!* "How do I know who you are?" Her ears were hot.

"I am Anton, and you must ask yourself another question; how do I know what I know? Unless I am who I say I am?"

"And who are you, Anton?"

"Tell me your name and I will tell you who I am."

She cleared her throat. "Helen."

He grinned wide and nodded his head once. "And I'm the one who will help you fly."

She swallowed, looking up into his eyes.

"May I see your hand?" Anton asked

She opened her hand and glanced down at it. His large hand suddenly held hers gently. She tried to pull it free, but the man held her firmly and she saw that his eyes were not threatening. They were deep and dark and smiling. She let him take her hand. But he was not interested in her hand; his eyes followed her arm to the tiny pockmark from her old days on the needle.

Then the man who called himself Anton did a very strange thing. He leaned over and he kissed that tiny scar very gently. And Helen let him do it. His lips sent a shiver right up her arm and through her skull.

There was suddenly a small black card in his hand and Helen had no clue where it had come from. She took it. He held her eyes in his own for what seemed an eternity. Then he turned and left without another word.

It occurred to Helen that she had stopped breathing. Her heart was slamming in her chest. She looked at the card. It had an address on it—this man's address— and a simple map. The den of iniquity. She should throw it to the ground and stamp her feet on it, she thought.

Instead she shoved it into her pocket and walked numbly for the flat.

HELEN HAD calmed herself before entering the apartment, but a tingle rode her spine and she was powerless to dismiss it.

"Did you find the potatoes?" Jan asked without looking up. He continued his typing, reached the end of a section and slapped the carriage back. *Ding!* He low- ered his hands and looked at her. She held up the four large spuds.

"They'll make a fine soup," he said and clapped his hands together once. "I'll give you a tip, my dear. Use a low flame. It may take a few minutes longer, but we'll be using ladles instead of forks if you do."

She *humphed,* feigning disgust at him. "Come over here and I'll use a ladle on you, Jan Jovic."

He threw his head back, delighted. Then he clambered out of his chair and padded over to her. "Have I told you recently that you're the light of my world?" he said, taking her head in his hands. He kissed her cheek. When he withdrew his eyes were on fire. No, his passion for her hadn't dimmed, not even a little, she thought.

"I love you, Jan," she said.

Do you? I mean really, like he loves you?

He winked and returned to the table.

Helen slid into the kitchen and dumped the potatoes into the sink for cleaning. *Clack, clack, clack . . .*

The day fell to darkness as Helen prepared their supper. Outside, the cars beeped on through the evening. Inside, the room kept time to Jan's clacking. But

330

Helen was not hearing the sounds. She was still hearing the stranger's voice, soft and soothing.

And I am the one who will help you fly.

The card lay in her pocket. God forbid if Jan should find it! She eased into the bedroom and placed it under the mattress. He stopped his clacking and she rushed out, but he was only reading a page he'd written.

Do you want to fly, Helen?

The soup spoon slipped from her hand and splashed the hot liquid onto her arm. "Ouch!"

"You okay?"

"Fine."

She dug out the spoon and chided herself. *Stop this nonsense! Stop it! You are not an adolescent. You are the wife of Jan Jovic.*

Yes, but do you want to fly, wife of Jan Jovic?

In the end she butchered the soup. It was not crispy; it was not even too thick. But it tasted bland and not until Jan mentioned salt near the end of their meal, did she remember that she'd forgotten the spice altogether. She apologized profusely.

"Nonsense," he said. "Too much salt's bad for the heart. It's much better this way, Helen."

She retired at nine, leaving Jan to finish his chapter. But she could not sleep. Her mind settled into a dream of sorts, wide awake but lost in the stranger's world, in recounting every detail of their meeting. And then it slipped into Glenn's Palace and a mound of powder and she gave up trying to fight the thoughts. Instead she let them run rampant through her mind, even embellishing them.

She pretended to be asleep when Jan came to bed, but in reality she dozed for another two hours. The card lay under her mattress, and at one point she was sure she could feel it. And if Jan rolled over here, he would feel it! She started and sat.

"What is it?" Jan asked, suddenly awake.

She gazed about in the darkness. "Nothing," she said, and collapsed to her back.

Sleep finally overtook her near midnight. But even then she could not shake that man's haunting face.

Do you want to fly, Helen?

Yes, of course. Don't be silly. I would love to fly. I'm dying to fly.

Do you want to die, Helen?

I want to fly. I don't want to die.

I want to sleep.

CHAPTER THIRTY-SEVEN

JAN AMBLED down the avenue the following afternoon, stretching his legs, whistling into a light breeze. He'd asked Helen to walk with him but she seemed content to stay home. Perhaps even a little preoccupied with staying home.

The sights and sounds of Sarajevo came to him like a rich, soothing balm as they did every morning, healing wounds long forgotten. When he'd walked these streets five years earlier, the war's scars still mocked the city on every corner; blasted buildings and pitted roads.

But now . . . now his city was brimming with new life and a people fanatical about reestablishing their identity. There was some dissatisfaction with Tito and his government, of course—talk of an independent Bosnia. And there were occasional words between the Serbs and the Croats, even the Muslims. That had become a staple of the people; a prerequisite the land seemed to extract from its inhabitants. But the country was nothing like the war-torn shamble he'd left.

"Hello, Mira," he called, passing the bakery where the plump baker swept clouds of flour through her doorway. "Nice day?"

She looked up, startled. "Oh, Janjic, there was a gentleman looking for you. I sent him down the street."

"Oh? And did this gentleman have a name?"

"Molosov," she said.

The name rang through Jan's mind like a manic rat. Molosov was looking for him? So the soldier from Sarajevo had heard that he'd returned. They'd discussed the possibility a hundred times and now it was happening.

"Hmm," Jan finally managed.

"You send your wife down, and I will sell her something special, just for you," the baker said.

He chuckled. "Good enough."

Jan glanced up and down the street; it was empty. He left Mira and walked on, but with a stiff step now. Molosov. The name sounded strange after such a long time. And if Molosov had heard of his return, what of Karadzic?

The sun was out today. In Atlanta he would have been sweating like a pig. Here the warmth was like a smile from heaven. It had only been a month, and yet it felt like a year. He'd heard from Lorna, who had sent him the settlement statement from the ministry last week. She'd managed to pay off all of their debts and come away with nearly five thousand dollars. What should he do with it? Lorna wanted to know.

Give it to Karen, he'd written back. *She deserves it and more.*

As for himself and Helen, they had four thousand dollars still, which was barely enough to carry them through the year. Then they would see. Honestly, he had no clue.

Helen wanted to return to America, he knew that much. But then she was young and it was her first time leaving the country. She would adjust. He prayed she would adjust.

"Janjic."

He turned toward the voice. A man stood on the curb, staring at him. The street suddenly appeared vacant except for this one man. Jan stopped and looked at the figure. There were others striding in his peripheral vision, but one look at this man and they ceased to exist.

Janjic's pulse spiked. It was Molosov! The soldier he'd roamed Yugoslavia with, finding enemies to kill. One of the soldiers who had crucified the priest.

Now Molosov was here, grinning at him from the street.

"Janjic." The man strode to him, and a smile suddenly split his face. "That is you, Janjic?"

"Yes. Molosov."

The man thrust his hand out and Janjic took it. "You're back on the streets of Sarajevo," Molosov said. "I'd heard you'd gone to America."

"I'm back." In any other place this man would be his mortal enemy. They had never gotten along well. But they had been through a war together, and they were both Serbs. That was the bond between them.

Molosov slapped him on the shoulder and Jan nearly lost his balance. "You are looking good. You've put some meat on your bones. I see America has been good to you."

"I suppose," Jan said. "And you? You are good?"

"Yes, good. Alive still. If you're alive in Bosnia, you are good." He chuckled at his remark.

"You were looking for me?" Jan asked.

"Yes. My friend in the market told me about you a week ago, and I have watched for you. I am planning to go to America." He said it proudly, as if he expected immediate affirmation for the disclosure.

"You are? Very good. I am not."

Molosov wasn't put off. "This place is no longer for me. I was thinking you could help me. Just with information, of course."

Jan nodded, but his mind was elsewhere. "Have you heard from the others?" Jan asked. "Puzup, Paul?"

"Puzup? He's dead. Paul left the country, I think. To his new homeland, Israel."

"They were good men." He wasn't sure why he said that. There was some goodness under everyone's skin, but Puzup and Paul were not especially well endowed with it and Jan had concluded as much in his book.

Molosov withdrew a cigarette. "And you, Janjic, you have a wife now?"

"Yes. Yes, I'm married."

"A fat lady from America?"

Jan smiled with him. "As a matter of fact, she's from America. The loveliest woman I've ever known."

He chuckled, pleased. "American women are the best, yes? Well, let me give you some advice, comrade," Molosov said in good humor. "Keep her away from Karadzic. The beast will devour her!"

A spike drove down Jan's spine at the words. His feet felt suddenly rooted to the concrete. "Karadzic?"

The man's smile faded. "You two were not so close. Forgive me—it's been a long time."

"Karadzic is . . . he's in Sarajevo?"

"He's always been in Sarajevo."

Of course, Jan already knew that if the man were still alive, he would live somewhere near Sarajevo. But hearing it now sent a buzz through his skull. "And what's Karadzic up to these days?"

"The same. I worked for him, you know. For three years, until I couldn't stomach his nonsense. Karadzic was born to kill. He doesn't do well without a war, so he makes his own."

"And how does he do that?"

"In the underground, of course. He's Sarajevo's prince of darkness." The man laughed and drew on his cigarette.

"So Bosnia has its own Mob, is that it?"

"Mob? Ah, the American gangsters. Yes, but here it's all done with threads of nationalism. It legitimizes the business, you see."

"But his business is illegitimate?"

"Are you joking?" He looked around to be certain they weren't overheard. "Karadzic doesn't have a legitimate bone in his body. If you're looking for drugs in Bosnia, his dirty fingers will have touched them somewhere along the line, no question."

The heat started at the crown of Jan's head and washed over his face. Drugs! His mind flashed to Helen. It was the association alone, he knew, but still he was suddenly thrust to the verge of panic, standing there on the sidewalk beside Molosov. *Dear God, help us!* A dreadful sense of foreboding washed through him. And Helen.

"Just stay out of his way. Or better, go back to America; this place isn't safe for people like you and me." He jabbed Janjic playfully with the hand holding his cigarette. "At the very least, if your wife is as beautiful as you say, keep her out of his sight. He makes pretty women ugly very quickly." The man chuckled again.

But Jan didn't find any humor in his words. None at all. He was barely hiding his terror. Or perhaps he wasn't.

"I . . . I have to go now," Jan said and began to turn.

Molosov's voice lost its humor. "Hold on. You weren't easy to find. We have a lot to discuss. I'm very serious, Janjic. I am planning on going to America."

"I live in the flats on the west side of the market. Top floor, 532." Jan suddenly thought better of giving out the address, and he turned to his old comrade. "But keep this to yourself."

Molosov grinned again. "I will. Good to see you. I live on the east end of the Novi Grad. Welcome back home."

Jan turned back and took the man's extended hand. "Yes, good. Good to be home."

He left then, striding evenly for half a block. And then seeing Molosov disappear around the corner, he broke into a jog.

She has been acting strangely, Janjic. Helen has not been herself.

Nonsense! He was just piecing together impossible strings of coincidence.

She didn't come on this walk with you, Janjic. She did not want to.

Shut up! You're being a child!

Still he had to get back to see her. If anything happened to Helen now he would die. He would throw himself from their window and let the street take him home.

Jan reached their building and swung into the atrium. He took the stairs two at a time and had to pause after five flights to catch his breath. By the time he reached the tenth-floor flat his chest burned. He crashed into the apartment.

She was not in sight!

"Helen!"

His black typewriter sat alone at the table. "Helen!" he screamed.

"Hello, Jan." He spun toward the bedroom. She walked out, wide-eyed. "What's wrong?"

Jan doubled over to his knees and panted. *Thank you, Father!* "Nothing. Nothing."

"Then why were you screaming like that?"

He straightened, smiling wide. "Nothing. It was nothing. I ran up the stairs. You should try it sometime; excellent exercise."

She grinned. "You scared me. Don't smash in here screaming the next time you decide to exercise, if you don't mind."

"I won't," he said. He pulled her to his chest and stroked her hair. "I promise I will not."

CHAPTER THIRTY-EIGHT

THE DAY seemed to keep time to the *clacking* of Jan's typewriter, but it all came to a silent halt late that afternoon, when Jan clapped his hands with satisfaction, stood from the table, and proudly announced that he was leaving. His uncle Ermin had a car he wanted to sell them. An old bucket of bolts, Jan said, but the old man had fixed it up—given it a new coat of blue paint and tweaked the carburetor so that it actually ran. Perhaps having a car wouldn't be such a bad idea. They could drive out into the country and see the real Bosnia. Even Ivena had access to a car.

He said he would be gone for a couple of hours. Helen's heart was pounding already.

He kissed her on the nose, then again on the cheek, and after a short pause, again on the head. Then he slipped out the door with a wink, leaving her alone in the kitchen staring after him. The old wooden wall-clock with painted ivy leaves read five o'clock.

Horns honked through the open window to her right. She closed her eyes and swallowed, trying to shake the voice that suddenly whispered through her mind. And then it wasn't whispering—it was buzzing, like an annoying fly that refused to go away.

Helen leaned back on the kitchen counter. *You know that if you pull that card out you won't stop. You know you'll go.*

Of course, I won't go! Going would be suicide! Her heart thumped in her chest. How could she possibly be having these thoughts after a month of freedom? That's what her time in Jan's strange country had been: freedom. No Glenn, no drugs, no chains. And now a stranger who called himself Anton had walked out of the shadows and offered her chains once again. What a fool the man was to think he could just waltz into her life and expect her to follow.

337

Helen ground her teeth. What a fool she was to think she would *not* follow! "God, please . . ."

She ditched the feeble attempt at prayer and let her mind play with the card. *If I leave now I could see this place in the Rajlovac district and be back before Jan returns. I would just walk there and then walk back. Is it a sin to walk?*

But you won't just walk.

Don't be stupid, of course I'll just walk! That's all I'll do. A rush of desire flooded her veins, and she pushed off the counter toward the bedroom.

You want the chains, Helen?

She pulled the black card from beneath her mattress and straightened the covers quickly. Her hand trembled before her eyes. "Rajlovac," it read.

Don't be a fool.

But suddenly the impulse to at least walk toward the place hammered through her mind. She walked straight for the front door and eased into the staircase, thinking that she *was* being a fool. But her spine tingled at the thought of flying. And she was already hating herself for having come this far. Why would she even dare to think about any of this?!

Her feet padded quickly down the stairs. She cracked the door to the street and slipped into the dying light. She would walk east. Just walk.

Voices of caution whispered through Helen's mind, casting their inevitable arguments as her feet carried her east. But within ten minutes, she'd shoved the debate aside, preoccupied instead with the eyes that seemed to watch her progress. They were just strangers, of course, watching the Western woman—was it that obvious?—walk briskly with her head down. But to Helen it seemed as though every eye was focused on her. She picked up her pace.

The streets ran narrow, bordered by square tan buildings. Rajlovac—she'd heard that there was money in the Rajlovac. A short boxy car snorted past, spewing gray smoke that smelled strangely comforting. The structures were thinning. She was headed away from home and every step she took would have to be retraced, in the dark.

She should be home, peeling the potatoes for tonight's meal, listening to music, reading a novel. Being loved by Janjic. Helen grunted and watched her feet shuffle over the ground. No, she did not want to do this, but she *was* doing this and she *did* want to do this.

She pulled the black card out a dozen times and glanced at the sketched map on the fly. It wasn't until she had entered the Rajlovac district that she began think-

ing that coming here had been a terrible mistake. The sun sat on the western horizon, casting long shadows where the buildings did not block it all together. If there
was money in Rajlovac, it wasn't wasted on the buildings, she thought. At least not
in this industrial section where the card had led her. Here the old gray structures
appeared vacant and unattended. The occasional blown-out window gaped square
and black to the darkness within. A newspaper floated by, whipped by the wind.
Its cover picture of a man shouting angrily had been all but washed out by the
weather. Three men stood across the street, arms folded against the cool, wool caps
on their heads. They watched her pass with mild interest.

You should be back with Jan, Helen. How long have you been gone? Less than an
hour. If you turn back now he'll never know.

But her feet kept their pace, shuffling forward as if pulled by habit. Right into
the falling darkness, ignoring the fear that now snaked down her spine. This was
not right. A large building suddenly rose at the end of the dead-end street she'd
entered, ominous against the charcoal sky.

Helen stopped. This was it. She stood alone on the asphalt and faced the ten-
story blackened building. Gray cement towered on either side, chipped and
pocked by years of abuse and war. The sound of water trickled faintly along the
curb, sewer water by the musty smell. She took a hesitant step forward and then
stopped again.

Thirty meters ahead a flag waved above a large door; a dirtied white flag with a
black object on either side, but she couldn't make out the shapes at this distance. She
took a breath to still a tremor that ran through her bones, and she walked forward.

You have to turn around, Helen. You've had your walk. It's time to go home and
prepare the evening meal. Go and let Jan hold you. He'll do that, you know. He will
hold you and he will love you.

Her feet ignored the plea and stepped forward.

If night had not fallen over the rest of Sarajevo yet, it had come here first. She
wondered absently if this was how it felt to walk into your own grave. Other than
the trickle of sewer water the night lay still. Perhaps she'd gotten it wrong.

A chill suddenly streaked down her spine. The markings on the flag were
skulls, she saw. Black skulls waving in the breeze. A human form clothed in dark
wool lay in the gutter to her right, evidently dead to the world. Helen stopped for
the third time, blinking against the warning bells that rang in her head. Another
body was propped in the far corner, barely visible.

Helen stood before the metal door and stared at the brown paint, peeling like scabs from a rusted surface. A throbbing beat came from deep within the building, barely audible, but somehow comforting.

You aren't walking any longer, Helen. Now you're going in. That wasn't the deal.

She reached a trembling hand forward and pushed gently on the door.

Do you want to fly, baby?

The door swung in quickly, startling her. But it had not given on its own—a man stood in the shadows looking at her with dark eyes. At first he said nothing, and then, "Who invited you?"

"A . . . Anton," Helen said.

A faint smile crossed the man's face. "Yes, of course. Who else would find such a beautiful woman. You know what we do here?"

Helen's heart skipped a beat. *Do you want to fly? Or do you want to die? We do both here.* "Yes," she said, but her voice held a tremor.

"Then follow me." The man turned and walked into the building. Helen crossed the threshold, her mind screaming foul. But still her legs seemed to control her movements, as if they possessed a mind of their own. That was foolishness, of course; she was telling her legs to move because she wanted desperately to move forward. Into this dungeon.

The hall was very dim, dressed in the same peeling paint that covered the outer door. They passed several limp bodies, strung out on the floor. He led her into a stairwell where he stepped aside and pointed down a flight of steps. Helen glanced up the stairs that ascended to her right, but he stabbed his index finger into the darkness below.

"Down," he said.

She swallowed and began her descent. The door banged behind her and she turned to see that the man had left her. She was alone, surrounded by silence. A dull consistent thump came from the walls—the sound of heavy pulsating music. Or the sound of her heart.

She lowered her foot to the next step, and then the next, until the steps ended in a landing before another door. She knew at a glance that the heart of the building lay here. Anton was here, beyond this fortified entry, sealed into thick concrete. A small window on the door grated open, exposed a pair of bloodshot eyes for a couple of seconds, and then snapped shut. The door swung in.

This is it, Helen. If you enter now you won't be able to make it back in time to peel the potatoes.

She stepped inside and stopped.

340

Helen stood in a tunnel roughly hewn from the rock beyond the building. Red and amber bulbs strung along the ceiling not three feet over her head cast an eerie light down the passage. Wet concrete ran underfoot, curving to the right twenty feet ahead. The dusty odor of mildew mixed with the smell of burning hair filled her nose. Her senses tingled with anticipation.

"Hello, Helen."

She spun to her right where another smaller tunnel gaped in the shadows. The man who called himself Anton stepped from the dark, smiling with a square jaw. He wore a black robe over the white shirt now, like some kind of vampire. The orange light glinted off his round eyes.

"I did not expect you to come so quickly." He reached a hand out to her. Behind him, tiny feet scurried along the tunnel. Rats. The tinkle of water was louder here too, she noted. That sewer water was making its way down somehow.

Helen hesitated and then took his hand.

He chuckled and the sound of his voice carried down the hall. "I promise you that I will not disappoint you, my dear." Anton kissed her hand with thick red lips. "Come."

She walked forward on soles tingling numb. The sound of her own heart thumped with the faint music. He led her along the dimly lit passage to a door made of wood with heavy cross members. He gripped the wooden latch, winked at her, and shoved the door open. "After you, my dear."

Helen stepped past the large man into a smoke-filled room. The sweet smell of hashish wafted through her nostrils. Here the yellow lights peered through a haze of the stuff, casting a soft glow about the room. The ceiling hung low, seemingly hewn from sheer rock and supported by a half dozen pillars. Bright red-and-yellow rugs covered the stone floor, nearly wall to wall. Thick white candles blazed on old wooden end tables. Tall earthen pots filled with purple and green feathers stood by each of the pillars; brass and silver plates adorned the walls, reflecting the myriad of flickering flames. It was a gothic kind of psychedelia.

A dozen bodies reclined on stuffed pillows and chairs, unmoving to fuzzy throbbing music, but fixated on her. Helen gazed at them and immediately felt a kinship—their eyes swam with a language she knew well.

She felt a hand on her shoulder, and she twisted her head to meet Anton's black stare. He smiled thinly but did not speak. His eyes lowered to her arm and he traced it lightly with a thick finger. Something about the way those eyes sparkled sent a shiver down her spine and she shifted her gaze from him.

One of the figures—a man—rose and walked slowly toward her, grinning dumbly.

"What's your price?" Helen asked.

Anton chuckled softly. But he didn't answer.

The other man walked up to her and lifted a hand to her cheek. His finger felt hot. *You're in this now, Helen. You're home. Whether you like it or not, you are home.*

"You want to know what the price is?" the man said. A large scar ran across his right cheek and it bunched up in a knot when he smiled. "I am Kuzup. I am your price, princess." He bit the tip of his tongue.

Anton seemed to find humor in the man's statement. "This one's beyond you, Kuzup. She's too rich for your blood."

Helen smiled with them, but her skin tingled with fear. "And even if you could afford me, I'm not for sale," she said.

They both laughed. "Down here we're all for sale," Kuzup said.

A small prick flashed up Helen's arm and she jerked. Anton's big hand closed over her mouth from behind. "Shhhhh. Let it go, princess."

He'd put a needle into her arm. His hand was not rough, only coaxing, and she let herself go.

"Shhh." His hot breath washed over her ear. It smelled like medicine. "Do you feel it?"

The warmth ran through her body in comforting waves. "Yes," she whispered. She didn't know what Anton had given her, but the drug quickened her pulse. This was good. She was into this. *I'm flying now, baby.*

He released her and the room swam. Kuzup was giggling. Anton held a small syringe, which he tossed into a pot to his right.

Helen sauntered out onto the floor and eased herself onto a thick cushion. The music worked its way through her body like a massage. An obscure thought occurred to her, the thought that Jan would like this. Not seeing her with strangers like this, but feeling the euphoria that drifted through her bones now.

"How much?" she heard Kuzup asking.

"Are you made of gold? Because you'll need a mountain of it to match what I've been offered for this one."

"Bah!"

Helen lost interest in their babbling. To her right, a woman lay on her back, staring wide at the ceiling. Mucus ran from her nose and for some reason Helen found some humor in the sight. The woman was beautiful, with golden hair and brown eyes, but she'd been reduced to a stiff board, gawking at the low-hung black stone. Did she know how absurd she looked, sweating on the floor?

And you, Helen? You're less foolish? She rolled into a ball, feeling suddenly euphoric and sick at once. Like a self-conscious dog, lapping at some vomit—such a comforting treat, as long as no one knew. But he would be home soon, wouldn't he? Jan would be home to tell her about the blue car his uncle had sold him. They could take romantic trips to the countryside now.

A high-pitched cackle cut through Helen's thoughts. She saw a woman dressed in red with her arms entwined about Anton's neck. Her hair was long and black. She was kissing him on the nose, and then on the forehead and down his cheek, whispering words through pursed lips. The woman threw her head back and laughed at the ceiling. They both looked at Helen, pleased with themselves.

"So she has come without a fight, our American beauty," the woman said, loudly enough for Helen to hear. Then the woman turned to Anton and licked his right cheek with a wet tongue. He did not flinch. He only smiled and watched Helen. The lady in red was speaking to him, calling him names. Names that made no sense to Helen.

Except one name. She cooed it in a low voice.

Karadzic.

She called him Karadzic and that name rang a bell deep in Helen's mind. Perhaps an endearing term Janjic had called her once. Yes, Janjic Jovic, her lover. *Karadzic.*

CHAPTER THIRTY-NINE

SHE WAS gone when Jan burst into the flat to announce his smart dealing over the car. He'd struck a deal with his uncle Ermin: no money for thirty days, and if the car still ran, he would pay one hundred a month for six months. It was a good trade, given the unavoidable fear that the rattling deathtrap might fly apart at any moment.

But Helen wasn't in the flat. His breast-beating would have to wait until she returned from the market. Darkness was falling outside, and she didn't often go down to the street after sunset. She hadn't cooked yet either.

Jan sat at the table and picked away at his typewriter. He was nearing the end of the book. One more chapter and it would be ready for the editor. Not that he had an editor. No publisher, no editor, not even a reader. But this time the book was for him—for the writing. It was a purging of his mind, a cleansing of his soul. And it all came down to this last chapter. Ivena would have to live with the fact that his story was now done. Not his full life, of course, but this ravishing love story of his was now over. It had found its fulfillment back here in Bosnia.

He glanced at the pile of completed pages, stacked neatly beside the typewriter. The title smiled across the cover page. *When Heaven Weeps.* It was a good name.

If there was a real caveat, it was in the simple realization that he didn't know what he would write in this last chapter. Up to this point the book had fairly written itself. It had rushed from his mind and his fingers had hardly kept pace.

Helen isn't back, Jan.

Jan stood from the table and walked to the window. The market closed at eight, but the shoppers had thinned already. *Where are you, dear Helen?* He glanced at the watch on his hand. It was ten past seven.

And what if she's gone, Jan?

His pulse quickened at the thought. No. We are beyond that. And where would she go? *Father, please, I beg you for her safety. I beg you, don't allow harm to come to her.*

It occurred to him that he was sweating despite the cool breeze. He spun from the window and rushed from the flat. He would go to the market and find her.

Jan entered the open-air market three minutes later, quelling memories that brought a mutter to his lips. He strode quickly through the street, craning for a view of her. Of her unmistakable blond hair. *Please, God, let me see her.*

But he did not see her.

He approached Darko's vegetable kiosk, where the big man was busy filling boxes with squashes for the night.

"Darko, have you seen Helen?"

The man looked up. "No. Not tonight."

"Earlier, then? At dusk?"

He shook his head. "Not today."

"You are sure?"

"Not today, Janjic."

Jan nodded and glanced around. "She was home three hours ago."

"Don't worry, my friend. She will return. She is a beautiful woman. Beautiful women always seem to find distractions in Sarajevo, yes? But, don't worry, she is lost without you. I have seen it in her eyes."

A distant voice snickered in Jan's mind. *And if she is beautiful, keep her away from him.* It was Molosov, and he was suddenly laughing. Heat washed down Jan's back. He fought off a surge of panic. He spun to Darko, whose grin softened under his glare.

"You know Molosov?" he demanded.

"Molosov? It's a common name."

"A big man," Jan said impatiently. "Brown hair. From the east side of Novi Grad. He was here yesterday. He said he had a friend in the market."

"No."

Jan slammed his palm on the merchant's table and grunted. Darko looked at him with surprise. Jan dipped his head apologetically and ran from the kiosk. *Please, Father. Not again, please! I cannot take it.*

He stopped at the next kiosk and questioned vigorously of Helen and

Molosov to no avail. But that small voice in his head kept snickering. He ran through the market, fighting to retain control of his reason, desperate now to find either Helen or Molosov. Of course it was just a hunch, he kept telling himself. But the hunch burrowed like a tick in his skull.

If anyone knew Molosov, they weren't talking easily. Until he spoke to the beggar at the west side of the market.

"You know Molosov? A big man with dark hair from the east end of—"

"Yes, yes. Of course I know Molosov." A smile came to his ratty face.

"Tell me where to find him."

"I can't—"

"You think I'm playing? Tell me, man!"

The beggar pushed Jan's hand aside. "Perhaps a little money will loosen my memory."

Jan shoved his hand into his pocket and snatched a fistful of bills. He held them in front of the beggar's growing eyes. "Take me to him and this will be yours."

Twenty minutes later, Jan stood before Molosov in a small tin shack with a dozen men betting on a game of cards. A bare bulb burned above them. At first mention of Karadzic's name, Molosov ushered Jan outside by the arm. "You're trying to have me killed?" he demanded.

"I have to know where he is! You know—you must tell me!"

"Lower your voice! What's this about?"

Jan told him, but Molosov wasn't forthcoming. Karadzic's place was not common knowledge. He tried repeatedly to dismiss Jan's fears, but the quick shifting of his eyes told of his own fears. In the end, it took the thousand dollars Jan had pocketed for the car to persuade the big soldier. Jan withdrew the wad and offered it to the man. "Take it. It will buy your passage to America. Tell me where he is."

Molosov looked at the money and glanced around nervously again. "And what if she's not there?"

"It's a risk I'm willing to take. Hurry, man!"

Molosov took the bills and told him, swearing him to tell no one.

Jan turned then and ran into the night, east toward the Rajlovac.

And what if Molosov is right? What if Helen isn't there? What then, Jan?

Then I will weep for joy.

But dread pounded through his chest. He didn't expect to be weeping for joy. Weeping, perhaps, but not for joy.

THE DEAD-END street Molosov had directed Jan to was pitch black when he swung into it thirty minutes later. He pulled up and flattened his palms on his chest as if by gripping it he could ease the burning of his lungs. His breathing sounded like bellows echoing from the concrete walls.

A flag, Molosov had said. With skulls. Jan could see nothing but foreboding black. He stumbled forward and then stopped when the dim outline of the banner materialized over a door, thirty yards ahead. Three bundled bodies lay on the sidewalk, he saw. Another in the gutter, either dead or wasted.

A picture of Karadzic filled his mind, square and ferocious, screaming at Father Micheal. He had fought that image for twenty years now. The notion that Helen was in there with the beast suddenly struck him as preposterous.

Jan walked forward. *And if he is inhuman, what is Helen?*

He grunted and rushed forward. Lights flashed in his peripheral vision; the war was coming to his mind again and he blinked against it. Jan shoved the door open and stepped into a dark hall. The faint beat of music carried through the walls. He stood and willed his eyes to adjust; his breathing to slow.

At the end of the hall stairs rose to his right and descended to his left. Down. With Karadzic it would be down. He crept down the steps and ran into another entry. The music sounded louder, keeping beat with his heart. He tried the door. It was locked.

A small window suddenly grated open, casting a shaft of yellow light over his chest. Jan stepped back. The door swung open.

You don't belong here, Janjic.

No one appeared. Ahead a tunnel had been carved from the rock, lit by colored lights. Whoever had opened the door probably stood behind it, waiting. Jan stepped through. The music thudded now.

You really have no sense in coming here, Janjic.

The door slammed behind him and he whirled around. He could see no one. Another door led into the wall behind the entrance and he tried it quickly. It was locked.

"Lover boy has come for his woman?"

The voice echoed in the chamber and Jan spun around. *Father, please! Give me strength.*

347

"Janjic. After so long the savior has returned home. And to save another poor soul, no less."

This time he could not mistake the familiar rumbling voice; it was tattooed on his memory. Karadzic! *Steady, Jan. Hold yourself.* He took a deliberate breath and let it out slowly. He stood and gripped his hands into fists.

Feet crunched faintly and then stopped directly in front of him. He took a step backward in the darkness. Pale yellow light suddenly flooded the tunnel.

The figure stood before him, an apparition from a lost nightmare. He was tall and boxy, balanced on long legs and dressed in black, with a wicked grin splitting a square jaw. It was Karadzic.

Two distinct urges collided in Jan's mind. The first was to launch himself at the larger man; to kill him if possible. The second urge was to flee. He had faced Karadzic once and lived to tell the story. This time he might not be so lucky.

Jan moved his foot a few inches and then stood rooted to the earth, tensed like a bowstring.

"So good to see you again, my friend," Karadzic said softly. "And you have come so quickly. I had expected to force your hand, but now you have jumped into my lap."

Jan couldn't speak. He could only stare at this incarnation of terror. The man had lured him here. He'd used Helen against her will to bring him in, he thought.

Jan spoke quietly. "You always had your way with women. You prey on the weak because you yourself are only half a man."

"And you still have a tongue, do you?" Karadzic said. "I did not bring your woman here, you poor fool. She came to me, perhaps in search of a man. I can see why she left you."

"You lie! She did not come on her own."

"No? Actually I had planned on luring her with the old woman, but it wasn't necessary."

The old woman?

An arm suddenly clamped over Jan's mouth and yanked his head back. He swung his elbow back and was rewarded with a grunt. A hand punched his kidneys and he relaxed to the pain.

"Perhaps you would like to see your Helen?"

The arms from behind jerked his hands behind him and lashed his wrists together with rope. They shoved a rag in his mouth and ran a wide strip of tape over it. Karadzic walked slowly up to him. His old commander breathed heavily, his lips parted and wet. Sweat glistened on his forehead. Without warning his arm lashed out and he struck Jan on his ear. He gasped in pain.

"You would do well to remember who's in charge," Karadzic said quietly. "You always were confused about the power of command, weren't you?" He thrust his face up to Jan's, his smile now gone. The man's breath smelled sweet of liquor. "This time you'll wish you were already dead."

Jan winced. Karadzic struck again, on Jan's cheek.

The man spun and marched down the tunnel. "Bring him," he said.

The hands behind shoved Jan and he stumbled forward. They propelled him quickly down the dim passage, to a steel door beyond which Karadzic had stopped. Then the door opened and Jan was pushed roughly into the room. He scanned the interior, breathing shallow, fearing what he might see here.

A dozen sets of eyes stared at him, blank in their state of stupor. Candles flickered amber through the white haze. The music seemed to resonate with the black rock walls, as if they were its source.

Then Jan saw the body moving slowly on the floor not ten feet from where he stood and he knew immediately that it was Helen.

Helen!

Oh, dear God! What have you done?

He screamed despite the rags in his mouth, but the weak sound was lost to the music's dull thump. He threw himself forward against the hands that held him, struggling frantically to free himself. *Oh, dear Helen, what have you done? What have they done to you?* His vision blurred with tears and in a sudden fury he flailed back and forth. She needed help, couldn't they see that? She was lying on the ground moving like a maimed animal. What kind of demon would do this to his wife?

Angry shouts sounded behind him and a rope flopped around Jan's neck. They dragged him back, straining against the rope. The door crashed shut and he was shoved down the corridor. Jan tripped and sprawled to his knees. *She was smiling, Janjic. Writhing in ecstasy and smiling with the pleasure of it.*

They pulled him to his feet and kicked him forward. *Helen, dear Helen! What have they done to you?*

They've done to her what she deserves, you pathetic fool. They have given her what she has wanted all along.

He was forced down a long tunnel, and then another that branched to the right. The passage ended in a cell hewn out of solid black rock. By the light of torches they strapped his arms to a twelve-inch-wide horizontal beam bolted to the wall. Two men restrained him while Karadzic looked on. But the fight had left Jan and he let them jerk his limbs about as they pleased.

His mind was on Helen. She had fallen again. He'd brought her two thousand miles to escape the horrors of Glenn Lutz, and now she had found worse. A death sentence for both of them. And why? Because he hadn't loved her dearly enough? Or because she herself was possessed with evil?

Ivena's words came back to him. "Helen's not so different from every man," she'd said. But Jan could not picture *any* man, much less *every* man doing this. And if Ivena was right and this was a play motivated by God himself, then perhaps God had lost his sense of humor.

They suddenly ripped the tape from Jan's mouth and pulled the rag free. His lips felt on fire.

"You really shouldn't have tried to stop me twenty years ago," Karadzic said. "See what it's cost you? All for an old priest and a gaggle of old ladies."

"I've paid for my insubordination," Jan said. "You took five years from me."

"Five years? Now you'll pay with your life."

"My life. And what do you hope to gain by taking my life? It wasn't enough to kill an innocent priest? Blowing the head from a small child's shoulders didn't satisfy your blood thirst?"

"Shut up!" Even in the dim light he could see Karadzic's face bulged red. "You've never understood power."

"The real war is against evil, Karadzic. And it seems you don't recognize evil, even when it crawls up inside of you. Perhaps it's you who don't understand power."

Karadzic didn't answer, at least not with words. His eyes flashed angrily.

"You don't have the courage to take your anger out on me, face to face," Jan said. "You hide behind a woman!"

The commander looked at Jan for a moment and then placed his hands on his hips and smiled. "So. Our valiant soldier will fight for his lover's life. He realizes that I'm going to kill her, and now he'll use whatever means at his disposal to persuade me otherwise." Karadzic leaned forward. "Let me tell you, I don't bow to humiliation so easily, Janjic."

"No? But the priest humiliated you, didn't he? You marched into the village intent on sowing some horror and instead you received laughter. You've never lived it down, have you? The whole world looks at you as a coward!"

"Nonsense!"

"Then prove yourself. Let the woman free."

"And now the soldier attempts manipulation. I told you, your woman's here of her own choosing. Your *mother*, Ivena, I took by force. But not dear Helen."

"Ivena? You have Ivena? What could you possibly want with an innocent woman?" Nausea swept through Jan's gut.

"She was to lure your lover, my friend. But now she'll serve another purpose."

"You have me. Release them, I beg you. Release Ivena; release Helen."

Karadzic grinned. "Your Helen is far too valuable to release, Preacher."

Preacher? "You have no complaint against her. You have me. I beg you to let her go."

Now the big man chuckled. "Yes, I have you, Janjic. But I was offered a hundred thousand dollars for the death of the preacher *and* his lover. That would be your Helen. I do intend to collect this money."

A hundred thousand dollars? Jan was too shocked to respond. Then he knew it all in a flash.

Lutz!

Somehow Glenn Lutz had his finger in this madness.

"Lutz . . ."

"Yes. Lutz. You know him, I see."

A growl formed in Jan's stomach and rose through his throat. His blood felt hot and thick in his veins. Then he lost his reason and began screaming, but the words came out in a meaningless jumble. His heart was breaking; his heart was raging. He wanted to kill; he wanted to die. He suddenly threw himself against the restraints, thinking that he had to stop the man.

Karadzic was going to kill his mother and his wife.

A blow crashed against his head. Karadzic's fist. Jan shuddered and settled back, silent. A balloon of pain swelled between his temples.

Another fist smashed into his jaw and stars dotted his vision. Jan slumped forward and lost his mind to the darkness.

CHAPTER FORTY

JAN COULDN'T tell if he'd regained consciousness or if the black before his eyes was still the darkness of his mind. He thought he blinked a few times, but even then he couldn't be sure. Then he heard ragged pulls of breath and he knew that he was hearing himself.

He was still strapped to the beam, hands spread wide. His shoulders ached badly and he made a feeble attempt to shift his weight back from them. An immediate surge of pain changed his mind. He sagged on the beam and fought to clear his mind.

The room echoed with his own heaves of breath. The sound brought a chill to his bones, a déjà vu that suddenly had the hair on his neck standing.

He had been here.

When?

It came back to him like a fist from the darkness: He was in the dungeon from his dreams!

For twenty years he had dreamed of this very place—he knew it was the same. The same sound, the same beam at his back, the same pitch-blackness. The details had sunk to obscure depths during these last dreamless months, but they came raging to the surface now. The dreams had been a premonition of his own end.

Death awaited at the end of this mad journey. He'd been given love—a graft of God's heart, Ivena had said. And now he'd found death. The price of love was death. Jan's chest tightened with remorse. What a fool he'd been to bring Helen to Bosnia. To Karadzic! *Oh, dear Helen, forgive me! Oh, God, help me.*

A soft voice whispered in the darkness. *"It is a only a shadow of what I feel."*

Jan caught his breath and lifted his head.

"No more than a faint whisper."

The voice was audible! Jan held his breath and scanned the darkness but saw nothing. He was hallucinating.

"You feel this pain?
"Your worst pain is like a distant echo. Mine is a scream."
This was not a hallucination! It couldn't be! *Oh, my God! You're speaking! I'm hearing the voice of God!* A tear slipped down his cheek. He stilled and listened to the loud inhaling and exhaling of his breath. He could see nothing but blackness. Then he spoke in a whisper.

"And my love for Helen?"
"A small taste. You could hardly survive more. Do you like it?"
Then it was true! "Yes! Yes, I like it! I love it!"

A small voice began to giggle behind the other. A child who laughed, unable to contain his delight. It fell like a balm of contentment over Jan. God and this child were seeing things differently, and it wasn't a sad thing they were seeing. Tears fell from Jan's eyes in streams. He began to shake, smothered in these words whispered to his mind.

His world suddenly flashed white and he gasped. At first he thought it might be the war memories, but he saw immediately that it wasn't. The field of white flowers stretched out before him, ending in a brilliant emerald ocean. The sky rushed toward the distant water, in rivers of red and blue and orange.

He shifted his feet and looked down. A thick carpet of grass squeezed between his toes, so rich and lush that it appeared aqua. Within three meters, the bed of red-and-white flowers began, swaying ever so gently with a light breeze. They were the flowers from Ivena's greenhouse. The sweet odor of rose blossoms swept through his nose.

Still the sky fled to the horizon, like a sunset photographed in time-lapse but never ending. Jan stared at the surreal scene and let his jaw fall open. It was not of this world. It was of the other. And it was part of his dream.

He heard a faint note on the air, like the distant drone of a huge wind. He was thinking that the sound might be coming from the field when he saw it, a single black line on the horizon moving toward him.

The line stretched as far as he could see in either direction. Slowly it grew, moving in with increasing speed. Jan caught his breath. Tiny shapes emerged from the faceless line. They flew toward him, below the streaming sky, against the tide, as though riding an airborne tsunami.

Jan jerked back a step and froze, unsure what to do. Then the sea of figures was upon him, rushing a hundred feet over his head, silent except for an aerodynamic moan, like a mighty rushing wind. He yelped and crouched low, thinking they might clip his head. But they were a good hundred feet up. It was the sheer volume of them that cast the illusion of proximity.

He stared, dumbstruck. They were children, mostly. He could see their blurred bodies streaking over him in hues of blue and red. A faint bubbling sound suddenly erupted from the children, running up and down the scales, as if magical chimes were moving with them. Only it wasn't a chime; it was laughter. A hundred thousand children giggling, as if their sweep down upon him was a great joke they now delighted in.

Jan's mouth spread in a smile. A chuckle escaped his mouth.

The laughter grew in response. And then Jan was laughing with them.

The line suddenly ended and he saw that the leaders had looped up into the sky, like a wave curling back on itself. They screamed in for another pass. A man with long hair led the flight, and at his right a smaller figure clung to his hand, squealing in fits of laughter; he saw them both clearly this time. They looked at him directly and their eyes sparkled with delight. When it seemed they were close enough to touch, Jan recognized them.

It was Father Micheal and Nadia!

Suddenly Jan wanted to leap up and join them. He stood to his feet. He was laughing with them, right there in the stone room; he knew that because his shoulders were feeling the pain from his body's jostling. But in his mind—in this other world—he jumped and flung his hands up futilely. He *had* to join them!

They looped back again, but this time they stopped high above and hovered like a cloud that covered the sky. The sound fell silent.

Jan pulled up, astonished. What was happening?

Then a thin wail cut through the air. And another, and another until the sky moaned with the sound of weeping. Jan stepped back, stunned. What had happened?

He lowered his eyes to the meadow. And he saw what they saw. A body lay on the flowers, ten feet from him, and he knew. It was Helen, and heaven was weeping for her.

Two emotions collided. Delight and grief. Love and death.

Jan's world snapped back to black, and he inhaled quickly. He was back in the dark room. The vision of heaven was gone.

THAT WAS *your dream, Jan. The dungeon and then the field. It was this. You have somehow waited for this moment since the day you saw Father Micheal and Nadia die. You were meant for this. This is your story.*

"God?" His voice echoed in the chamber. He was speaking as if God were physically in the room.

Yes, and so he was. Is.

"God?"

But only silence answered him.

A sense of desperation welled up in his chest. A yearning for the laughter, for the voice of God, for the smell of the flowers from Ivena's garden. But they were gone, leaving only the lingering memory of Helen, lying on the grass. She was not laughing. Was she dead?

And what if she was? What if that was the meaning of this vision? Karadzic had killed her and now heaven was weeping. He straightened in his straps, suddenly panicked. In that moment he knew what he would do.

"Karadzic!" he screamed. His head ached with the exertion. "Karaaadzic!"

Fire burned at his shoulders. But he had to do this, didn't he? It was the thinnest of threads, but it might be Helen's only hope. "Karaaaadzic!"

A fist pounded on the door. "Shut up in there."

"Tell Karadzic to come. I have something to tell him."

A moment of silence. "He wants nothing from you," the voice said.

"And if you're wrong? This will mean everything to him."

A grunt sounded, followed by a long period of silence. Jan called out twice more, but the guard didn't answer.

The door suddenly rattled with keys and then swung in. Shafts of yellow light fell across Jan's body, and he lifted his head.

Karadzic stood in the doorway, slapping keys in his right hand like a baton, legs spread. "So, you wish to beg me for your life after all?" He chuckled and his voice echoed in the chamber.

"I'm no longer interested in my life. Only Helen's."

"Then you're a fool and I pity you," Karadzic said.

"Helen was always the prize. That's why Lutz offered you money for her death. If he can't have her, then he'll kill her. But believe me, if that dirty pig thought for a moment that he could have her as his own, willingly, he'd never kill her."

Karadzic's lips twisted to a grin. "Is that it, Lover Boy?"

"Lutz would pay much more for Helen alive. I'm sure of it."

The smile softened on Karadzic's face. "Don't try tricks with me, soldier."

"Don't take my word. Ask Lutz himself. If he's paying you a hundred thousand dollars for our deaths, then he'll pay two hundred thousand for Helen's heart. I promise you."

"And I'm not interested in your promises. You think your sly tongue will play to your favor?"

"I'm not speaking of my promises, you idiot," Jan said. Karadzic's eyes narrowed. "I'm telling you what Lutz will say when you talk to him."

"And what makes you think I'll talk to him?"

"Your greed will see to it."

"And your stupidity will see to your death."

"You would be a fool not to call Lutz. Demand double for Helen's willing return and he'll agree to pay you."

"Even if you're right, how do you propose I force the woman to return to Lutz? You say he's a pig."

Jan gathered himself and straightened against the beams. His shoulders throbbed, as if needles had been run through his joints.

"You persuade Helen to openly renounce her love for me." Saying it made Jan sick.

Karadzic stared dumbly. "Renounce her love? You're talking women's talk."

"If she were to renounce her love, it would break her spirit. That's why the priest wouldn't renounce his love for Christ. Haven't you understood that yet? It wasn't only words he was refusing to give you; it was his heart. If Helen renounces her love for me, she won't be able to live with the shame. She'll go eagerly back to America. And in America there is only Lutz for her." How could he even say such words? Living with Lutz would be a death of its own. But then God could still woo her, couldn't he?

Karadzic was no fool in the art of bending minds; the war had taught him well. His eyes darted back and forth. "So you propose I break her heart by forcing her to renounce you? You think I am so naive?"

Jan took a deep breath. "No, you can't force her. She must do it willingly. So play one of your games, Karadzic. The same game you played with the priest. Perhaps you'll recover the shame he heaped on your head."

Karadzic blinked rapidly. Jan had struck a chord there.

Jan continued quickly. "You can't force her, but you can motivate her. Tell her that if she doesn't renounce her love for me, you'll kill her." He swallowed hard.

Karadzic licked his lips, understanding already. Jan went on.

"You tell her that, but if she chooses to die rather than renounce her love for me you do *not* kill her. You release her. And if she does renounce her love, then you release her to Lutz. Either way she lives. Either way you may kill me." Jan forced a smile. "It's a game of ultimate stakes. She chooses to live and you become very rich; she chooses to die and you still get your ransom, but not for her. Only the half paid for me. She is free."

"Her choice to die for you will set her free," Karadzic stated with a glint in his eyes. "But her choice to live will hand her over to Lutz. Or I could just kill you both and collect the money already offered."

"You could."

Karadzic stared at him for several long seconds. Then he backed out of the room. "We will see," he said, and he was gone.

The door closed and Jan slumped against his straps.

KARADZIC ENTERED the dimly lit quarters beneath the earth and stared at the large American seated cross-legged in his leather chair. The man stood to his feet and faced him. He looked albino in the yellow light; very white from his blond hair to his pale skin, this pig. Karadzic had never suspected that another man could send a chill down his spine, but Glenn Lutz did, every time he turned those black eyes his way. He did not like that.

"Well?" Lutz asked.

"He has a proposal for you," Karadzic said, walking for his liquor cabinet.

"He knows that I'm here?"

"No. Of course not. He thinks I will call you."

"He's not exactly in a position to give proposals, is he? What's his proposal?" Lutz demanded.

"He says that you will pay me double for the woman's heart."

Glenn breathed loudly in the chamber. "I didn't make a thirty-hour trip to cut out her heart. I came to kill her. Straight and simple. Once she's dead, I don't care what you do with her. He's ranting."

"He's not suggesting that I cut her heart out. He's suggesting that I play a game with her." Karadzic poured scotch into a glass and faced the bulky American. "The same game that I played with the priest in the village."

Lutz stared dumbly. He wasn't connecting. "I paid you to bring them in. Fifty thousand American dollars for each. Now I'm going to kill them both. I'm not interested in games."

"And what if the game gave you Helen back? Hmm? What if she came willingly to you as yours and yours alone? What would you pay for that?"

Glenn pulled and pushed the stale air through his nostrils as if they were old bellows. His eyelids fell over those black eyes like shutters and then snapped open. The man had lost a part of himself somewhere, Karadzic thought.

Karadzic spoke again. "He says that you will pay me two hundred thousand dollars if I'm able to persuade her to renounce her love for Janjic. He says that if she renounces her love for him in the face of death, she'll lose her will to love him and return willingly to you."

Glenn stared at Karadzic for a long time without moving his eyes. Finally he spoke. "And if she refuses?"

"Then we set her free. We kill only Janjic." He took a sip from the glass.

"I came to kill them both," Glenn said, but his conviction seemed tempered.

"Janjic is right. If the woman renounces her love for him, her spirit will be broken. She will be yours for the taking." Karadzic smiled. "But either way I will kill him. You will have her alive or dead. Either way you will win."

"I thought the game was to set her free if she chooses to die."

"That was Janjic's request. But if she chooses to die rather than renounce her pathetic love for one man, then we will give her that wish." It really was like the priest, wasn't it? Karadzic felt his pulse thump through his veins. A sort of vindication.

"And why should I pay you—"

"Because you could not do it," Karadzic interrupted, suddenly angry. "She would never renounce her love with you standing there." He had no idea if that was true or not, but suddenly the money was sounding very attractive. And playing the game again carried a poetic justice that was starting to gnaw at his skull. "I will kill Janjic regardless. And I am offering you the chance to have your woman alive and willing. It's your choice. One hundred thousand for both dead, or two hundred thousand for Janjic dead and Helen in your arms."

Glenn turned from him and put his hands on his hips. The man wasn't beyond trying to kill *him*, Karadzic thought. Lutz would pull the trigger without a thought. But this was Bosnia, not America. Here the American would play by his rules. Or die. If it wasn't for the promise of the money Karadzic would have killed the fat slob already. It would be a pleasure to watch the pig die.

"I'll double my payment for Helen," Glenn said, turning. "One hundred thousand for her if you can make her curse the preacher. I'll pay you our agreed fee of fifty thousand for the preacher. That's one hundred fifty thousand. No more."

He said it all as a man used to authority, and Karadzic almost told him to swallow his money. But he didn't. He might do that later.

"Fine," he said, and walked for the door. "I will expect you to keep your promise." Lutz was boring into him with those black eyes when he turned back to him. "Do not leave this room," Karadzic said. He left and a chill of fury ripped down his spine.

Maybe he would just kill them all. When it was over and he had his money. But now he would play. The thought brought a grin to his lips.

Poetic justice.

CHAPTER FORTY-ONE

HELEN FELT hands moving her, jostling her around, but her mind still drifted in lazy circles. They had changed her position, she knew that much, and now she grasped for threads to the real world. The room with all of its colored lights and feathers wasn't easily distinguished from her dreams.

She was standing, or lying on her back. No, standing, with her arms thrown to either side, immobile. Odd. Helen turned her head slowly and closed her eyes against the tiny flames of light. The candles looked like fireflies skittering across her horizon. She moaned. When the pinpricks behind her eyes cleared, she looked again and the room came into soft focus.

The black walls glistened with the glow from several dozen white candles staggered at various heights, their flames flickering like jerky dancers. A couple of figures moved in the shadows but most of the others she'd seen were no longer present. Helen tried to shift her feet to rid a tingling there, but she found she couldn't. She lowered her head and studied her bare feet. Yes, they were bare. And pressed side by side, hanging limply. Off the ground.

The last detail cleared her mind and she blinked. Her feet were bound together, suspended off the floor! Her arms . . . She lifted her head quickly and looked at her right arm. Half-inch rope had been wrapped around her forearm and a huge crossbeam. She turned her head. Her left arm was bound to the same beam.

A chill ran up her spine. What was happening to her? She pulled against the restraints, but they didn't give, and her head throbbed with pain for the effort. They'd ripped her tan cotton slacks at the knees, baring her calves. The white of her blouse was smudged with dirt, and the sleeves shredded to her armpits.

What is happening? Helen began to whimper, not because she wanted to whimper, but because she wanted to ask and nothing else would come from her mouth. She desperately searched the room and caught the looks of the two men, but they only stared, unblinking.

"H . . . help." Her cry squeaked like a pathetic little toy, and she began to weep softly through trembling lips. "Please help." But the room was empty except for these two men calmly looking at her.

She knew then that her life was about to end. There was a feel to the air unlike any she'd ever known. A biting chill but hot, so that her skin glistened with sweat. She shivered. The room smelled like rotten meat, but tinged with a medicinal odor she recognized as heroin. Evil filled this dungeon, dark and lurking, but very much alive. And she had come here eagerly.

Helen's body shook with fear and shame. *Oh, Jan, dear Jan, what have I done? I am so sorry.*

How many times had she said that?

She bit her lip, hard enough to draw the tangy taste of blood.

The door opened to her left and a large figure stood in the frame, backlit by the hall's orange light. Karadzic.

Suddenly she knew who this man was. He was Karadzic! *The* Karadzic! He was Jan's commander in the book!

A woman was shoved past him, stumbling to her knees. Her dress was ripped up one side, but it looked vaguely familiar. The two men who'd been in the room stepped forward and hauled the woman to her feet.

Helen saw her face, streaked with blood so that it looked torn along a jagged line. She caught her breath.

It was Ivena! Ivena was here!

"Ivena!"

Ivena turned her head slowly and looked at Helen. Then her eyes widened and immediately wrinkled with empathy. Ivena's mouth parted in a silent cry. "Dear Helen . . . Oh, dear Helen, I am so sorry."

Helen turned to the door where Karadzic still stood in shadows. "What are you doing to her? She's an old woman. You can't—"

"Don't be afraid for me," Ivena said, now with a soft voice. Helen faced her. There was a glint in Ivena's eyes and it wasn't from the firelight. "I fear for you, dear Helen. For your soul, not for your body. Don't let them take your soul."

A white light flooded Helen's mind with that last word, as if a strobe had been ignited. She jerked her head up.

The room had vanished. She gasped.

A field of white flowers stretched out before her, surrounded by a brilliant blue sky.

Her vision snapped back to the room, where the big man, Karadzic, was stepping in, followed by the woman in red. They both wore clown grins.

But Helen remained here less than a second, before the white world popped back to life like a flashbulb. The flowers swayed, delicate in the breeze, bowing to a prone figure not ten feet away. She heard what sounded like a child sobbing quietly, and Helen quickly scanned the surreal sky. It was turquoise now and it flowed like a river toward the horizon.

Helen dropped her eyes. The woman on the ground was dressed in a pink dress with little flowers and . . .

It was *her!* It was her, *Helen!*

The soft sobbing halted for a brief second, leaving only deathly silence. The world had frozen with Helen in it, standing agape, lying near death.

And then the screaming started. A hundred thousand voices wailed at once, desperate in their agony. In her mind's eye Helen covered her ears and doubled over. The sound ripped through her nerves like a razor. They were weeping for that prone figure. For *her.*

"God, dear God, forgive me!"

Instantly she was back in the dim room, with her last cry echoing around her. Karadzic and his black-haired woman stared at her, their smiles gone. They had heard her.

"God can't hear you, fool!" The big man was dressed in a black robe with the lady in red at his arm. Two others had followed them in and now took their posts to Helen's right. Then Karadzic stepped to the center of the room and faced her. "You think calling out to God will save you? It didn't save the priest, and he was better than you."

The two men who'd waited near the back had Ivena by her arms now. They jerked her to the side where they stood her up facing Helen. But the glint in Ivena's eyes did not fade.

The candles flickered silently. Helen sagged from the cross, heaving with emotion. But it really wasn't from the madness in this room, was it? It was from that vision. It had left her sight, but the weeping still crashed through her heart.

Karadzic approached Helen, wearing a twisted grin again. He was very tall, so that his face came level with Helen's. He lifted a thick hand and ran his fingers down Helen's cheek.

"Such soft skin. It's a shame, really." Karadzic spoke very softly, and he wiped the tears from Helen's cheek. It made little difference; fresh tears spilled in silent streams. He leaned closer, and Helen could smell the musty odor of his breath.

"Today you will die. You know that, don't you?" he whispered.

Karadzic's eyes were no more than six inches from Helen's; they roved in their sockets, searching Helen's face. He ran a thick tongue delicately over his teeth; sweat glistened on his upper lip. "In one hour you will be dead. After we've had our fun. But you can save yourself. You're going to decide whether or not you want to stay alive now. Do you understand?"

He looked into Helen's eyes, waiting.

Helen nodded. A squeak of air escaped her throat. Fear spread through her bones, replacing the sorrow brought on by the vision. She glanced over at Ivena, who stared at her with that fire in her eyes.

"Helen," Karadzic whispered. His mouth popped lightly with the parting of his lips and tongue. "Such a pretty name. Do you want to stay alive, Helen? Hmm? Do you want to go back to your lover?"

Helen nodded. She glanced over Karadzic's shoulder and saw that the others hadn't moved. The faint hiss of burning candlewicks played over her mind. The man was breathing deliberately through his nostrils.

"Say it, my darling. Tell me you want to stay alive."

"Yes," Helen said. But it came out like a whimper.

Karadzic smiled. "Yes. Then you remember that, because if you don't, I'm going to let Vahda break your fingers off, one by one. It will sound very loud in this room. You will think that you're being shot, but it will only be your bones snapping loudly." Somewhere in there his smile had vanished.

Helen realized that she was no longer breathing.

Karadzic turned and walked back. A pistol was shoved in his belt, large and black. Helen's breath came in sudden short pants. Chills swept over her skull. *Oh, God! Please save me. I'll do anything!*

Karadzic turned around by the woman, Vahda, and for a long moment they stared at Helen, unmoving. Shadows flickered with the candle flames, dancing across their faces.

Karadzic reached out to the guard on his right and took a revolver from him.

Helen's heart crashed into her throat. Her breathing shortened—she was hyperventilating. Glenn's eyes were black. No, it was Karadzic, and his eyes were like holes. Why were they doing this? What had she done to anger them?

"Now, Helen, we brought you here to kill you. And we're going to do that." He spoke very softly, very matter-of-factly. "But since your husband was kind enough to tell my story to the world and bring me such fame, I've decided to give you a choice. You did read his book, didn't you?"

She didn't respond. Couldn't.

"Good. Then you'll remember that I gave the priest a choice. You do remember that?"

Karadzic took a step forward. "Look at me, Helen." She did, still trembling. "Here is your choice. It's quite simple. If you renounce your love for Janjic, I will set you free."

She blinked at the man. Renounce her love? For Janjic! She could do that easily—they were just words.

"Do you understand? Tell me that you don't love him—that you would curse him if he were here—and I'll set you free. Do you understand?"

She nodded impulsively.

You can't renounce your love, Helen.

Of course I can. I have to! She refused to look at Ivena, but she could feel the woman's eyes on her.

"Very good."

"You . . . you won't hurt him?" Helen asked.

"Hurt him? If you reject him, what will it matter? He'll be dead to you anyway."

Her head began to throb. She closed her eyes, desperate to wake up from this nightmare.

"Helen."

She opened her eyes. Karadzic had lifted the gun and rested its barrel on his cheek. He tilted his head, and looked past his bushy eyebrows at her.

"You know what happened to the priest. I know you do. I killed him."

She didn't move. The air felt very still.

"But I want you to be sure that I will do what I say. I want you to know that when I say I'm going to kill someone, I will kill them." His mouth was open in a slight smile.

"Look at Ivena, Helen."

Helen turned toward Ivena. The older woman looked directly at Helen with an eagerness in her eyes and the hint of a smile on her lips. There was no fear; there was only this absurd confidence that glowed about her. A fresh surge of tears spilled from Helen's eyes.

The guards stepped aside and Ivena stood on her own feet, wavering.

"Do not weep for me, Helen. The weeping is for you," Ivena said.

From the corner of her eye Helen saw Karadzic lift his arm to Ivena. A *boom!* crashed through Helen's skull and she jerked back. Ivena's neck folded back. The side of her head was gone. She fell to the floor like a sack of flour.

Then Helen's mind began to explode with panic. There was laughter, but she couldn't remove her eyes from Ivena's limp body to see where it came from— maybe from Karadzic and his woman. Maybe it was from her.

Ivena! Dear God, Ivena was dead!

Oh, God, please save me! I please beg you to save me! Please, please!

JAN STRAINED against the ropes, ignoring the pain that throbbed in his joints. It had begun, he knew that much. He could feel the tension in his gut, and it made him nauseous.

Dear Father, I beg you, save her. I beg you!

He heard a distant report: a gunshot far away. Had they shot her? Jan dropped his chin to his chest and groaned aloud. Bile filled his throat and he threw up. He spit the bitter taste from his mouth and groaned again. It was too much.

Karadzic would do whatever possible to encourage Helen's denouncement of love, even if it meant harming her. And Ivena, what would he do to Ivena? The thought of that bullhead touching Helen revolted Jan, actually made his body quiver on its moorings.

He let his head loll and begged God for the moments to pass quickly. If she renounced her love, she would be gone forever and Jan thought he might as well die without her. Which was precisely what would happen. Karadzic would butcher him.

But if Helen chose death instead? Karadzic might break his word and kill her. But there were no other options. At least they would die as one, in love.

Father, you cannot allow her to die. She is your Israel; she is your church; she is your bride.

A picture from the Psalms, of a giant eagle screaming from the sky to protect its young, spun through his mind. *You have cast this madness, Father. Now save us. You have made me Solomon, desperate for the maiden; you have made me Hosea, loving with your heart. Now show me your hand.*

Silence.

Jan hung from his restraints, wanting death. He could hardly think for the pain. If Karadzic would free his hands, he would claw the man's eyes out! Jan ground his teeth. He would pummel that thick face! *How dare he touch—*

The world abruptly stuttered to white.

The vision!

Laughter crashed in on him from all sides. The field of flowers and this hilarious laughter. A wave of relief swept over his chest and he chuckled suddenly. Then the sentiment thundered through his body and he could not contain it. It was pleasure. Raw pleasure and it boiled from his bones in bubbles of joy!

Jan doubled over, as far as his bound arms allowed, and he laughed. The room echoed with the sounds of a madman, and he couldn't help thinking that he'd finally lost his sanity. But he knew at once that he could not be more sensible. He was drinking life and it was making him laugh.

Every fiber in his body begged to die in that moment; to join that laughter forever. To roll through the field and rush through the blue sky with Father Micheal and Nadia.

The vision vanished.

He blinked in the darkness. *You know Nadia spoke of laughter, Janjic. You know Father Micheal laughed. And then they both died. The laughing precedes death.*

Then let me die, Father.

But save Helen. I beg you.

THEY HAD left the room for a while, to give her time to think things through, the woman said. Ivena's body lay in a pool of blood to Helen's right, her eyes open and dead. The candles cast wavering shadows across the room. And Helen stared with round eyes, a sheen of sweat glistening on her skin, breathing in ragged lurches.

She had passed out once, from hyperventilation, she thought. When she came to, she wondered if the whole thing had been a bad dream, but then she saw the body and she started crying again.

The problem was quite simple. She didn't want to renounce her love for Jan. Her mind revisited his incredible kindness and his passion. Renouncing his love could very well be death in and of itself. At the very least she could never face him again.

But then she didn't want to die. No, she would never allow them to kill her.

The door banged open, and Karadzic walked in with the woman and two guards. One of the guards walked to Ivena's body and began pulling it to the side. "Leave it!" Karadzic said.

The guard released the body and joined his comrade on Helen's left.

Karadzic took up his position before her, like an executioner eager to get on with it. Vahda was biting at a fingernail, obviously excited. They stared at her in silence for a moment.

Karadzic spoke in a low rumble. "Now, Helen. We're going to begin breaking your fingers, I prefer the knife and we might get to that, but Vahda has persuaded me that a woman will do anything to keep her fingers."

Helen began to shake again. The nails in the beam at her back were squeaking with her trembling: an obscene sound that sent chills down her legs.

"Oh, God!" she moaned. "Please, God!"

Karadzic lifted his eyebrows. "God? I told you, God isn't listening. I think your God—"

It was all she heard. Because the world exploded again. It flashed white. She was back in the vision!

Only this time, the field of white flowers was swimming in the laughter of children. Helen caught her breath. There was another sound there with the children—she recognized it immediately. It was Ivena! Laughing with the children. Hysterical.

And the prone figure had vanished. And that was funny, she thought. No, that was delightful. That was perfectly incredible! That was better than anything she could ever have imagined.

She heard her own laughter, joining the chorus. Not because it was so funny, in fact funny was a terrible word to describe this emotion erupting from her belly. She felt as though she'd been yanked from an acid bath and plunged into a pool of ecstasy. This intoxicating world of intense pleasure.

This is heaven.

"Stop it!"

The voice snapped Helen back to the room.

"STOP IT!" Karadzic stood trembling. "You think it's funny?"

Helen was chuckling. The woman hung from his cross covered in her own sweat, shaking like a leaf. A moment before, it had been terror twitching those muscles; now it was laughter.

The scene ran through Karadzic's mind like a sick joke. He had seen this before. In a small village not so far away, twenty years ago.

"Shut up!"

She stopped and looked around like an idiot, as if unsure of where she was. The absurdity of this sudden turn in her demeanor brought a chill to Karadzic's bones. What in God's name did she think she was doing?

"You laugh like that again, I'll put a bullet in your stomach! Do you hear me?"

Helen nodded. But her eyes were no longer round and wide. They looked at him with mere curiosity. He would have to put the fear back into her. He would break two fingers, one on each hand. Her index fingers.

Karadzic took a step forward, noting that his own hands still trembled. He closed them into fists. "We will see how you feel after—"

"I've made my decision," she interrupted calmly.

He blinked. "You have, have you?"

"Yes."

"Not so fast." This was not sounding good. "I have Janjic. Do you know that?" The pitch of his voice had elevated, but he didn't care.

"You . . . you have Jan?" She swallowed, and for a second he thought she might burst into tears again. "I love him," the woman said.

"You're a fool," Karadzic muttered through clenched teeth.

"I will die rather than renounce my love for Jan."

This was impossible! "You won't just die! You'll have all of your bones broken, one by one, you little coward!"

Her eyes stared at him without moving. Tears spilled from each, leaving fresh trails down her cheeks. But she did not blink.

"If you think you'll find some perverted satisfaction from hurting an innocent woman, then do it," Helen said.

"You think you're innocent? Did I drag you here? You've killed your own lover by coming here."

Her cheeks sagged.

Karadzic continued quickly. "Janjic will die and only you can save him. Renounce him, you fool. They're only words! Don't be an imbecile."

"No!" she screamed. "No." She began to cry again. She was going to break.

Her face wrinkled with pain. Karadzic could smell the change in her and he encouraged her gently.

"Save yourself," he said. "Renounce him."

She inhaled sharply and settled slowly against the ropes. She looked directly into his eyes and Karadzic swallowed. There was a new woman behind those eyes and she was stronger than he'd thought.

"You know I can't do that," she said quietly. "Kill me. I'll die for him—it's long overdue."

The tremble started at Karadzic's head and worked its way down to his heels. If he hadn't been immobilized on the spot, he might have lifted his pistol and shot her then.

Vahda was not so paralyzed. She shrieked and flew past Karadzic with claws extended. Her fingers dug into Helen's neck and she raked them down her chest, leaving trails of blood.

Karadzic stepped forward and brought a heavy hand across Vahda's head. The woman sprawled to the floor. "She's mine!" he shouted. "Did I tell you to do this?"

He stepped back, trying desperately to gather himself. He was losing control of the situation, the one thing no good commander could allow. His breathing came thick and slow. White spots floated in his vision. Vahda pushed herself to her feet.

Karadzic faced Helen. "So. You think you are smart. Choosing your death. Well, I *will* kill you. And I will allow Vahda to break your bones. But you won't die until you've witnessed the death of your lover. Would you like that?"

The woman did not react.

He screamed it. "I said, would you like that?"

She blinked. But otherwise she only peered at him. Her neck was bleeding badly from Vahda's fingernails.

"Get the prisoner," Karadzic snapped.

Two guards quickly left the room for Janjic.

"Vahda, dear. Remember, this is my game, not yours. You must remember that." She didn't acknowledge him. "So now you may break two of her fingers, but only two," he said.

She turned to him with a glint in her eyes.

"Yes, darling. You may. And her knees."

CHAPTER FORTY-TWO

THE FIRST thing Jan saw when the two guards dragged him into the room was a tall woman in red with long black hair. She was facing the wall. He saw Karadzic to the left, wearing a sinister grin by candlelight. Then the woman moved aside and he saw Helen.

She'd been tied to a thick wooden cross. Her head lolled to one side, and she stared out into the room, expressionless. She hadn't seen him.

There was blood on her neck. And her knees . . . *Oh, dear God!* Her knees were a bloody mess. Jan panicked then. He growled and flung himself forward.

His attempt was rewarded with a stiff blow to the side of his head. He slumped between the guards and Helen's image swam in his vision. She was looking at him now. Slowly a thin smile formed on her mouth. *Dear Helen! My poor Helen!*

Her index fingers were oddly disjointed. Nausea swept through his stomach. He turned from her and saw the body folded over itself in the shadows. It was a woman, lifeless, dressed in . . .

It was Ivena! That was Ivena lying in the corner with her head bloodied. *Oh, dear God! Dear God!*

Jan closed his eyes and lowered his head. The sorrow rose through his chest and rushed from his eyes, as if a dam had broken deep in him. He hung from his arms between the guards and he wept.

"Do you like what you see, Janjic?" Karadzic asked quietly.

Shut up! Shut up, you devil from hell!

"Don't listen to him, Jan. Listen to me." It was Helen's voice!

He lifted his head and blinked.

"Shut up!" Karadzic said.

But Jan was looking into Helen's eyes, and he saw something there. Something new. Something that reached into his chest and squeezed his heart. It was the way he'd felt in the restaurant on their first date, the same feeling that had given him weak knees in the garden under a full moon. It was the same beating of his heart that had pounded in his ears while she leaned over his shoulder looking at the coffee machine.

And yet it was coming from her heart, not just his. He could see the love in her eyes and in the lines around her lips. She seemed hardly aware of her broken bones. She was swimming in a new dimension.

He began to cry, and the guards shifted awkwardly on their feet.

"Jan." It was Helen again, weak yet speaking his name. His body trembled.

"Jan, I love you."

He lifted his head to the ceiling and began to wail out loud. Waves of joy washed through his bones.

The guards released him suddenly and he crashed to the ground. He hardly felt the force of the fall. She loved him! Dear God, Helen was loving him!

He wanted to look up at her and tell her that he loved her too. That he would give anything to hear her say those words again! That he would die for her.

Jan's lips pressed against the stone ground and his tears pooled. He rolled to his side and tried to push himself up. He couldn't. But he had to. He had to stand and rush over to Helen and kiss her face and her feet and her wounded knees and tell her how terribly much he loved her.

Karadzic was screaming something. Jan opened his eyes and saw that the man had thrust a pistol in Helen's cheek. But Helen's eyes were on Jan.

She didn't seem to care about the gun. And it occurred to Jan that he didn't either. In fact, it all seemed rather absurd; this big man shoving his black weapon at Helen, as if doing so should bring her to her knees. She was tied up, how could she possibly fall to her knees? She was strapped to the cross, bleeding, and she was smiling.

A bubble of laughter escaped Jan's lips.

For a long, awkward moment the room fell to silence. Karadzic and his woman stood shaking, glaring at Jan, at a loss. Helen looked into Jan's eyes.

Karadzic suddenly spun, gripped the pistol in both hands, and squeezed the trigger. A deafening report boomed through the room.

The slug tore into Jan's side, burning as if someone had jabbed him with a branding iron. He gasped and clutched his side.

"Dear Father, save us," Helen's trembling voice whispered. Her chin rested on her chest. "Love us. Let us hear your laughter."

"Silence!" Karadzic screamed.

The door suddenly banged open and a ghost from the past stood there, huge and white and round-eyed. It was Glenn. And a moment later Jan knew that he was in the flesh. Glenn Lutz was *here!*

Helen had looked up and was staring directly at Glenn. "Show your hand. Show the power of your love. Let us hear your laughter. We've died already, now let us live." She was praying for the laughter.

Karadzic had spun to Glenn, who stood dumbfounded, glaring at Helen on the cross.

The room fell to an eerie silence.

"Kill her," Glenn said in a breathy voice. His face suddenly contorted with hate, and he stepped up between Karadzic and Vahda. "Kill her." His voice rose in pitch and he began to shake. "Kill her!" he screamed.

Karadzic stood rooted to the ground.

The sound came like bubbling spring, gushing from the rock. It was laughter. It was the same laughter from the vision. But it wasn't from the vision. It was from Helen. Helen had lifted her head and was laughing open-mouthed.

"He, he, he, he, he, ha, ha ha ha ha ha!"

Jan held his breath with the suddenness of it. It was the picture from the cover of *The Dance of the Dead,* only here, painted on Helen.

If Glenn's senses hadn't already snapped, they did in that moment. He roared and swung a huge fist at Karadzic's face. Bone smashed bone with a sickening thud and Karadzic staggered backward. Like an unleashed tiger, Glenn sprang at Karadzic while the commander was still off balance. But Karadzic set himself and the two large men collided.

Glenn shook like a leaf now, his lips pressed white with desperation. With a thundering roar, he ripped the gun from Karadzic's grasp and jumped back.

Helen's laughter echoed through the room, and Glenn jerked the pistol toward her in a blind fury.

The reprieve was what Karadzic needed. He snatched another gun from behind his back and jerked it up in line with Glenn. But the American's gun was already steadied.

A boom crashed through the room. Jan's heart stopped its beating. *Oh, God!* He clenched his eyes shut. *Oh, dear God!*

Laughter pealed about him. Helen's laughter. In death? She had joined Ivena and—

Jan snapped his eyes open and stared at Helen. Her eyes were closed and her mouth was open and she was still laughing.

Then Glenn's huge body fell, like a side of beef. His head bounced off the concrete a foot from Jan's. His eyes were open and there was a hole in his right temple.

Helen was still laughing, seemingly oblivious to the struggle around her. Her mouth was open with delight and tears wet her cheeks.

Karadzic faced her, sweat pouring from his skin. He took a step back and his eyes skipped around. It occurred to Jan that he was terrified. The big man opened his mouth in a moan.

Jan looked at Glenn's torso again, and this time he saw the black handle wedged under his shoulder. The gun!

Jan glanced up at Karadzic. The man trained his wavering gun forward, as if struggling against an unseen force. They had been here before. Only this time it wasn't the priest's laughter Karadzic would silence. This time it was Jan's wife's. The realization passed through his mind and he thought his chest would explode. Still Helen did not stop her laughing.

Jan reached out his right hand and grabbed for the gun under Lutz's body, keeping his eyes on Karadzic all the while. The man was transfixed by the sight of Helen. At any instant the gun in his hand would buck.

Cold steel filled Jan's hand. His world swam. He found the trigger and pulled the pistol out in one quick motion. A groan broke from his throat and he heaved the gun up in Karadzic's direction. He yanked the trigger.

Boom!

The slug hit his old commander somewhere below the waist, but Jan kept jerking on the trigger. *Boom! Boom! Boom! Boom! Boom!*

Click. The gun was empty.

Karadzic staggered back, wide-eyed, his own weapon unfired. He stared at Jan, wavering on his feet. Several blotches of red spread on his shirt. His nose was twisted and bleeding.

The man fell face forward on the concrete and lay still.

The room grew quiet.

Karadzic's woman had gone white. She eased toward the door, glanced one last time at Karadzic's lifeless form, and ran from the room. One of the guards ran out behind her, blinking in disbelief.

Only then, with Helen hanging from the cross, Jan lying in a pool of his own blood, and the last guard cowering against the far wall, did it occur to Jan that they were alive.

He dropped the gun and pushed himself to an elbow. He saw Helen looking at him in silence, and immediately collapsed to his side. Pain shot up his spine and he groaned.

Helen looked at the remaining guard, who still stood trembling. "Please, please," she begged. "Please help us."

The guard suddenly rushed across the room with a drawn knife and Jan's pulse spiked with alarm. The man ran to the cross and his blade flashed. It severed the cords. Helen fell free. The guard caught her, quickly lowered her to the ground, and ran from the room.

Jan's world began to drift. The universe had been created for moments like these, he thought. It was an odd thought.

Jan felt his head being lifted and he opened his eyes. She'd managed to crawl to him and lift his head in her arms. She was sobbing.

"Forgive me! I'm so sorry, Jan. Forgive me! Forgive me, forgive me, forgive me. I was so wrong. I was so, so wrong."

Her words floated in and out. She'd never said such things, but then she'd never been who she was now. Jan's body trembled, but this time with an unspeakable joy. The fruits of love. The universe was indeed created for moments like these.

He stared up at her, a dumb smile spreading across his face.

Helen leaned over his face. He felt her hot tears fall on his cheek. Then her warm lips on his own. And on his nose.

"I love you, Janjic."

She kissed him again, around his eyes.

"I love you, Jan Jovic. I will love you forever. With Christ's love, I love you."

She began to cry again and Jan lost consciousness, in the arms of an angel. In the embrace of true love.

CHAPTER FORTY-THREE

Six Months Later

A LIGHT New England breeze swept over the tall black cliffs that held the Atlantic Ocean at bay, and lifted Helen's hair from her shoulders. Before her, as far as she could see, whitecaps dotted the blue sea. In either direction, green grass rolled with the hills. It was the ideal setting to convalesce, she thought. Beautiful and healthy and perfectly peaceful.

She sat in the gazebo across the small glass table from Jan and breathed the salty air deep into her lungs. He sat in his wheelchair and stared at the ocean, wearing a loose cotton shirt and looking stunningly handsome.

Fifty yards behind them, their white colonial house sat stoically on the lawn. She would be in there preparing supper for them about now if it weren't for her knees. But they'd hired Emily to do more than nurse them to health, Jan insisted. On a day as bright as today Emily would probably serve them on the sprawling veranda.

Helen faced Janjic. "I love you, Jan."

He turned to her and his hazel eyes reflected the sea's green, smiling in their wrinkles. "And I'm mad about you, my dear." He extended a hand and rubbed her pregnant stomach. "And you, Gloria."

They'd already decided it would be a girl and they would call her Gloria, because of the glory that had set them free.

Helen smiled. "Thank you for bringing me back."

"What, to America?" He chuckled. "Did I have a choice?"

"Sure. We could have stuck it out in Bosnia." She looked out to sea. "Of course, you wouldn't have gotten the new book deal for *When Heaven Weeps*. Nor the movie." She smiled.

"And I wouldn't have the luxury of living my life in peace with my bride and my child," he added. "Like I said; did I have a choice?"

"No, I guess not."

"My only regret is that you're not well enough to serve me hand and foot." He smiled wide. "A celebrity deserves no less, don't you think?"

"Jan Jovic, how could you say such a thing? Don't worry, my knees are better by the day. I'll be at your beck and call before you know it." They laughed.

Helen stood and walked behind him. Ivena's red-and-white flowers cascaded over the thatchwork, spreading their sweet, musky scent. They'd brought a shoot with them six months ago and planted it along the south wall of the house and here, by the gazebo. Only Joey's Garden of Eden also featured the new species of lily and there it had nearly taken over the botanical garden's east wall.

Helen drew Jan's hair back, bent over and kissed behind his ear. "It's you I worry about, my dear. I don't know what I would do without you."

"Then let's make sure you don't have to live without me," he said. "I've lived through worse. You think a hole in my liver will hold me back?"

He said it with courage and she smiled.

Helen leaned over and kissed his other ear. "Well, I promise that I will love my wounded solider until the day that I die. And I have no intention of going any-time soon."

She laid her head on his hair and closed her eyes. How could she have possibly betrayed this man? The memory of her treachery sat like a distant pain at the back of her mind—always there but incomprehensible. An insatiable love for this man had replaced her addiction in whole.

The details of the last few months were written in black-and-white for the world to read in Jan's new book. The fact that Glenn's estate owned the legal rights to *The Dance of the Dead* was now irrelevant. His old book wasn't the complete story—he'd told them clearly enough at the news conference. *When Heaven Weeps* was. And as a new property it wasn't under the restrictions of the old contract he'd signed with Glenn's company.

Neither Roald nor the council could argue with that. Jan had graciously omit-ted their most ugly moments from the story. But not the woman that they had scorned. Not Helen. Jan had put her on nearly every page, both her ugliness and her beauty. Mostly her beauty, Helen thought.

She kissed the crown of his head.

He pulled her hand. "Come here."

She walked around the chair and sat in his lap.

He took her chin and looked into her eyes. "You're everything to me. You're my bride. You make my heart pitter and my knees weak. You think I would leave that for the grave?"

"No. But maybe for the laughter."

"I have the laughter already. I carry it in my heart, and it's for you."

Helen smiled and leaned forward. "You're very sweet, my prince." She kissed him lightly on the lips and then pulled back. His eyes were on fire with love.

"I love you. More than life," he said.

"And I love you. More than death."

She kissed his lips once again. She could not help herself. This love of theirs—this love of Christ's—was that kind of love.

CPSIA information can be obtained at www.ICGtesting.com
Printed in the USA
LVOW040108010613

336427LV00002B/4/P